CHEETAHS NEVER WIN

A Magical Romantic Comedy (with a body count)

RJ BLAIN

CHEETAHS NEVER WIN
A MAGICAL ROMANTIC COMEDY (WITH A BODY COUNT)
BY R.J. BLAIN

Witnessing a double homicide dumps Aaron Clinton into the middle of a gruesome murder investigation. To stop the budding serial killer from striking again, Aaron's forced to join forces with a reformed cop and a colony of cranky cats.

Warning: this novel contains cats, murder, more cats, mayhem, cheetahs, mischief, felines, a serial killer, romance, humor, puns, generalized hilarity, and whipped cream used in inappropriate fashions. Proceed with caution.

ONE

Why couldn't I get one of the more
interesting jobs?

MISS SHARON GRAY locked onto a shoe store
at Park Lane, a woman on a mission refusing
to accept defeat. Someone was going to lose,
and I wasn't sure if I pitied her wallet, her
new shoes, or the horrified woman in the
store. Under the guise of checking my phone,
I photographed the pair, the building, and to
make things more difficult on myself later, I
snapped a few shots down the sidewalk
where the Saturday shoppers congregated.

My client's target recruited the store employee, and I worried she'd stay there all day.
Had I been wise, I would've dumped the
problem onto Sassy's lap. Sassy liked shoes.
Sassy even enjoyed keeping other women
company while they shopped for shoes.

Sassy also found—or created—trouble
wherever she went. Chaos nipped at the
cheetah's heels. If I called her, she'd storm

into my quiet afternoon of information gathering. Miss Gray matched the usual shadowing target, a pretty woman with expensive tastes and as much of a magnet for trouble as my feline partner.

Women like her put me on edge, usually because they viewed me as candy for their arm. When they found out I was a private investigator, most lost interest—or immediately made assumptions.

As I often did when following someone, I questioned every decision leading up to the acquisition of my private investigator's license. Generally, I enjoyed questioning people and seeking secrets.

Unfortunately, most of my cases involved figuring out who was cheating who, and if my client was correct, Miss Gray spent her evenings with Senator Sterling, a married man up for reelection in a few months.

My client wanted Senator Sterling's job, and he meant to get it through any means possible. Investigating Tom Heatherow on the side might land me in hot water later, but I'd seen a few too many PIs burned by politicians to take any chances.

A single conviction would lose me my license, and I meant to keep my reputation spotless.

I second-guessed my decision to accept my client's offer, a sum sufficient to cover my expenses for an entire month and then some. A few incriminating photos would wrap the job. Mr. Heatherow would need a lot more than a single sex scandal to win a senate seat. As I hadn't been paid to offer advice, I'd let him learn from his mistakes.

Senator Sterling was already on route for a divorce. I'd located the filing after ten minutes of work. In his case, it was a matter of who had cheated who first.

One day, people would learn cheaters never won. With men like me around, secrets always surface. It was just a matter of when.

Why couldn't I get one of the more interesting jobs?

Oh, right. The firm of defense lawyers still wasn't talking to me after I'd proven without a shadow of a doubt their defendant was guilty of embezzlement, blackmail, and extortion. Add in an accessory to murder charge and evidence presented to the prosecution, and I'd burned more than a few bridges with the firm.

They couldn't touch me for following the law, but they refused to hire me again.

I found the entire situation ridiculous. The job of the defense wasn't to clear guilty men of crimes, but to ensure the punishment fit the crime.

My job was to find the truth. That was it, that was all.

I figured my parents had pegged me right from the start. In any other life, I would've become a cop.

If they'd gotten their way, I would've been a married cop, but I'd learned the hard way the cheated never won and to never trust a woman on the prowl. Ladies enjoyed their dalliances as much as men, and once the lies started, all bets were off.

I'd evicted myself from the dating pool, determined to stay single until I died of old age. It might've worked if not for Sassy. I still didn't date, I still lied to myself that I never would, but every time I crossed paths with my partner, I wondered.

I reined myself in, packed up my misgivings, and chucked it into the bin to worry about later. To offer the illusion of purpose, I ducked into the shop beside the shoe store, browsing the selection of overpriced watches while waiting for Miss Gray to finish making her purchases. Ten minutes later, she remained in the store, and when I checked, the store's employee looked ready to throw up.

What Miss Gray had done to terrorize the woman interested me far more than infidelity. While I tried to limit my interactions with someone I photographed for a job, I couldn't leave the poor clerk to suffer.

Damn it. Sassy didn't need yet another pair of heels, yet I had no other excuse to play rescuer or snoop. I'd lose hundreds of dollars, but I always budgeted for excess expenses when shadowing someone.

I just hadn't planned on making contact with Miss Gray yet, and I disliked when something snarled my plans.

It would take work, but I'd convince myself buying shoes for Sassy technically counted as a business expense. Technically.

Realistically, I couldn't mark a pair of shoes on my taxes, which meant I'd be buying Sassy another pair of heels out of my pocket.

Bracing for the worst, I stepped into the store. Both women stopped and stared, and Miss Gray's gaze roamed over me while she licked her lips. Having been treated like a dessert at a buffet more times than I cared to count, I could handle the situation one of three ways: I could run, I could ignore her, or I could smile, which would inevitably be treated like an invitation.

Whoever invented the social requirement to smile needed to be taken out back and shot.

"Howdy, ladies." I tipped the brim of my baseball cap, forced a smile, and turned my attention to finding the perfect pair of shoes for Sassy, expecting her to beat me with them when she found out I'd unwillingly flirted with someone I was tailing. After she finished beating me, she'd probably kill me. Before killing me, she'd remind me I suffered from an allergy to women first.

"What's a handsome man like you doing in a store like this?" Miss Gray murmured, and to make certain I understood she wanted to catch my attention, she fluttered her lashes.

The poor store employee deflated, but it was better than an imminent loss of her lunch.

"A friend of mine's dating someone new, and I thought I'd congratulate her with a pair of shoes. She lives for shoes. What would you ladies suggest? I'd like to make them something special." I paused, faked a cringe, and added, "Preferably something special but affordable."

According to their expressions, the world had ended in a blaze of glory. Rather like my laptop, a relic in dire need of replacement, they struggled to comprehend my question.

Maybe if I'd stop buying Sassy shoes I'd have more money to spend on replacing things like my laptop.

The employee's brain finished rebooting first. "This way, sir."

She led me straight to the front window and pointed at a pair of black heels. "This is a classic heel good for everyday use. If you want something a little wilder, I just got in a pair of leopard print."

Leopard spots would infuriate my cheetah partner, which tempted me into making the purchase to watch her reaction. "Anything in cheetah?"

"If you're willing to spend a thousand, yes. It's a three-inch stiletto, open toe."

"She wears a size 8. I checked five different brands to be sure."

"Do you remember any of the brands?"

"One had a funky red bottom." Despite feigning ignorance, I could list almost every brand she owned; the more expensive the shoe, the more passionate she became, and I loved watching her when she forgot herself and rambled about the latest and greatest.

"A size 8 should fit. I'll be right back, sir." The employee, Danielle according to her name tag, scampered off.

Miss Gray glanced at my left hand. "How is a nice man like you still single?"

Her question led me to believe she thought any man without a ring was fair game, something that often led to single women taking married men to bed. Fighting the urge to sigh, I forced another smile. "I haven't met the right woman yet."

While the truth, I also lied right through the tiny gap between my front teeth. Sassy churned through boyfriends, mostly cheetah lycanthrope, and came to me with her current war cry: cheetahs never win.

I gave it another few years before she realized she could date every cheetah male on Earth without finding one loyal pre-mating. I'd done my research.

The females mated with one male for life.

The males slept with each other until a female convinced him it was time for a lifetime of cubs.

Sassy only dated lycanthropes.

The only woman I wanted, lycanthrope or not, only dated lycanthropes.

I'd need a miracle to dig out of the relationship mire I'd made for myself. Until then, I'd pretend being hopelessly single was what I wanted.

Miss Gray took her time looking me over. Again. "You could come give me a try tonight. There's a party. It'll get rowdy, I'm sure. You got yourself a suit? If so, I've got the ticket. My date cancelled."

On the PI front, a cancelled date was a bust. "Well, that's a pity. Know why?"

"He's a cheap dick. Fucker picked some other broad."

I could think of a few reasons why. "I'm sorry, ma'am."

Miss Gray wrinkled her nose. "Turns out the bitch is his fucking wife." Clicking her teeth together, she shook her head and averted her gaze. "In our club, the rules are clear: either the wives are in or the men are out. Why can't everyone just follow the rules?"

Why did I always meet the odd ones? Oh, right. I was a private investigator. I courted trouble on a daily basis. I'd been around long enough to deduce she had kinkier tastes than most. Dallas also had more swingers clubs than I cared to count, and I'd been invited to at least half of them during jobs. I'd gone exactly once as an observer.

Some liked to be watched, and I'd sworn to reject any job that might drop me into a den of depravity. Obviously, I hadn't vetted Tom Heatherow and the potential for uncomfortable situations thoroughly enough.

Why had I accepted his proposal, anyway?

Oh, right. A month's worth of income, which I needed to pay for Sassy's new pair of thousand dollar shoes.

Damn it.

"Swingers club?" I made a show of looking over the cheaper shoes, and a pair of baby blue flats caught my eye. I picked them up and turned them over in my hands. Sassy sometimes wore a dress the same color, one capable of transforming me into an emotional wreck. "Are these a good shoe?"

Miss Gray snatched the shoes. "On the lower end, but yeah. They'll do. These ones would be in an 8, too. Your friend has trouble dating?"

"You have no idea," I muttered. "Is the party tonight with your club?"

"Yeah. It is. There's no sex tonight, though. You interested?"

Damn it, damn it, damn it. Why couldn't I keep my license with a conviction? Mr. Hearthrow deserved a one-way trip to hell. "As a matter of fact, I am. When and where?"

"The Ritz-Carlton at nine. It's a mixer. It's how we find new people to partner with. You'll be a hit. It'll be a good way for you to see if you like it." Miss Gray handed over the shoes and dug into her pocket, retrieving a small white envelope. "Arrive thirty minutes early."

I slid the invitation into my back pocket, already hating myself for what I did for money. A hidden camera would do the talking for me if Senator Sterling showed up. I doubted it if I held his ticket, but I couldn't be certain.

The ticket could've belonged to another man easily enough.

However, if he had acquired his own ticket and brought his wife, things would become interesting for my client, who would lose his sex scandal angle. Miss Gray's commentary led me to believe infidelity factored, but considering the relationship between Mr. and Mrs. Sterling was all but over, the information I gathered wouldn't create much of a scandal.

I needed proof of a scandal. Proof got me paid, and I couldn't break the law while I worked, which made the job challenging on a good day.

Oh, well. I'd figure something out.

Danielle returned with Sassy's new shoes, and as I suffered from a complete lapse of good judgment, I got her the blue pair, too. She might kill me over it later, but for a few minutes, one of us would be happy.

TWO

That girl's going to kill you one of these days.

NOTHING SOURED my day quite like gunfire and bodies.

The gunfire, two ear-piercing shots, led me to the bodies. The busy steps ascending to Park Lane's parking lot made a terrible place for a murder. As though in celebration of the deaths of a young woman and her son, confetti rained down from the nearby second-story roof.

In the moments it had taken me to round the corner, the killer had escaped, two bodies and scraps of paper the only evidence of his deed. A single glance told the bitter truth: bullets to the head killed instantly, merciful as far as brutal murders went.

With a heavy heart, I retrieved my phone and called the police.

"9-1-1. What's your name, your number,

location, and the nature of your emergency?" a man asked in a gravel-rough voice.

I gave him everything he'd asked for before stating, "There's been a double homicide at Park Lane near the parking lot. A woman and her child were shot in the head."

"How long ago? Did you witness the incident?"

"No, sir. I was down the street, heard the gunfire, and found them on the steps."

"Has anyone else been injured, Mr. Clinton?"

"No, sir. The shops are crowded, but it doesn't seem like anyone else has been hurt."

"Please stay where you are. Do you know if anyone is armed?"

"Sir, we're in Texas. I'm probably the only one who isn't armed. No one I can see actively has their firearm out. I didn't see the shooter, but I think he fired from the roof."

"Why do you believe that?"

"The woman and child were shot through the top of their heads, sir. Someone has also dumped scraps of papers onto the steps."

The scraps still rained down, caught on the breeze and swirling towards the sidewalk and parking lot.

"Officers are on route to your location, sir. Can you please give me your description?"

I complied, wondering if the cops would

identify me from my hat, or their knowledge of me as a PI with a reputation of sticking my nose where it didn't belong.

BY SOME MIRACLE, everyone on the street gave the bodies a wide berth. It didn't save the evidence from blowing away, and several scraps of the confetti, made of newspaper clippings, found their way into my pocket, stuck in my hair, and otherwise turned me into walking evidence.

Sirens announced the arrival of the police, and I sighed my resignation when a midlife-crisis-turned-cop led the charge. During his political career, Maxwell Smith had single-handedly set back women's health by a decade, triggered an endemic of newborn fatalities, and otherwise destroyed stable family life for Texans before a severe case of humility and morality led him to paying penance working the streets as an officer of the law.

When I could ignore his sins, I liked the man despite his enjoyment of giving me a hard time.

"Aaron," he greeted, taking the steps two at a time to join me. When he spotted the bodies, he whistled. "That's brutal. You didn't see the shooter?"

I knew the drill; to keep my PI license intact, I needed to clear myself as quickly as possible. "I'll verify everything I witnessed and my innocence by angel at the station. I was down the lane buying bribes for Sassy."

"That girl's going to kill you one of these days. Stick around and don't touch anything," he ordered.

Beyond the confetti pieces I'd pocketed, fouling evidence was last on my list of things to do. "I have an engagement at eight-thirty. Wish I could give you something concrete, but I was around the corner when the shooting happened. I didn't see anything."

"I'd call that partner of yours to cover for you. I think you'll be busy, even with angelic verification. The chief wants us thorough on the cases involving kids. My shift ends at seven, and I have no idea who you'll be with if you're still in questioning."

In Maxwell Smith's language, he wanted to talk off the record about the murders, he'd probably pull strings to make sure I got out the same time he did, and I'd save myself a lot of aggravation if I went with what he wanted. I couldn't imagine what he wanted to talk to me about. I'd find out soon enough.

I dug out my phone and dialed Sassy's number.

"What do you have for me, Aaron?" my partner growled.

"I need help with a job, and I bought you two pairs of shoes for a stay of execution. There's been a double homicide at Park Lane. I was around the corner and called it in. I need you to put on your new shoes and go to a party for me. Formalwear. I'll also need you to extend my apologies to someone."

"Sure. I can do that. I can be at Park Lane in twenty. Call me if they take you to the copper shop."

"What about your date?"

"Cheetahs," she hissed.

"Caught him with his tongue down his buddy's throat?" I guessed.

"Basically. If this didn't happen at least once a week, I'd ask if you were following me." She sighed. "Again. I'm impressed you didn't shadow me today."

"Had I been available, I might have. I have to practice shadowing, and someone has to bail your ass out when you forget to watch where you're walking. I'm concerned. The one pair of shoes has a heel."

"You're joking about shoes when I know you can't stand them. You're rattled. Who was shot?"

"A mom and her kid."

"Shit."

"Yeah."

"All right. Twenty minutes, Aaron. No one likes the cases with kids, so sit tight, don't touch anything, and play nice with the police officers." Sassy hung up, and I returned my phone to my pocket.

It was a good thing I wasn't a cop. If I got a hold of the killer, I doubted the bastard would make it to trial. Some things I couldn't forgive, and young lives ended early topped the list.

NO MATTER how many times I swore off women, whenever Sassy came around, I forgot all the reasons why and risked dying from suffocation. Holding my breath while watching her, a haphazard blend of feline grace, clutzy charm, and tanned Texan cowgirl, might kill me one day.

If she liked me half as much as my bribe of shoes, I'd be set for life. She snatched the bag and invitation out of my hands, bouncing from foot to foot while digging for her prizes. The gathered cops, working hard to make sense of a senseless murder, stopped and stared.

I remembered I needed to breathe. "Sassy. We're at a crime scene."

Without looking away from my bribes, she pointed behind her. "There's a spent casing in the step's shadow in the confetti someone missed."

Sure enough, she pointed right to the missed evidence.

"I'm going to buy you a cheap pair of shoes for that." I marveled at her photographic memory, the original reason I'd joined forces with her. I tailed people better than she did, she caught the little details I missed, and we both did well at interviewing and intel gathering for defense attorneys, which made up half our workload.

Without that damned case from a few months ago, it would've made up the entirety of our workload.

"These are good. Your best friend was about to find it anyway."

Maxwell sighed. "You don't have to live up to your name, Sassy."

"Screw you, Max. Has Aaron gotten around to requesting an angel yet?" She abandoned her examination of her new shoes to give the cop her full attention. "I'll be accused of having rabies if he hasn't."

"It was the first thing he did when we arrived. I already called it in. Keep your rabies to yourself, Sassy. If you need a dose of neutralizer, go to the clinic. I'm not your personal supplier."

I tensed, ready to grab my partner around the waist so she wouldn't assault an officer and lose her PI license. "Sassy, if you need to vent about your scumbag date, come over to my place tonight after the party."

I wanted to suggest she wear her blue dress with her new shoes, but that would send the wrong but also right message. If she came over, I kept a stock of treats meant to keep cranky cheetahs happy. A happy cheetah purred, and if I got lucky, she'd shift for me.

I'd never live it down if Sassy figured out I'd violated my sacred vow of never loving a woman again. If she realized I wanted to offer what she hunted with other men, we'd fight. By the end of said fight, I'd either be left on the curb or infected with lycanthropy. I hedged my bets on the curb.

We'd partnered together because we were utterly incompatible.

I wore my clothes to death. She worshipped new shoes. She drank. I grabbed a beer every blue moon. I still snuck smokes in the back. She was allergic to cigarette smoke and always caught me.

I'd forced her to coin cheetahs never win thanks to an ill-timed cig.

Neither of us acknowledged a painful truth: we wanted the same thing.

Sassy tugged on my jean jacket. "You okay, Aaron?"

"I hate when kids are brought into it. What a fucking waste." I told the truth yet I lied. I did hate when kids became involved in

the problems of adults. I hated my helpless-
ness more. If I'd moved faster, if I'd been
closer, could I have stopped one of them from
dying? I had no idea if the shooter had
gunned down mother or son first. It didn't
matter. I replayed the seconds between their
deaths and my arrival over and over again.

If I'd arrived ten seconds sooner, could I
have done something to save one of them?

The past I couldn't change would haunt
me for a long time.

Maxwell thumped my shoulder. "If you
ever get tired of being a PI, join the force. You
could do good things. I have."

I wished I could forget Maxwell's past. I
bet he wished he could, too. The chasm of
bad choices and circumstance divided us, but
I pushed my feelings aside and buried them
for a while. He tried to pay penance for his
sins.

I couldn't say the same for most.

"We'll see. Maybe if I finally get tired of
figuring out who cheated who and snap." I
shrugged. "I respect your beat, Max. You've
got a tough job."

He carried the burden of saving lives on
his shoulders.

I searched for the truth on behalf of the
defense. If Max and his fellow officers found
the killer and an attorney approached me for
the case, I wasn't sure what I'd do. I wanted

the truth, but the idea of helping a lawyer defend a killer of children didn't sit well with me. I didn't trust myself to look for the unbiased truth.

It might result in an innocent going to jail.

"Give it some thought. The two of you would make a good pair."

Sassy growled. "I don't have the hybrid form, Max."

"Tough luck. Well, I still think you'd make a good cop despite your feline disposition. Go on and get out of here before you earn a case of rabies along with your scratching post."

"You're an ass, Max. And Aaron isn't my scratching post."

"Why not? He'd be a good catch for you. We've all heard you yowling about how useless unmated cheetah males are. I've witnessed it for myself. Aaron is capable of tying his own shoelaces without help."

I counted to ten, my estimated time for Max's jab to sink in and blow a fuse in Sassy's head. I made it to eight before my partner hissed, stomped down the steps, hissed again, and howled, "Men are *jerks!*"

"I can't tell if you're a help or a hindrance, Max," I admitted.

"I'm helping. I planted the seed you're a viable solution to her dating problems. I've bought my wife shoes from that store, Aaron, and a man doesn't just buy any old girl shoes from that store without a lot of love and money involved. A lot of money. That said, she's out of your league, but I tried. Good luck. You're going to need it. Now, let me see where we're at and get you to the station for a proper questioning session. I'll check on the status of the angel while I'm at it. There's been a wait for them lately."

"Off the record, any reason why?"

"Stalkers. Women have started asking for angels to prove they haven't done anything to deserve the unwelcome advances of their stalkers. It's a mess."

Sometimes, I really hated Texas, its back-water ways, and so many who insisted on treating women like fodder or accusing them of guilt for the crimes of men. I'd heard Sassy rant.

No matter what, it was *her* fault.

She wore too much. She wore too little.

Her shoes were too flashy. Her shoes weren't flashy enough.

She'd made eye contact. She hadn't made eye contact.

Sassy counted herself as lucky. Lycan-thropy gave her an easy out plus sharp claws and teeth. It helped, but I still worried.

Everything circled back to her belief that she never won at life, beginning before birth and being infected with the lycanthropy virus, the middle child of a pair of cheetahs determined to up the percentage of feline lycanthropes without help.

"This city pisses me off."

"Cool your heels, Aaron. Get through questioning, and as soon as I'm off shift, we'll go grab a beer. Well, I'll grab a beer while you nurse a coffee."

Fuck it. "I'll have a beer, but you're buying and driving."

"Well, I know you're having a rough day when you decide it's time for a drink. No worries. I'll get you home safe and sound."

THREE

A man can hope, can't he?

MY QUESTIONING SESSION lasted less than ten minutes. I supposed the cops had interviewed other witnesses before getting around to me, confirming my alibi and story before asking me to confirm my name, something that made us all laugh.

Everyone in the station knew who I was. My willingness to give my statement before an angel, who confirmed the truth of my words, made things easier on everyone. I classified as a second-tier witness, and I offered to give them copies of my photographs. They refused on the grounds I hadn't been in the right location and lacked images of the victims.

I'd keep copies of the pictures in case I'd somehow photographed the killer during my time at Park Lane. It annoyed me that the cops didn't want the potential evidence.

They had no proof I had pictures of the killer, but they lacked proof I *didn't* have pictures of the killer.

I scored a few brownie points and a donut for not giving them a hard time on a shit case. After my questioning, I waited for Maxwell so he could live up to his word on buying me a beer. To kill time, I checked over the images, wondering if some secret lurked in plain sight.

"You ready?" Maxwell appeared at my shoulder. "I doubt your phone holds the secrets of the universe."

"A man can hope, can't he?"

"The DA is miffed you're involved, but he changed his tune when he saw the interview recording. He even said if we could nab you to run cases involving kids, our solve rate would skyrocket. He liked you were willing to share your photos."

"The DA is involved already? It's early."

"That's what I was thinking, too. Mostly. I'll explain at the bar. How does the place by your apartment sound? I can drop you near your truck, and we can meet there."

"That works. I think I can handle staggering two blocks home."

"I'll make sure you get there. While the DA's happy with you for a change, don't test your luck with him on this one." The way

Maxwell arched a brow led me to believe he wanted some unofficial help.

I could do that. "I'll keep my nose clean."

"You always do. Why'd you think your photos might be useful?"

"I took pictures of the crowd while investigating. I'll see what I can find and tip you off if I learn anything important."

"This is what I like about you. You always do what's right. I'd be a much different—and better—man had I known back then what I know now. I really hope we find this bastard before he has a chance to go after someone else."

He would. They always did. Then I thought about it and wondered why Maxwell assumed the killer was a man. "He?" I asked.

"Women are creatures of passion given flesh. If it were a woman, she would've gotten in their faces and killed them at point-blank range. No, my gut feeling says a man did it."

I'd take the sane route and collect evidence. While women were creatures of passion in the flesh, men were as well.

Everyone had the capacity in moments of passion to do the unthinkable, but the mother and child hadn't died from someone's unleashed, raw emotions.

They'd been killed in cold blood, and the murderer had left them in a shower of paper confetti, irrefutable evidence of meticulous planning.

Women could be meticulous. Women could be cruel. Women were equally capable of planning murder as men.

I wouldn't argue with Maxwell over it; it wasn't worth wasting my breath. "Well, if there's anything I can do, ask."

"We'll talk at the bar," Maxwell replied.

I wondered what he knew that I didn't, but I'd find out soon enough. All I could do was hope he wouldn't ask for something I couldn't give him.

A RUSTED-OUT family car tailed me halfway across Dallas, and I took a few detours to shake off the vehicle. Once satisfied I'd lost the driver, I headed home, grateful my apartment building had an indoor garage. It wouldn't stop anyone from finding me, but it'd make their work a little harder.

Maxwell waited for me in the bar at a table tucked into the corner. "That took longer than I expected. What held you up?"

"I picked up a tail. I figured I'd give him a tour of Dallas." Had I worked in any other profession, I might've been more worried about it, but I'd dealt with it time and time again, usually in the form of an angry

boyfriend, side man, or soon-to-be ex-hus-
band wanting to blame me for his abusive
ways. If the tail showed up again, I'd get the
plate numbers and report it to the police. If it
related to one of my jobs, the incident would
become part of the case one way or another.

I needed to fit in some time at the range
and start carrying again soon, especially if I
kept having to deal with clients like Tom
Heatherow.

"Get a look at him?"

I shook my head and sat across from
Maxwell. "Not really. No front tags on the
vehicle."

"Welcome to Texas. You worried?"

I shrugged. "Not yet. If I see the junker
again, maybe. What do you want to talk
about? You obviously want it off the record
and on the sly, else we would've been in the
break room entertaining your badge
buddies."

"Thank you for not calling my co-workers
badge bunnies this time."

I grinned. "I save that for when I'm in the
break room and they've annoyed me. I also
try to wait for Sassy to be around because she
enjoys the entertainment."

"Obviously. That's because she's the one
who usually gets mouthy with the police. A
damned pity she doesn't have the hybrid
form. She'd be a real asset on the force."

Trying to imagine Sassy as a police officer gave me a headache, and I hadn't even gotten around to grabbing a beer. "I'm afraid to ask."

"You're both smart, you're both good at getting information, and you both under-stand the importance of finding the actual truth and not what the DA's office wants you to find. Or your attorneys, although word down the line is the local firms are still giving you the cold shoulder for finding evidence against a client and turning it over to the po-lice, thus losing the defense the case."

"It's right in my contract. It's not my fault they didn't read the contract closely enough."

"I bet the lawyers were not happy when you told them that."

"Precisely. I think they blacklisted me more for beating them at their own game than exposing their client. As I told them, they hired me to find evidence. I found it. It's not my fault they didn't like the evidence I found and that their client was so guilty they had no chance in hell of being able to reduce his sentence."

Maxwell sighed. "I sometimes believe the law enforcement system and judiciary sys-tems have nothing to do with justice and everything to do with personal prestige."

I suspected the former politician under-stood that better than most. "You won't hear me arguing with you. What do you need that's important enough for you to cross town to have a beer with me?"

"I'm worried the shooting at Park Lane is just the beginning. In the past few months, we've gotten a lot of calls about women being stalked. It's following the same trend as the killing; every report has involved single mothers with children. Most are only bothered for a week or two before the stalking stops."

The first thought to come to mind bothered me; when I did work for a client, I usually wrapped up the initial profiling within a week or two unless I needed to uncover deeper, darker secrets. "PI?"

"Doubtful. There's too much overlap, but it could be a pair of PIs working together. Some of the detectives brought your name up, but when we showed the women your pictures, only two of them recognized you or Sassy, and they confirmed you weren't the ones stalking them."

"That's something. But why involve Sassy?"

"We all know you send her in to do your dirty work if the woman you're shadowing either likes shoes or is skittish around men."

Considering Sassy could charm the shoes off other women without much work, I couldn't blame them for assuming I'd use her like that. Sassy did pick up that role when needed, although she volunteered as often as not. "Are we cleared off the suspect list?"

"You're clear. You two were cleared early. That said, you're being monitored, so keep your nose clean. You've ticked most attorneys in the area off one way or another. The local prosecutors would love to have your license revoked."

Of course they would. I'd been a thorn in their side since the day I'd been licensed as a PI. The rare cases I found incriminating evidence against the defense's client didn't make up for the number of times I'd put a kink in their cases. I flagged a waitress for a beer to buy myself time and some liquid fortification, which I'd need to get through the conversation. "Same shit, different day. Let me see if I understand this correctly. You want my help while some dicks from the DA's office want to sink me?"

"That's right. We're going to need all the help we can get on this one if the stalking case is connected. So far, we've identified at least three PIs involved with the stalking cases, and we have had over a hundred unique reports in three months."

It'd take a lot more than three PIs to profile over a hundred different single mothers. "How many women total?"

"At last count, one-ten."

I whistled. The waitress returned with my

beer, and as promised, Maxwell paid. Aware I'd be buzzed halfway through the bottle, I sipped with care. "Well, you have my attention. What do you want me to do? I can't profile that many women even with Sassy's help."

"I want to hire you to do what you do best. I want you to stick your nose where it doesn't belong while staying within the letter of the law. I'll give you the intel I can. Try to find out what connects these women, why they're being profiled and stalked, and anything else you can dig up about them. We're spinning our wheels, and we just don't have the manpower needed to check them all. I know you have other work, but I'd appreciate however many hours you can give me. We don't have jack shit about this, and with one of the women who'd reported already dead, we're worried we've been given advance notice of future hits."

As a general rule, I tried to avoid the police during an investigation; they typically viewed me as an obstruction to their cases, especially when they thought I might find something they'd missed. For Maxwell to want to hire me, he believed something big was going to happen, something that his partners on the force wouldn't be able to handle alone.

That Maxwell came to me told me one truth I couldn't ignore: he believed more children would be targeted and killed. We didn't see eye-to-eye on a lot of things, but the cases with kids always worked out the same way.

When kids were involved, I did my best work, and I would toe every line possible to see justice served.

I took a sip of my beer and got ready to make a deal I'd likely regret later. "I'm in. I'll find out what I can. How do you want me to deliver the intel to you?"

"Use the anonymous hotline. That way, if anyone does come poking around, it'll take them more work to link us. Technically, what I'm doing isn't illegal, but it's toeing some lines I'd rather not people be aware of."

With Maxwell's background in ruthless politics, I bet he understood the risks of his actions better than most. "Yeah, your buddies aren't going to be happy with you if they find out you hired me. The DA's office would have a conniption, and so would your chief."

"Nonsense. Despite how often he gets annoyed with you for messing up his investigations, you do good work and have better ethics. He's just pissed you're not on the force and choose to play with the defense. Anyway, you haven't asked me how much I'm paying."

With kids involved, I would've done the work for free and faced Sassy's wrath for losing us money. I lifted my beer in a salute.

"If I don't ask, you get this one on the house. That bastard killed a kid."

"Well, you're getting paid for this one. You're getting seven thousand, Sassy is getting seven thousand, and I'll add two more payments each in a few days so the banks don't hold them for too long. For every solid lead you bag, I'll add an extra grand."

I raised both brows. "I couldn't have possibly heard that right. You're paying us twenty-one thousand each plus lead bonuses?"

A former politician with a reputation of being good with money had the cash, but he'd never used his personal assets on a case before.

"You heard me right. I want this solved as quickly as possible. You two make a damned good team, especially on the cases involving the kids. You're motivated, and you won't sacrifice an innocent to wrap a case faster. You in?"

"I already told you I was in. Sassy'll jump at the chance to work this one, too." While lycanthropes often got the short lot, when it came to kids and family, they scored top marks for determination.

"Got your wire details handy?"

I dug out my wallet and retrieved the pair of cards with our payment details on them, which Maxwell photographed with his phone. I waited for him to pocket the device before asking, "Do you have a map of the incidents?"

"I'll email it to you from a dummy account. Expect it in the morning. I'll also send over everything else I can."

"I hope you realize people are going to ask why you hired us later. It's going to be impossible to hide it forever. It could wreck your reputation in the force," I warned.

"There's nothing on the books barring me from hiring you with personal funds. I'd rather pay you than be too slow on the draw. I can handle the heat. You just keep things legal on your side of the fence."

I'd be earning every penny of my pay and sweating every minute of the job, but some prices were worth paying. "I'll keep my nose clean. Sassy will, too." It'd be a little harder for the cheetah; as soon as she found out we were hunting someone killing kids, she'd plunge right into the deep end. Reining in her enthusiasm to solve the case in record time would challenge me in more ways than I cared to think about.

With no other choice, I'd cross that bridge when I got there.

"Good. What do you think about the murders today?"

I wished I could forget the memory of the bodies on the steps while confetti rained down on them. "Someone planned it well," I admitted. "A professional. The shots were fast and accurate. At first glance, I'd peg it as ex-military. The shops were busy, and the shooter picked the ideal place to wait for them. Just about everyone shopping at Park Lane takes those steps at least once. The public place implies he wanted the bodies found fast. Why? That I can't tell you. The confetti bothers me."

"It bothers us, too. I can tell you this much. The pieces were printouts of two types. One had the number one on it. The other had a date with no year: April 10th."

"Newspaper clippings?"

"Yes. We haven't been able to identify which paper they came from yet, but the font matched in all the samples we've found so far. The paper's going in for analysis to see if they came from the same newspaper batch or not. Considering the number of pieces, I don't think the paper will be the same, but it's possible."

"Do you think it's the start of a serial killer spree?" The serial killers who wanted to be remembered left clues and taunted the police. They had an agenda, and they wanted to let the police know they were a step behind at all times.

Maxwell sighed. "If the shoe fits. I think it does. I'm concerned the stalking incidents are the killer looking for ideal victims for his spree."

"Had the woman killed today filed a stalker report?"

"If so, I haven't been told yet; another pair is working on that portion of the investigation. But, not everyone reports, and there's been so many stalking cases, I'm worried that the cases may be connected."

"Get me as much intel on the woman and her son as you can. In the meantime, I'll see what I can dig up."

"Will do. And Aaron?"

"Yeah?"

"Make sure your conceal carry permit is up to date and you've gotten in your hours at the range. Don't take any unnecessary risks. Whoever this guy is, he means business. Try to talk Sassy into wearing a vest while you're at it. You, too."

When Maxwell wanted me wearing protection, it meant trouble. I couldn't tell if he was indulging in paranoia or he knew something he wasn't telling me yet. It could go either way with him. I sighed. "I'll talk to her about it."

"Just be careful. I worry this is only the beginning."

I LEFT the bar after finishing my beer and took a headache home with me. If I left without delaying, I could contact Sassy and take over the meeting with the swingers and spare her from attending the party. Within minutes, my headache would develop into a migraine, the kind determined to stick around for days. Bracing for the inevitable rush and misery involved with arriving on time, I called her cell.

"The copper shop released you already?"

"They did. I might be able to make it to the hotel on time if I head over now. I'm almost back to my apartment."

"Don't worry about it. I've already contacted your lady friend and introduced myself as a friend—one hoping to land you permanently but still willing to share for a while. At least until you're contagious." The laughter in her voice promised Sassy knew she'd been fibbing and waited for me to call her out on it.

Sassy didn't share, not when it came to her men.

"Why do I get the feeling you've already discussed my assets?"

"Well, we've certainly been discussing your ass."

I wasn't sure if I was to interpret that as the cheetah having an actual interest in my ass, a situation I wouldn't mind in the slightest, or if she was trying her best to sass me straight to a migraine. "What's this about the contagious commentary?"

"They like the thrill. It took her a few minutes to warm up to me, but when she saw the shoes you'd bought for me today, she relaxed. I told her you had gotten an emergency call at work."

At least she'd been honest enough about that. "You're sure you'll be okay at that party? It's not really your crowd."

"It's more of my crowd than it is your crowd. Remember, cheetah? The males of my species love things like this, especially when there aren't any women involved. I'm sure. You head on home and try to relax. You sound ready to come unhinged. I'll check in with you later. Then we can talk about this in-ter-est-ing party you sent me to. In detail." She added a bit of a growl, and as always, I had no idea if she was yanking my chain because she could, or if she meant to get the payback she was rightfully owed.

I smiled. Lycanthropes. Send the loyal types to a swinger's party, and it was the end of the world. "I secured us a contract for forty-two thousand dollars today, and it has potential lead bonuses."

Sassy sucked in a breath. "You have my attention."

"You won't get paid if you kill me for sending you to that party."

Her laughter dulled the edge I'd heard in her voice. "Well played. All right. You win this time. You live. For now."

"You're so gracious, Sassy. Whatever would I do without your forgiveness?"

"Be bored, lonelier than you already are, and completely bereft of positive female attention in your life."

I needed positive female attention from anyone other than Sassy? I supposed having positive attention from my mother might do me some good, but my mother had an issue with lycanthropes and already considered me halfway into my grave from partnering with the feisty cheetah. I smiled and strolled towards my apartment. "Positive female attention isn't just a myth?"

"You're an ass."

"But I'm an ass who got us a big contract. I'm also an ass who bought you *two* pairs of shoes."

She sighed, and I imagined her rolling her eyes and praying for patience. "Good job on the contract. I'll properly appreciate your work tomorrow. Oh, by the way, go into your apartment through the window or you'll be tarred and feathered."

Damned cat. "Tarred and feathered? What

the hell did you do to my apartment this time?"

"You'll only step in whipped cream going through the window."

I wondered how I'd get in through the window without having the ability to land on my feet if I fell during the attempt. "Anything else I should know?"

"Tread with care."

Sassy must have done some research and discovered what sort of party I'd sent her to in advance, resulting in her paying me back before she'd left for her unwanted date with a group of swingers at a mixer. "Remind me why I gave you a key again?"

"I keep your life interesting. Have fun!" Sassy hung up, and I considered banging my head against the brick wall of my apartment complex. One day, she might remember I lived on the second floor and none of the windows were near the stairwells. Given the choice between being tarred and feathered or falling to my death trying to enter my apartment through the window, I opted for the extra clean-up but higher chances of survival. Taking off my jacket, I set it out of the way and unlocked my door.

All remained quiet.

On most days, I believed peace and quiet to be good things. With Sassy on the prowl, it meant trouble and humiliation.

I cracked my door open and peeked inside, examining the frame, latch, and knob. In true prankster fashion, she'd rigged a bucket overhead designed to fall on the unwitting when they opened the door. I stood on my toes and worked my hand beneath it. If she'd used actual tar, it had cooled, which would've resulted in a hard knock to the head but little mess. Unwilling to take any chances, I eased the bucket off the door and lowered it so I could peek inside.

Fluffy cotton candy obscured my view of whatever else might lurk within. To make things more interesting, Sassy had gone through the trouble of lining the inside with plastic wrap. As Sassy took food sanitation with surprising seriousness for a predatory feline who liked her meat bleeding on her plate, I assumed she'd decided to prank me with edibles. I plucked out a pinch of the cotton candy and munched on it.

One treat pleased the cheetah over all other treats: chocolate syrup. I'd bet the entire contract with Maxwell she'd decided to tar me with her favorite treat to maximize my exposure to her favorite food. That mean she had one goal in mind: revenge through tongue bath.

I shook my head, checked it for additional traps, and once satisfied the entry was safe, I retrieved my coat and hung it on the empty rack. I assumed she'd relocated my property to protect it from the tar and feathering I'd rightfully earned.

After I got some payback of my own on the damned cat, I'd thank her for having some common sense. I'd also ask what I'd done to deserve her at her worst. The party had earned me some trouble, but not a complete booby trapping of my apartment. I could think of a few things that might warrant the booby trapping of my apartment.

Actually, I could think of a lot of things that might earn me her at her worst, and not showing up to save her from a miserable date topped the list, with sending her to a swinger's party coming in a close second. I'd earned the tarring and feathering for saddling her with Miss Gray.

Damn it.

There was only one thing I could do. I texted Sassy and asked her to come by my apartment before she headed home, begged for a ten-minute warning, and to provide her with a reason to make the trip worth her while, I told her I wanted to discuss the new contract.

She confirmed she'd stop over and estimated she'd be at the party for four hours.

Four hours gave me the time I needed to figure out what to do with the cotton candy, a bucket of chocolate syrup, and an obscene amount of whipped cream. The whipped cream would go down the drain; after sitting out in my apartment for an unknown period of time, I wouldn't feed it to a dog. The rest left me no other choice.

I'd wear it and pretend I had Sassy's general inability to avoid disaster.

FOUR

You're such a cat.

AS REQUESTED, Sassy warned me ten minutes before she arrived. As I valued my floor, I dumped the bucket of cotton candy and chocolate syrup over my head in the tub, used towels to mitigate the worst of the damage, and waited in the entry for her amusement.

She arrived right on schedule, opened my door, and stared at me with wide eyes. A giggle escaped her lips, and she clapped her hands over her mouth.

Excellent.

"You're such a cat," I announced. "Did you forget I'm not a feline? How am I supposed to enter through the second-story window with any expectation of not falling to my death?" I fought against my need to smile. A neutral expression would work best for my needs, which involved screwing around with Sassy and leaving her wondering how I'd handled my introduction to cotton candy and chocolate syrup. "How was the party?"

"Senator Sterling showed up with his soon-to-be ex-wife. I got some excellent photos of them jousting with their tongues. I also scored photos of their other partners. They're the talk of the town. They're splitting so they can remarry, and their new partners used to be married to each other. It's surprisingly amicable, and I think they're participating in some hot foursomes. I believe they intend on remaining a sexual partnership beyond divorce. They just want some new waters for general house life from the looks of it."

Tom Heatherow would have a field day with the intel, but nothing in our contract stated I couldn't leave a subtle warning for the senator. Then again, I doubted the senator cared. He could spin his relationship choices like a champ, and the mess would resolve itself without my help.

Political sexual scandals only hurt when the target actually cared. Senator Sterling didn't seem to care. The general population wouldn't care, either.

Hell, most men I knew would be cheering the man on for working the system and having a side woman with her man's blessings. Personally, I didn't roll that way, but it was none of my business what consenting adults did.

"Hey, Aaron?"

I grimaced at having been caught wool-gathering. "What is it?"

"Why did you dump chocolate syrup and cotton candy over your head?"

Damned cat, figuring out my ruse with no effort on her part. "I figured you deserved to see the fruits of your labor."

"Well, the fruits of my labor didn't seem to make much of a dent on your floor. Dumped it in the bathtub?"

"Yep."

"Two towels to contain the mess, too, from the looks of it. Heaven forbid you get syrup on the floor. Don't move," she ordered, strolling in the direction of my chocolate-decorated bathroom. She peeked inside and laughed. "Well, that will keep you busy for a while. What happened to the whipped cream?"

"I dumped it down the drain. I figured it'd gone bad sitting out."

"Let me see if I understand this. You dis-armed my trap, restored your apartment to order, dumped the potentially but probably not spoiled whipped cream down the drain, and waited until I was on my way here to pour it over your head?"

"That sounds remarkably accurate," I admitted.

"You're even more of a cat than I am."

"I don't think a self-respecting cat would do this." I pointed at my chocolate-covered hair. "I figured I deserved this for sending you to that party."

"It beat my date," Sassy muttered. "Did you know there's a group of swingers interested in contracting the virus? I recommended they ask the male cheetahs. They'll sleep with anything that moves as long as they sign a bloody waiver."

Her tone, close enough to a growl I might luck out and see her shift, warned me her date had gone even worse than I'd thought. One day, she'd win, and she tempted me to be the one who won her.

How would be the question.

As always, I cursed myself, my professionalism, and my dumbass promise to never cross the dating line with her. If she figured out the truth, what would she do? It amazed me she hadn't already figured out I'd developed an unfortunate interest in her, one that grew with the same tenacity of a dandelion in the cracks of a sidewalk.

When we'd first partnered together, she'd been concerned; with her dismal luck in the dating world, I couldn't blame her for being worried. Her promise of immediate retribution no longer worried me.

She did things like leave traps of cotton candy and chocolate syrup for her unsuspecting victims.

I wanted to laugh at the absurdity of the situation, but I faked a sigh instead. "There can't be many cheetahs left for you to date, Sassy. You might need to start expanding your horizons for a male of another species."

Sassy wailed and yanked at her hair. "Maybe if they'd stop kissing each other long enough, I'd go on a second date with one of those loser male cheetahs! Can't they leave their boyfriends at home for at least a few hours? Mom had the same problem, too."

I appreciated Sassy's mother having found a way to overcome the natural tendencies of unmated cheetah males, but I worried Sassy would follow her mother's footsteps without it being targeted in my general direction. "How did your mother solve the problem?"

"She kidnapped him. Then she held him hostage for a while. Once she made it clear he was a captured male she intended to keep, she warned him if he involved his tongue with anyone other than her, she'd geld him after she had at least one litter, cruelly using him as a sperm donor."

Having met Sassy's father, the threats, posturing, kidnapping, and hostage situation likely tripped his trigger, revved his engine, and ensured Sassy's mother got her way. However, the threat of gelding made me grimace. "Well, I promise I've never done anything to deserve being gelded, and I plan to keep it that way."

Sassy snorted and waved her hand. "I wouldn't geld you, but after the day I've had, I need chocolate."

I already regretted turning myself into a living treat for Sassy's enjoyment, and she hadn't even shifted yet.

AT EIGHTY POUNDS, Sassy ranked in at the lowest of the low on the lycanthrope cheetah scale, smaller than mundane adults by at least three pounds. I suspected her size drove off some suitors, but I theorized she'd bulk up once she picked a mate and settled down for life. The few times I'd seen Sassy's mother as a cheetah, she could eat mundane cheetahs for lunch, and Sassy's father was at least thirty pounds heavier than her mother.

Then again, if Sassy stayed petite, I wouldn't mind it at all. Eighty pounds was enough feline for any man to contend with, especially when she insisted on taking over my lap at her convenience.

As keeping her happy topped my current

to-do list, I leaned towards her so she could use her tongue to give my face a washing I'd regret for days. Sandpaper had nothing on her, and long after she'd stripped off the top layer of skin, she continued on her mission to enjoy every drop of chocolate syrup she could.

To make it clear I was a treat she intended to enjoy, she pressed the tops of her claws into my leg to make certain I stayed put and didn't attempt to escape her not-so-tender grooming.

I consoled myself with digging my fingers into her fur and pretending I groomed her. While her fur was coarse compared to most dogs and cats, I enjoyed petting her, something I refused to admit to anyone. Adhering to our typical routine, I kept my mouth shut.

No matter how perky and lively Sassy behaved, she needed silence sometimes, something few others understood. When she was ready to talk, she'd wander to my bathroom, shift, come out, and talk. How she dressed would determine how the rest of my evening went. If she claimed my bathrobe, I'd dig out the pint of ice cream I kept in the freezer and pretend I didn't require sleep to function. If she wore her clothes and headed for the door, I'd pretend nothing had happened.

When Sassy lost her spunk, I worried. Some days, I worried enough I considered breaking a glass in such a way we both bled. It didn't take much blood to crank the risk of infection, and infection with lycanthropy would change all the rules of engagement. According to my observations of the local cheetah coalition, I'd have no more than ten years to convince her to pick me before I became an insufferable male cheetah like the rest of them.

It would be a challenge.

Two hours after beginning her assault using only the powers of her tongue, Sassy retreated to my bathroom, emerging a few minutes later wearing her clothes. "Call me tomorrow about the contract. I have a date at four with a wolf. We'll fight, but at least he's not a damned cheating cheetah."

"How does twenty after four sound?"

"About right. He suggested fast food to meet up and get to know each other."

Ouch. He could've at least suggested a family diner. "I guess he's expecting a fight, too."

"It is what it is. Thanks for the chocolate."

I chuckled and waved her off. "I'd say any time, but I need at least a few layers of intact skin."

"I'll give you a week. I'm thinking peanut butter and chocolate mousse next time."

She'd need a lot longer than two hours to lick that mess up. "I'll keep a stock of lactose-free milk in the fridge in that case. Just no whipped cream left out as a trap. It might spoil. If you want whipped cream, leave it in the fridge like a reasonable adult."

"Worry wart." Sassy headed to the door, hesitated, and then let herself out, mumbling something under her breath.

I wanted to hit the asshole cheetahs who'd stolen her fire and left her tired, lonely, and worn. Too many promises divided us, and I didn't know how to overcome them without leaving a shattered mess in my wake.

Fuck it. Tomorrow, I'd go buy her another pair of shoes, a purse that matched, and pay her parents a visit. Maybe they'd have a solution to Sassy's lack of a love life that didn't involve extending me an invitation to a gelding.

FOURTEEN THOUSAND DOLLARS, seven thousand for me, seven thousand for Sassy, waited in the company bank accounts first thing in the morning. I checked my clothes for scraps of paper, confirming Maxwell's tip about the number one and April 10th. The lack of a year frustrated me even more than the ambiguous date and number. Why April 10th?

The number seemed dreadfully obvious;

the pair was only the first of the deaths, an omen I hoped wouldn't come to pass. Maxwell's willingness to hire me out of pocket led me to believe the police wouldn't catch the killer in time to prevent another murder—or murders.

Had the mother or child been the real target? If the child had been the target, why? What could a child have done to deserve death?

The number could mean something else, but until I uncovered more evidence or Maxwell contacted me with additional information, I had no choice but to focus my efforts on the date. I sent Maxwell an email asking if he'd learned any names; he'd be able to guess I meant the mother and child without anyone who might read it understanding what we discussed.

Realistically, I expected it would take him until afternoon at the earliest to give me enough information to start my part of the work.

Until he contacted me, I'd make the most of my time and begin my plan to convince Sassy to forgive me when I broke several key promises trying to free her from a future of dating cheating cheetahs and wolves. While I had nothing against wolf lycanthropes, I couldn't imagine the amount of property damage a cheetah and a wolf might create given more than twenty minutes together. To get the shoes and purse, I needed to venture to Highland Park Village. Daily interaction with Sassy gave me an unfortunate idea of her dream shoe, which was more of a strappy, heeled sandal in red with clear bits of plastics holding it together along with some gold trim. As I couldn't give her the shoes of her dreams without its matching purse, I'd be getting her the red calfskin handbag also decorated with gold.

My credit card would cry when I swiped it, and I'd spend a long time paying it off when everything was said and done. One hour and over five thousand dollars later, I drove my truck into the heart of cheetah territory to pay Sassy's parents a visit.

A wiser man would've written up his last will and testament before making the drive across town.

The last time I'd infringed on his territory, Sassy's father had kicked my ass so hard I'd needed emergency surgery to repair my teeth. I couldn't leave the shoes or purse in my truck, so I'd hope he'd delay my beating long enough to put the bag somewhere safe. I gave myself low odds of successfully dodging a second beating.

Once mated, cheetah males defined overprotective. Toss in the rarity of daughters among cheetahs, and I courted disaster and long-term rehabilitation.

Her father's truck and her mother's car were in the driveway, and to my relief, none of her brothers' vehicles were parked on their front lawn. Had they been around, I might've turned tail and run for the hills. If any of them noticed my departure, they'd chase, as cheetahs enjoyed the hunt above all else.

I wanted Sassy's attention, not the attention of her chronically single brothers in search of a good time with anyone who would look at them. If wolves had the same population controls inherent in their species as cheetahs did, the general infection rates would plummet—or be strictly male with a few frustrated females scattered throughout the population.

Bracing for the worst, I got out of my truck, went to the door, and knocked.

If anyone asked me to guess Oliver Chetty's species, I'd pick grizzly bear every time. Made of muscle, taller than me by at least six inches, and prone to lumbering, I struggled to accept he transformed into a sleek, spotted cat capable of outrunning the wind.

He looked me over, raising a brow. "You're the last person I expected to see at my door today. What brings you around here without my kitten in tow?"

I held up my one defense, the bag clearly

marked with Sassy's favorite brand of shoes. "Please don't get any blood on these. I bought them for Sassy, and I'd like her to receive them unstained."

As far as pleas went, I thought mine went over well. Thirty seconds went by without me bleeding at all.

"Come on in and tell me why you think you're going to be bleeding today," Sassy's father ordered. "Put the bag on the gun rack and lock your weapon up if you're armed."

"I'm not carrying today."

I was grateful looks from lycanthropes couldn't kill; Sassy's father would've had me in my grave in ten seconds flat.

"Why the hell not? My kitten gets cranky when you don't carry."

"Your kitten also likes scaring me for fun and booby trapping my apartment, making carrying a dangerous prospect."

"That's the honest truth."

As ordered, I set Sassy's shoes and purse on the gun rack. I kicked my shoes off before following Sassy's father into his kitchen. Once upon a time, the massive room had barely held everyone. The long table with twelve chairs had since been replaced with a round one meant for four. I found the opened space depressing and lifeless compared to my older memories.

Then again, it meant I didn't have to deal

with Sassy's nine brothers plotting my demise in some fashion or another.

"Take a load off and tell me what brings you my way. Coffee?"

"Please." I sat at the table and marveled that he hadn't started tenderizing me yet; last time I'd come over, he'd pounced on me the instant I got through the door and whooped my ass for not keeping Sassy out of trouble—trouble I hadn't even known she'd gotten into.

Surviving the Chetty family would be my second challenge, especially once Sassy's father found out I meant to break a few promises to catch a cat by her tail and keep her around.

I was so damned doomed I had no idea how I'd make it through the day.

Drawing in a slow breath to steady my nerves, I announced, "I have to call Sassy later this afternoon to rescue her from a date with a wolf. Since she's desperate enough to try dating a wolf in the first place, here I am. She's sworn off dating the uninfected, I promised I wouldn't think about her in a romantic fashion, and it's gotten to the point I'm bailing her out of bad dates at least three times a week. I'm at a loss of what to do, and the only feasible solution I've got involves contracting an incurable disease."

"I'm not sure how contracting lycanthropy could possible help with this train wreck that's my kitten's dating life. Bless her heart, she's determined, but she's got the worst luck I've ever seen."

I doubted Sassy's luck could get worse even if she tried. "I thought I'd blame the virus—and whoever infected me with it— when I breached my basic promise to never mix my work and private life. I'm also supposed to be the one man she can trust. I figure it'd be a hell of a lot safer for her if she stopped dating dead-beat cheetahs with mature viruses. From my understanding of the situation, I'll have ten years following my infection to convince Sassy to take pity on me before I join the ranks of dead-beat cheetahs."

Sassy's father chuckled and brought me a mug of black coffee with a high risk of being toxic sludge thinly disguised as coffee. All asking for cream or sugar would do was increase my odds of suffering through an even worse beating later. "Thank you, sir."

"I see you've put some thought into this. When was the last time you were tested for lycanthropy?"

"I'm tested every two years when it's time to renew my private investigator license."

"And when's your next renewal?"

"I just renewed. Two months ago," I admitted.

"Good. Here's the deal. If you want the

virus, you gotta fight like you mean it. I'll find you a donor with a spiking virus of our strain, but you're the one who has to make him bleed. I don't care how you do it. Sock the brat in the face for all I care, get overly enthusiastic with power tools doing errands around this place, whatever it takes. You'll be putting your license on the line, but that's not my problem. You're right about my kitten, though. She won't bend, so you'll have to. That you're here tells me you've done figured that out already. What happened to you swearing off women for life?"

As Sassy's father referred to his sons as brats, I expected the 'fight' would be more accidental in nature. While cheetah males preferred each other over the rare ladies among them, each and every one of them went to extremes when it came to trucks, power tools, and recreational vehicles.

My future looked like a dark, pain-filled place for the next little while.

"Sassy happened," I confessed. "I just spent several thousand dollars on three pairs of shoes for her since yesterday. Don't ask how much the purse cost, please. I'm trying to forget about it for a while."

"Cheetahs enjoy offerings. My wife tried to bribe me into marrying her, but she ultimately had to get bossy with me."

I supposed a kidnapping and hostage situation counted as bossy. I waited for her father to continue, biting my tongue so I wouldn't start the tenderization portion of my day prematurely.

"Sassy's virus is an odd one. She's all cat in her genetics, but she's all wolf in her behavior. Her momma? Her momma went around the block before becoming contagious and her virus matured enough to make her monogamous. Sassy's never been with a man because cheetah males disgust her. Don't ask me about her opinion on the wolves, as I won't have that language in my house."

"Cheetahs never win, according to her, and she can't tolerate it." I sighed and shrugged. "Letting the cheaters win, that is. So she plays it the straight and narrow way and won't bend. So here I am. I'm going to toe the line and hope she views my efforts as bending the rules rather than cheating. If she thinks of it as cheating, I'm sunk."

"Unless you get together with another lady while the virus matures so you skip the ten-year dive into the main coalition."

The truth sucked, especially when Sassy's father bludgeoned me with it. "Exactly."

"So, you have more than a few problems on your hands. Sastria's stubborn, but you know that. Your first problem is broaching this to her. What's your plan?"

"First, I'll blame her brothers, their power

tools, recreational vehicles, or trucks for my status as newly infected. That'll be the truth, so I won't be lying to her. That I'm willingly putting myself in harm's way will annoy her, but she never said I couldn't. If anything, she'll like that I'm trying to get along with her brothers. Anyway, after it's been confirmed I caught the virus from one of them, I'd blame them and propose an expansion of our current partnership to include full benefits and responsibilities. In part, I'll beg so I don't become yet another dead-beat cheetah male a few years down the road. I'm probably going to have to promise she can geld me if I cross her lines."

She would, too.

"Will you cross her lines?"

"I certainly have no desire to be gelded, sir."

"No sane man does."

I hesitated to label Sassy's father as sane, but I played along, pretending he hadn't goaded Sassy's mother into kidnapping him and holding him hostage until he agreed to settle down. "I've done some limited research on the lycanthropy virus. As far as I know, there are three legal ways to contract the virus, and one of them is off the table."

Sassy wouldn't sleep with anyone, and while it made me uncomfortable thinking about it, I had no doubts she was still a virgin.

Her father had it right; Sassy acted like a wolf more than a cheetah when it came to men, and she'd keep the first man she slept with for life. In that, we were well-matched. I'd done my time around the block before swearing off women, and the next time I settled down, it would be in a permanent relationship.

"Son, you've been doing yourself too much damned reading. I could go grab a knife, cut you up, and bleed all over you. As long as you had a chance to decline, it's legal. There ain't no damned law on the book stating you can't get infected if you want to. Them laws are all about making sure the virus ain't forced on anyone unwilling. But here's your real problem. My kitten's stubborn, but she's smart. For *you* to be coming over here and daring to ask *me* about the virus means you're serious about her. She'll come around, but she's going to be having one of her hissy fits for a while over it."

Hissing mad I could understand. Sassy wouldn't be hissy. She'd be murderous, and I gave myself even odds on if she'd target me or her father first. "My other option is to be infected during an accident. An accident created by my own stupidity is fine, but from top to bottom, it'd have to be an accident."

"Charlie got himself a new ATV a few weeks back. He'd be right interested in taking you for a ride on it. That thing loves bucking him off, and without fail, he comes back bloodied to hell. The seats got permanent stains on it, I reckon."

"Survival's important, sir."

"Right you are. And that thing is a death trap. But if you don't come up with a safer way to handle it, I reckon that's your best bet for getting infected while it being a genuine accident. But since survival is important, here's what I can do for you. I've got plenty of toys a pair of idiot boys can bleed over. You and him are the perfect pair to be young and reckless over my tools. You'll even be able to tell an angel the truth when we're done, and you won't even peep a hint of a lie. And well, if you knock yourself out while playing and Charlie bleeds all over you, well, these things happen. My kitten needs herself a sturdy, reliable man. Given my way, you'll be in the ER when you're supposed to be calling my kitten this afternoon, so I'll take care of tellin' her the part about how you and her brother decided to act your shoe size rather than your age."

I could see Sassy forgiving me for an accident. Eventually. Who could blame me for wanting to play with her father's power tools. He had a lot of them. He had an entire shed of them waiting for my use. He had so many power tools I could build an entire house without needing to go to the hardware store.

"Why help me, sir? The last time I came over, you rearranged my face."

"Don't worry yourself about that, son. I was testing to see if you were tough enough to handle my kitten. The way I see it, she's hoping her white knight gets a little dirty working to earn her. She'll learn she's signed up for a handful one of these days."

I drank the toxic sludge he called coffee to buy myself a few moments. "Did I pass?"

"Sure. You had the balls to come back over after I busted up your face. It took you a while, but I busted your face pretty good. A man has to dust off after that. The others I've busted up just hid and whimpered like newborns, and not a one of them has even dared to come onto the block. I've caught you dropping my kitten off in your truck several times. It took you half the time to work up the nerve to come here solo, too."

I needed to stop underestimating Sassy's father. "Were you expecting me to pay you a visit?"

"I sure as hell have been hopin' you would, truth be told. My kitten likes you something fierce and hasn't figured out she don't have a hope in hell dating anyone else. I give it no more than two or three years until her virus snaps and she goes loco and pounces. I figure all you're doing is keeping her virus from straining itself landing you. It'd be quite the mess if she went loco because her virus was itching to mate. I'm partly to blame. I raised her to be stubborn. Her brothers are aware you're on her menu, but they value their lives so they keep their mouths shut. She been clingy lately? That's usually the first sign a kitten's ready to become a queen among felines."

"She licked chocolate syrup out of my hair and off my face for two hours last night and left in a mood."

"I thought your face was lookin' a bit off today, redder than normal. You still a tee-totaler?"

"I had a beer yesterday before I dumped chocolate syrup and cotton candy over my head so her hard work at booby trapping my apartment wouldn't go to waste."

"Seems you had yourself an eventful day yesterday."

"I'd say. A little boy and his mother were gunned down at Park Lane. I was working down the street when it happened."

"I take it you and my kitten are going to be involving yourselves with that one?"

"Yeah. We are."

"Good. Ain't right hurting the little ones. You let us know if we can help."

"The killer left confetti made from, what I can tell, newspaper scraps. One has the number one. The other has a date: April 10th.

No year. That's where I'm going to be start-ing. Maybe if I can figure out why that date is important, I'll be able to get some leads."

"Well, you'll want to be checking the Sunday papers for that date; no one's printed daily papers in years. It's all digital now or on Sunday only. If it's a newspaper it's printed on, that's where you'll go first. Could be someone just using newspaper stock and printing it themselves. Any sign there's any-thing else on the sheets?"

"I've got samples at home to check. It's on the list for later today."

"Dean's an artist. Hand over your keys, and I'll send him over to have a look-see. You check them for prints?"

"No. They were in my clothes and likely contaminated, but the cops have samples, so if there are prints, I'll find out about it."

Sassy's father raised a brow. "You gone and got yourself somebody on the inside?"

"For this job? Yeah. I got somebody on the inside ready to feed me intel. It was that bad."

"The ones that involve the little ones al-ways are. So, tell me. How do you like your recklessness? I've raised nine boys, and every single one of those brats liked their reckless-ness in a different way. If you want to sell my kitten on the idea it was an accident, then you need to be reckless in a way that's all you. The accident will come. After all, my brats will be involved. I've got everything you might need. As a note, my wife is expecting a new shed by the end of the week, and I couldn't help but notice you brought your truck."

I raised my brow, sipped my coffee, wished I'd had the balls to decline a drink, and struggled to keep from grimacing over the assault on my taste buds. "Yours too tired to hit the lumber yard?"

"Damn straight my truck's too tired to hit the lumber yard, but she won't hear about getting me something new until she's got her new shed and we've torn down the barn down the way and put up something new. Noah done wants to get himself some new horses and some head of cattle, and his place don't have the space for all the livestock he's fixing to get."

When Sassy's father issued an invitation to help with the manual labor, it was accepted. Without question or argument. "Why not? I don't have anything else to do today beyond bailing Sassy from a bad date." Sassy's father didn't need to know I was supposed to be getting more photos for Heatherow on top of hunting a serial killer. "You're going to call for Dean?"

"Charlie, too. I reckon it'll take them two hours to come on by. Plenty of time to hit the lumber yard and get a load in."

"Why don't we take a ride to my place,

pick up the samples, and get the first load on the way back? It's more efficient that way."

I'd also get to keep my keys and keep Sassy's brothers out of my apartment.

"Sounds like a plan. I'll go put my kitten's new toys in the safe and give the brats a call so they can make themselves useful for a change." Sassy's father headed for the door to fetch the shoes and purse.

I found it funny even her father wouldn't come between Sassy and her shoe and purse fetish. Fortunately for my peace of mind, only a fool would steal from a cheetah lycan-thrope's home. 'Never steal from someone who can run faster than you' needed to be hung from his door.

Maybe I'd make him a sign for Christmas; he appreciated twisted humor almost as much as his daughter.

FIVE

One cub would tear through here
and leave nothing but rubble.

SASSY'S FATHER prowled around my apartment, a scowl fixed in place. "This ain't big
enough for cubs or kittens."

One day, I might understand why Sassy's
father referred to his daughter as a kitten and
his sons as cubs. I figured it had something to
do with rarity; that Sassy's father had a
daughter at all seemed impressive. The Dallas
coalition had one breeding pair: Sassy's parents. No one knew how Sassy's mother had
picked up the infection, although most bet it
was luck of the draw from a magical hot spot.

Sassy gave the local cheetah population
hope there'd be another generation, although
no one wanted to be the sacrificial lamb from
my understanding of the situation.

Cheetahs. Either they were unmated and
randy with their colony fellows or they lived
and breathed for children.

Unless I wanted to stir the old man's ire, I'd have to nip his concern in the bud. "Moving is an option."

"Better be. One cub would tear through here and leave nothing but rubble. Sassy's just like her mother, and once she gets her hands on you, there'll be a lot of cubs in your future. I'm hopeful for at least several kittens, too. The coalition's thinking about looking for women wanting the virus."

"That's only going to work if you've got some cheetahs willing to leave the coalition lifestyle to settle down with a permanent mate."

"It's like you actually pay attention. I'm impressed. A few of the older males are thinking about it. Sassy's too young for them, and everyone in the coalition's already figured out she's got her heart set on you despite her being too dense and stubborn to figure that out yet. Truth be told, I expect you'd be invited to help with work in the yards until an accident happened to make sure my kitten gets what she wants. With you as her breeding male, there's some hope some of the teen boys will pick themselves kittens before the virus takes hold too strong."

Great. Sassy's father already had us boosting the local cheetah population. I wondered why he thought I might be able to change how the virus ticked for cheetahs. "I see you cats have been gossiping again."

"That's what us cats do best. If there's gossip to be had, we have it. But, being serious here. This place wouldn't last ten minutes with a single cub, and I'm concerned it won't survive my kitten for long."

Considering she'd booby trapped my apartment with cotton candy, chocolate syrup, and whipped cream, I was inclined to agree with him. I needed to check into the reality of lycanthropy-infected children before Sassy's father filled my head with dread and nonsense. Shaking my head at the insanity, I retrieved everything I had on the Park Lane murders, photographed the scraps so Sassy's brother could review them, and fetched my tool kit along with my work gloves. "There are a lot of steps between our current situation and even the thought of cubs. Frankly, I give myself a fairly high chance of being rejected because she partnered with me only after I promised there would be no relationship between us."

"She was wrong. She'll even admit it one day. Technically, doing reckless things with her brothers isn't breaking your promise. At the end of the day, my little kitten will appreciate your ingenuity."

His little kitten would bankrupt me in a month if I kept buying her shoes to avoid in-

stant death. Maybe I'd buy her a stupidly expensive dress to go with her new shoes. An
entire ensemble might distract her long
enough for me to confess my every sin and
beg for forgiveness.

It was her fault I'd grown to love everything about her. I bore no responsibility. Any
sane man would love Sassy given time.

"That's the expression of a defeated man,"
her father stated in his coolest tone.

"The wolf's taking her to a fast food joint.
I spent thousands on shoes. I'm wondering if
I showed up at one of her dates with the
shoes if she'd kill me."

"I already agreed to help make certain
you're infected during a terrible accident involving power tools. You're going to give my
kitten gray hairs with your fussing."

Why had I gone to Sassy's father for help?
Oh, right. Desperation. "Think your colony of
cubs would be interested in helping to track a
killer and double-cross some politicians? I'm
going to need to free up some time on my
schedule if I have to recover from a tragic accident involving power tools. Can we keep
the accident to something that has minimal
recovery time? Sassy might kill me if I miss
too much work and dump our contracts on
her lap."

"They'd do it for fun. What's the deal with
the politicians?"

"I need incriminating photos of one, an opportunity for said politician to defuse the situation, and no links back to me. My hire gives me a bad vibe, and my current photo and intel pool isn't robust enough for my liking."

"That's not like you."

"No, it's not, but I've got a bad feeling about this whole mess," I admitted. "I'm going to forward my gallery of the pictures I took at Park Lane. My hire had me following a woman hoping to secure compromising photos."

"Woman's name?"

"Sharon Gray."

"Lycanthropy positive, non-contagious, wolf strain. Hunting for a mate. She's been eyeing the colony, as she's the adventurous type. She's active in political circles. If he's a politician, she's probably slept with him. She's a single mother of three."

"She has kids?" I blurted.

"She gave them up for adoption at birth to a mated wolf pair in Houston. Her twin sister and her mate. Her sister's barren. The missus and I took a turn with her younger child; she didn't want anyone knowing about him until she could get a hold of her sister and make arrangements for adoption. The other two are twin girls, two years older than the boy."

My eyes widened. "She gave them up for adoption to her sister? But why?"

"She loves her pups something fierce, and she loves her sister, too. Far as I reckon, she doesn't want them embroiled in any scandals, so she hid her pregnancies and made sure no one outside of the lycanthrope circles knew they'd been born. This way, she gets the best of both worlds. The pups think of her as their godmother, so she gets to see them, they view her sister as their mother, and since they're twins, no one can really tell from a DNA test they're Sharon's pups."

"Now I'm really confused," I confessed. "Does Sharon's sister also have pups of her own?"

"No. She developed ovarian cancer before she'd contracted the virus, and she had her ovaries removed. There won't be any pups of her own, unfortunately. So, Sharon did the only thing she could; she had a few pups so her sister could become a mother."

Whenever I thought lycanthropes couldn't surprise me any more, they always did. "I'll confess, she doesn't seem like the type of woman to do something so selfless at first glance."

"She's a tricky one, and she'll do whatever it takes to protect her family. In that, she's as wolf as one can get. I'd make sure you don't take your search beyond the local area. Some things are best left secret."

On that, we were agreed. I also made a mental note to stop underestimating Sassy's father. "Know anything about Senator Sterling?"

"Typical political playboy, bisexual, and he likes his kinks rough. That's common enough knowledge. He likes the publicity, as it gets him more sexual partners without having to work for it. His wife likes her kinks, too. If he's your target, go to town. He likes the attention, and in his case, any publicity is good publicity. I can get you a list of his clubs, and I bet you can talk him into posing for you with partners who want the notoriety, too."

Pinching the bridge of my nose, I breathed in deep and considered flinging myself out of the nearest window. "Just how common is this knowledge?"

"Very common among lycanthropes; he's a risk taker and isn't against infection, so the unmated play it safe with him. He gets on well with the coalition because he can flit in and out of the couplings without bringing any drama with him. His wife tags along with some of her girlfriends as voyeurs, too. Wouldn't be any of my business, but Sterling wanted a round with one of my older brats."

Shit. "Over eighteen?"

"My brat was twenty-two when he made

the rounds. He's never eyed my younger brats, and he's careful about antagonizing the mated pairs. His general rule of thumb is that unless his future partners are over the age of twenty-five, he gets the okay from the parents. It's weird, but I'd rather weird ethics than no ethics. Now, all that said, he did have an interest in my little kitten after she turned eighteen, but I warned him off. He's not her type."

"She can't stand cheaters."

"Yep."

I could easily see Sassy having a major altercation with a politician like Senator Sterling. "Please tell me he didn't approach her directly."

"She don't know nothin' about him; I told him he'd be wise to steer clear. She'd take his balls for a trophy, wait for them to rot, and then feed them to him if he barked up her tree. As you say, she don't like cheaters none at all, not even when the partner is in on it. One plus one is two with her, and the only additions to that come nine months later."

I recognized a hint when I heard one, although I doubted I'd be helping him with his grandchildren problem anytime soon. "How long ago did Sterling come around asking about Sassy?"

Sassy's father waved off my concern. "Don't you worry yourself about it, Aaron.

That man's been looking for pretty young men and women since he was a pretty young man himself. He aged, his interests didn't. But he is a stickler for consent and only plays ball with people who don't mind getting into the line of fire with him if a scandal pops up. It's a game to him and his partners. People try to nail him on a scandal, and he'll show up with his wife and the person accused, and they'll make out on the street corner together until someone takes their picture. It's hard to make it a scandal when none of the participants care. Add in the fact he lands pretty young men and women, and he ultimately gets nods of approval from those who want to join the swingers, too. Sure, the religious and ultra conservative hate him, but it's not like they were voting for him anyway."

I foresaw a headache in my future. "My hire's basically wasting his time and money trying to sink Sterling, then."

"Easy cash for you and my kitten. You don't get the easy jobs often, so be happy with this one. It's nothing new. Hell, he's probably been looking for younger partners since you were in diapers. It'll be easy to dig up current photos of him with young women who look more like younger girls, and if you want to make it spicy for him, I can give you a long list of names within the coalition who'd love to have fun with the religious conservatives. They hate us anyway."

"Of course." Cheetah lycanthropes couldn't act more gay if they tried, and some did just because they were cats who enjoyed offending delicate sensibilities. "What do you suggest?"

"I'll ask around the coalition and put out some feelers. That should land you some good pictures Sterling knows about. It'll let you keep your reputation intact and pass over good intel without screwing the senator over. It's easy to prove he's done no wrong doing, but it sure looks bad at first blush."

"Want my job? I think you could do it better than I can right now."

"That's what us old men do, son. We drink beer and gossip, and there ain't nothing as entertaining as talking about the talkers and learning who cheated who. If you need dirt on the local politicians, just ask. We're cats. We live to poke our noses in places we don't belong."

Interesting. As I'd already unveiled a little too much, I'd toe the wrong side of the line for a change. "What can you tell me about Tom Heatherow?"

"Steer clear of that one. He'll do anything to win. He's the kind of talker we hate the most. If he ever had a sense of decency or ethics, he's never showed sign of them during his dealings. Well, not quite. When it comes to money matters, his word is good. But if you don't have it in writing, expect a slow fuck, and I don't mean the good kind."

Great. I needed to review the contract again and make certain we kept to the letter and the spirit of the damned thing. "Nice to know. Anything interesting on the campaign front?"

"Not particularly. It'll be a few weeks before the first shots are fired. Should make for interesting news."

"Let me know if you hear anything."

"Will do. I'll tip off my little kitten if there's anything good on the grapevine."

"Thanks. I'll owe you one."

"Nonsense. I'm going to owe you one for settling my little kitten down, and don't you be tellin' a soul I said that. I'll deny, deny, deny."

He would, too.

PARANOIA DIDN'T USUALLY DICTATE my actions, but when Sassy's father openly disliked someone and issued warnings to take care, the wise listened. To cover my ass, I loaded the photos I'd taken to the gallery I shared with Sassy and backed them up to several different servers. I repeated the process with the finalized contract and sent Sassy a message relaying her father's advice.

Satisfied I'd done everything I could for the moment, I took my tools to the truck along with some rope to lash down any over-sized supplies Sassy's father might need, rolled up the cover, and stored it in the cab in case we needed it.

"We're going to be late," I predicted, doing my last check of the truck. After having lost one windshield to a dick who hadn't secured his tools in his bed, I'd decided I wouldn't be that man. If it went into my truck, it stayed in my truck until I was ready to remove it.

"Don't you worry about it. The brats know we're headed to the lumber yard. I heard that older one cackle over it. Says I couldn't keep it to an hour at the lumber yard even if I tried, and he promised to make you a good cup of coffee as a reward for putting up with me and my shopping."

Of Sassy's brothers, only Charlie would make me coffee the way I liked it. The rest of them tried to top their father's tactics of creating poison disguised as coffee. The gesture was more up Dean's alley, so I assumed the pair was working together to prevent me from running away after dealing with their father at the lumber yard.

"Which yard am I taking you to?"

"Let's hit the one in North Dallas off the 75. They're running a sale."

With luck, traffic wouldn't add an extra hour to our trip, and I hopped into the cab, waited for her father to buckle in, and started the engine.

I loved the growl of a good diesel, and my truck delivered each and every time. If I hadn't had an audience, I would've spent a few minutes listening, and when confident no one watched, I would've pet the dashboard.

While a few years old and painted silver because I couldn't find a good used diesel on the lot in any other color, when someone needed a good truck that could handle some heavy loads, they were wise to come knocking on my door.

"We're inevitably going to scratch your truck putting him through his paces," Sassy's father announced. "What's his name again? Carl?"

"Carlos. Carlos is a good, strong name for a good, strong truck. That, plus every damned Carlos I've ever met could kick my ass in a fight. I learned my lesson well: don't mess with anyone named Carlos. And any-way, don't you worry about his battle scars. I cover them with a paint pen once a month."

"There'll be dents, too. What'll you do about them?"

"I know a guy."

"If you spoil my little kitten like you do this truck, she'll be insufferable."

Considering I'd willingly poured chocolate syrup over my head and endured several hours of tongue bath to try to make her happy, I couldn't imagine a world without an insufferably spoiled Sassy in it. "Should she become insufferable, does that mean she'll get to dodge the monthly barbecues?"

"No. It'll just mean she'll annoy us more at them, showing you off like we've never seen your ugly mug before."

"You make it sound like I'll be attending the monthly barbecues."

"Your truck can haul the coolers better than mine. That'll be your price of admission. My little kitten makes pies because it keeps her quiet for more than a few minutes."

"You say that like it's a good thing."

"I see there's no hope left for you. Perhaps I should've taken the initiative. How many months of whining might I have avoided had I taken the initiative?"

"Count the number of failed dates for a good estimate," I suggested.

"Ain't nobody got time for that."

I chuckled and navigated through the max of side streets to reach the 75, grunting my satisfaction over the flowing traffic. Any time the highway treated me well, I called it a good day. "While true, don't tell Sassy that."

"I don't got a death wish this week. It'll be rough enough calming her down. Until you're shifting, she'll freak if you stub your toe. With the size of our family, we'll get you down to fifteen years max. Maybe ten if we push our luck."

Last I'd checked, most estimates for the full development of the lycanthropy virus rang in closer to forty years. "How?"

"Transfusions. We've got someone of every blood type in the coalition. If you're a common blood type, we might even have you shifting in a few years, as long as you're compatible with Sassy."

"We're the same blood type," I admitted. "We had our blood type tested in case of emergency. Mostly to see if I could give *her* a transfusion, but turns out we have the same blood type."

"Then that means you're my blood type, and you'll be set. We'll jumpstart your virus, so we'll only be limited in how often Sassy can donate without tapping her virus. Once your virus is matching hers, she'll start getting touchy about anyone coming near you. Having a few cubs will settle her down. I give it two years before she goes loco and corners you. If you surrender now, I can fill her ears with hostage situation locations you might enjoy."

"I've always wanted to go to Hawaii," I admitted. "Seems like if I'm going to be held hostage, getting in some surf and sun in an exotic location seems like the way to go about it."

"It'd also make it difficult for you to run away. She can pitch it as a vacation and transform it into a kidnapping and hostage situation. That'll work. I'll have her mother work the idea into her head. We'll help her along with a pair of tickets for Christmas in a year or two. Mind you, before she snaps and goes loco. She's stubborn, so she'll need some nudging in the right direction."

"How long have you been planning grandchildren?"

"Oh, I reckon I started when I figured out she'd picked you and couldn't figure out how to land you. I've been entertained."

In more ways than I cared to think about, marriage to Sassy meant marriage to her family and the entirety of the colony, which was formed of multiple male-centric coalitions that overlapped thanks to the promiscuous nature of unmated cheetah males. At last count, the entire state had six women, only two of which were able to shapeshift. The other four infected women, still several decades from their first shift and trying to claim a male without having to resort to kidnapping and taking hostages.

I wished them the best of luck. They'd need it.

Sassy represented the only woman of her generation in the colony, and it still amazed me she hadn't been able to find a cheetah.

I shook my head at the utterly feline situation. My hopes of getting to North Dallas without hitting a traffic snarl died within ten minutes, and I grunted at the honking of horns. Most targeted a semi going well below the speed limit in the center lane. I changed to the fast lane, accelerated to the speed limit, and kept an eye on my side mirror and the center lane for my first chance to pass without being a dick about it.

Most Texans would've settled with being a dick about it, but I respected the weight and raw power of my truck, which could pulverize a small family car without much effort. Responsible driving helped make certain my truck stayed in pristine condition, too.

I left people alone, and they left me alone, which I found to be an ideal situation.

The semi's driver decided he had a gas pedal, inching up enough that I abandoned my effort to pass without breaking the speed limit, opting to wait for him to move along and return to the center lane where I belonged.

"No sane cop'll ticket you for going five over."

I just loved when someone, especially my future father-in-law, told me how to drive. "I have rope in the back. Surely a cheetah can run fast enough to keep up with me and my slow ways."

"I will pay good money to watch you say that to my little kitten."

I grinned and kept an eye on the semi, which pulled up alongside me. Traffic slowed ahead, boxing me in, and I drummed my fingers against the steering wheel while waiting for the inevitable slow grind to a halt. "Well, isn't this just delightful."

"You seem to have developed a concerning case of British."

"That's my grandfather's fault," I replied, keeping an eye on the vehicle ahead of me with a tendency to treat the brakes like they were meant to be slammed every other minute. "He comes overseas once a year and tries to brush his accent off on us."

Traffic resumed motion, and I eased my truck back up to speed, expecting someone to do something stupid to slow us all down again.

So focused on the vehicles ahead and behind me, I didn't notice the semi swerve into my lane until it was too late. Metal screamed against concrete with a shower of sparks before everything went black.

SIX

Car accidents sucked.

A DIM MEMORY of throbbing pain in my throat, the fumes of leaking diesel and smoke, and waves of heat chased me from sleep. If a memory, it lacked the substance I expected, but I'd never dreamed of anything quite so real before.

Too much seemed real, but the lack of physical feeling cast everything in doubt.

I considered the issue and decided it didn't matter; memories and dreams couldn't physically hurt me, and time would dull the edge of any memories in the same way popping a few painkillers eased a headache. When I followed that logic, odd that it was, it didn't matter if I smelled diesel and smoke. The waves of heat worried me. That fringed uncomfortably close to the physical, which in turn could become reality.

I focused on the vivid details, hunting for actual memories rather than the hazy recollections of a dream. The throbbing in my throat, the stench of smoke and diesel, and the heat led me back to one place: my truck, the 75, and an unplanned trip to a lumber yard.

One by one, my memories filtered through the fog in my head, and I didn't appreciate them at all.

Big trucks crunched under the full force of a semi, and the memory slammed into me rather like my poor pickup had crashed into the median. That explained a lot.

Car accidents sucked.

A car accident, or in my case, a truck on truck demolition derby, explained a lot. My death certificate would cite an infuriated cheetah as the cause of my demise. With luck, I'd be pumped so full of drugs I wouldn't feel a thing when Sassy got a hold of me.

The last time I'd landed in the hospital, a released convict had taken a few pot shots at me; the defense attorney hadn't expected me to uncover evidence the bastard deserved longer than the two years he'd served for murder. That job had been the one to earn me a blacklist among the attorneys, as they hated when they got the case wrong and their own hires proved it. I expected to cool my heels and work outside of the law system for a few more years over it, too.

Some lawyers needed the win more than they wanted justice to be properly served.

Hospital-grade painkillers explained a lot. The damned things left me in a daze, prone to drifting off mid-sentence, and incapable of maintaining coherent thought for more than a few minutes at a time. With my luck, when I finally got around to opening my eyes, I'd face a disconcerting number of hallucinations. Some hallucinations were easier to cope with than others. Even drugged, I tended to recognize that a rabbit made of glitter and blood didn't actually exist.

Sassy found my odd ability to identify the absurd while drugged amusing, and she attempted to confuse me by bringing the absurd into my personal space and testing if I could tell the difference between a drug-induced hallucination and reality.

Opening my eyes took enough effort I contemplated giving up and letting the drugs have their way with me. Before I could do just that, the drag of a rough cheetah tongue over my cheek killed any hope of escaping back into sleep.

Ouch.

Someone needed to tell Sassy her tongue classified as a torture implement when used on my face.

Sassy's purrs rumbled, and she exchanged her tongue for her cold, wet nose. I waited for the inevitable, and sure enough, she licked my cheek again.

My uncooperative body, with the help of hospital-grade drugs, refused to do my bidding, leaving me easy prey for the feline's affections.

"Sassy, leave part of his face intact. You do not need to lick his cheek off. Licking him isn't going to wake him up faster. The doctors said sometime today, so knock it off. You should be grateful they're letting you shed all over the hospital room."

I marked Sassy's father off my list of things to worry about. Then again, lycanthropes were a lot more durable than run of the mill humans like me.

Sassy growled.

"Now look here, missy. You're only in here because the doctors like his vitals and body temp when you keep him company. Your job is to lie there, be quiet, and purr. Behave. Leave his face alone."

For a moment, I thought she might actually listen to her father, but then she chirped. I interpreted the sound as one of defiance, as when left with no other recourse, Sassy talked back. Talking back always got her into trouble, but when in doubt, Sassy sassed.

Someone needed to tell her father I liked when Sassy sassed and to stop discouraging her from sassing in my presence.

"I mean it, Sastria. You're going to wake him up pawing all over him like you are, and he'll probably be startled, then he'll try to react, but with that tube still stuck down his throat, he'll just make himself even more miserable. Will it make you feel better if I ask one of the nurses to check in on him again? I know they haven't been around for a while, but that's because he's improving. No news is good news right now."

Sassy chirped again, more inquisitive in nature than defiant.

"All right, all right. I'll go pester a nurse for you. Yowl if you need me, and mind all those gadgets he's hooked up to. No pawing, and keep your displays of affection to nuzzling. No teeth, no claws, and try to leave him a few layers of skin."

In a classic Sassy stunt, she placed her paw on my chest. The pressure hurt enough to cut through the haze in my head, and my body chose that moment to report a myriad of stronger pains, the worst of which throbbed in my throat. In a way, the pain reassured me; numbness typically accompanied full paralysis, a terrifying consequence of neck injuries. My arms and legs filed their protests along with my chest and throat, another sign I'd recover from the crash.

The next time a semi crawled along, I'd wait or exceed the speed limit passing.

Lesson learned.

Time distorted as it often did when subjected to the influence of painkillers, and when I finally got around to blinking, I'd upgraded from a sassy cat to a cranky woman. While I hadn't been able to verify if I'd actually had a tube down my throat, I was pleased to discover I was free from any invasive objects outside of a pesky IV line.

I amused myself glaring at the catheter in my arm, my conscious state unnoticed by Sassy or anyone else. Sassy waged war with a white-coated doctor, and when I got around to examining him, his freakishly pale skin and wispy white hair distracted me from listening in on their argument. His hair blended with the wall, and I wondered how he combed it without breaking the fine strands. I could understand why the old man let his hair run free; the instant he applied any product, I bet he'd resemble a drowned rat.

"Miss Chetty, I'm not asking you to leave permanently. You would benefit from a few hours outside of the hospital while Mr. Clinton undergoes testing. You can't accompany him, and you, frankly spoken, could use a shower."

A stressed, busy Sassy sometimes forgot she could out-stink a rotting skunk during a heatwave given twenty-four hours and weak

deodorant. One day, she might win the deodorant war. Maybe.

Instead of buying her shoes, I needed to
invest in every type of deodorant manufac-
tured so she could date the perfect deodorant
rather than deadbeat cheetahs destined to
drive her insane. She'd emerge better for the
odd relationship with varied hygiene
products.

Until I could find her the perfect deodorant capable of withstanding her when
stressed, I could help the doctor evict my
sassy cheetah for a while. "I thought the
skunk imitation contest was scheduled for
next month."

My tongue cooperated, a miracle all
things considered, but my voice emerged
raspy and soft.

Sassy still heard me, and she whirled
around, her eyes wide. "Aaron!"

"I think I'm late with our client's pictures."
Expressing my work concerns might get her
on the move. Maybe.

Sassy perched on the edge of the hospital
bed, and she flicked my forehead. "I took care
of it; Dad got us some good leads. Our client
signed off, and he paid the full balance owed
plus a bonus for the extras. He got right
cranky about it, too. The bastard probably
thought we'd violate our contract with you
down and out for the count. He came

through despite being a jerk about it, though. Thanks for uploading the contract terms, by the way. It saved me having to get my damned brother to hack into your computer to get to them. We need to make sure future contracts are in the joint folders by default."

"I got lazy. Sorry. He gave you problems?"

"Not particularly. Reminding him of the contract terms cleared the matter up, as it reminded him of the pesky little details he hoped I wouldn't remember.

Miracles could happen, although Tom Heatherow's audacity and attempt to get out of the bill worried me.

"It wasn't a big deal, Aaron. It took me less than five minutes to clarify the contract terms, and once he saw our work, he paid the bonus voluntarily. I'm just annoyed he assumed we'd flop on the contract because of the accident."

"The semi won. That's not fair," I complained in an effort to convince her I'd be fine without having any idea what was actually wrong with me.

"You remember what happened?"

While certain the doctor wanted to be the one to ask the questions, I ignored his displeased expression and focused on my partner instead. "I remember a semi rammed me into the median. That's it."

"Your truck flipped into oncoming traffic."

Okay. While I'd expected crunching into a median would be dangerous at best, flipping over the median hadn't even occurred to me as a possibility. I blinked. "I'm still alive?"

"Aaron!"

"I thought it was a valid question," I whined. All things considered, after surviving through a semi flipping my truck into oncoming traffic, I needed to invest in a few lottery tickets.

The doctor cleared his throat, and while Sassy narrowed her eyes, she gave him her attention. "You were exceptionally fortunate, Mr. Clinton. If the passenger in your vehicle had been incapacitated, you would have died. You're doubly fortunate he knew basic first aid and CPR. Unfortunately, due to the severity of the accident, it's probable you were exposed to the lycanthropy virus."

Nice. Life had given me a lemon in the form of a semi ramming my truck into the medial, but I'd gotten a cool glass of sweetened lemonade with the bonus of not having to trick Sassy at all to be exposed to the virus. "Cool. I can enter the date Sassy bachelor pool. Even the right species. Hey, does that give me automatic parental approval?"

Silence answered my question, which was when I realized what should've been a private thought had exited my mouth without permission.

Damned painkillers, escorting me right to the executioner's block. So much for my nice glass of lemonade. As I couldn't make the situation any worse, I added, "Oops."

Sassy faced me, her mouth hanging open with her eyes wide. I added her reaction to the pro column.

Maybe I might survive for a few more minutes, especially if I tossed in a bribe. "I bought you those fancy clear shoes with the red soles and their matching purse. Please don't kill me for what the drugs made me say."

The doctor cleared his throat again. Why did doctors like clearing their throats when they wanted attention? Did all doctors have a chronic throat problem from trying to explain medical issues to their patients? "It could be up to a year before we can confirm if you were infected, Mr. Clinton. There are factors involved. We're not certain how much blood transferred during the accident or if your genetics offer any resistances to the virus. There's also the matter of blood loss. If you're a viable host, the virus may replicate faster to encourage your recovery. That's rare, but it can happen. You were in critical condition upon arrival, which makes this a slim possibility. In twenty-four hours, we'll be able to test for early incubation. That said, we'll only test if you desire. Some patients prefer not knowing right away, and this early in infection, you won't be contagious. Your first mandatory testing will be in a year."

"Incubation? Like an egg? But they're cats, not chickens."

Sassy clamped her mouth closed.

"No, Mr. Clinton. The incubation period is when the lycanthropy virus develops in the body. Once you're contagious, the virus is considered to be fully established. It's matured when you have your first shift."

"Okay. Good. I don't want to go into an egg."

Sassy dissolved into a fit of giggles. "No eggs, Aaron. I promise."

"Wait. I like omelets. I like cake, too. I need eggs for those."

"You can still eat eggs."

"Just you try to take my omelets," I warned.

The doctor cleared his throat again, and I worried my doctor would need a doctor at the rate he was going. "Miss Chetty, if you would please leave so we can begin testing, it would be appreciated."

"But Dad isn't here yet."

"As Mr. Clinton will be in testing, Mr. Chetty will be unable to accompany him. There's no visitation during testing."

For a moment, I thought Sassy would

fight the doctor's edict, but she wrinkled her nose and sighed. "Fine."

I forced my arm into motion and poked her to get her attention. "Please. Go shower. You're going to make the skunks feel bad about themselves."

With a low growl, she jumped off the bed, stormed from the room, and slammed the door behind her. "I'm going to have to buy her a new pair of shoes again, aren't I?"

"Not of all life's problems can be solved with buying her shoes, Mr. Clinton."

"Bite your tongue!"

The doctor chuckled.

THE TESTING SESSION lasted several hours, but the hour-long explanation of my injuries exhausted me. Internal bleeding and a head injury took the top spots at the most severe, and the head injury took the blame for my stint on life support with the assistance of a severely cut throat. I'd have a scar for a while; assuming I contracted lycanthropy, the virus would eventually remove the mark, but for a few years, I'd carry a reminder of how I'd almost lost my head in the accident.

One fact rose above all the others: without Sassy's father, I would've bled out before the paramedics had arrived at the scene. How the

hell was I supposed to thank him? Fancy
heels wouldn't work. Tools might, but I'd
need to replace my truck before I worried
about buying anyone anything.

For a shamefully long time, I contemplated ruining my career with a count of kidnapping. Taking Sassy somewhere quiet for
some rest and relaxation seemed ideal. Who
needed a career anyway? Escaping from reality would help. Unfortunately, I estimated I
wouldn't escape the hospital for another
week unless I got lucky.

Instead of running away like I wanted, I
endured an MRI and numerous other machines tasked with checking on my health
and making sure I stayed alive. Sometime
after the MRI but before anyone could update
me on how long I'd be stuck in the hospital,
the painkillers sucker punched me.

The next time I regained coherency, the
room suffered from a cop infestation, the
head annoyance of the District Attorney's office, and a cranky Sassy determined to drive
them off. As such entertainment couldn't be
purchased on a regular day, I watched with
interest.

Sassy bristled at the DA, her hands balled
into fists and her entire body shaking, a
surefire sign she might finally snap and go
for the DA's throat. "Maybe if you'd wanted
his pictures, you should've accepted his open

offer to have them the day he was in the station and questioned," she snarled. I couldn't tell if she meant the jab at the DA or the cops, although I decided it didn't matter; she'd nailed them both with her single statement.

Within ten minutes, she'd sprout a fur coat and spit curses at them as a feline, something I'd enjoy. Unless they got lucky, it would take her an hour to cool her temper, and they'd regret annoying her into wasting their time.

Robert Allamant, the DA and a royal pain in my ass, sighed. "Miss Chetty, the new evidence—"

"The new evidence can kiss my ass!" she yowled. "He offered the police evidence, which was refused. He could've died because of that fucking refusal. What if the pictures showed the killer?"

"Miss Chetty—"

"Don't you even Miss Chetty me, you ass! You and your cops dropped the ball. Because you dropped the ball, Aaron's truck is scrap, and who the hell knows when he'll be going home?"

Yep, my partner was ten seconds shy of sprouting fur and rampaging in a hospital. "Watch out, Rob. She might bite, and honestly, if we end up stuck with each other while you're being treated for rabies, we'll try to kill each other given an hour. You'd win with your current advantage."

Being the one laid up had its perks; the argument slammed to a halt, and Sassy spun to face me, her eyes redder than I liked. Sassy didn't cry often, but when her anger surged enough, she, according to her, sobbed because it was illegal to kill people who pissed her off.

"Aaron?" Too many questions hung in the air, and I organized them by priority, which meant I ignored them and focused on her red eyes instead. "If any of them made you cry, I'm accepting a rain check on beating the responsible parties."

She sassed me with a roll of her eyes. "Your mother sent Easter lilies because she's evil."

Allergies. Right. I blamed the drugs for forgetting about Sassy's allergies to pretty flowers. "She actually visited?"

My mother couldn't stand lycanthropes, and she went out of her way to torment Sassy, resulting in me spending more time with Sassy's parents than mine. Considering I'd had a strict 'flee from Sassy's father' policy until recently, I found it amazing my parents had even found out about the accident in the first place.

"Under protest and armed with Easter lilies." Sassy wrinkled her nose. "She cried, tried to take me home with her, cried some more when the doctors said she couldn't take me home with her, and then cried some more when your father and cousin made her leave. Your brother's coming off deployment to see you."

I locked onto the one man in the room who might be able to save me: Maxwell. "Help."

The cops laughed while the DA narrowed his eyes and frowned. "What's the problem?"

Wonderful. Great. Stupendous. I eyed the machine responsible for dishing out the painkillers, wondering how to make it do its job and knock me out again. I'd seen that look on the DA's face before. I'd become his current big case.

"He gets pissy because I'm better than he is at everything," my brother announced from the doorway, dressed in a flight suit and looking ready to take out a military outpost without help. "You don't look dead to me. Mom said you were dead or dying." He patted his gun, which could reduce a human skull to mist at the single pull of its trigger.

"You're not supposed to bring the mister into a hospital, Mark," I replied, pointing at his gun. "You're supposed to leave your baby with the military."

"Oh, this one isn't my baby. This is one I borrowed from somebody here. My baby is still in Canada. They wouldn't let me take her onto the plane for some reason."

"Space in the cockpit?" I guessed.

"They bitched and moaned I wanted to bring a bag with me as it was. So, I got this call from Mom about you being dead or dying."

"If I'm dying, don't tell me, and if I'm not dying, don't help. What hell hole did they pull you out of this time, and why is your baby in Canada?"

"I was guest training some Canadians. I bet my baby is slutting it up with some Canadians right now at the range. She's randy like that. I called in a minion and caught a flight over."

"Mugged a fighter jet?"

"Borrowed. I didn't have to resort to mugging this time. I even nabbed a pilot, too. I got away with it because the pilot's a good test pilot, and I promised Sheppard could borrow him to beat on some new recruits until I was finished here. I needed to take some leave anyway, and you made for a decent excuse."

"Gee. So glad I could help."

"What's this howling I heard down the hall about you and the copper shop dropping balls?"

I closed my eyes, sighed, and contemplated escaping out the window. Unfortunately, my brother would enjoy chasing me, dragging me back to the hospital, and ensuring I stayed put until a doctor convinced him I wasn't actually about to die. "Mom brought Easter lilies and riled Sassy up. Before that, I was napping."

"The yelling woke you up?" Mark stepped to my bedside, and on route, he shoved his flight helmet onto Sassy's head. "Simmer down there, kitty."

My partner sighed. "I hate you, Mark."

"That's Lieutenant Colonel Mark to you."

"Like hell it is, you egg-headed buffoon."

That Sassy hadn't gone straight for my brother's throat as usual impressed me.

Mark grunted and arched a brow. "She's even sassier than usual. What's gotten your kitty so riled up?"

"I'm guessing a close brush with death in the form of a car accident, potentially a failed murder attempt from the little I've gleaned from the screaming. Hey, check it out. The DA is visiting me, and we haven't tried to kill each other yet. Isn't the CDC supposed to be notified when miracles happen?"

"Why is Robbie visiting you anyway?"

"I'm guessing he wanted to fight with Sassy. Sassy's giving him a hard time about some photographs. I'm rather entertained right now."

"You're also higher than a kite. They have you on the good painkillers, I see."

"You're probably right."

"I'm always right," my brother replied. "Thank you for noticing."

Sassy yanked my brother's helmet off her head and flung it at him. "You smell worse than a skunk."

I arched a brow. "Why'd you leave it on your head for so long, then?"

"Shock something like a helmet could smell so bad," she admitted.

Mark tucked his helmet under his arm and grinned. It amazed me the unconventional projectile hadn't made a mess of the expensive medical equipment doing important things like keeping me alive. I considered the situation, and as my brother didn't just come off deployment for any old reason, including me doing some time in the hospital, I figured there was something more than just an accident bringing him back from Canada. "Why are you here, Mark? I could see them punting you home for my funeral if you weren't deployed in the field, but I'm obviously not dead."

"I showed my CO the pictures of your truck and suggested I might overly tenderize some Canadians if I didn't get a week off and a ride home. He gave me two weeks as long as I attempted to behave myself, three if required. Word down the line is a serial killer tried to add you to his tally."

"You officially know more about this than I do. While I'd guessed there was a possibility the accident hadn't been accidental, the serial killer part is new." The serial killer part had been a possibility from the start, but I hadn't expected to get drawn directly into the line of fire—not yet, at least. The assholes, newly released criminals, and anyone else with a grudge usually waited until I'd actively stuck my nose where it didn't belong.

Rob scowled, giving my brother his undivided attention. "How did you find out about that?"

"It hit the news, our mother called me, and I asked a few insiders for extra intel. I want a copy of the pictures, Aaron."

"I'll give you copies of the pictures that exclude contracted information. If you want the pictures without my work in them, you'll need a warrant. Same with you, Rob. Don't pick on Sassy too much in exchange."

"She's the one who can't help being stubborn," the DA muttered.

"She also can't give you the pictures without a warrant because of the confidentiality clauses in our contract. I know which pictures I can give you without violating our contract terms. She doesn't. If you want those pictures, you need a warrant. Got your laptop handy, Sassy?"

"I have yours handy, too."

I chuckled, unsurprised my partner would lug around both of our laptops just in case I might be coherent enough to need my piece of shit. "Yours runs faster. Get the pictures loaded so the circus can go home."

The cops relaxed, and the tension in the room eased to tolerable degrees. Maxwell chuckled, and he took a post near the door, shoving his hands into his pockets. "The circus came to visit you and ask questions. Let's start with an easy one. How are you feeling?"

"These painkillers are great."

"Sounds like it. What do you remember about the accident?"

"A semi took offense to my truck and rammed me into the median. I don't remember anything after that."

"Your truck is deceased. The semi flipped you into oncoming traffic, and frankly, we're considering it a miracle there was only one fatality. Someone speeding rammed into you head-on and was instantly killed. You got lucky. Your truck had spun after flipping, and they'd crashed into the bed," Maxwell informed me.

I grimaced. "I'm not sure I want to see the pictures," I admitted. "How many pieces was my truck in after that?"

Sassy sighed and perched on the edge of my bed. "There was enough left of it to make it a bitch getting to you. They had to tear the cab apart to get you out. I abused my power of attorney privileges to file your insurance claims. Mr. Stuffy over there wants to put one of his asshole hotshots on the case when they catch the bastard."

"Semi hit and run?" I guessed.

"He sure did, and he left a confetti mess all over the highway. You were assigned the letter x and a date, too."

Great. I'd become a statistic, although I'd dodged death unlike the mother and child at Park Lane. "Which date?"

"June 21st."

"That's odd." It was especially odd as that was my parents' anniversary date. "What are your thoughts?"

Sassy shrugged. "Not sure yet. We're working on it."

"Well, it's Mom and Dad's wedding date." I pointed at myself. "Yours truly was born nine months later."

Mark snorted. "Anniversary, twerp. I beat you out of maternal prison six years earlier. I'm just generous and don't mind sharing my birthday with you."

There was only one thing left for me to tell my brother. "You suck, Mark."

"I suck so much I flew all the way back from Canada to visit you. How can I help with the investigation?"

"Stay out of the way," I ordered, as did most of the cops and the DA.

Mark scowled and waggled his finger at me. "You must have planned that. I'm hurt."

"No, you're just a bossy know-it-all." I directed my gaze to his gun. "Armed with a ridiculous rifle."

The DA shook his head and laughed. "If you want to make yourself and that ridiculous rifle useful, babysit your brother until we find out if he'll be targeted again. Also, I trust you have the appropriate paperwork to carry that in public places?"

"You mean my gun isn't the appropriate paperwork?"

"Mr. Clinton," Robert warned.

"I have all the authorizations I need to take the gun off the base and into public spaces. I'm currently badged as part of the military police and I have blanket jurisdiction for Texas. Word down the line is they want this terrorist shut down, and yes, the military is classifying this killer as a terrorist, and we've gotten nods from the CDC and the FBI to be involved. They want this guy dealt with. Immediately."

"And that leads us right back to you, Aaron," Maxwell announced. "Did you see the semi's driver?"

"No, I didn't."

"Notice anything unusual?"

I thought about it, and I remembered to avoid nodding before irritating my healing throat. "The only thing I noticed was he was driving slow, and when I got into the passing lane, he went back to highway speed. I found it annoying. I'd meant to ease off and just wait for my exit at that point, but I got boxed in by impatient drivers behind me and a traffic snarl ahead."

"Waiting for a truck like yours?" my brother speculated. "How bad would the crash have been if Aaron had been in the right-hand lane?"

"Easily lethal," Maxwell replied. "Both sides of the highway in that area have concrete barriers and heavy traffic. The median was still the worst place to have the crash, but the exit lane wasn't exactly safe, either."

Sassy handed me her laptop, and I went to work sorting through the photographs, creating a file for those without Sharon Gray in them and another for images I'd need to doctor if the DA wanted them without a warrant. "Here's the deal, Robert. I can send you the images that don't have confidential information in them without a warrant, but I'm toeing gray territory. If you want these pictures as evidence to present in court, I request you get a proper warrant and official copies. That said, if you're not against me doctoring the images, I can remove my client's interests from the photographs and still let you get information on those in the crowd. If you want the full images, you'll need another warrant, one that can legally invalidate the confidentiality clause with my client."

"I'll get the warrant for the general photographs by the end of the day. Please send me the doctored images, but make it clear they're doctored so I can acquire a warrant for those, too," the DA replied. "That should cover your professional reputation."

I found the nice version of the DA creepy at best. "Since when did you care if my professional reputation remained intact? On a good day, I piss in your cereal because I'm good at my job."

"I cared when you lost your primary stream of income doing the right thing and going against the defense's wishes to cover up their client's crimes. I'll swing by the firm blacklisting you and make it clear that I'll be informing the general public about their unethical practices and efforts to circumvent the law. They won't bite. They never do. But I'll have word spread around about the case where you chose the law and justice over the contract. Costs me nothing, costs them a lot, and makes it clear they need to pay better attention to their ethics rather than their win percentages."

While I wanted to say the same about the DA's office, I kept that thought to myself. "Remind me later not to piss you off, Rob."

"You piss me off whenever you walk into the room, but I don't hold it against a man for doing his job well. I just get ticked you always manage to get in my way."

I grinned, unable to deny the accusation. "Why are you here, anyway? It's not like you to pay personal visits when you could grab one of your minions to do it for you."

"Whoever did this is going to rot in prison for a long time since I can't get the death penalty in Texas. That's why. I may not like you most of the time, but you and his other victims deserve justice. You're my only living clue in this mess, so we're going to be seeing a lot of each other in the future. I suggest you get used to it."

I foresaw numerous headaches in my future. On the plus side, Sassy would bristle daily, providing me with an unmatched view and superb entertainment. "In good news, you know if I'm working a case and the fucker is guilty, you'll find out about it. I don't like making your job harder, but the punishment should fit the crime."

Rob sighed, but he nodded. "I do respect that. Just so you're aware, I have filed for a warrant for your client list for the past six months, and it'll include a demand for the complete content of the contracts. I should have the approved warrant in a few hours."

Great. That'd make my life a mess for the next while, as part of our contracts involved notifying them if we were served a warrant revealing any information about our clients. "Sassy?"

"I'll get the contracts sorted and start the notification letters," Sassy replied. "Twenty-four hours to get everything sorted. Honestly, most of the work is done, but I have to give our clients twelve hours to challenge the warrant with the judge, not that it'll get them anywhere. I'll make the calls as soon as we're done here and shoot them emails to cover our end of things."

"I can work with twenty-four hours," the DA replied. "I'll have the warrant served in the afternoon to make things easier on you. I'll ping the judge and let him know you're aware you're being warranted and are gathering the information we need and fulfilling your contract terms. He wants to move on this as much as we do."

Sassy tapped the top of her laptop's screen to get my attention. "Anything else you want me to prep for them?"

"Only if we're warranted. How are we on outstanding contract issues?"

"Just the one."

I gave Sassy a great deal of credit; she didn't even glance at Maxwell.

"That one's mine, and I've already disclosed I've hired you to gather extra information through legal means. I was scolded by the chief, but as long as you stay legal, all tip-offs will be pursued."

"Rob, can we exclude Maxwell's contract from the warrant?"

"While it'll be gathered as part of the warrant, I'll hold it aside. I'll inform necessary parties only as needed. That said, I want a copy of the intel."

I arched a brow. "Max?"

"Give it to him. His office is digging through old cases for links, and I'd be giving him the intel anyway. I'm all for efficiency. Whoever this guy is, he means business."

I worried at that; since waking up in the hospital, everyone had been careful to avoid mentioning the Park Lane case to me directly. "Was there another killing?"

Maxwell sighed and nodded. "Unfortunately. Three more mothers and four kids, and we suspect one of the kids was an unintentional target; the main victims were one shot instant kills. We're speculating the killer wasn't sure which kid was his actual target and decided on the fly to add to the body count. The first shot fired wasn't lethal, but the second was. The triple homicide happened this morning and will be on the afternoon news."

Shit. Once was a maybe, but four mothers and five kids killed was a trend—and evidence of a probable serial killer with an agenda. "A number and date at each shooting location?"

"Correct," Maxwell confirmed.

I sighed, able to think of only one legal but questionable method I could help the investigation along, and the woman who could pull it off sat beside me. "Sassy?"

"What?"

"You know that colony of cranky cats I often complain about?"

"If you mean my family, then yes, I do."

"Have them hit up the local wolves and suggest this asshole might go after their puppies next."

Sassy's eyes widened. "That's a ruthless tactic to open with. I like it. Anything else?"

"You still friends with any of those lionesses you bitch about because they can roar and you can't?"

"I'm friends with most feline lycanthropes in the state. Everyone loves me. Why?"

"The cops are going to need a lot of tips to catch this fucker, and I think it's time I proved to you that cheetahs can win—if they're of a feline bent on the hunt. You'll have to do most of the work until I can bust out of this joint, but I'll help as I can."

"You're literally asking me to herd cats."

I laughed. "Yes, I am."

She spat curses, tossed a few hisses in my direction for good measure, and snatched her laptop, packing it away while protesting my cruelty between breaths. She howled over my evils for the entire hospital to hear, stomping towards the door.

I, along with everyone else in the room, took a few moments to appreciate the view.

I counted to thirty before chuckling. "That's one hell of a woman."

My brother rolled his eyes and everyone else in the room shook their heads, likely suspecting I'd lost my mind. To be fair, I likely had.

SEVEN

All in all, I thought I'd earned a good
sulk.

SOMETIME AFTER THE third round of questioning, which boiled down to telling them I
didn't remember each and every time, I
conked out on my inquisitive guests, most
likely in mid-sentence.

I couldn't remember.

Another round of testing confirmed I
wasn't going to fall over dead, and thanks to a
blend of magic and medicine, I escaped the
hospital five days following the accident.
Most of the time I spent either by my lone-
some, with my brother, or with Sassy. Sassy
ultimately got suckered into handling my affairs, which kept her out of the hospital more
often than not.

The day of my release, my unwanted
brotherly attachment, accompanied by his
baby rifle, wheeled me out of the hospital as
the institution couldn't handle the thought of

me walking out of the place like they'd actually cured me.

"You could've let me wheel myself out," I muttered.

All in all, I thought I'd earned a good sulk.

"And lose the chance to rib you over this for years?"

"That would be nice, now that you mention it. Can I get up now?"

My brother pointed at an SUV parked nearby. "That's my rental, and no, you can't drive."

"I'm pretty sure I'm too drugged to drive anyway. Where are we going?"

"To hell. Mom and Dad demanded the presence of all offspring for dinner. They're not convinced the hospital has been feeding you appropriately. They're probably right, as you're even scrawnier than usual."

I lurched to my feet, ditched the blasted wheelchair, and limped to Mark's rental. "What happened to going home? Where I live, not where the people who spawned us live."

"There's a cat infestation, and I'm tired of being hissed at by pissy cheetahs. There was a wolf flirting with a panther the last time I checked on your place."

A wolf was flirting with a panther in my apartment? While I'd asked Sassy to involve the wolves, how had it devolved to interspecies flirtation in my apartment? Oh, right. I'd asked Sassy to herd cats.

My fault. I should've known better than to expect anything else.

"Why was a wolf flirting with a panther? Wolves aren't felines, Mark."

"He was willingly conspiring with a cat. And, I gotta say, that lady is packing heat in all the right ways. I'd be interested in a round with her if she wasn't the marrying type."

"You are such a slut, Mark."

"I know. It's great. Anyway, I'm sorry, but we're going over to our parents' place. For the sake of our eardrums, pretend you like it." Mark unlocked the vehicle and hovered until I climbed inside. "You doing all right? You look like death warmed over."

"I'm alive and only spent two days comatose. I'm great. And don't you even think about expressing any concern to a doctor I might not be ready to leave the hospital. I will take your baby rifle, shove it up your ass, and fire."

"Noted. And technically, you were only in a coma for thirty-one hours, and you regained consciousness much faster than expected. Were they able to confirm lycanthropy infection? The asshole doctors won't give anyone but you or your power of attorney the results, and Sassy refuses to ask."

"I refused the second test," I admitted.

"The first test, taken when I was brought in, was negative. They'll test again in a year, but they're estimating a ninety percent chance of infection. The doc wanted to claim it was basically a guarantee, but some people have natural immunities to the virus and he didn't want a lawsuit. My white blood cell numbers are completely haywire, which is a solid sign of infection in his opinion. But then he acknowledged I suffered from enough internal injuries it could just be my body fighting off every infection known to man right now."

"So, he has no idea and was just spewing shit out of his ass trying to sound fancy."

"Basically."

"Joe's an army medic. Get him to check you over. He knows every trick in the book for field operations, so if you've still got something wrong with you, he can patch you up properly. He also has the right virus strain, being your kitten's brother and all. Once we're at our parents' place, I'll ping the base and see if he's in the area. If so, I'll ask for him to come pay you a visit as soon as he can get free from his duties. My bet's on the white blood count being from all those internal injuries you managed to survive. Good job on that, by the way." Mark started his rental. "If you're not up for visiting our overbearing parental units, I'll give you to the cats."

I debated which was most likely to kill me,

resigning myself to the reality of having dinner with Mom and Dad. "I'm more likely to handle the overbearing parental units than the felines destined to freak out the instant I step through the door."

"That's one way to put it."

"The doctors want me to go back in for another round of lycanthropy testing next week, claiming internal injuries and potential other infections making a mess of early detection with the added bonus of increasing my chances of infection. I politely declined, using that quack's own complaints against him. If Sassy's father bled on me enough to infect me, according to him, his virus might try to heal my injuries, tap itself out, and go into hiding while recovering and replicating. As such, it won't be detected even next week, and since it's incurable, I see no need to be poked and prodded for lycanthropy on top of the other poking and prodding they need to do. I managed to annoy everyone with that one."

"You're good at annoying people, especially when you use their own logic against them."

"I thought I was being nice, saving my insurance company several thousand dollars of unnecessary testing." I stretched my legs and settled into my seat, debating if I wanted to take a nap. "I'm not up for the traditional beer, but I'll let you kick my ass at a game of pool if Dad still has his table. You can fill me in on your intel about this serial killer at the same time."

"You're not even up for pool, Aaron. You'd try to play from a stool and lose even worse than you usually do. As for the intel, yeah. We need to talk. I've been helping the cats; they've been working my leads, but we haven't gotten very far. We think the common link is the kids, though."

Shit. "What's the link?"

"They're all between the ages of six and ten, and there's no father listed on their birth certificates."

I jumped to a conclusion I didn't like. "The mothers may know who the fathers are—or is. But why kill the kids, though?"

Even as I asked, I got the sinking suspicious I knew why: corpses couldn't talk, and most wouldn't exhume a child's corpse to perform a paternity test if it wasn't done as part of the autopsy, and from my understanding of the situation, the paternity tests would only be done if there was just cause. While I thought there was plenty of just cause in the suspicious circumstances, I had no idea if the police and the coroner's office would agree with me.

"Judging from your sickened expression, you have a few ideas about why. I submitted an anonymous tip that the police might want to do a paternity test. Will they? I don't know. We might get lucky. I doubt it. Even if the kids all had the same father, they need a warrant and just cause to identify who the father is. *I* think the grounds are solid, but I doubt a judge will agree with me. I can think of too many reasons why someone might want to kill kids because of their father."

I could, too, which bothered the hell out of me. "Shit."

"Yeah. My thoughts exactly. We had some ideas, but I'd like to hear yours without my ideas influencing yours."

"The first thing to occur to me would be someone wanting the direct evidence of infidelity gone. Both mother and child. Next, I'd look at revenge. It could be a hatred of single mothers by a father cut out of their child's life, for example. In theory, it could be a psychopath. Could also be a fanatic, I suppose. Someone who believes in set family units, likely someone belonging to an extremist religious cult. After that, my ideas are all variations of those themes. Instead of a father behind the killings, it could be a business partner or someone trying to hide evidence to save their reputation. A family member might want to remove the family shame, too." I scowled over the baser cruelties of humanity. "It could be one of a hundred different things."

"Which is probably why the police won't bite on the paternity warrant," my brother muttered.

I thought about the break in the pattern: me. I was the product of a marriage, a second-born son from conservative parents who'd waited until marriage to jump into bed, something considered a rarity by most. I had no children; the few times I'd slept with a woman, we'd both been careful, and I'd made certain there hadn't been any unexpected surprises nine months later.

I didn't fit any of the possible scenarios.

"Has anyone looked into the mercenary networks to see if anyone hired a hitman for a large-scale job? I'd buy into a serial killer, except there's one issue: I don't fit any of the possibilities. A serial killer would ignore someone like me, who doesn't fit their story. Their profile. Their cause. Serial killers are a special breed of criminal, and they don't operate the same way a mercenary might. Had a serial killer wanted me out of the way, he—or she, as it's entirely possible the murderer is a woman—wouldn't want to pollute their headlines with my death. They'd find another way to kill me, one that doesn't fit the same dialogue as the other killings." I shrugged. "That's just my opinion, of course. But here's one thing to remember: the first killing was a professional job, Mark."

"Yes, it was a very professional job. The hit on you was professional, too. The police found a tracker on the rubble of your truck. I only found out because I got a tip off; the model was military-grade, likely stolen from a supply depot. Word got down the line to me, which fits really well with your mercenary suggestion. I'd been wondering if the serial killer had started out as a mercenary, but I think your idea fits better than mine. A serial killer with military connections might be able to get that tracker, but that sort of thing is more likely to fall into the hands of a mercenary. A mercenary, or mercenaries, had occurred to me, but the rest of the killings have been true to form for a serial killer with the exception of you. A mercenary mimicking a serial killer would throw the investigation off."

"What I want to know is this: was using the same method on me by accident or design?"

My brother flicked at his steering wheel but didn't put the SUV into gear to leave. "I don't have an answer for that. But if it was by design, why do it? And you don't trash a truck like yours in that way by accident. It was definitely by design."

"I liked that truck," I muttered. Without

any idea of why a mercenary *or* serial killer would want to eliminate me using the same calling card, I focused on more immediate life problems. "Did Sassy tell you how badly I'm getting fucked on my insurance?"

"You're fine on the insurance front. They classified the incident as no fault for you, and they gave you forty grand for your truck. It won't fully replace your baby, but as I'm a generous, wonderful older brother, I have decided I'm covering the rest. By that, I mean I needed to keep Sassy busy and your new truck will be ready for pickup soon. Tomorrow soon. Happy early womb eviction day. I added some extras, and I got full replacement insurance from the dealership on any incident where it's deemed you're not at fault."

Hell had surely frozen over. "You replaced my truck?"

"Your kitty did most of the work, and it kept the hysterics to a minimum."

"Sassy?" Since when did Sassy suffer from hysterics? I could see Sassy panicking, especially if there was a threat to her chocolate or shoe supply, but to have hysterics? "You can't be serious."

"Sassy having hysterics is not something I'd joke about. She flipped when she found out you and her daddy had been in a fatal collision. She saw your truck on the news before she'd been contacted by her mother."

Yep, that would make Sassy freak right the hell out. "Holy shit. What happened?"

"She, according to her father, showed up at the hospital as a cheetah and sang the sad song of her people until a nurse found her mother in the waiting room. Then, in what I can only think of as a complete lapse of sanity and judgment, crawled onto Dad's lap and continued to sing the sad song of her people. Dad was not happy to have a lap full of distressed cheetah. When she wasn't singing the sad song of her people, she was either chirping or hyperventilating and panting."

"Please tell me someone recorded this."

"Mom did, but she's holding the video hostage."

"Well, that's not very nice of her."

"She's agreed to show it to us should we show up for dinner."

I pointed in the direction of our parents' house. "Onward, driver! Take us to the video."

"Asshole," my brother muttered.

To my dismay, I discovered laughing hurt.

A DARK BLUE Chevy Silverado with crew cab and full bed devoured space and took over my parents' driveway. I bet when someone started it, the neighbors three streets away would hear it rumble. Everything from the chrome trim to the heavy-duty tires proclaimed the vehicle needed to be put to immediate use.

"Black and blue, just like you," my brother announced. "The black comes from the leather interior, it has your precious diesel engine in it, and some other junk Sassy kept squealing over and insisted you'd like. Honestly, I think I need one, too."

That was *my* truck? I pointed at it. "That's the truck? But you said tomorrow."

"Apparently, I lied. Unless someone else got the same truck I bought you. Sassy must have picked it up early. She's on all the paperwork. It made things easier. Also, you score full points for making her your power of attorney. She's a beast at paperwork, and she took no prisoners at the dealership. She charmed and bullied her way to a good deal on it."

"That's seriously the truck?"

Mark parked on the grass and killed the engine. "It really wasn't supposed to be here today." Sliding out of the rental, he bellowed, "You're such a fucking cat, Sassy!"

"Fuck you, stinky helmet head!" Sassy yowled from inside.

My parents, the conservative religious types, had allowed Sassy into the house? I waited for the screaming over the liberal use of curses to begin, but other than my brother and Sassy, the house remained quiet. "Stinky helmet head?"

"Mom said she couldn't call me a reject from the gene pool. We've numbed her to our foul mouths. Honestly, I heard Dad muttering curses under his breath the other day, so I think they've finally been cured of their pristine language."

About time. I sighed, shook my head, and unbuckled my belt, preparing for Sassy's inevitable assault. "You probably should clean your flight helmet. It is gross." Expecting my sore body to charge me yet again, I eased out of the SUV. It went better than I expected. "Why is Sassy here?"

Before Mark had a chance to reply, Sassy charged out of the house, skidded around the truck, bolted across the yard, and launched herself at me. A better man would've caught her. I sidestepped. She thumped into the seat and sprawled.

On second thought, I needed to dodge her near open doors whenever possible, and I took a moment to enjoy the unrivaled view. "Hey, Sassy. You missed." I'd pay for teasing her later, but I appreciated what a good pair of tight jeans did for her legs, and on second inspection, I noticed she wore the blue shoes I'd gotten for her. They, too, did wonderful things for her legs. "Hey, you're wearing the blue pair."

"They're nice. Thank you. I like them a lot. Daddy said I didn't get to see the new ones until you gave them to me yourself." Sassy slid off the seat and dusted herself off. "Sorry. I got excited."

As cats had limited modes of operation, including ready to sleep, asleep, or zooming everywhere, I resigned myself to the inevitable. "Pounce gently. I'm still sore."

According to the doctors, I'd be sore for at least another week.

Sassy faced me, examining me from head to toe. "Where's not sore?"

"His mouth," my brother announced before strolling towards the house. "Our mother is likely spying through the window. The probably newly infected would enjoy if you examined his mouth with yours, and there's an added bonus of offending my mother tossed in, free of charge."

"I'll enjoy murdering you in front of our mother," I replied, careful to keep my tone neutral. "Finish giving your final speech before I kill you."

"You couldn't kill a fly in your current state," my asshole brother countered.

"Sassy?"

"I promised your mother I wouldn't try to kill the stinky helmet head."

"Why would you do something like that?" I complained. "Anyway, I'm sore, not dying. Just hug gently. What other dumb things did you promise my mother?"

"If I want to shift, I have to go to the bathroom and leave my clothes folded in a neat pile. I'm not allowed to ruin her floors with my claws. There's something about trying to watch my language." She hesitated, looked me over again, and took the koala approach to hugging, wrapping her legs around my waist while burying her face against my neck.

As pouncing, in and of itself, wasn't a gentle act, I accepted my stupidity with a wince. To keep her from falling, I wrapped my arms around her and gave her a squeeze.

"She's not too clear on the definition of gently." Mark snagged my cheetah by her waist and pulled.

While I let her go, she held on tighter. "Mine. I'm not letting go. No. Go away."

Pain sucked, but I appreciated her possessiveness.

"You're going to knock him over," my brother warned. "If you want to continue your koala impression, which is a very good one, mind you, please wait until he's inside. It'll be easier on him."

Sassy eased her hold enough so my brother could yank her off. I staggered, catching my balance on the SUV. My brother hauled Sassy towards the house, and she kicked and screamed her defiance.

"Try not to fall asleep on the walkway. You know how Mom feels about that," my brother hollered over Sassy's fussing.

"Put me down." The cheetah squirmed and kicked, and I wished her the best of luck freeing herself from my brother, who viewed his body as a canvas for muscle building and physical exertion. Honestly, it amazed me he even fit in a fighter jet.

"I'll put you down in the house. Damn, woman. Gently doesn't mean climb him like he's a tree. I know you're excited, but try to have some limits."

Sassy twisted in my brother's hold and beat on his arms while kicking her legs without earning her freedom. The situation amused me too much for my own good. "He could run off with you, and you'd be stuck. Don't let her escape, Mark. That's my cheetah."

"She's your cheetah? I thought you were her pet human," my brother replied, setting Sassy down at the door. "If you want attention, woman, wait until he sits down first."

"But I was being gentle."

"It's true. For Sassy, that was gentle. I think I did well. I didn't fall over."

"You turned gray, Aaron. Go sit before you fall down," Mark ordered while shoving

Sassy inside. "Mom, Dad! I've brought the twerp."

"You don't have to shout. We're standing right here," my mother said, stepping away from the front window, thus confirming my brother's suspicions. Most of the times my mother had visited, I'd been down and out for the count or didn't remember much, and she scrutinized me from head to toe. "You're looking better."

After a close brush with an affectionate cheetah, it impressed me I'd fooled my mother. "They wouldn't have let me out if I wasn't at least looking better."

"Sit. Your brother's right. You look like you're about to pass out on my floor, and you know how I feel about people passed out on my floor."

My mother loathed anything that damaged the pristine state of her precious hardwood floors, so I obeyed, picking the couch as my new base of operations to give Sassy space next to me if she wanted. "Where's your father, Sassy?"

"I convinced him to stay home. I had to yell at him. They tried to follow me. I wasn't having it, not this time."

I was afraid to ask who 'they' was, as her mother and father only started the list of candidates. "Thank you for stopping them."

As I suspected would be the case, Sassy

plopped onto the couch beside me. "You're welcome. How are you feeling? Does it hurt much?"

"The doctors gave me painkillers if I need them, there are some antibiotics in there, but I haven't filled the prescriptions yet. I'll get to it. Honestly, escaping the hospital was tiring enough."

My brother snorted and perched on the arm of the couch. "Yet you bitched about the wheelchair."

"I have to keep a little of my pride intact. It's battered."

Sassy smiled and patted my knee. "You've had a rough week."

"Rough is one way to put it. I couldn't help but notice there's a really pretty truck outside." I arched a brow. "Do you happen to know anything about that, Sassy?"

"Who, me?" Her smile widened to a grin. "I don't know what you're talking about."

"Really? I think you're yanking my chain, Miss Sastria."

"I'd never."

"Well, I like the color."

She giggled and snuggled into the couch. "I remembered you were upset when you couldn't get that shade of blue in the old truck. Your brother wanted to paint it puke green."

"Thank you for not painting it puke green."

"My fashion sense totally factored into my status as your power of attorney, and everyone here knows it. Obviously, I'm the only one qualified to pick the appropriate colors for things you own."

"I thought your fashion sense existed to provide me with appropriate bribe material." I feigned a frown, narrowing my eyes to offer the illusion of being suspicious. "Shoes, purses, and other accessories exist so I can provide bribe material."

"That, too."

"I bought you those weird clear shoes with the red sole you wanted. I tossed in a bonus of a red purse to go with them." I tried to relax but tensed from the worry she'd be unhappy with my attempted bribe.

"So I heard. But why?"

If my attempt to make the cheetah mine and mine alone soured, I'd blame the drugs again. Sassy understood drugs, and with a little luck, she'd opt to forget I'd bought the shoes before the accident. "I think I wanted to use them as a bribe to remove you from the general dating pool. Beating a bunch of braindead felines for upsetting you is hard work, but then you wanted to go on a date with a wolf. Braindead felines seem a little easier to beat on than a wolf. Seriously, Sassy? A wolf?"

"I ran out of heterosexual felines, don't ask about the bisexual ones, and I only went on the dates with the homosexual ones to make their mothers feel better—and to cover their real dates with each other. Well, most of the time. There were a few incidents of pure desperation. Those didn't work out well."

"Well, I bought you a terrifyingly expensive pair of shoes to put an end to that crap."

"That's very sweet of you. You didn't have to, Aaron."

Like hell I didn't have to. "My shoes make you happier than dates with those men."

Sassy snorted. "Obviously. Your shoes don't attempt to lick the back of an unexpected boyfriend's throat."

Even without my painkillers hampering me, I doubted I could figure out how a pair of heels could engage with an over-amorous cheetah. "They're very reasonable shoes that cost an unreasonable amount."

"You're so tired you've given my new shoes sentience."

"I wouldn't say no to some coffee if you wanted to show me a little mercy. You'll need a crane to get me up at this point. I'd also like to know what I've missed."

"I'll make some coffee," my mother announced, marching towards the kitchen.

"I would've showed you mercy, but I'm banned from the kitchen."

I sighed, completely unsurprised she'd gotten evicted from my mother's kitchen. "How did you get banned from the kitchen?"

"I put my paws on the counter and checked out the contents of the fridge. She'd asked for someone to get her some milk! She just wasn't expecting me to fetch the milk while transformed. I didn't damage the jug, either. I was gentle."

The thought of Sassy mouthing my mother's milk jug made me smile. "You're such a cat."

"I am. You've missed a lot, although I'm glad you've missed it. That annoying DA prick keeps bothering me, and those damned cops keep getting these ridiculously specific warrants. They sent over six of the damned things yesterday." Sassy pouted and stared at the coffee table, and knowing my mother, Sassy had already heard the riot act about feet on the coffee table.

"You won't have feet if you put them on Mom's furniture, and if you don't have feet, you won't need shoes," I warned.

"Vicious. Evil and vicious, that's what she is."

Since announcing the purchase of expensive shoes to remove Sassy from the dating pool hadn't ended my life, I decided to test my luck. "For the record, should I be infected with lycanthropy, I'm trusting you to preserve my heterosexuality. I don't want to be attacked by angry females like your father was. He made it very clear to me: female cheetahs are vicious."

"To you, all women are vicious and dangerous."

"You're especially dangerous. I keep buying you shoes. So many shoes." I slumped my shoulders and faked a pout. "I'm—"

"Don't you even, Aaron! If you say what I think you're going to say, I will find a way to torture you for life."

I fought to avoid smiling, as keeping her around for life was my goal. "I'm going to go bankrupt trying to bribe you into forgiving me for my every sin."

"You're an idiot. You don't have to bribe me with shoes."

"It's the only thing I know that works!"

Sassy rolled her eyes. "You're hopeless. I'll accept your bribe of shoes as an excuse to reject bad dates, but every time I'm challenged about my rejection, you have to go on a very public date with me so I don't look like I'm a liar."

I considered her offer a complete success of my first goals. The next goal would be to have her reject every other man to make a pass at her. "How often are you challenged when you give someone a rejection?"

"Twice last week, resulting in two unwanted dates."

"And the week before?"

She shrugged. "Four, I guess. Maybe five."

Uh oh. I wouldn't have enough money to buy shoes if I took her on good dates two to four times a week. I'd enjoy it more than I should, but I'd have to watch my money carefully—or find out what her favorite inexpensive outings were so I wouldn't go bankrupt within a month. Then again, I spent thousands on shoes. Surely I could be more selective about the shoe acquisitions and spend my money wisely to plan appropriate dates. "This week?"

"The ones from this week don't count. I told them I needed to visit you in the hospital, which was the truth."

"Humor me."

Laughing, she shook her head. "I stopped counting after ten. They wanted to 'distract' me."

I could think of a few reasons men might bother Sassy, and the lycanthropy virus only played a small role. A good pair of heels elevated her to a daydream, although her temper and tongue could easily transform her into a nightmare. "Dare I ask?"

"I suggested they could distract each other if they were that bored."

Of course she had. Sassy sassed, and how she sassed directly related to her stress levels. When Sassy turned snide, she needed shoes or an outlet. "I'm sorry I worried you."

"Someone tried to kill you," she whispered.

I wanted to point out someone had tried to kill her father, too, but I kept that thought to myself. "I probably either saw or photographed the killer, and I get the feeling they're the type to want to get away with their crime."

Unfortunately, the idea that the killer wanted to get away with a chain of brutal murders added strength to my idea we weren't dealing with a serial killer, but a hired mercenary or assassin.

"Or they didn't care if you lived or died as long as you are out of the way."

I glanced at my brother, who decided he had a lot of dirt under his nails in need of immediate attention. "Your thoughts?"

"I think it's plausible there's a psychopath, likely a professional, with an agenda on the loose, but he wants to fuck with law enforcement without getting caught. I think you know something, but we can't figure out what, which leads us back to a twisted serial killer who decided to add you to his tally. The mercenary idea, as I said in the car, makes sense, but we just can't prove anything either way. The photographs we looked at didn't lead to anything, although there are a few individuals we couldn't identify in your shots."

When searching for a criminal or solving a mystery, I dreaded three words above all: I don't know. The lack of knowledge often led to incorrect convictions. Sometimes, the innocent went to prison. Sometimes, the guilty walked free.

Too few were willing to request an angel; angels told the truth and nothing but the truth, and everyone had their secrets.

I sighed, wondering if we'd find the truth before even more women and children were murdered. "Sassy, did the DA get warrants for information on our clients?"

"Yes. They got a warrant for all clients within the past two years. The clients have already been notified about the circumstances. The DA was particularly interested in Tom Heatherow."

The DA would love to crucify a newbie politician, especially one actively attempting to smear a rival candidate. "I can't see how he might be a factor unless he copy-catted to get out of the bill. And even if he did, why ruin his potential political career saving some money? He's invested millions into his campaign, and that's out of his own pocket. I didn't look too closely at his campaign funding," I admitted.

Sassy and my brother exchanged worried glances. Before I could question them, my mother brought in a tray burdened with mugs and placed it on the coffee table.

She placed a #1 Grandmother mug in front of me. My brows inched upwards. First, I wanted to know where she'd gotten the damned thing, as my brother and I had no children due to our dedication to all things contraceptive. Second, when a conservative like my mother, who practiced her religion with the fervor of the truly devout, started dropping hints, she meant business. When a woman with a strong aversion to the evils of the lycanthropy virus dropped them without shame, I knew to worry.

Sassy got a bright pink mug decorated with unicorns..

With a smirk, Sassy picked up her mug and lifted it in a toast to my mother. "The odds of a girl are really low, but I can take a hint."

Sassy handled my mother better than I did. Since when did *my* mother even *think* of accepting a lycanthrope as a potential daughter-in-law—or drop hints she wanted a granddaughter?

My brother snickered. "They're zero unless you convince my brother he isn't actually allergic to women. I wish you luck. But any-way, you don't date the uninfected."

"Apparently, I do now, but only when ass-holes refuse to accept no as an answer. I ex-pect I'll be forced to date the same person into eternity. There are that many assholes in Texas," she complained.

My mother unloaded the tray and tucked it under her arm. "What a terrible tragedy. Would you like some cheese to go with that whine? If you need to have ten boys before you have a girl, I'll just have to suffer through somehow."

Shit. My mother had done some basic re-search into cheetahs, and she'd found the math to her liking. If she pressured us for a girl, she'd get more grandchildren than I could count out of the deal, and as Mark wasn't going to ever enter the father pool if he had a choice in the matter, that left my mother with me, and she'd dipped her toes into desperate waters, willing to let go of her prejudices for the sake of the family line con-tinuing.

Since criticizing my mother would land me in a world of hurt, I turned my annoyance onto my brother. "You should settle down and have a few kids. You're the older son. Why are you shirking on your manly duties to our beloved mother?"

My mother snorted.

"I'm a slut. I'm not marriage material. As our beloved, wonderful mother raised me right, I take every precaution. The last thing any of us needs is me having an unexpected child."

Sassy laughed and nudged me with her elbow. "You'd make a much better single dad compared to Mark. He manages to stink up everything, even his flight helmet."

I could only think of one answer that wouldn't have *someone* in the room out for my blood. "But I don't want to be a single dad. Single dads have to pay child support. Married dads get a wife, a kid, and tax breaks. I think they get other things, too."

"Free sex," my brother said.

I shook my head. "Most expensive free sex known to man, but possibly cheaper than child support?"

Mark stared at me, his brows furrowing. "How much is child support?"

I shrugged. "How much do children cost?"

As we only knew one woman who'd have a realistic answer for us, my brother and I stared at our mother for enlightenment.

"Children are cheaper when married," she announced.

Considering my mother was rather traditional and conservative, I doubted every word to come out of her mouth when it came to children. "Justify that statement, please."

My mother smiled. "Married couples require babysitters less frequently, and daycare can be avoided in some cases. Babysitters and daycare facilities can run up to twenty an hour. That's only the beginning."

I held up my hands. "I surrender."

"Smart boy. When you take frequency into consideration, I assure you free married sex is much cheaper than child support *or* prostitutes."

Mark snickered. "Can't argue with that one."

The last thing I wanted to think about was my parents having sex despite appreciating the results. "Noted."

"And now that I've disgusted my sons, let's discuss this serial killer that's on the loose. I'd rather not get another call like that in my lifetime. Where are you in the investigation? How can we help?"

Mark sighed and shrugged. "We don't know anything concrete. Our current speculations are disturbing at best. Ironically, the attempt on Aaron's life might be the clue we need to find the killer."

Leaning back, I frowned and considered my brother, wondering why he'd left that tidbit out on the drive over. "I'll bite. Justify that, please."

"The date left is our parents' anniversary, nine months to the day we were born. The other dates match up roughly before the kids were born, too. None of the kids have a father listed, although you do. Your date, however, confirmed the trend; we knew, without shadow of a doubt, your date of conception." Mark hopped to his feet, headed for the door, and retrieved a laptop from his battered backpack. He took over the rest of the couch, plunked his computer onto the coffee table, and booted it. "I've built a victim profile with some help from the police and the DA. It's unpleasant."

"How so?" I peeked at my brother's screen to discover a pornography collection. "Seriously, Mark?"

"They're a mix of the murder victims and stalked women who may be potential targets. It's not *my* fault they worked their way through school or decided to do this for whatever reason. Not my business. Some were prostitutes, a few were strippers, there was a bucketful of escorts, and one campaign manager. That's the odd one of the lot, but ironically, she's the one that drew the police's attention to Tom Heatherow. All of the children killed were between the ages of six and twelve. In the politics world, that's essentially one full Presidential election cycle, classified as two years for the main campaign and the full term building up to the start of the next cycle, which technically has a two-year overlap since people start campaigning early."

"What does the Presidential election cycle have to do with anything?"

"The campaign manager worked for a failed Presidential hopeful in Texas during that time period. His campaign went nowhere, but he pocketed a hefty funding bonus from the attempt; he essentially dropped at the end of the overlap period when it was clear he wouldn't be able to make a second bid for the Presidency."

"Who?"

"Abraham Sarmassen."

"Never heard of him," I admitted.

"He's Tom Heatherow's biological father. Heatherow's illegitimate, and his mother married before he was born. Sarmassen was married to someone else at the time, and the scandal ended his second Presidential campaign run out of the gate. After looking over the evidence, I'm thinking he only got through the first part of the cycle because he had no chance in hell of winning his first bid, but his second bid was looking far more promising."

Well, that little discovery explained why Heatherow wanted to sink Senator Sterling using a sex scandal. "All right. Tie it together for me. What does this have to do with the killed kids?"

"Heatherow is participating in a campaign for the senate, which is usually considered a precursor for a Presidential run later. If he wins the senate, he can do his own bid for the Presidency. He hired you to get dirt on his opponent so he'd be a shoe-in for the senate."

"Sassy? How is Tom Heatherow's involvement with us such common knowledge?" I complained.

"The fucker got a warrant, and he got clearance to be privy to the intel. Sorry, Aaron. Nothing I could do. With the notifications filed, the courts can make the list public as the subpoenas are filed. To cover their suspicion, *everyone* is being subpoenaed to get a basic statement on what they hired us for. I expect Heatherow will take the easy out and claim we were doing background investigative work on rival candidates, which is completely legal; everyone does it, so no one will think twice of it, especially him. Heatherow already contacted me and informed me he'd be present for the hearing with his statement. He also sent a card wishing you well. I turned it over to the DA as an early Christmas present to see if it had Heatherow's prints on it for their records."

"If no one has told you this today, you're such a smart woman. Good work."

Sassy smiled.

"I really want to know how the fucker got a warrant when he's in the damned military."

Sassy's smile blossomed into the kind of grin I loved most, promising trouble of some sort. "He's sleeping with the enemy."

I matched her grin and arched a brow at my brother. "Jumped straight into the DA's bed, Mark? Classy. Hey, whatever works for you. After associating with so many cheetahs, I'm used to being the only single straight man Sassy knows."

Sassy wrinkled her nose and huffed. "Dad's straight."

I laughed. "Your father's only heterosexual because your mother resorted to kidnapping him and taking him hostage until their viruses bonded them for life. You're going to have to resort to drastic measures if you want a cheetah."

Or she'd have to wait until her brothers tenderized me and I caught a severe case of lycanthropy. Either would work. With a little luck, some good would come from the accident. Most considered infection with lycanthropy a bad thing.

I wasn't most men.

"Can I continue or do you two need some time?" my brother grumbled.

"I still want to know how *you* got a warrant."

"Technically, the DA nudged the police to

get the warrant, but he requested military policing assistance and dropped my name, thus earning me the right to poke my nose in your business. The FBI is involved, as is the CDC. Hell, everyone's involved at this point. I'm the only one who really thinks Heatherow is a major player in this game though, and I mean as the hire not as the hitman. I think the killer hates targeting kids but is too professional to dump an accepted job. The DA thinks I should stop concocting conspiracy theories, but he looked really uncomfortable as he listened to them, which tells me he's probably warming up to the idea because none of the other ideas fit."

I considered that, and one thing stuck out to me. "What does Heatherow have to do with the murdered women?"

"My preliminary research indicates he's fucked them all."

"Mark," my mother warned.

"I have photographic evidence of the fucking, and I have reason to believe Heatherow hired Aaron to find out if Miss Sharon Gray has kids. Fortunately for Miss Gray, Aaron didn't learn at the time that she does. She has twin daughters and a son, and the daughters are likely Heatherow's. I believe she wasn't using contraceptive because she wanted to help her sister have a family. No father is listed on the twins' birth certificates.

Since you have a reputation of being thorough, I suspect Heatherow assumed you'd notify him if she had children. It's worth noting she had the kids before contracting lycanthropy, and rumor down the line is she's looking for a father so she can have some babies of her own."

"He hired me to follow her regarding Senator Sterling."

"Gray is a politics groupie, and he remembers what happened to his father. The senate is a common stepping stone for people seeking a Presidential nomination, although plenty of governors, mayors, and other lower politicians make runs as well."

As I could easily understand someone running a ruthless campaign to secure power, I found the idea of murdering women and children for the cause abhorrent at best. "Are you going to tell me anything else I'm not going to like?"

"Yes. If it *is* Heatherow behind this, we still have to catch the killer doing his dirty work, and no one knows where he's going to strike next."

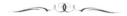

THE DA SHOWED up ten minutes before dinner, and he brought a small army with him. Unfortunately for me, Sassy had stolen my truck and prescriptions, leaving me to fend for myself.

Maxwell took Sassy's spot on the couch, and I found it an unsatisfactory exchange. "You're looking better."

I counted heads, wondering why the DA had brought six cops with him. "I have a feeling I'm about to feel a lot worse. I see you've recruited minions, Robert."

"I'm impressed the cat left you unattended. Four of the cops were to keep the kitty from ripping my head off."

"What did you do to deserve it? Anyway, she's taking my new truck on a joy ride under the flimsy excuse of filling prescriptions. She should be back in time for dinner. What brings you over here?"

"The infestation at your apartment directed us here," Robert replied, and he shot a glare at my brother. "We'd been under the impression you'd be taking him home from the hospital."

My brother smirked and shrugged. One day, Robert would learn he'd never browbeat my brother, who spent his daily life browbeating military men who all thought they could do his job better than he could. "His truck was ready early, Sassy was driving Mom loco, and he didn't feel up for an ambush. I gave him the choice on dealing with the infestation or our parents, and he opted to run away from the infestation. Wise, really. What do you have for us?"

"This is the oddest thing I've ever done as a DA, but Chief Braneni asked for a favor, offered some friends to make it clear he means business, and sent me on over. Aaron, how would you feel about a slight shift in your career?"

I arched a brow and eyed my coffee mug, which had an insufficient amount of coffee left to handle weird questions from the DA. "I might be infected with lycanthropy. It'll be a requirement for at least a year after infection is confirmed unless I luck out and get an exemption for my PI license. Why?"

"Chief Braneni got smacked with some diversity quotas to fill, and he needs a new pair. The requirement is at least one lycanthrope without the hybrid form and someone to partner with them, with a high preference for an infected pre-shift lycanthrope. When he heard you were likely infected from the accident, he started making phone calls. You would need an eighty percent chance of infection rate to qualify."

"Which you know I meet."

"Chief Braneni may have mentioned doing an official request for the information from the hospital and procured the warrant for the information under the new diversity initiative. The judge saw who was being warranted and the purpose for the warrant and said it was the best warrant he had to deal with for the entire month." Robert chuckled and shook his head. "You've got yourself a few too many friends on the bench, Aaron."

"I find solid evidence and make sure it's legitimate before submitting it to the attorneys or police. That helps."

"And that trait is what would make you ideal in police investigations. You have the experience needed, and you're a known entity. If the force has to get used to non-hybrid lycanthropes, it's easier to work with someone the cops are already familiar with. And let's face it. Sassy? She's got the skills but didn't get lucky on the hybrid form."

"Cheetah hybrids are rare." By rare, I meant non-existent. "Explain the diversity issue."

"It's simple. He's got a minimum number of women he needs to hire, and there just aren't a lot of qualified applicants right now who meet base requirements. Sassy qualifies, but was barred due to lycanthropy. With her, she checks off two boxes, and he gets a good cop on the team. It'll open doors for other women, too. We're behind on women in the force here, and we're especially behind on infected officers. We just don't have enough bodies to handle cases dealing with infected citizens. That needs to change. Chief Braneni also wanted me to tell you he wrote in a box for pissing off the local defense attorneys, as before they got pissy over you losing them a big case, you were a major asset for them. Now you'll be a major asset for the prosecution. It's a win-win for me, and you would be the force's guinea pig for how well a pre-shift lycanthrope can work on the force. It'll also let them test out a newly shifting lycanthrope. Also, he asked me to tip you off: when he had the warrant served, you were flagged as a potential for early onset lycanthropy. It's not confirmed, but should your virus replicate faster than normal, you'll have liability coverage. There's also a note that your doctor wanted to do a test in a week, but you opted to wait for confirmation at a later time. He wants to know why."

I pointed at my brother. "He's going to talk to his military doctor friends with specialization in infection cases."

"I am?" my brother asked.

"Yeah, you are. Those doctors just wanted to get me out of their hospital as soon as possible, so I'd like a second opinion, and you know the right people to ask about a second opinion."

"Wow. Since when did you develop a severe case of doctorly paranoia plus good common sense? Mom? I think Aaron's grown up on us!"

"Stop annoying your brother, Mark," our mother hollered from the kitchen.

"Mom likes me more than you right now," I informed my brother. To make it clear I had the upper hand, I lifted my mug and saluted him with it before taking a sip.

Robert snickered. "I see your mother is hoping for a litter of kittens."

"Well, Mark?"

"I know a guy. He'll be in touch," my brother promised. "But seriously? Good thinking. You were let out in record time, and you're moving worse than a cripple. I'd rather make sure you don't need to go back into the body shop."

"If you find solid evidence he shouldn't have been released, let me know," Robert ordered. "I'll have the information added to the case we're building. If there's an issue, that'll cover him legally."

"Want full military certifications on the examination?"

"Please."

"Consider it done."

Robert turned his attention back to me. "I'm hoping you'll talk to your partner about this opportunity. You're between contracts, and I've been told the next academy cycle starts in a month. Think it through. I can't promise what the pay grade will be like, but the opportunity is there, and unless I'm way off my mark, Sassy wanted to be a cop."

Anyone with a pair of functioning eyes could guess Sassy wanted to be a cop. Still, I foresaw disaster in my near future. "I'm going to hazard a guess the defense firms wouldn't overturn the blacklist?"

"When I told them I'd try recruiting you for the police force since they're dumb fucks, I got to enjoy watching them turn a charming shade of gray-green. Even if you decline the invitation, I suspect you're going to walk away a winner. On the force, I expect you'll be bumped straight to investigations. You're known for one thing above all else: the truth prevails. That's a win for me. I get fewer overturned convictions. It's a win for the defense, too. Cases you run won't be just about the verdict. It'll be about making sure the right person's punished for the crime. The inclusion of non-hybrid lycanthropes is still in its infancy, but you and your cheetah are the best to showcase the cause. However annoying, the felines are good at sticking their noses into places they don't belong. You two have a healthy, long-term partnership, so the force isn't gambling there."

Hell might've frozen over while I'd languished in the hospital. "Who are you, and what have you done with Robert?"

"I better not hear you mouthing off to a

guest, Aaron," my mother barked from the kitchen.

No matter what I said, I lost. "Well played, Robert. Well played."

The DA smirked. "Accidental, but I'll take it. What are your odds of joining?"

While I found the odds better than I liked to admit, I worried about Sassy. "I'll talk to Sassy about it, but I expect I'll have to peel her off the ceiling when she finds out. Anything else bringing you my way?"

"While the DA's office doesn't hire PIs, I have a personal job for you and Sassy, and we all pitched in for your fee."

'We all' could be a lot of people, the six quiet cops hanging out in the living room numbering among them. "I'm listening."

"It's worth mentioning I'm covering most of the bill," Maxwell admitted. "And I wired the full amount to your bank account yesterday. This is too important to get into a jurisdiction war over."

I could make some guesses: the police, the DA, and quite possibly the CDC and FBI wanted someone on the outside snooping into the serial killings. "What do you want me to do?"

Robert and Maxwell exchanged looks, and when Maxwell shrugged, Robert replied, "Information gathering. We have a list of potential victims. First, we want you to check in on them. Watch for people watching them. Try to figure out some leads for us. Most important, we want to watch for people watching *you.*"

Ah. They needed bait, and I was the one who got away. "I'm in. I want this fucker caught."

"So do we. I won't lie. I expect this will be dangerous," Robert admitted. "Despite our rocky relationship, I don't willfully endanger people."

"The way I see it, I'm getting paid for the inevitable. This fucker is killing kids." I drew in a breath and held it until I could better control my temper. "How many of the kids don't have a father listed on their birth certificate?"

"All but one," the DA admitted.

"Are you running paternity tests on the bodies?"

"We don't have just cause."

I owed my brother. "Tom Heatherow's father lost a Presidential bid over his existence. He's illegitimate. It's election season. What if someone is getting rid of the DNA evidence? If you have the paternity tests done and the results on file, you won't have to exhume the bodies of children later. Maybe you can't do anything with the information right now, but if you *do* get just cause to pursue it, you have the intel."

Everyone in the room, even my military-hardened brother, winced.

A better man might've taken mercy on them, but I couldn't afford to. "It's true. Maybe the father's DNA isn't in the system. Maybe you can't justify obtaining a warrant to identify the father if he *is* in the system, but if those kids share a father, you might have an important lead."

"And I don't need a warrant to identify if the victims are related," Robert admitted.

"Right. What's the victim count up to?"

"Twenty-four women, twenty-five children, and you. You're the odd one of the bunch, and you're the only survivor."

That I'd survived made me the odd one, but the dates on the scraps of paper would likely lead us to the culprit. "Did you check into the dates?"

Robert sighed. "Yes. Using yours as proof of concept, we compared them to the birth certificates of all victims. I hate how right you are, but the paternity test will likely confirm things we'd rather not have confirmed. The dates match within eight and a half to nine and a half months of birth."

"Of the kids."

"One mother and child were born several days apart, but yes, we believe it's for the children."

"Why have you delayed the DNA testing,

Robert? It's pretty glaring. It'd be the first thing I checked."

He shook his head. "It's not that easy. Even if I have it done, it won't do us any good. We can't use the information until we have just cause for a warrant identifying the father. Even if we identify the father, the CDC doesn't do genetic testing of infants. They want that registry, but it's not going to happen any time soon. The current age for DNA registry is eighteen unless a crime is involved. If we attempt to get information on children with unknown fathers of that age range, all we're doing is turning them into targets and inciting mass hysteria. We don't have the resources to run that many DNA tests, either. There could be hundreds of children with unknown fathers of that age range in Dallas."

"Is there no way to get the information without exposing them as targets?"

Robert shrugged. "Not without knowing who is behind the killings and why. The why is a solid speculation, but not confirmed. Not without running the DNA tests and figuring out the probability of relation."

Shit.

The front door opened, and Sassy poked her head inside. "Two cops are blocking my spot, and Aaron'll get cranky if I have to park his dainty truck on the grass." She tossed a white paper bag to my brother. "You're temporarily adult supervision. Read the labels and figure out what Aaron needs to take."

Maxwell got to his feet, laughed, and dug out his keys. "Give me your keys, Dan. I'll move the cruisers onto the grass so the truck stays clean for a few extra hours."

One of the quiet cops guarding the door laughed and gave Maxwell his keys. "Don't you scratch my baby."

"Does your baby have enough paint left to scratch?"

"I think there's a patch or two on the hood."

Maxwell shook his head and went outside to move the cruisers so Sassy could park.

"Anything else you need, Robert?"

"As a matter of fact, yes."

"What?"

"Do you have any children that might be targeted?"

I scowled at the question, but I shook my head. "Not that I'm aware of."

My brother snickered. "You're joking, right? Aaron? Have kids? While I don't think he's a virgin, if you ever need advice on contraceptives, he's your man."

What had I done to deserve my brother at his worst?

"Good. That's one worry off my mind," Robert admitted. "When do you think you can get in your hours at the range? You need them if you're going to think about that job offer."

Sassy bounced into the living room and plopped onto the couch beside me. "I just drove a cop car. I stole the keys, and I moved it so I could park faster. They drive like shit compared to your truck. What job offer?"

"You're so badass the cops want to see if you'll terrorize the locals if you're wearing a uniform. They want me to make sure you sass the civilians into submission without serious incident. However, you may want to limit your grand theft auto incidents in the future, especially when the cops are witnessing it."

Maxwell strolled in and laughed. "Public pitching?"

"Witnesses if she kills me for even mentioning it."

"What would we be? Contractors?"

"No, Sassy. Cops."

Her eyes widened. "Say what?"

"They want to test non-hybrid lycanthropes on the force, and my infection possibility rate qualifies me. We already work well together. It seems there's an academy training session in a month. We have a contract or two with Maxwell to finish first."

"Or two?"

"They need bait. I agreed. It'll be a change

of habit, but what do you think about working for the prosecution for a while?"

"You have got to be yanking my tail."

"Robert?"

"Talk to Chief Braneni for details," the DA replied. "It's a real offer."

"I can become a cop? Without the hybrid form?"

"Times are changing. There are enough lycanthropes now and not enough hybrids to fill law enforcement needs. With Aaron likely infected and your skills from your private investigations business, you can fill a gap in the force."

Sassy pointed at me. "And I'd be partnered with him?"

"That's the idea. Lycanthropes are often paired together like that, as mated pairs team up together. While you two aren't mated, you've been working together for a long time. It's best to keep good teams working together. You two make a good team. Anyway, Chief Braneni asked me to talk to you so you have a chance to think about it. And with that done, we'll get out of your hair. The chief will be in touch."

EIGHT

"Are you going to give her a name?"
"Mine."

THE PILL COCKTAIL Mark stuffed down my throat packed a punch, and had I been thinking clearly, I wouldn't have gotten into my new truck with Sassy behind the wheel. I would've crawled upstairs to my childhood bedroom and slept it off. But no, I abandoned common sense and followed the cheetah like a lost puppy in need of attention.

Instead of taking me home, she drove me to her parents' place and parked my baby on the grass.

"But she'll get dirty," I complained. "You can't get her dirty."

"Decided she's your side chick, have you?"

"She's too pretty to be a man."

Sassy laughed and killed the engine. "I can't argue with that logic. She's a very pretty truck. Are you going to give her a name?"

"Mine."

"That's not a name for a truck, Aaron. That's ownership status. And yes, she's yours. You poor thing. Your medications are having their way with you. Don't worry. You can go to bed in a few minutes, and no one is going to touch your new baby while it's parked in front of a lycanthrope-infested home."

I liked she acknowledged her parents' home had a lycanthrope infestation. "Why are we here?"

"I'd like to see this serial killer invade my daddy's house with my brothers on guard along with some friends. We're having a sleepover party. I haven't had a sleepover party in years. You wouldn't come between me and a sleepover party, would you?"

A wise man went along with what the agitated woman wanted. "Of course not. But why do you think my apartment's unsafe?"

"I never said that."

"I might be drugged sky high, but I haven't been completely reduced to a one-celled amoeba yet. You brought me here and called in your brothers. You think my apartment's unsafe."

Sassy scowled. "Mark lied to me. He promised you'd be so high you wouldn't notice. No one is going to try anything in a house full of lycanthropes. Daddy asked the local wolves for backup. There's a pack prowling the neighborhood tonight. If anyone shows up and sniffs around your truck, we'll know about it."

When Sassy got it into her head to be stubborn, it took a lot of coaxing to get anything out of her. I either needed to push the point or let it go, and if I tried to let it go, curiosity would eat away at me until I found out the truth somehow. "Any reason you think there will be problems tonight?"

"You survived. That's going to piss this guy off. He's a pro. You got away. Of course there will be problems. And I say no. There won't be problems because I asked my daddy to make sure there won't be any problems."

Damn it. Sassy was on a collision course for chaining herself to me, probably with literal handcuffs she'd steal from Maxwell. "If he didn't want me to have a chance of survival, I'd be dead, Sassy. This guy doesn't miss. I think he just wanted me out of the way for a while."

"Nope."

When Sassy made up her mind, it's be easier to move a mountain, change the ocean's tides, and perhaps relocate the moon. Maybe I'd try my hand at wrangling a hurricane first. "All right. Anything else I should know?"

"You're sleeping in my room, but Daddy says there will be no shenanigans in my room, so I have to sleep on your feet and keep them warm while a cheetah."

As the fastest way to ensure shenanigans in Sassy's room was to tell Sassy she couldn't indulge in any shenanigans in her room, I gave it two days at most before she snapped and went after me. Sassy's father needed to be thanked somehow, and I bet I could find some tools he didn't already own. "I'll do my best not to kick you, but you'd be more comfortable sharing the bed properly than hunched over my feet. If you're concerned my feet will get cold, we can use another blanket."

"Your feet are closer to the door. If someone does come after you, I want to be ready. I even sharpened my claws earlier."

"Did you have your mother paint them?" For some reason I didn't understand, nail polish survived the transformation, and nail polish stuck surprisingly well to cheetah claws.

"They match your truck."

Nice. "Good choice."

"I certainly thought so. Daddy wants to see you when we get in, and I'm not invited. Try not to pick a fight, okay?"

Considering Sassy had gone Daddy's Little Girl to the extreme, I'd do better than my best behavior to keep her from snapping. How she'd snap, I had no idea, but I wanted to be off my medications so I could fully enjoy it when it happened. "I can manage that. Well, I won't pick a fight on purpose, but I'm heavily drugged. I do stupid shit when drugged."

She laughed. "We know. Your mouth gets you into trouble every damned time. Daddy's probably in his den. I'll show you where it is, then I'll go shift."

"All right." As being heavily medicated might save me from Sassy's mother but wouldn't spare me from her father, I went through the usual guest ritual, making sure I took my shoes off, removed any stray dirt so I wouldn't track it over the floors, and handed over my wallet and keys to Sassy so I wouldn't lose them. "I will lose them in my current state."

"They could stay in your pocket, Aaron."

"I'll lose them."

"All right. I'll put them in my room for you."

While I'd been to the living room, guest bathroom, kitchen, and dining room, I'd never been through the rest of the house, and Sassy led me to a door, which descended into the basement. She took the steps two at a time and knocked. "Daddy? We're here. If you don't need me, I'll go upstairs and shift. I've got Aaron's wallet and keys. He didn't want to lose them."

I wondered at the little girl Sassy had once been, likely an avid worshipper of her father. The street went both ways, as only an idiot would miss how much her father adored his little kitten. I needed to, when opportunity allowed, thank her parents for doing everything just right with her.

A vibrant, stubborn, headstrong woman with indomitable pride didn't happen by accident.

"You come on in, Aaron. Get yourself ready for bed, Sastria, and I hope you've abandoned your hope of going to your apartment tonight. If you need something, I'll send some of your brat brothers over, but you're staying here for the rest of the day."

Yep, I definitely needed to thank Sassy's father in some way.

Sassy bolted up the stairs. Smothering my chuckle, I shook my head and opened the door.

A book lover's dream waited inside, and two armchairs took up the limited free space. While he had a fireplace, I appreciated he'd gone the electric route; smoke could damage books, and from the looks of his collection, he'd spent thousands finding the perfect titles to grace his shelves. Sassy's father lounged on one of the armchairs, and he gestured to the seat beside him. "You've got to be tired. Sit, sit. How are you feeling?"

"Like my brother spiked my medications with more medications," I confessed, grateful to get off my feet. Once seated, my body reminded me how sore and abused it was. "Thanks for keeping me from bleeding out. Appreciated."

"You're welcome. You are looking better, though you're still grayer than I like. How's my kitten holding together?"

"She's all right."

"I find that unlikely, as tense as she's been. Last time she was over, she wanted to go to her apartment and bake every single type of pie you like and feed them to you."

That explained the ban from returning to her apartment. "The DA came over and pitched an offer from the copper shop; they want to use us as guinea pigs for non-hybrid lycanthropes on the force. Sassy never wanted to be a PI. She wanted to be a cop. So, she's excited right now."

"I stand corrected. You still serious?"

It took me all of ten seconds to confirm to myself I needed the infection almost as much as I needed my next breath. The offer from the police had cinched the deal, as I refused to risk Sassy's chance of having her dream job. I had my reservations, as I understood what else being a cop entailed, but some sacrifices were worth making.

For Sassy, I'd do a lot more than deal with the burdens of becoming a cop.

"One of my brats has a field transfusion kit with him and knows how to use it. He's already confirmed I can donate, as he got a copy of your medical file from my kitten, which had your blood type listed. The plan is to give you transfusions as often as safely possible until your next testing to help the virus take hold. Here's where things will be tricky. Sassy's already locked onto you, and she'll become anxious until you're a properly mated pair. This is due to your incubating virus and hers reacting to each other. Your job is simple. Keep your attention focused on Sassy. Bribe her with shoes as necessary, but stay concentrated on her. Your virus will figure it out from there. Being blunt, kidnapping followed with a hostage situation is becoming a family tradition, so play along when she finally snaps."

"As long as it happens when I'm not scheduled to work, okay. I'm all right with that."

"I'll make sure her mother suggests our kitten take care with the timing."

"I take it we're going to use the crash to hide the transfusions?"

"That plus a little magic and an ointment to close the injection sites. My brat will be monitoring the transfusions to maximize how much we can give you and jumpstart your infection. In good news, your injuries likely mean we can make more ground tonight. He thought the other option might creep you out."

"I'm not a vampire, nor am I bisexual."

"As such, we're going the transfusion route."

"I'd say do your worst, but I don't think I can handle your worst today," I admitted.

"You'll be fine. Just try to relax. You'll be upstairs napping in no time at all."

ACCORDING TO SASSY'S BROTHER, Joe, the hospital shouldn't have released me, and if an opportunity presented itself, he wouldn't be against beating sense back into my collection of doctors, none of which had any business being a doctor if they couldn't verify the complete halting of internal bleeding before releasing a patient. Using an eclectic mixture of magic, blending natural ability and practitioner tricks, he examined me from head to foot, muttering curses the entire time.

When a military field surgeon cursed over my health, I worried.

When the military field surgeon could likely lift my other doctors over his head and snap them in half, I worried a lot.

"Should I just go buy my casket now? Because seriously, with how you're cussing, I feel like I should just save everyone the hassle, and buy my own casket in advance. And since I spent so much money on your sister's shoes, I'll probably opt for a cardboard one for cremation. It'll be cheaper."

Sassy's father snorted. "Don't be dramatic, Aaron."

"He's not necessarily wrong, Dad. Perhaps a little dramatic, but he's not necessarily wrong. I'm going to document and authenticate my findings with an angel so I can build a malpractice case. He's got more leaks than I like, and it's serious enough he really shouldn't have been let out of the hospital. Fuck, did they not even bother with a blood test? Any medical mage worth their license would take one look at you and know you're leaking like a sieve. Did they just go off an imaging check and ignore the signs of internal bleeding? Fuck, I wouldn't even need to do a blood test. I would've just checked your blood pressure and laughed at the idea of releasing you in this condition. On blood pressure levels alone, you're already a candidate for a transfusion." Joe spat more curses. "It's like they want you to fall over dead or develop early onset lycanthropy. I won't even need to cover anything, Dad. He's a mess. Why is he even here? Why would they release him? What sort of doctor is that fucking stupid?"

"I'm assuming he's here because the hospital decided he no longer needed to stay there," Sassy's father replied. "Complete your examination. I'll run upstairs and tell your mother she might need to donate as well so she doesn't have her evening wine. Aaron, I'll give your brother a call and notify him there's a problem. I'm also going to bring him over just in case. I'll also convince him it's wise he not yap about what we're doing."

Mark would love watching me be used as an experiment by a bunch of cats. "I'm sure he'll eagerly become an accomplice."

"Good. Need anything from me, Joe?"

"Bring down some bottles of water, please. In the meantime, I'll figure out how much of a transfusion he needs. I might be able to pull it off just using your blood if your virus levels look good after the first round, but I'd rather Mom be ready if needed."

"I'll take care of it," Sassy's father promised before rising to his feet and strolling towards the door as though he didn't have a worry in the world.

"If you work through Mom and Dad, Dean's good to donate, but Charlie's virus is too low for my liking. I checked before coming down here. While Sassy's probably good to donate, I'd like to leave her in the dark about this as long as possible. She'll flip, and when she flips, her virus flips, and the last thing you need right now is a mauling, which is exactly what would happen if she and her virus flip right now. Mate claims are rough," Joe said, shaking his head and sighing. "But seriously. You're a mess, and I'm going to be filing about this. You shouldn't even be out of the hospital."

"I guess that explains why I felt like shit trying to walk to the rental?"

"Yep. I'm glad your brother called me. Frankly, if I wasn't a field surgeon used to working with the infected, I'd be carting you back to the hospital in an ambulance just to be safe rather than sorry. Bleeding like this can easily become fatal, and it can become fatal in minutes. Frankly, I don't even understand how you're as alert as you are. If I had to make a bet, you're infected, the virus is replicating as fast as it can to help counter your internal bleeding, and when I start the transfusion, your incubating virus and Dad's virus are going to get together, have a party, and jumpstart your infection nicely with an added bonus of helping the internal injuries heal."

"I'm going to ignore all the parts about this potentially being fatal and concentrate on what's important. Your odds on infection probability?"

"When I go grab the scanner I have on loan, my bet is it's going to squeal like a stuck pig when I bring it near you."

"Which is good."

"Very. Unless you don't want lycanthropy, in which case, I'm sorry."

Joe wasn't sorry at all, and I laughed at his unrepentant tone. "Please tell me I have decent odds of surviving tonight."

"You do. I've healed a lot worse in the field. You should recover with no impairment or permanent damage. The lycanthropy virus will help with that. While Dad's upstairs, I'm going to be blunt with you. Dad asked me to poke around in your memories and see if I can find anything out about the driver. I know you've said you don't remember anything, but it's common with brain injuries for memories surrounding a traumatic event to be forgotten. I'm capable of poking around your head and sifting through old memories. I'll go through everything from now until shortly before the crash in order to learn whatever details I can. What I find will be private unless I feel it will help us find this asshole. Everything you saw, felt, and thought will be mine to know, and that disturbs people."

I raised my brows. "Well, I love your sister and bought her nice shoes hoping she'd forgive me for deliberating contracting lycanthropy, except that part of the plan got derailed. I'm terrified of your father. Beyond that, try to stay out of client matters, please."

"You didn't have to tell me your secrets."

I snorted. "You're a cat. You're going to tell everyone anyway. Just keep a lid on the client matters. If you think poking around in my head will find the killer, have a ball. I just don't promise you'll like what you see."

"True, that. All right. Make yourself comfortable. Relax if you can. I'll try to keep this as painless as possible, but it depends on where the bleeding is. Some areas are more sensitive to magic than others, and the harder I have to work, the more painful it becomes. If it's too much for you to handle, I'll drug you until you can't see straight to make sure Sassy doesn't figure out something's wrong. Try not to scream. I'd rather you bit me like you mean it than scream. You screaming will set Sassy off."

"Noted. Hit me with your best shot, just don't kill me, please. I've had my fill of close brushes with death for a while."

UNEXPECTED NAPS MADE it difficult to monitor if Sassy's brother rummaged through my head. According to my body, I'd endured a second crash, although my chest and stomach took the brunt of the pain. My throat twinged, an alarming enough sensation, but since no one around me panicked, I focused on regaining coherency. It took a lot longer than I liked, and when I finally managed to crack an eye open, Joe fiddled with a line attached to my arm.

It hurt.

"Ouch," I informed him.

"It only stings a little. You'll be fine." Joe straightened and shook his head.

"Am I leaking?"

Joe's shoulders slumped, and he sighed.

"It's never a good sign when the military surgeon looks defeated. You're making me think I need to purchase a casket."

Shooting a glare at me, Joe perched on the arm of his father's chair, careful to avoid the blood-filled lines. "I'm not defeated. I'm annoyed and tired. You were leaking, but you're not leaking now. I've patched you up, but you're going to be stuck in bed with limited mobility for the next week unless your incubating virus gets its ass in gear and finishes the job faster. Assuming Dad's virus levels stay stable, he'll be your morning donor. Dean has evening duty, and Mom will be the extra as needed. I'm going to call in for your medical record, but do you remember if they ran you through any imaging machines?"

"They did, yes. The last one was the day

before I was released, I think. I'm not really sure what all the machines do," I confessed.

"All right. I'll talk to Mark, and I'll have him start investigating your doctors and their connections. There's no way those active bleeds should've gone undetected. You had a minor bleed in your brain, and just don't fucking ask me about the rest of the mess. You'll be fine, but you need rest, and you need to let the virus do its job. Also, I'll make sure Sassy knows to keep her attention extra gentle."

"But she has been gentle," I protested.

"Aaron, she climbed you like a tree, and because you're an idiot, you liked it despite it hurting like hell."

"Well, yes. She was wearing the blue shoes, and she was excited. Honestly, I was a little excited, too. Have you seen my new truck?"

"Who hasn't? You can see it from the end of the street. I'd say you're overcompensating, but honestly, you put your trucks through their paces whenever possible. And I can't begrudge how much you enjoyed your first look at that beauty."

"Is a trip to the hardware store out? I need new tools. My old tools had a terrible accident. I would find a trip to the hardware store very restful."

"Order new tools online."

Sassy's brother wasn't just a military man,

he was a hardened, cruel professional, potentially aligned with the darkest forces of evil. I frowned and wondered how I could defeat the darkest form of evil.

Sassy's father laughed. "Don't get pouty, Aaron. As soon as Joe clears you off bed rest, I'll take you out for some tools. It'll give us a chance to see if anyone is following you before you go diving back into trouble."

From the day I'd met him, Sassy's father had called me trouble. His fatherly intuition must've warned him I'd meant to stick around. I considered my options and decided he'd win no matter what I did. "I'll make a list of tools I'll need."

"That might keep the trip sane. Perhaps. I need a new planar."

"Dad," Joe complained. "You don't need a new planar."

"Your mother decided I need a new planar."

Joe crossed his arms over his chest. "And what is Mom going to tell me when I ask her about your old planar?"

"That she broke my jackhammer breaking my planar."

Joe turned to me, and we stared at each other. When it became clear Sassy's brother was at a complete loss, I sad, "I can help him pick out a new planar and a jackhammer, and until you think I'm able to drive, I'll give Sassy the keys to my truck."

"You're not helping, Aaron."

"Sure I am. Do you really think your old man will leave the hardware store without breaking the budget otherwise? After fitting a planar and a jackhammer in the bed of my truck, he'll have to leave space for my tools. It's probably cheaper to get him a new planar and jackhammer than it is to leave him with half the bed of a truck to fill."

"I hate that you're right."

I nodded at the line sticking in my arm. "When do I get free of this thing?"

"In an hour, and keep it quiet. My sister is sulking at the top of the stairs as a cheetah. Mom banned her from coming down the steps, and Dad threatened to make her sleep in the guest bedroom alone if she didn't behave. I had Dad tell her I was doing a thorough examination, and since she has no idea how long those actually take, she's assuming I'm just being thorough. I'll have to wipe your arm down with antiseptic to mask the scent of blood, but it should do the trick. If she does smell your blood, I'll just say I did a blood test. If she smell's Dad's blood, I'll tell her I was checking his virus levels. Since everyone got a round of virus levels being checked today, she won't think twice about it."

I could live with an hour. I hoped.

A CHIRPING Sassy waited at the top of the stairs, and I scratched behind her ears, fighting to keep from laughing. "Everything's fine," I promised. "I'm wiped and in dire need of some sleep, but everything's fine."

Sassy's father came up behind me and thumped his hand against my shoulder. "Take him to your room and remember to be gentle," he ordered. "Let him sleep as long as he wants, and try to limit how much weight you rest on him. He's not a pillow. Tonight, you're limited to putting your chin on his shoulder. Purring is acceptable. Other than that, keep your paws and teeth to yourself."

Sassy shook herself, rose, and retreated in the direction of the staircase leading upstairs, and I followed, too tired to hide my grimace.

Joe shadowed me. "I'll check on you in the morning. I'm also going to call in a few prescriptions for you. Sassy, you'll need to pick them up in the morning. While you're running errands, I'd like a copy of his medical insurance."

Twisting her ears back, Sassy glared at her brother.

"We'll talk about it tomorrow, just please get me a copy of his medical insurance. Snag me a complete copy of his medical record while you're at it. Oh, and the contact information for his lawyer would be nice, too. In the meantime, keep Aaron company, keep him warm, and try not to shred your bedding. And no, the scripts aren't anything to worry about. He needs some supplements while he recovers. It's annoying they weren't already prescribed, but it's no big deal. He'll just bounce back faster while taking them."

Sassy chirped and bobbed her head.

After being poked and prodded, I viewed the potential of Sassy puncturing me in her typical feline enthusiasm minimal at worst. "It's fine, Sassy. Your brother's paranoid, as is my brother. You know how those military types get, and since our bothers get along, well, they gang up on their unsuspecting victims. I'm their choice of victim this week. Let them be worrywarts. As for the medical records, they're worry warts. Don't ask me about the lawyer. Joe probably wants our lawyer's info because he likes handsome men."

"Funny, Aaron. Why am I helping you again?"

"You like that I tell the truth with an added bonus of being easy on the eyes. Unfortunately for you, I'm unwavering in my heterosexuality."

"How annoying. Dad, I'll drop by in the

morning. Sassy, unless he stops breathing, he's fine. Should he stop breathing, yell for Dad. He's good at CPR."

Sassy's father sighed. "Stop trying to give your sister a panic attack, Joe. Aaron, go to bed."

As only an idiot argued with Sassy's father, I did as told.

SASSY HAD ONLY herself to blame for my unconscious behavior. Had she not used me as a climbing pole, I wouldn't have sought revenge in my sleep. Waking up holding eighty pounds of cranky feline added some spice to my morning. She growled and beat me with her tail, an understandable reaction to being held hostage and unable to escape.

All in all, I found the situation pleasing, as she kept me warm.

As my nose was already buried into the bristly fur of her neck, I decided to enjoy the moment and take a few deep breaths.

"Sassy, will you stop your complaining already?" Joe grunted and tapped his foot on the floor. "Obviously, he likes where you're at. What's the problem? You're always whining you can't attract single men, but now that you've got one wrapped around you, you're whining about it! You even got him into bed with you. You should be celebrating. Aaron, let her go already. It's noon. You need to take your medications and have breakfast. Your parents came over earlier this morning, but they left when they found out you were still sleeping. They looked in, saw you'd wrangled yourself a cheetah, and bailed."

"My cheetah," I mumbled, rubbing my nose in Sassy's fur. "Warm."

"And you're obviously still asleep. You need a hot bath and breakfast. After, I'll do another examination and see how you're doing. Sassy, I really need you to go pick up his scripts while I figure out why his body temp is low enough he's using you as a heater."

While I grumbled complaints, I released her. "Sorry, Sassy."

She rolled over and dragged her tongue over my face. Twice.

"I deserved that."

Joe chuckled. "Get a move on, Sassy. I'll make sure he's all right. Oh, and do me a favor?"

Sassy chirped.

"Mom put in an order with the butcher. She'll give you the address. Pick up her purchases in Aaron's truck, please? You'll have a few undercover cops tailing you watching for anything suspicious. Stay off the highways."

Flattening her ears, she hissed at her brother.

"Are you sure you want to date that hissy cat? Less complaining, more running errands. I have to go to work sometime today, and Dad'll whoop my ass if I don't check on your pet human. You even put clothes out for yourself last night to make this morning easier. Smart. Now, move your ass. Seriously. You're on dinner duty. You know what'll happen if Mom feels like she wasn't hospitable to a guest."

Sassy bolted out of bed, slowed long enough to grab her clothes in her mouth, and fled.

"I see our mothers share similar beliefs about hospitality."

"Added bonus of my mother knowing we can take a whooping and not have a bruise by morning. In good news, my mother would only whoop our asses if we really earned it."

"Switch?" I guessed.

"And we had to pick it out ourselves. Only took once to make it clear we never wanted the switch again." Joe laughed, leaned out of Sassy's bedroom, and stared down the hall, shaking his head. "And off she goes."

The thumps on the stairs concerned me. "Did she just fall down the stairs?"

"Yep."

"I'm okay!" Sassy yelled.

"Is she even dressed? How could she get dressed that fast?"

"Not precisely. She was yanking on her pants when she tried to take the stairs, resulting in her headlong flight down the entire damned thing. She's tough. She'll be fine." Louder, he added, "Put a damned bra on, woman!"

"Screw you, Joe!"

"Sastria, you dress yourself properly before leaving this house," Sassy's mother hollered.

"Honestly, she did better than usual. Last time, she hadn't gotten her pants all the way on before bolting out the door. Cheetahs? We're not body shy. You'll get used to it."

I hoped I never got used to it; Sassy in a bikini could reduce me to a gibbering mess in five seconds flat. Fortunately—or unfortunately, as the case often was—she rarely went swimming. Cheetahs and water didn't mix, although I hoped to buck the trend since I enjoyed a good weekend at the lake.

At least Sassy liked fish.

With as much dignity as I could muster, I replied, "I think I'll manage somehow."

"It'll be such a burden on you, I'm sure."

A door slammed downstairs, and moments later, my new truck rumbled to life. "It'll be a terrible burden. Do you think she'll try putting her shoes on first?"

"She's not the brightest crayon in the box sometimes. Could happen if you keep her shoes out. She's a bit single-minded once she's off to avoid a whooping."

"She's not at any risk of a whooping from me."

Joe snickered. "Cheetah, Aaron. We like it rough. But, you'll know when she wants a whooping from you."

While he provided way too much information for my comfort, I filed his comment away as a warning. Then again, maybe I was more of a cheetah than I cared to think about. If Sassy wanted to get rough with me, I'd probably enjoy it. "Good to know."

"It's considered polite to ignore nudity unless you're admiring your mate or a coalition partner. Since you'll never have a coalition partner, you can admire Sassy all you want. Just keep public displays of affection to a minimum. We try not to overly offend the uninfected."

By uninfected, I assumed he meant people like my parents, who viewed lycanthropes as a direct violation of their religion's tenets. They welcomed headless angels with open arms, but everything else went onto their list of prejudices.

It amazed me my parents had let Sassy into their home. That my mother had warmed up to her enough to start dropping hints at grandchildren astonished me.

"That's not what Sassy tells me about her dates," I muttered.

"Sassy's an idiot and goes to lycanthrope-friendly bars and restaurants. We're more relaxed. She's also exaggerating some. Well, a lot. Kinda. I mean, her dates are totally guilty of kissing each other and ignoring her. That part's unfortunately true. It's her fault, though. She informs the various coalitions when she's taking one of their men out on a date. They show up. If she wanted to steal a coalition cheetah, she'd be stealthier about it."

One day, I would understand Sassy. I'd probably be a candidate for admission to a mental institute, but one day, I would understand her. "How bad is she exaggerating, do you think?"

"Only as much as needed to get your attention and escape from a date she didn't want to be on in the first place. We're promiscuous, Aaron. We're one of the few lycanthropy species that'll screw anything that moves until a determined cheetah female comes around. And since most cheetah males have no interest in human females, well, it's a vicious cycle. Sassy's been locked onto you for years. Mom's getting impatient, but it takes time for a female to decide to stake her claim. All this is doing is speeding up the process. Since Dad's a mated, breeding male, his virus is already wired to be interested in a singular female, in this case, Sassy. We speculate because you're inheriting so much of Dad's virus, you'll have no interest in the coalitions. The instinct to join a coalition takes time to develop, and it happens because of the low number of eligible females. Since there's an eligible female already interested in you, you're going to fixate on her. It's already happening. You wrapped yourself around her the instant you clocked out for the night. Dad invades Mom's space all the time. He's wired to protect her."

I scratched the back of my neck, but since Joe had already poked around my head, I saw no need to hide anything from him. "To be fair, I'm an unrepentant pillow hugger."

"Well, your pillow is now much warmer and furrier, and if you're anything like Dad, you're going to develop severe separation anxiety if you're away from her for more than a few hours. This is fairly unexplored territory, as there are so few unmated breeding females. I'd say I'm sorry, but I'm not. I'm of the opinion you're one of the few acceptable options around here for my sister." Joe checked out the window. "Good. She's gone. Time for you to get a transfusion. Dad's virus is spiked to the high heavens this morning, so it's an ideal time to boost your incubating virus. I've never had a chance to seriously attempt inducing early onset maturing of the lycanthropy virus before. I accessed the CDC's files last night after you went to bed; you check every last box on what they think is required for it to happen. I went ahead and called in the possibility, informed them of the medical malpractice suit I'll be filing on your behalf due to the severe internal bleeding, and got an authorization to use Dad as a legal donor. You'll have to sign some papers, but you're cleared, and they'll make an exception for your license with a few conditions, especially since you're being courted by local law enforcement. They jumped on the non-hybrid test like flies on shit."

Of course they had. "How much earlier? The virus typically takes decades to mature, correct?"

"Up to forty years in some. It's considered a new lease on life; once the virus matures and shifting happens, aging is often somewhat reversed or halted. It's a case by case scenario. In your case, aging will halt. I've got a high sensitivity scanner on route, but it and its technician will be a few days getting here. Ideally, Dad's spiking virus is going to replicate in your body, finish healing the damage from the crash, and take root. If we get lucky, we could see matured virus levels within twenty-four hours."

"*That* soon? And by matured, you mean I might sprout a fur coat?"

"That's exactly what I mean. You're to be-have like you're contagious until we can get the high sensitivity scanner over for a better look at your virus levels."

"All right. What should I do to keep from passing the virus on to someone else?"

"Stick your tongue only down Sassy's throat, only take Sassy to bed, and don't bleed on anyone. Kissing won't actually spread the virus, but I'm siding with my sister on this one. She's hopeless, and she needs to get some action and land you already. You have one job to do. Don't mess it up. I've heard this lecture enough times from Mom that I'm going to spare you from hearing it from my mother. Cheetah ladies do *not* want an overly considerate male in bed. Sassy's going to be a handful, and all you're going to do is frustrate her if you take the overly gentle route with her. I'm sparing you the descriptions of what my mother likes. You're welcome."

"Anything else I don't want to know but you're going to tell me anyway?"

"Some details about the downsides of early onset lycanthropy. The CDC's file had a lot of information, and I have concerns."

I considered crawling under the blanket and covering my head with Sassy's pillow. "When a military surgeon tells me he has concerns, I worry."

"That's because you're a chronic worrier."

"While true, could you not? I'm already dealing with potentially bleeding to death from internal injuries."

"You're not potentially bleeding to death anymore."

"Anymore."

"Valid point, but you'll be fine. Should I warn my sister you're a whiner?"

I laughed. "I'm pretty sure she already knows."

"All right. The downsides are going to be pretty uncomfortable for you. My theory is the virus slowly adapts the host to shapeshifting, taking a long time to mature so the first shift isn't traumatic. You won't have that luxury. I suspect when you go through your first shift, it's going to be brutally painful, and you'll be trapped as a cheetah for a few days. You'll also be easily confused, potentially delirious, and prone to succumbing to a cheetah's base instincts. There's no gradual adaptation. You're going to be sick as a cheetah, and when you shift back to human for the first time, you're going to get sicker. You're going to be so sick you'd rather participate in another crash." Joe shrugged. "It's not going to be fun for you, and you'll likely require sedation. Worse, Sassy is going to freak out. If you haven't mated properly before your first shift, her virus is going to spike, it's going to spike hard, and she'll be driven to claim you. While you're ill. It's going to get ugly."

"Well, that explains the whole protective brother trying to talk me into sleeping with his sister thing."

"Yeah, that's not exactly the most comfortable thing I've done in my life. This is one of the more unique situations I've been in. I'm just glad I figured out you were it for my sister a long time ago, else I'd be even more uncomfortable than I already am."

"I'm so relieved I'm not the only one who finds this conversation disturbing."

Joe sat on the edge of the bed. "Sassy will be a problem. You'll need to be prepared. Once you shift, she's going to smell your pain and the spiking virus, and she'll be prone to panicking. We've already seen how badly she's panicked as a result of the crash. Her virus is going to spike, and her only concern will be protecting you."

Laughing, I shook my head. "I'm her property at this point, aren't I?"

"You figured that out quickly."

"Anything else I need to know? This is survivable, right?"

"It is. Early onset is due to the virus going into overdrive to preserve your life. After your first shift and your body finishes adapting, your virus will go into remission to recover. That's when Sassy's protective instincts will peak. She'll guard you while you're adapting. During a normal first shift, lycanthropes don't need to recover long as their viruses are naturally robust. They're also more stable; the slow growth of their virus gives them a chance to control their new impulses. You're going to be a powder keg set to blow. Obviously, do everything you can to stay away from the uninfected during the adjustment period. Until your virus is convinced you are Sassy's mate, you'll be annoying."

"*I'll* be annoying?"

"So Mom claims. I think you and my sister will be too busy keeping each other company to annoy bystanders. The annoying part will be your inaccessibility. I think you'll be fine, and I'll be on hand to make sure your transition goes as easily as possible. You ready to be poked and prodded again?"

"Only if you're going to make sure I'm not going to bleed out from any new leaks."

"That is the plan."

"Then we better hurry so we're done before Sassy gets back."

"Don't you worry about that. Tonight, we feast like kings, and Sassy will be gone for hours doing Mom's bidding so she doesn't earn a whooping."

Poor Sassy.

NINE

Are you sure your parents aren't wolf
lycanthropes?

WHILE JOE SUBJECTED me to another transfusion, I read about the victims, one profile
from the police and the other from my
brother, who had done a hefty amount of
footwork to give me something to do while
on bedrest. In most cases, the intel overlapped, but I found my brother's profiling
gave me a more complete view of the murdered women and children.

I needed to remind Maxwell that a good
investigator learned the full story of a crime
and not just the parts that fit a certain dialogue or made the prosecutors happy. The
defense would seek every clue in every
cranny to make the prosecution work for the
conviction.

"You all right, Aaron?" Sassy's father
demanded.

I checked the clock hanging on his den's

wall to discover an hour had slipped away. "I ignored you, didn't I?"

"I'd be offended if I didn't recognize when a man's taking his work seriously."

"I can't tell if Maxwell just doesn't have access to better intel or if my brother needs to leave the military and join investigations." I picked up Maxwell's files with my left hand so Joe wouldn't have reason to yell at me again. "The more I look over these files, the more I think my brother has the right idea. I'd bet my entire career Tom Heatherow has something to do with this mess. Is someone covering up his activities on his behalf? Framing him using his past? Is it him trying to make the evidence disappear? I can't tell. But, our best lead is Sharon Gray, and if Tom Heatherow finds out she has kids, she might be the next victim."

"We can't let him find out about her kids," Sassy's father growled.

"I'm thinking I'm going to impose on Mark. He's old enough he could have fathered them. Adding three kids to his rap sheet to cover for them is up his alley. He may not want kids of his own, but he won't care if his reputation is smeared by a few rumors. He's slept around so much it amazes me he doesn't have at least one or two he doesn't know about. What I need to figure out is how to talk him into it, how to talk *her* into it, and how to do it without the kids finding out. They're adopted now, and they don't need that sort of drama in their lives. Ideally, Tom Heatherow is the only one who finds out my brother 'had a few kids' with Sharon Gray. If we can get them all in on it. Mark's enough of a slut no one is going to think twice about it if he claims they're his."

"That's a terrible idea," Sassy's father grumbled.

"If it keeps her and those kids from becoming victims, it's a great idea," I countered.

Silence.

"Are you sure your parents aren't wolf lycanthropes? You're fixating like a wolf. You're also just as protective of pups and mates as a wolf," Sassy's father complained. "We're not wolves. We're felines. We're master strategists."

I arched a brow. "At what? Knocking shit off shelves?"

"Dad, you're not allowed to give him a whooping until he's fully healed and has shifted for the first time," Joe announced.

"You will pay for that, boy," Sassy's father promised.

Maybe Joe's decree would help me survive the whooping I'd rightfully earned. "Wolves are the strategists. Felines are opportunists with a short attention spans."

Joe smacked the back of my head. "You're

really going to earn yourself a whooping you'll regret. Dad, your virus is spiking, and he's taking it over like a champ. If he wasn't already swooning over Sassy and those damned shoes of hers, you'd need to lock your other sons up by tomorrow to keep him from getting randy. Frankly, you're going to have to lock Sassy up tonight—or we can all camp outside tonight while they destroy the house. I don't care which, but I refuse to be in the house while Aaron stalks my sister."

"Progress is that good?"

"I'm willing to bet he'll set off a low-sensitivity scanner at this point. Even before the transfusions, considering the internal bleeding and his ability to withstand such low blood pressure for so long, he would've been a high probability of early onset. We're just speeding things up a little. We might want to warn Sassy."

Judging from the way Sassy's father sighed, Joe's announcement had sliced off a few years of his life. "I'll just tell her she needs to haul ass and become a properly mated woman already. I'll even do it over dinner, so call in witnesses."

"Witnesses to what? Your immediate murder when she snaps and tries to kill you at the dinner table?" Joe blurted.

I couldn't figure out if the man was trying

to help or hinder. "Am I even going to survive today?"

"Aaron, don't start again. You're not going to die," Joe complained.

"Well, he might. Cheetah females during a claim are vicious. I like it. We can go camping with the wolves and leave the bedridden in bed to be ridden."

"I never want to hear you talk about my sister like that ever again, Dad. That's wrong. No. No. Go to hell, Dad."

Sassy's father rolled his eyes. "You've been sitting there hinting at him your sister needs to mate immediately if not sooner, and now you're getting offended when I say it how it is? That's what's going to happen if we leave them alone in the house if your estimates are correct. You can patch him up in the morning if she gets a little too eager with her teeth. Best of all, if that happens, transfusions are her problem. I'm tired of patching his leaks, Joe. Fix this travesty. How are those leaks doing? If they aren't all patched, I'm going to give him a whooping, dump him in your sister's room, call her home, and lock them in until one of them snaps, then she can give him his next transfusion."

For a hardened military man who dealt with death daily, Joe wilted the more his father spoke. "I'm so sorry, Aaron."

"I'm curious about if I'm still bleeding to

death," I admitted. "I'm willfully ignoring the rest."

"You're not bleeding to death. Your holes are all plugged, and from what I can tell, the virus is doing its job. If Sassy does get her ass in gear tonight, I'll skip the morning transfusion unless necessary and run a scan in the evening to see how you're doing. That said, if you're contagious tomorrow night, I'll need to call in a CDC rep to get you registered for early onset. There's legal paperwork; it's a lot of liability clearance for you. I've already started the groundwork, so it won't be an issue should you be close to your first shift."

"Scan him before dinner. If he qualifies, call in the rep before Sassy gets her hands on him. It's entirely possible she won't let anyone near him for a few days, or she'll do so grudgingly. The investigation of that serial killer might help on that front, but I wouldn't count on it," Sassy's father warned.

I sighed. "Are you sure this'll help with my license? Otherwise, it's pooched for a year."

"It'll help with your license *and* with the law enforcement recruiters. You'll be the worst case scenario for lycanthropes in the field, and if you shake out, others should shake out, too. It'll be fine. Anyway, you're going to hold your license without issue. You're not at fault for infection, and you're probably early onset. We'll know for certain tonight. Anyway, Sassy's already cleared and partnered with you, so you'll have a stabilizing factor. She knows what to do if you have problems."

"What's the catch? There has to be a catch."

"Your insurance premiums are going to suck."

Well, shit.

THERE WAS something to Joe's belief I might stalk his sister. Five hours after being sent off on her errands, she came back with my new truck, and I stared at her more than my new vehicle. She wrangled the first overfilled canvas bag into the house by herself before her brothers descended on the bed and retrieved the rest.

Without any fear in her eyes, she looked at her mother and hissed, "You are Satan."

Sassy's mother smiled. "But I'm Satan who will feed you and your brothers a feast tonight. We have guests, and you were the only available person."

Sassy pointed in the direction of my truck. "Six of my hellspawn brothers are here. They could've done it! Why are they all here? Please don't tell me the entire lot of those assholes are coming tonight."

"Everyone's coming tonight if they want to step foot in this house for the next year. Mr. Clinton's parents and brother will also be coming. We'll be having dinner in the back, so you need to help your brothers get the tables set up. Your father refuses to set up the other dining room table."

Scowling, Sassy stepped into the kitchen, and I enjoyed watching her go. "Just how much did you order, Mrs. Chetty?"

"Enough to feed my boys, their coalition, you, your family, and that glutton of a daughter I somehow produced. We might have leftovers. Don't you worry yourself any. We've got the pits already lit and ready to go, and everything will be ready by dinner. You just sit and rest."

The sitting and rest thing I could do like a champ. While the transfusions helped, I wanted to go back upstairs, take Sassy with me, and go back to sleep. Even before the crash, I'd enjoyed her company as a cheetah while I slept. Some men made their own security, but I saw no shame in my awareness of her eighty lethal pounds of claws and teeth. I wondered if that would change post infection.

A lot would change, and I wondered what sort of man I'd become on the other side. In fact, I'd already changed.

I'd gone from shirking from the idea of

handling the burden of a cop to embracing it for Sassy's sake. It disturbed me how easily I'd been swayed, but I wouldn't break her dream because of any misgivings on my part. She wanted to be a cop. I wanted justice for the wronged, which had led me into becoming a private investigator in the first place. The method of acquiring justice would change, and I'd have to resist the things I disliked most about the police and how they handled investigations.

Accessing information would be easier, but I'd be limited in other ways.

Somehow, I'd make it work.

Sassy stomped back into the living room. "Why are there ten tables out back, Mom?"

"Because we're going to need ten tables, Sassy. Why else would I have had your brother set up ten? The buffet table still needs to be set up. Would you rather keep Aaron company or help?"

"We don't have a buffet table, Mom."

"We will in about two hours. Your brothers and your father will be making it as soon as all the meat is in the kitchen."

I raised my hand. "I'll help."

"You already helped. You loaned Sassy your truck this morning. You have been ex-cused from manual labor for this evening," she replied, smiling at me. "You have to be tired. Why don't I make you a glass of sweet tea? I'll have one of the boys take you a chair out back and you can watch."

"That's the best I'm getting, isn't it?"

"I love when the babies know their place," Sassy's mother purred. "Why don't you and my little kitten worry about those files you were poring over this morning? I asked that sweet brother of yours to make sure you have everything you need to do your work, and he says he added a present to it. Sassy, darling, do be a dear and fetch those briefcases Mark brought."

"Where are they?"

"Your father's office."

Sassy ran off, and I once again admired the view. "You could send her on little errands all day. I wouldn't mind at all."

"You're going to be such an easy catch for her once she gets it into her head she needs to catch you. Do try to give her a challenge, Aaron. It won't hurt her to have to bend some to earn you."

"I think she's had enough trouble lately." I remembered her reactions to me while in the hospital, and if I never saw her worry like that again, I'd be a happy man. "Do you know where Mr. Chetty stashed her new shoes?"

"Of course, dear. Would you like me to get them?"

"Please, ma'am."

Sassy's mother went to the stairs leading

to the den and yowled, "Fetch Aaron's bag, dear!"

It amused me my mother and Sassy's mother were birds of a feather. One day, I'd have to ask my mother if she'd learned household management from a special school for Texan women. Then again, a wise man kept his mouth shut and didn't stir the ire of a southern woman.

I couldn't tell if I needed to blame the virus for my lack of self-preservation.

Sassy beat her father back to the living room, and she held a briefcase in each hand with one tucked under her arm. "Your brother's crazy, Aaron. What the hell does he think we're going to need to do investigative work? These things weigh a ton."

"I believe he said there were new computers in them plus papers of various sorts. He was concerned Aaron would get bored and wander off."

"Mark vastly overestimates my ability to wander off," I muttered. "I should get up and help you, Sassy, but I'm not really feeling it right now."

"Don't," she hissed. "You were gray this morning, and now you're more of a gray-green. Joe? Joe! Get your ass in here, Joe!" she howled.

Sassy's father came into the room carrying the bag I'd left with him from before the crash. "You're a cheetah, kitten. You don't howl like some wolf at the moon."

"But, Daddy, look at him. He looks awful. He's green."

A stream of Sassy's brothers came inside, overburdened with plastic bags. I nodded to Dean and Charlie, who flashed me knowing grins. The rest of Sassy's brothers blended together, younger carbon copies of their father. "If you expect me to remember your names, you're out of luck today," I announced. "I can only tell Charlie and Dean apart because Dean's got his mother's eyes and Charlie used a weed whacker on his head. And Joe has a military cut. The rest of you seem to have emerged from the cloning vat properly."

"That would be the drugs talking," Joe announced.

Sassy's father gave me my bag and rescued Joe from his. "You're fine, Aaron. Blab all you want, and we won't think nothing of it."

Mercy from any male member of the Chetty family worried me. "Thank you, sir."

"Joe, he's green. Why is he green?"

Joe glanced at me, and I figured he wanted my permission to rile his sister up. I had no idea how she'd take the news, but I nodded anyway. While I waited to confess why I looked like death warmed over, I peeked into the bag to make sure everything was as I'd left it. Someone had added a second pair of shoes with red soles, and I glanced at Sassy's father.

He answered me with a shrug.

Whatever. Two pairs of shoes was better than one pair of shoes, and two pairs of shoes might overload her so much she'd enter orbit and crash faster, which would give everyone some peace and quiet. Personally, I hoped someone startled her into shifting so when she did crash and burn, she'd do so as a chee-tah. Eighty pounds of cheetah was somehow easier to handle than the woman. I could carry eighty pounds of cheetah around, al-though I'd likely coerce one of her brothers into doing the hauling for me.

"All right. Sit yourself down next to Aaron and take your new shoes," Joe ordered.

Sassy growled but obeyed, and I set the bag on her lap. "It's not that bad."

"It is that bad. It's like this, Sassy. I got the information from your lawyer because I'm filing a medical malpractice suit against the hospital. They released him with potentially lethal internal bleeding. There's no way any reasonable testing would have missed the in-ternal bleeding. They knew he was bleeding, and they released him anyway. He had a minor brain bleed and severe abdominal bleeding. Yesterday, you were evicted upstairs so I could work on him. The bleeding is re-solved, but because of exposure to our father, the virus had ample opportunity to take root. He's green because the virus is working over-time replicating and taking care of his in-juries. Right now, I have him heavily drugged so he's not really feeling it. One of the med-ications I had you pick up was to control the nausea and vomiting associated with early onset lycanthropy."

Sassy sucked in a breath and froze, her eyes widening. "Early onset lycanthropy?"

"Infection was essentially inevitable. When he arrived yesterday, his blood pres-sure was dangerously low. I had a choice of taking him back to the hospital or hooking up a field line to Dad. I opted to hook him up to Dad and let the virus sort the mess out. The bleeding's under control, but he's going to be sick for a while. We're going to do a proper virus check tonight."

The instant she realized what a confirmed infection entailed, her face fell, and judging from her expression, she believed her dreams of becoming a cop shattered to dust.

"Confirmed early onset won't hurt your chances of becoming a cop, Sassy. If anything, it improves them," I said. "They want to see lycanthropes in the force, and having one bordering on first shift or post-first shift is ideal for their needs, and there are already rules in place for early onset infections. Your brother's been handling the paperwork. Since you've been shifting for a while, you'll be responsible for me. You'll have paperwork to sign, I'm sure."

"He's right. You'll be responsible for him in the field, and after he goes through training on how to prevent the infection from spreading, it won't be a problem." Joe sat on the arm of the couch beside his sister and poked her in the arm. "You need to keep an eye on him and help him with the grunt investigation efforts. Until I clear him off bed rest, which should be in about a week, you'll have to do the brunt of the physical work. At this stage, we don't want to exhaust his virus. Since Dad's the donor, we think he'll demonstrate more like a breeding male than a coalition male, but we'll have to keep an eye on him. Fortunately, because his virus is incubating so quickly, he won't be at high risk of becoming a coalition male. Coalition males develop when there's a lack of breeding females around."

"I know that," Sassy snapped. "Fucking coalition males."

Years of frustration laced her tone, and I fought my urge to smile. I tugged on her bag. "Look at what I got you."

"You really didn't have to, Aaron."

"But I wanted to. You like them." While I wanted to believe I foresaw fewer trips to the shoe store in my future, I got the feeling I'd have to get more creative about my acquisition of presents for her.

Cops likely didn't get paid nearly as well as private investigators who took on high-level clients.

Sassy pouted but peeked into the bag. "There's two pairs of shoes! You said one and a purse! And there's the purse. Aaron? Aaron!"

I laughed. "I'm only responsible for the clear pair. I didn't know about the other pair until I peeked into the bag right now. You'll have to investigate who added those."

The ploy distracted her for all of five minutes while she examined her new shoes. Once she satisfied herself, she returned them to the bag and placed it between her feet. "Give it to me straight, Joe. How bad was the bleeding? Really. None of this sugar coating bullshit you like to do when you think I might be upset. I'll be really upset if you lie to me right now. I'll ambush a fucking angel if I must to get the truth out of you."

"It was bad enough I told Mark to investigate the hospital and the surgeons to find out if someone there might be connected to the accident. Without the lycanthropy virus, I don't know if he would've survived being released. Mark asked me to do a full examination because he didn't like how Aaron was looking, a good move on his part. So, I've already been in touch with the CDC, and they approved the transfusions. Dad's virus was spiking, which helped our case. That leaves you."

"What about me?" Sassy demanded.

"Dad's virus isn't going to be able to handle many more transfusions, and while we're willing to donate, your virus is likely the best for the job. First, you're a breeding female. Second, he's demonstrating like a breeding male. If you donate, he's yours for life. You'll have to take some additional steps, but if you want him, you can have him. If you don't, I'll interview some coalitions to see which one is best suited for him."

I wanted to reach over Sassy and throttle her brother for even suggesting I join a coalition.

Sassy went for her brother's throat, kicking her shoes halfway across the living room in her determination to kill Joe. "Like hell you will!"

The pair tumbled off the couch, crashed onto the end table, and hit the floor hard. I cringed at the shatter of glass as the lamp met its end along with some trinkets out for display.

"They came from the thrift store," Sassy's mother announced. "You just don't keep nice things near the couches."

Well, that was something.

I leaned over the couch to observe the brawl between brother and sister. "Should we stop them?"

"No, leave them," Sassy's father ordered. "She needs to work out her nerves. Joe, don't let her roll in the glass."

I sometimes forgot how strong lycan-thropes could be. With no evidence he combated his struggling sister, Joe hopped to his feet, snagged Sassy around her waist, and relocated her to the other side of the living room before allowing her to get a hold of him and drive him back to the carpet.

I wanted to be like Joe when I grew up. If I could move an infuriated Sassy without effort, I'd be able to keep us both out of trouble. "That should be a sales pitch for lycanthropy."

"Military training," Joe countered. "I'll tell your brother you need an instructor. It'll do you good on the force, too."

"Want me to take care of the glass?" I offered.

"No," everyone in the room replied, even Sassy.

I scowled but stayed on the couch. "I see how it is." Since I'd been outvoted, I grabbed the nearest briefcase and opened it to discover a new laptop, one that'd probably cost my brother a small fortune. "I sense brotherly disapproval over my choice of laptops."

Sassy snorted. "Your laptop was a piece of

shit compared to mine, and mine was due for an upgrade. I paid your brother back for my machine, but he wouldn't let me buy yours. He said something about having to give you an escape from maternal prison gift from last year since he missed it."

"He's missed it most years of my life. He was too busy celebrating his."

"Just accept it, Aaron. Please."

Damn it. I couldn't say no when Sassy said please. "All right."

"You gave him a transfusion from Daddy? What were you thinking, Joe?"

"I was thinking he was already infected and needed a transfusion immediately. You were too unstable to sit through the hours needed to do it safely. There's also the issue of being an unmated female. You giving him a transfusion would make it so you're bonded to him for life. You don't make that decision when it's a critical need. You can think about it until after dinner. If you're not willing, Mom and Dean are willing to donate. Charlie's virus is too tapped to right now, but the others are fine. If we run out of donors from the family, I'll start hitting up other coalitions to get him as much diversity as he can."

Cheetahs struggled with virus diversity, that much I remembered from Sassy's bitter complaints over the dating pool, which was limited at best. While Dallas had several strains of the cheetah lycanthropy virus, her family counted as the freshest of the lot.

Cheetah females rarely approached human males, which further limited the strain pool.

"No." Sassy went for her brother's throat again, and Joe fended her off. "You're not letting a coalition corrupt him!"

"Then you, Dean, and Mom need to make sure his tank stays full. He lost a lot of blood to internal bleeding, and while I'm pretty sure the leaks are patched, his body is trying to adapt to the lycanthropy virus. He's going to be iffy for a while."

Sassy growled but gave up trying for Joe's throat. "Explain iffy."

"Fever, chills, and stalker-like tendencies."

"Stalker-like tendencies?"

"Sassy, next time you walk out of the room, sneak peeks at Aaron. He's so busy admiring your ass he won't notice you looking at him. Also, it grosses me out that I'm admitting this, but you obviously dressed to get attention today."

"I grabbed the nearest damned thing so Mom wouldn't whoop my ass!"

Sassy's mother laughed. "You tried going out the door half naked, kitten."

"I really don't want my ass whooped this week."

"And how old, exactly, were you when you

last got your ass whooped?" Sassy's mother challenged.

Sassy's eyes widened, and she gulped. With a whimper, she attempted to hide under her brother. "We were never supposed to talk about this ever again."

I needed to know. "I will do any chore you let me, just please tell me this story."

Sassy's father laughed, retrieved Sassy's new shoes and purse, and handed me the bag. "She was four, and she ran out in front a car because she hadn't looked both ways before chasing after a ball. She was always behind the curve on situational awareness. Charlie got clipped getting her out of the way. Fortunately, Charlie wasn't contagious, so I didn't have to pay to have the neighbor's truck neutralized, but he broke his ankle, and there's nothing whinier in life than a vain male cheetah who can't run at his leisure. Sassy got a spanking for not watching traffic before crossing the street."

"Had to pick the switch?" I guessed.

"It's like you grew up in the Chetty household. After she got switched, she got to do Charlie's chores until he escaped his cast, and to add insult to injury, I made her wash the neighbor's truck and supervise its repainting since Charlie scuffed the paint. Watching paint dry is not a fun activity for a young feline."

I bet. "Can't say I wouldn't have whooped her for that one," I admitted.

"Aaron," Sassy wailed.

"Sassy," I replied, mimicking her tone. "If you hadn't run out in traffic, you wouldn't have gotten your ass whooped."

"Traitor."

"Don't run out in front of traffic, and you won't get spanked."

Her eyes narrowed. "So if I run out in traffic, I'll get spanked?"

I pinched the bridge of my nose, wondering how I'd wandered right into that trap unawares. I blamed the medications. "This is your fault, Joe."

"If you run out in traffic, you won't get spanked," Joe announced. "If you want spanked that bad, just ask him. Sometime after the rest of us are far, far away, because the last thing I need to hear or see is my sister getting a spanking."

"Damn it, Joe!"

"What? You started it."

"That's not fair."

"Sure it is. You got your older brother's blessing. You should be thanking me. Just not on your knees or anything. Aaron will get ideas, and he's in no condition to control any new impulses. You also don't want him controlling new impulses right now. It's good for him to get a feel for what it's like. Also, you need to be more concerned about the investigation. We have jack shit on this killer, and we don't know where he'll strike next. Mark's been nagging me about getting Aaron back into action sooner than later, but until I'm certain he won't start bleeding again, he has to stay put. You're his best chance to get back on his feet."

"The entire police force and the FBI are on the case. Why is Aaron so damned important?" Sassy hissed her displeasure and crossed her arms over her chest. "I don't see what we can do that they can't."

That made two of us. "The more eyes on this, the better. It's not that we can do something they can't, Sassy. It's that I'm the one who got away. The sooner I'm back to investigations, the faster we can possibly lure the killer out. We have exactly one potential lead, and I only have one way to protect her, although it'll smear Mark's reputation doing it."

"And Mark's willing, by the way. I already asked. He's working on making contact with Miss Gray as we speak. With luck, the groundwork will be in place on that by dinner tonight," Joe announced. "We're still worried she'll become a target, but if Mark can't protect her, no one can. Miss Gray's getting to the point she's ready to settle down and have puppies of her own, so maybe your brother will get lucky for once in his life and settle down."

"Mark, my brother, settle down? Have you lost your mind?"

"The lycanthropy virus can convert even the rowdiest of players into a loyal family man," Joe replied. "In your case, you'll just become extra loyal with a side dish of overprotective and having entire litters of children. Just look at my dad."

"You're going to scare him off," Sassy's father warned.

The warning revitalized Sassy's desire to murder her brother, and shaking my head at the insanity, I resumed my investigation of the briefcases Mark had left to me so I could begin doing my share of the work.

TEN

I was getting exactly what I'd
asked for.

I NEEDED a trip to the library to check out
the newspaper archive, but I'd have to make
do with digital files until Joe and my brother
relented. I doubted either would let me out of
the Chetty home until I'd staked my claim on
Sassy or goaded her into making claims on
me. I found their obstruction obnoxious, but
at the same time, I was getting exactly what
I'd asked for.

Only a fool would complain.

The digital archive of the newspapers annoyed me as it excluded the original typeset-
ting; uniform, digital fonts ruled all the
prevalent papers. I did find one thing of use:
at least one paper had a corresponding date
to the murder victims. As the dates had been
from nine months prior to the victim's birth,
I decided to do some math and check the papers for articles from the estimated birthdays

of the victims. As I couldn't leave the house and wanted nothing to do with the war raging between Sassy and her brother, I read the entire newspapers from front to back.

A political article with a familiar face caught my attention, and I dug through the photographs of the women until I found her.

Renata Kirkville had announced her departure from political management a few weeks prior to the birth of her child for personal reasons, and one newspaper had bothered to report about it—on the day she'd given birth. In the background of the photograph, taken on the street, was a second familiar face.

I hated finding links in the oddest of places, but I wanted to kiss the newspaper who'd captured the photograph and posted it. Grabbing my new phone, I called the anonymous tip line for the police, and I used the line that handled tipoffs by recordings rather than discussing the situation with an operator. I listed the newspaper, gave the victim's name, the date the issue had run, and indicated Tom Heatherow was in the background of the image, a potential person of interest in the serial killing of single women and their children.

By the time I hung up, I'd captured everyone's attention.

"You can't be serious," Sassy blurted.

I turned my new laptop so she could see the screen. "Recognize them?"

According to her curses, she recognized our client in the background. "That fucking piece of shit. But she's not pregnant in that photograph."

"Exactly. And while the newspaper didn't expressly confirm her pregnancy, isn't it interesting they picked a photograph showing Heatherow in the background? They may as well have put their speculations on a billboard. And why opt to run the article on that specific date? According to this, she'd announced it weeks prior but only chose to run it the day she'd given birth. This newspaper was still printing daily, so it was a deliberate choice. She must have gone into labor the evening before the print run was set. Is there a way we can confirm that?"

"For us? No," Joe announced. "However, Mark can probably get the intel legally—or at least in so clever a way no one will know we accessed the information. The police can probably get the records as part of the investigation. Let Maxwell know directly; the anonymous line might take time to get through to him."

I tapped a text message to Maxwell requesting he look into Renata Kirkville's labor along with a heads up I'd left a tip on the anonymous line and a request he delete the message after receiving it. "Done."

"It's probably a coincidence that article ran right on the boy's birthday," Joe warned.

"As much as it is a coincidence Tom Heatherow is in the picture?"

The silence promised everyone wondered as much as I did over how much of a coincidence it could be. Joe hesitated, his brows furrowing. "Some of the dates were estimates."

"And I found this one exactly nine months following the date left with the victims. What if they all coordinate with a similar newspaper? What if it isn't actually the date of conception but a clue to get us from the conception to a matching article about the victims—or to someone related to the victims."

"Like Tom Heatherow," Sassy growled.

"Exactly."

"Once is a coincidence," Joe reminded me.

"Investigations is all about finding out if the coincidences become a trend and how those trends lead to the story of a murder. Every murder has a story, Joe. Sometimes the story is as simple as a mugging gone wrong, but sometimes, it's far more than that. We realistically need to check every newspaper from the date listed *and* nine months later to make certain there's a trend. And if there is, what is the trend? What sort of puzzle are we solving? Why is the killer giving us clues like this?"

Sassy grabbed her new laptop along with a printout of the victims, the dates of birth of the children, their corresponding numbers and dates left at the crime scene, and general profile. "The killer's telling us a story, and he's trying to give us enough clues to figure it out. But why would he do that? It's a trademark of a serial killer, but you broke the trend."

"Did he? We haven't looked for any newspapers with my date of birth yet." I dug through the online archives and found six newspapers with matching dates. "Honestly, I have no idea what I'm looking for, but if the killer's trying to send a message through old newspapers, perhaps the link isn't in our birthdays but what was in the news on our birthdays. Not a day goes by without some form of political news in the media, and that applied even when I was born. The real question is this: what happened when *I* was born that might be a part of that story?"

"Graduations," Sassy blurted. "Tom Heatherow would have been graduating when you were born. Is there a section in any of those newspapers congratulating graduates?"

"Wait, what? Graduates?"

"College graduates, Aaron. He's a lot older than we are. He would have been graduating college when you were born."

I'd peg the man to be in his late thirties, which would've put him as a high school graduate when I'd been born. "Just how old is he?"

"Mid-forties. He aged well. He's not infected with lycanthropy as far as I know. He might have been mentioned in a newspaper. According to my tentative research on him, he graduated on the Dean's list. Since he's from Dallas, he might've gotten a mention."

"Which school?"

"University of Texas at Austin."

"Rank in the school?"

"Best of the best. The guy's smart."

"Type of degree?"

Sassy frowned and grabbed a stack of papers, sifting through them. "Business degree from the business school. I don't remember which type of business degree."

"Decided to go into business, then when his father ran for President, he was exposed as a bastard son?"

"Sounds about right."

A headache brewed, and I wondered if I could function if I begged another little white pill out of Joe and his stash of painkillers he fed me to keep the whining at a minimum. "What are our other options?"

"News about his father in political format. If he's shown with a woman, perhaps there's an element of the story. If we get both, then we probably have a really strong story, but I wouldn't count on that. That would be too much of a coincidence."

"How long was his father in politics before his Presidential run?"

Sassy shrugged. "I haven't researched much into his father. I didn't think it was relevant."

I wouldn't blame her; without the other clues in place, I wouldn't have thought it relevant either. "We're going to need that data. Can you look for that while I read these newspapers?"

"On it."

"No, you're not," Sassy's father announced. "It's time to put the research away. Dinner will be ready soon, and your mother really might give you a whooping if you make her late feeding the guests. Aaron, your parents are on the way and should be here within the next twenty minutes, so you should go take a warm shower and get yourself as presentable as you can. I had the brats steal some clothes from your place last night. It's up in Sassy's room. Sassy, you can help set the tables. Joe, you keep an eye on Aaron. You may as well do those doctorly things you claim you're so good at."

I packed away my laptop and jotted down a note of what I needed to look for after dinner. "I just hope we can figure out the trend tonight so we can start looking at other articles to identify potential leads to additional victims."

"Me, too. We'll get this guy, Aaron. One way or another, we'll get him."

"It could be someone covering for Tom Heatherow," I reminded her.

"I don't care if it's him or not. I just care how he fits into this. If we find out where he fits in the puzzle, we can figure out the entire puzzle. That'll lead us to the killer, and it'll lead us to the killer in a way where we have more than circumstantial evidence." Sassy smacked the pile of papers on the coffee table. "This shit is circumstantial evidence at best. We need solid leads, and we won't get it until we figure out this mess. This guy is a professional, and until he makes a mistake, we're fucked."

"Language," Sassy's father warned.

"Well, we are. We haven't even been able to find the damned truck that hit Aaron. It's like the fucking thing just disappeared into thin air. It's not on any of the recordings, and there's no evidence of where he exited the highway. How the hell does a big white semi just disappear like that?"

Joe frowned. "Wait. White?"

"Yeah, it was white," I said.

"No, it wasn't," Joe replied.

I frowned. "What do you mean by that?"

"I mean the truck wasn't white. It was red, painted with produce on the side. I know you rattled your head pretty hard during the crash, Aaron, but that's a pretty big difference. It was red with produce on the side, one of those farmer's market trucks they use for the weekend markets in town."

"Schuckle's?" Sassy asked.

"Yeah. You know the one I'm talking about."

Sassy's father frowned, and his brows furrowed. "But the truck was white, Joe."

"Not according to Aaron's memories it's not, and I've got the truck's tags from his memory, too."

"I noted his tags, too. What were they?"

"F03-0268."

"That's not what I remember," Sassy's father muttered. "And the truck was white."

"And what does this tell you, Dad? I'll wait."

I sucked in a breath. "Illusionary magic. Someone disguised the truck, and then he dropped the magic to make the truck disappear."

"And he's able to affect the traffic cameras so it picked up a white truck with the wrong tags, so when he dropped off the radar, he was back in his regular truck. A little extra magic, and he could disguise the damage to the truck from ramming Aaron into the median. Alternatively, he could have a manipulation talent that allows him to change the color of the paint on the truck. I can think of four or five classes of magic that could accomplish the same goal."

"Why did you wait until now to tell us?" Sassy demanded. "What the fuck were you doing poking around in Aaron's memories? You asshole!"

"Finding out he loves your legs in your jeans, has as much of a shoe fetish as you do, and his general intentions with you, my sister. The intel on the truck was just my excuse to find out what he was up to."

"I bought you really nice shoes, please don't kill me," I begged.

"Aaron."

"I'm sorry."

"Which jeans?"

"The ones you pounced him in with the blue shoes, which, for the record, he really appreciates. He was too busy admiring you in your jeans and those shoes to care you'd about killed him jumping on him like that," Joe announced.

"I have three other pairs just like them."

I reached for her bag of new shoes only to

have my hand slapped. "I just wanted to hand you the clear pair."

"Heels outdoors would result in a broken ankle. No. I'll wear them for you later."

"Tonight later or later later?"

Joe laughed. "As I said, Sassy. He has a shoe fetish almost as bad as yours, but he only likes shoes you're wearing. But being serious. The truck was red with produce painted on the side of it."

Sassy's father scowled. "Explain how you're seeing that in his memories while we're remembering something completely different."

"I'm accessing the memory directly without the visual cues and markers. Memories are stored in a different section of the brain than eyesight and sensory input. The sensory input portion of the brain is what's being affected. I directly accessed the memory, and as the magic affects a different part of the brain, it's unfiltered. It doesn't hurt that I'm fairly resistant to that sort of magic due to military training. I have to be able to detect and see through illusionary magic to make certain I'm properly treating injuries. Illusionary magic is sometimes used offensively to prevent soldiers from being treated, causing additional casualties. So, because of my training, while it's possible the memory itself is flawed, I'm able to see through it anyway."

"Is there a chance that the scraps of paper have been influenced by such magic?" Sassy asked. "There's a lot of them."

"Actually, yes. That's a possibility."

I grabbed my phone and called Maxwell.

"Aaron?" Maxwell answered. "What is it?"

"The semi that hit my truck is red with produce painted on the sides. A Schuckle's truck, and the tag number is F03-0268. Probable illusionary magic according to Sassy's brother, Joe. Is there a chance we can get access to a full set of the paper scraps? It's possible that they're affected, too, and Joe might be able to see through it."

"Illusionary magic? Are you serious?"

"It explains why the truck disappeared from the highway cameras. It disappeared because he changed the appearance of the truck, and he probably used magic to cover anything unusual."

"I'll run the tags. Is Joe willing to verify this through an angel?"

"Joe? You willing to verify with an angel?"

"Of course. And an angel can verify the memory, too, if you allow it."

"I'll ask an angel to review the memory, too. He was poking through my head trying to find out more information," I admitted.

"Have him review the first killing. You

might really have seen something you don't remember. Be careful, Aaron."

"I'll ask him. And you, too, Maxwell."

"Will do. I'll swing by later to talk about this." Maxwell hung up.

I set my phone on the coffee table. "He thinks you should review my memories of the first shooting, as this may mean I really did see something."

"Or your camera did, just like you speculated. I haven't seen the photos yet."

"Sassy? Can you print a full copy of the pictures for Joe?"

Sassy glanced at her father.

"I'll do your share of the dinner work while you get those printed out. Go shower, Aaron. Joe, how long will it take to rummage through his memories?"

"Twenty to thirty minutes."

"Do it before dinner, and I'll tell your mother it couldn't wait. If you find something, you get law enforcement on the move. That's too important to leave sitting for long."

"Shower after, Aaron. You're not going to like the next half an hour, and you'll want that shower to help you recover."

"If it helps catch the killer, it's worth it."

THE FIRST TIME Joe had poked through my

memories, I hadn't noticed him doing it. I assumed the transfusion and my weakened state had numbed me to his work. With time running short, he abandoned his finesse and stirred through my head with a red-hot poker. It hurt too much to scream, and my life flashed in front of my eyes, a confusing blur of images, sounds, and sensations.

He stopped and slowed every time I'd thought about his sister, and the instant I felt up for the task, I'd beat him black and blue over it.

When he got to the crash, I lost a few minutes of my life as the pain associated with the memory intensified beyond my ability to handle it.

I woke up to Joe slapping my cheeks.

"I really hadn't wanted to do that, but it's the only way I can access your memories. I have to rewind them," he confessed. "Once you went down, I got what we needed. I'm sorry. If I could have prevented it, I would have."

"That sucked. Can we not do that again?"

"That's the idea. I rewound as far back as your first contact with Tom Heatherow."

That would likely bite me in the ass later. "So, you're saying you own my ass for the foreseeable future."

"Something like that. You're pathetic. I just thought you should know that. You really went through all that work to avoid her traps, cleaned up after her, and waited until she came over to dunk yourself so she could lick the skin off your face."

"Basically, yes."

"You were infected before the crash."

I blinked. "Pardon?"

"You were infected before the crash. That's Dad behavior. That's ridiculously similar to Dad's behavior. That's breeding male cheetah behavior. When were you last tested?"

"Not that long ago."

Joe's eyes narrowed. "No. That's definitely infected long-term behavior. That's not 'standard human hates women Aaron' behavior."

"It was one of my more desperate stunts," I agreed.

"How long have you been buying my sister shoes?"

"Years," I admitted.

"I'd probably kill you rooting through your memory for years, so I can't look to see how the hell you contracted lycanthropy."

"You seem a little sure I contracted lycanthropy."

"Aaron, my sister's tongue is worse than sandpaper. She can flay muscle from bone with that tongue. That's what it's there for. You should have been bleeding after she licked you for two hours. It hurt, but that was not the reaction of a standard human being licked. The virus was already there and healing your face. You barely had a mark on you after that. Slightly reddened cheeks. That's a sure-fire sign of lycanthropy to me. But how the hell did you avoid detection? You're checked how often?"

"Every two years when I'm renewing my license."

"And you've been partnered with Sassy since you started college. Can you think of any time you might have mixed blood with Sassy?"

"Not that I'm aware of. She's really careful about transmitting the virus. I'm not allowed to go anywhere near her if she thinks I might contract the virus." I shrugged. "She panics if she thinks she might pass on the virus to anybody."

"And everything I saw in your memories supports your look-but-don't-touch mentality. So where'd you get it? It's obviously our strain; Dad's virus boosted yours. And if it's not early onset, how long have you been infected? What type of scanner did they use on you?"

"I don't know. I don't know anything about the scanners."

"Did they do a blood test?"

"No. It's one of those press to the skin ones."

"Insensitive, low accuracy. It won't detect lycanthropy until you're a stage below contagious," he replied. "That can be up to five to ten years post initial infection. Any chance your past girlfriends were lycanthropes?"

"Even if they were, I took all the precautions."

"No oral sex?"

While I disliked discussing my past sex life with Joe, I ignored my annoyance and replied, "Absolutely not."

"When was the last time you had a girlfriend?"

"Maybe five years ago. We were starting our business in earnest. She had another guy on the side, and I gave up at that point."

"It's likely you were infected at least a year or two prior to that, then. A year or two into infection is when the loyalty element really starts kicking in. With Sassy around, your virus likely considered her a viable mate, which would explain why your heterosexual tendencies remained intact. Male cheetahs only join coalitions when there are no eligible females around."

"And sisters don't count as eligible."

"Correct. Dad's always been pretty picky about who he lets near Sassy. Frankly, I'm astonished you got his approval."

I rolled my shoulders and cringed at the

creaks and cracks. "Your father did rearrange my face that one time."

"When he popped your tooth out and had to..." Joe's eyes widened. "That clever son of a bitch."

I blinked. "What?"

"He could have easily infected you then. Easily. One scraped knuckle in your mouth and you'd be infected."

"But he didn't bleed."

"Are you sure?"

I blinked. "He showed the cops his hands. No cuts."

"Aaron, just who do you think I got my magical abilities from? Dad could've closed any cuts on his hands without breaking a sweat. A few scraped knuckles is nothing to him."

My headache intensified. "You think he infected me on purpose?"

"I know that's going to upset you, Aaron, but think about it from my father's shoes. Sassy's loved you since the day she laid eyes on you, and you respected her too much to go against her wishes. Dad's not the type to let my sister suffer over something he can control. He'd do a lot more than face the penalties for infecting someone with lycanthropy to make her happy. That doesn't make it right, but ultimately, you wanted the virus of your own volition."

"That's incredibly underhanded."

"We should beat the shit out of him later over it. My brothers will help."

"I might accept that offer. Where does that leave us?"

"Well, with only seven years under your belt, you weren't contagious, and he must have given you barely enough blood to infect you. That's a longer incubation time. Since we have zero proof of earlier infection, we'll treat it like an early onset rather than the wily manipulations of a stupidly clever feline."

I wanted to be angry with Sassy's father, but I hesitated. If I had been infected, I hadn't noticed the changes in my personality, and I'd always, always respected Sassy's desire to only mate with someone already infected with lycanthropy. Fresh out of college, I doubted I would have taken the dive without being pushed, but as time had gone by, Sassy had become a critical part of my life.

Ultimately, no matter which way I viewed the situation, I would've sought out the virus.

"I'm going to go punch your father in the mouth to see how he likes it."

"If you're going to go punch him in the mouth, do it before you shower, please. Also, give me a chance to tell Dean and Charlie. The three of us can hold him back while you get your hits in."

"Can you fix his teeth?"

"As a matter of fact, yes."

I cracked my knuckles. "Will breaking my hand on his teeth cause any problems?"

"Beyond needing another transfusion once you start bleeding on me? Not at all. Just make sure you don't bleed on your family. You're undoubtedly contagious now."

"You got it."

FOR AS LONG AS I lived, I'd enjoy the shocked expression on Sassy's father's face when I sucker punched him in the mouth for all I was worth. I staged my ambush for the outdoors, which would be easier to clean, and as I respected Sassy's mother, I waited until only Sassy and a handful of her brothers witnessed my deed. Despite my convalescence, I still possessed enough strength to make it hurt. My prediction of breaking my hand on his face came true, and the stab of pain focused me on my task.

Blood for blood sounded fair to me, and I pounced, ready to take out my frustration on the sneaky, conniving feline.

"What the hell?" Sassy shrieked.

"I went poking around Aaron's memories for information on the killer and discovered, while reviewing, it's very probable he's been infected for at least a few years. The most probable suspect is getting his face tender-ized. Lift a finger against Aaron, and Charlie, Dean, and I are joining his side, Dad. You can fend him off, you can't do anything more than that. Try not to lose your teeth. I'll fix them after he tires himself out. You're so thoroughly busted, Dad."

"I ain't done nothin'!" Sassy's father howled, grabbing hold of my chin to hold me at arm's length.

"You healed your knuckles after cutting them open on Aaron's teeth."

Silence.

As I hadn't ensured I'd knocked out at least one of his teeth, I took another swipe at him, not caring the motion hurt like hell. There'd be time enough later to worry about my busted hand.

"Daddy?" Sassy whispered.

Yep, Sassy wasn't taking the news well, and since her father caused her distress, I went for his throat like I meant it. Charlie and Dean snagged me under the arms and pulled me off. "Hey!"

"We keep confrontations non-lethal, Aaron. That's flat-out going for the kill. Fix Dad's teeth before you worry about Aaron, Joe," Charlie ordered.

"Hell no! Dad can fucking look at his teeth in a jar. You did *what* to Aaron?"

Joe wisely hooked his arm around his sister's waist to keep her from attacking their father. "Aaron got his hit in, so call it even, Sassy."

When her father refused to look anyone in the eyes, I had no doubt the sneaky bastard had done as Joe believed. "We're going to have a talk about this later," I promised. "Sneaky, conniving bastard."

"Oliver Chetty, what have you done?" Sassy's mother howled from the kitchen.

I grimaced. "Or not. I'll just let her take care of it."

Joe grimaced, too. "That's harsh, Aaron. Let me see your hand."

I held out my throbbing hand to him. "I definitely broke something."

"Well, considering two of your fingers are pointed the wrong way, I'll say I agree with your assessment. You need to learn how to punch without breaking your hand on your opponent's face."

"Think I hit him hard enough?"

"You broke your hand. You hit him hard enough. I'm going to have to check his face for breaks now." Joe sighed. "Charlie? You up for a splint job? You need to practice, and he needs to take a shower and get the blood off. No trailing blood through the house, and keep the uninfected away from him until everything's cleaned up. Sassy, get the neutralizer and make sure nothing's left over."

Sassy growled but headed for the house, and Dean followed at her heels. Her storming off did a good job of distracting me from my hand.

"Dad?" Joe growled.

"Fine."

"You really did it? You really busted your knuckles on Aaron's face to intentionally infect him?"

"A father's gotta do what a father's gotta do. Look at him. It was only a matter of time anyway. I was just helpin' him along."

Joe shot me a glance and mouthed a 'I told you so' in my direction.

As I'd already rattled my brain enough, I turned to Charlie and used his shoulder rather than give myself a concussion banging my head into one of the picnic tables. "Why me?"

"Good men are few and far between, and with daily exposure to Sassy, your virus wouldn't want anyone else. He's a bastard, but he's a clever bastard. Are you going to charge him?"

"No, I'm going with early onset and planning a complicated and utterly feline version of revenge," I muttered.

Charlie slapped my back. "It'll be fine. Let's get you upstairs and cleaned up. Don't drip blood on the carpet. It's a bitch to clean up, and Mom'll get cranky if her carpet's pink for a week again. I keep trying to tell her she'd just be better off buying pink, shimmering carpet with how often we use neutralizer around here."

"Sassy's mad."

"I noticed you noticing. You tensed from head to toe. Doubt you noticed, mad as you are, but you need to take a shower and cool your heels. Sassy's going to read your body language and want to commit murder because you're upset."

"I'm contemplating some form of nonlethal revenge. Sassy would cry if I killed her daddy."

"Revenge is better than planning murder, and yes, Sassy would cry if you killed her daddy. She'll forgive him eventually. She's more mad she didn't catch the bastard doing it."

Sassy's mother stormed into the yard wielding a pair of barbecue-covered tongs. "What's this I hear about you healing your knuckles, dear?"

Oliver Chetty would die at the hands of his wife in the back yard with a pair of tongs, and I gaped with wide eyes, unable to fathom how she'd do it.

"If Aaron can't kill Dad, you can't kill Dad, either. Right, Joe?"

"Tit-for-tat, Mom. Dad broke a few of Aaron's teeth, Aaron broke a few of Dad's.

He'll be less hissy after Sassy calms him down. Sassy!"

"What now?" Sassy howled from inside the house.

"Come claim your kitty and help Charlie splint his hand."

"First you want me to neutralize the damned grass, now you want me doing what?"

"Stripping your male out of his clothes and splinting his busted hand. If I set the bones right now, he'll pass out, he'll miss dinner, and Dad really will die at Mom's hands."

Storming out of the house with a white bag, Sassy wound up and busted the bag open on her father's face. "You are such an asshole!"

Pink sparkling powder erupted everywhere, and I sneezed as it scattered, billowing and coating everything in the area. My hand stung, and the rest of my skin tingled. Sneezing and breathing it in turned the tingle to a more nefarious itch, but it subsided within a few breaths.

Sassy's father sighed. "Did you really have to hit me in the face with the bag?"

"Yes, sir, I most certainly did." To make her point clear, she smacked him with the empty bag. "We are going to have words later, Daddy."

Was there anything more appealing than

watching Sassy swear vengeance on her father?

Growling, Sassy's mother waved her tongs in her mate's face. "What have you done, Oliver Chetty?"

"Do you want to tell her?" Joe asked.

"No, no. I don't want a round with the tongs, and I'm pretty sure I'm partially responsible for how that went down."

"Smart bastard," Joe muttered. "Remember that scuffle Aaron and Dad got into not long after Sassy graduated college?"

"Unfortunately."

"He bled and closed the wounds with his magic and didn't bother to tell anybody."

Sassy's mother frowned, and she narrowed her eyes. "What's the problem?"

"Judging from Aaron's memory and changes in his behavior, he was infected."

Sassy's mother smiled, her expression relaxing. "What's the problem? And here I thought it was something serious."

"Dad's head is so hard Aaron broke his hand."

That earned Sassy's father a whack with the tongs upside his head. "What have I told you about that damned thick skull of yours?" Then, since hitting him wasn't enough to satisfy her, Sassy's mother seized his ear with the tongs. "Inside, and don't you be bleeding on none of the guests. Someone make sure all his teeth are picked up and bring them to the downstairs bathroom. That's easiest to clean. Joe, don't you be slacking on your father's teeth. Those damned things ain't cheap."

"Yes, Aaron's incident taught us that very valuable lesson," Joe replied, and he went on a hunt for his father's teeth in the grass, stirring up neutralizer. "Sassy, you keep Aaron's temper cooled. Go put on a pair of heels for him. That'll keep him distracted while Charlie straightens his fingers and sets the bones."

Sassy hissed at her brother.

"What? It's true. That man loves nothing more than you in a pair of good heels. You didn't think he bought all those shoes just because he's disgustingly nice, did you? Underneath that disgustingly nice exterior is a sexually repressed man."

"Joe!"

Sassy's mother reached out and smacked the back of her son's head. "Stop goading your sister. Dinner's going to be late enough as it is, and we've guests in the living room."

"Sorry, ma'am," Joe mumbled.

"Move it! I've hungry mouths to feed sometime today."

Charlie put his hands on my shoulders, turned me around, and marched me towards the house. "I'll take care of Aaron. We're gonna need some time, Mom."

"Take all you need, Charlie. I'll keep your supper warm, don't you worry none. I suppose it's a good enough thing I was running behind anyway, entertaining while doing the cooking."

I fled while I could.

MAXWELL, the DA, several other cops, and my parents joined in the dinner mayhem, and I waved my newly splinted hand at the unexpected guests. "If Joe gives me any more of those small pills, you're going to have to write me up for drug use."

Maxwell sighed, Rob shook his head, and the other cops grinned. "What did you do to your hand?"

"Punched a lycanthrope in the mouth. Seemed like a good idea at the time. Didn't realize he had steel in his skull."

That caught the DA's attention, and he arched a brow. "Lycanthropes tend to be durable, Aaron. Why did you punch a lycanthrope?"

"He tricked me. Punching him seemed the only appropriate response, and I refuse to be sorry."

Sassy's father stepped out of the house, and I spotted zero evidence he'd had a few of his teeth knocked out. "Early onset lycanthropy, a short temper, some drugs, and a good reason. We already cleaned up the mess."

"That explains why the grass is pink and glittery," Rob admitted. "We're sorry for interrupting you at dinner time, but when Maxwell told us about the truck, I thought it was worth a trip out here in person. Chief Braneni is on the way, too."

"You're still involved with this case way too early. We don't even have an actual suspect yet," I complained. "You're supposed to only annoy me when there's an actual suspect."

"Remember what he just said about those small pills I gave him, Rob?" Joe said holding out his hand to shake with the DA. "I got that bottle directly from the hospital with a waiver from the CDC because he's early onset."

"How early are we talking?" Maxwell asked.

"With his temper as it is? Something's going to either piss him off or startle him into shifting by the end of the week. I've already registered him with the CDC. I've got clearance for him to work on the force as he'll be partnered with an experienced lycanthrope. We'll work with him to teach him how to avoid spreading the infection. I've got a list of waivers, the documentation to send to his insurance company, and I got my hands on the licensing records to prove he wasn't registering the virus a few months ago."

Rob rubbed his brow. "Well, Chief Braneni wanted to test lycanthropes. He's getting exactly what he asked for. How long until he's off the serious medications, Joe?"

"I'll fuse the bones in his hands after dinner, after which he'll probably be keen on violating my sister in some fashion or another."

"Joe!" Sassy screeched, lunging for her brother.

I hooked my left arm around her waist and hauled her to me. "No killing Joe. He holds the drug supply, and without those, I hurt."

While Sassy growled, she didn't struggle in my hold. "That's not fair, Aaron. He's bad-mouthing you."

I would never understand women, but I wasn't going to argue with her. Then again, what I had in mind wasn't a violation but rather a mutually beneficial exploration of the benefits of clothing removal. "I'm not into any forms of violation, but I am keen on other things."

Joe rolled his eyes. "Don't, Aaron. Please. She's my sister."

"You shouldn't have started it, then." I gripped Sassy a little tighter so she wouldn't try to kill any member of her family. "I'm hungry, Sassy. If you try to kill Joe, we miss supper."

"Aaron," she complained.

"I already broke my hand on your dad's face. I don't want to have to break my hand again on Joe's face. He'll stop wanting to treat me, and then you'll be stuck hoping I don't bleed to death."

Sassy stiffened. "Fine."

I released her. "It's okay. I'm not even mad at the jackass. I'm just going to plan payback at an unexpected time and place."

"Let me help?"

"Sure. But you can't attack Joe or anyone else today."

"*You* got to," she grumbled.

"Extenuating circumstances."

"Still not fair."

"I'm hungry, Sassy. Have mercy."

"You're a hungry whiner. Fine. I'll delay my assault for when the DA and the cops aren't watching."

I laughed. "Good idea. We'll tag team the bastard later."

"That works."

As Maxwell, the DA, and the cops wouldn't leave until I gave them what they wanted, I said, "I gave Joe permission to use his magic on me, and due to his military training, he's adept at seeing through illusionary magic. He says the truck is red, had produce painted on the side, and had a different tag number than anything I remember —or that Mr. Chetty remembers."

"We ran the tags. The truck was reported stolen a day before the crash and is still missing. We're going to be on the lookout for it, but it was probably scrapped to hide evidence."

"A junkyard would have to have noticed a transport coming in for scrapping," I replied. "Call for angelic verification no transports were scrapped at the yards."

"We probably will," the DA admitted. "You still think the truck was white?"

I shrugged. "I don't know what I think, but I had Joe go through my memories up until the shooting, and we're going to go over the pictures later. If they don't match up, we might find something to help us pinpoint the killer. It lends credence to the idea this is a mercenary hit, a vengeance killing, or a cover up and *not* a standard serial killer."

"Aaron also figured out what one of the newspaper clippings might be referencing," Sassy announced. "We checked articles from a victim's birthday, and there was one about the victim's mother. Tom Heatherow is in the background of the image the newspaper used, and the article implies she was pregnant and having a child. The layout leads me to believe they wanted to suggest Heatherow was the father."

The DA's eyes widened. "That might justify the warrant needed to do a paternity test. Good work. Got anything else?"

"Aaron had found that right before we took a break for dinner," Sassy admitted. "We're looking into it."

"Good. What do you need from us?" Maxwell asked.

"Access to the original newspapers," I admitted. "I was using the digital copies online, so I can't verify if they match the font and style of the dates used. Were the fonts different between killings?"

"Somewhat. We've established it's from different newspapers, but we're not sure which ones. We were looking at the dates listed, though, not fast-forwarding to the date of the child's birth. That potentially opens a lot of possibilities."

"I'll handle checking the newspapers. I'm stuck on bedrest for the next few days anyway. Mark is making contact with Sharon Gray to throw any unwanted visitors off her trail. We're hoping Mark can play the part of an old acquaintance."

"Acquaintance?" Rob asked.

"My brother's a slut, Rob. Hell, for all I know, maybe he did sleep with her. I'm pretty sure he's slept with half the women in Dallas."

"Right."

"He'll find the whole thing a challenge, plus it's something right up his alley. Frankly, it's astonishing I'm not an uncle twenty times over yet."

Rob sighed. "Someone needs to lock him up."

"Or send notices to the fathers of young women that he's more promiscuous than the average prostitute." I considered my options, found little I could say or do about my brother's reputation, and hoped he didn't hear from anyone about my blunt admissions about his sex life. "It is what it is. If he can remove Miss Gray from the target list, I'm all for him using his slutty ways for our benefit."

The doorbell rang, and I turned towards the house. A moment later, Maxwell's phone chimed.

"That would be the chief," Maxwell said before he checked to confirm on his phone. "Yep. It's the chief."

Sassy's father excused himself and went around the house to fetch the police chief while the rest of us settled at the picnic tables. While I expected the police chief, who carried a leather briefcase with him, I hadn't expected Mark to be with him. My brother blew kisses at me.

The temptation to show him my middle finger stirred, but I resisted the urge and waved him over. He detoured long enough to kiss our mother's cheek where she sat with Sassy's mother, likely planning grandchildren.

"How did you break your hand?"

"Payback for my teeth," I announced. "It was strangely satisfying."

"You broke your hand on Oliver's face?"

"Since when have you been on a first-name basis with Sassy's father?"

"Since forever. What got you to man up and take a swing at him?"

"The lycanthropy virus made him do it," Joe said. "He's riled up. Don't mind him, just don't provoke him unless you want to sprout a fur coat in a few decades."

"No, but thanks for the offer. A severe case of lycanthropy would give me a severe case of monogamy. That's so against my personal religion."

My mother sighed, and my father turned on the bench to arch a brow at Mark. "Is there something you'd like to tell us, son?"

"I'm considering a job in prostitution so I can be paid for my good work."

One day, I'd understand why my brother wanted to give our parents a heart attack. "What brings you over, Mark?"

"Work."

Chief Braneni took the seat across from me, chuckled, and made himself comfortable.

"I asked him to come over so we can discuss the case and your future employment opportunities. I wasn't expecting to see you adding to your injuries, however."

"Mr. Chetty's face demanded rearrangement. Unfortunately, Joe undid my hard work, but I have to wait until after dinner to fix this mess."

"You need to learn how to punch properly, son."

"Yeah, I figured that out about the same time I broke two fingers on his face. Does the academy teach us how to punch people properly?"

"No. As a general rule, we don't punch civilians. We do try to keep all force used to reasonable levels, and we've found punching people in the face is bad for publicity."

Sassy coughed, likely to smother a snicker. "Aaron told me about the offer. It's real?"

"It's real. I brought some papers for you to review. I got a call early about your condition, Aaron. Early onset lycanthropy?"

"Yeah. That seems to be the case. Joe thinks I'll be shifting by the end of the week."

"Sassy? You'll be able to keep him in line?"

"How long is the education process before we're in the field?"

"We have an intensive six-month course we're going to run you both through, and you'll be working with a few FBI instructors.

I called in some favors. With your experience in the private investigation field, we'll see how it goes. It might be as long as eighteen months depending on how fast you pick up the important skills. We're going to also test if we've got any dogs you might be able to work with. We've found partnering investigators with a dog is useful, and there's a lot of quality animals this year. Fewer washouts than we expected, so we might be able to find one that'll work with you two. If you get a dog, it'll add a few months to your training, but you'll be better off in the field."

"Two cats and a dog?" I asked. "Really?"

"While that has occurred to me, it's worth a shot. It'll let us test dogs with investigators, although we are still working out the kinks on how to bring a dog to a crime scene without disturbing evidence until needed. We've got a lot of kinks to work out. We'll be doing a lot of tests of new procedures with you two. Frankly, your early onset diagnosis will really help with getting lycanthropes into the field without the hybrid form. If you, with the most volatile virus conditions possible, can handle the work, it's a pretty safe bet that other lycanthropes can as well. I'm open to the idea, as it'll drastically lower causalities in the field. There's a heightened risk of the virus being spread, but the CDC's determined that the virus is going to continue spreading no matter what precautions we take."

I believed that; while it seemed simple enough to prevent the spread of the virus, it only took one fist fight to cause an infection. Or, in my case, an overprotective idiot of a father wanting the best for his daughter.

Sassy's mother rose and headed to the kitchen, and to my surprise, my mother followed her.

Sassy perked up, twisting on the bench. "They're about to feed us."

"There's also the matter of feeding lycanthropes in the field. Lycanthropes eat a lot. Have you put thought into how to handle the voracious appetites of post-shift lycanthropes?" I asked.

"Yes. The CDC sent over everything they recommend for their hybrid field agents, and they've informed me the same rules generally apply to lycanthropes without the hybrid form. She'll have some challenges, but as long as you're stabilized by the time your education is completed, I see no actual issues with your condition." Chief Braneni set his briefcase on the table, opened it, and handed me a stack of papers. "One set is for you, one set is for your partner. The offers are the same. This will give you a chance to discuss it, review the required waivers, and contact the CDC should you have questions I can't answer. We don't typically handle recruitment in this fashion, but some opportunities shouldn't be missed, and the CDC is riding my ass about getting non-hybrid lycanthropes onto the force to better police the lycanthrope population."

"Why us?" I asked, separating the papers to give Sassy her copy. The way she snatched them, her smile widening until I worried she'd overload from anticipation, promised no matter what the documents said, I'd be signing up for a new career by the end of the week.

All of my misgivings crumbled under the force of her hopes, and I found while bitter, the pill went down easier than expected.

Some cases I'd lose. Some I'd win. Some, like the murders leading to an attempt on my life, would inevitably leave scars only time could heal. I respected Maxwell for attempting to undo the harm he'd done before joining the police force. His path, something I'd shied away from, was littered with challenges I feared.

Every choice in life came at a price, and I wondered if Sassy and I would emerge changed people.

Even without the lycanthropy virus, seeing the cooling bodies of a mother and child ate away at me, breaking apart my hesitancies until the only place I could bring

about the change I wanted was in the very
place I'd never believed I'd go. The papers
would set my course, but beyond too little
pay for the risks involved, I couldn't see myself saying no.

I'd already paid too much to lose the opportunity to make a real difference.

Chief Braneni stared at me, his expression
a carefully constructed mask of neutrality.
"For all you've been a thorn in our sides for
years, you're both respected. We're all aware
of what you've done at a personal cost to
yourself. It's hard to find fault with your
ethics, and that's what our force needs: men
and women with ethics. You have that. Lycanthropes will be joining the force, but if I
can have you two as the spearhead of the recruitment drive, I believe those who come
behind you will have less to prove and an
easier time of it. Not everyone will love you
or the virus you carry, but you two are the
only names I hear time and time again who
meet the standards we need. If you two work
well, you're paving the way for others. And
make no mistake. Dallas is a hotbed of lycanthropy, and it won't be much longer until the
minority becomes the majority. There are ten
wolf packs, I've lost count of the damned felines, and more move in every day. We need
lycanthropes on the force, and while Dallas is
a hot bed, there ain't a single damned hybrid

in the city, and nobody knows why. They like the east coast, or are northern bred. A few stragglers who like surfing in California. Elsewhere? The CDC's not telling me. I guess they don't want to lose their aces up their sleeves. I could use a few hybrids for major incidents."

I chuckled at the displeasure in the chief's tone. "Too bad you can't figure out what makes a hybrid. Then you could coax the virus into doing what you want."

"We're not science experiments, Aaron," Sassy growled.

"But Sassy, haven't you wanted to be a hybrid?"

"No."

"Why not?"

"I don't ruin my clothes when I shift un-less I'm in a hurry and claw them to shreds. If I had the hybrid form, my clothing budget would be ridiculous. Right now, as long as I'm careful, I don't wreck my outfits when I shift in a hurry."

Heaven forbid Sassy ruin her clothes shifting. Unable to help it, I smiled. "That's fair enough."

"Clothing is serious business, Mr. Clinton."

Well aware of her shoe bill, I wouldn't argue with her over it. "Yes, ma'am."

"See, Chief Braneni? He can be taught. Be

glad you don't have hybrids. Keeping them clothed in uniforms would cost you a fortune."

"That is not something I'd considered," the chief admitted.

"Why would you? To understand what it's like to be a lycanthrope, you'd have to walk in our shoes a while—or at least keep us company for more than a few minutes at a time. If you really want to see what it's like to be a lycanthrope, go to a weekend barbecue. By the time you're done, you'll have a much better idea of everything involved, the precautions lycanthropes take around the uninfected, and a much broader worldview than you currently have. Talk to Dad. I'm sure he wouldn't mind planning one for you."

"Yes, I would," Sassy's father muttered from the other table.

"Penance, asshole!" Sassy howled. "Pay it."

I rolled my eyes at Sassy's antics. "It's probably a good idea for the force to know exactly what they're getting into with the lycanthrope population. But you can be assured of one thing: it'll be the most well-behaved party of lycanthropes on Earth with that many cops loitering around."

"Ain't that the truth," Chief Braneni said. "If you'll plan it, Mr. Chetty, I'll recruit as many officers as I can for it. Pot luck?"

"That's how we roll on the weekend parties, yes. Aaron, your contribution is hauling duty in your truck."

"I'm in," I announced.

"Of course you are." Sassy jabbed me in the ribs with her elbow. "Behave. You can't even drive your truck until Joe clears you."

"If I tell your brother I love him, will he let me drive sooner?"

"No."

"That's entirely unfair."

"Deal with it," Sassy replied. "In the meantime, I'll enjoy driving your big, manly truck around."

"You're cruel, evil woman."

Sassy smirked.

ELEVEN

Tricky cat.

THE NEXT TIME someone warned me about the volatile nature of a cheetah female preparing to stake her claim, I'd listen. I'd also remember Sassy's brothers adored her and would do anything to make her happy, including scheme on a way to ensure she got exactly what she wanted. When I thought it through, I realized someone in Sassy's family would've gone out of their way to ensure I picked up the virus from somewhere.

Her father lacked her brothers' patience.

Joe topped my list of general accomplices. I'd stopped paying attention to the pills he gave me to make my life a little easier until the virus finished having its way with me, and I fully healed from the crash. As promised, he fixed my fingers. He'd even warned me I'd be down and out for the count.

Waking up in my new truck hadn't been part of any plan.

"What happened to staying at your dad's place?" I groaned, fighting off the clinging influence of Joe's damned drugs so I could sit up straight.

"We did until two in the morning, and after Mom and Dad were out for the night, Joe and Charlie dragged you to the truck. I bribed a few friends to tail us until we reach our destination, after which they'll be prowling around to make sure we're not disturbed."

Tricky cat. "What time is it?"

"Three in the morning."

"What friends?"

"Two wolf packs. They're invested; if we join the force, they get a chance, too. I got two other packs working on the serial killer case, too. We're hoping if we can team everyone up and get some good investigative work done, we can present a stronger case for getting a larger crew of lycanthropes in the initial test batch."

"Just how many wolves are we talking about here?"

"Thirty in the two packs prowling the woods tonight, another forty-seven in the investigative crew. Maxwell's been the primary contact for the wolves. They want to pitch the wolves being trained like police dogs to fit that role with lycanthrope crews; it'd solve the problems Chief Braneni mentioned, and if all lycanthropes can learn the ropes, we can supplement the mundane dogs. It won't eliminate the need for the regular dogs, but it'll help—and give lycanthropes extra places to work on the force. With our numbers, every pair could have a lycanthrope added to their team."

I rolled my shoulders and winced as my back notified me it hadn't enjoyed sleeping in my new truck. "This is going to put a damper on investigating."

"I brought the work with us. I'm sure we'll have some time. I also distributed all the information to the wolves. They're invading the libraries tomorrow to get photos of all the newspapers from the entire range. They're also getting photographs of every newspaper between your parents' anniversary and your birthday, as well as the month after to ensure we don't miss anything."

"Thorough."

"I figured you'd get pissy if your work was screwed. They're motivated. I expect we'll have every page of every newspaper released for at least seven years by the end of the day. That's a lot of wolves with a lot of cameras, and they're going to upload the pictures to our server."

"Where are we going?"

"Somewhere nice and remote. If the killer

even sniffs at you, they'll be picking him out of wolf teeth for weeks."

Gross. While I thought the bastard deserved a brutal end, it wouldn't end well for the hopeful lycanthropes. "You did impress upon them the fucker needs to live to see trial, right?"

"They've been informed of the only cases where lethal force is permitted. They're wolves. They'll toe the line just right. I gave them the speech, Maxwell gave them the speech, and since Rob doesn't really trust any of us, he gave them the speech, too. Once they were done giving them the speech, Mark blasted in with a fuck it, leave him scattered throughout the state of Texas speech, as he's really miffed he almost lost you. If Mark gets a hold of this guy, he won't last long. He's carrying that damned rifle around with him and is itching to use it."

"Why did anyone think it was a good idea to give my brother a carry permit for that gun?"

"Rob asked the same question."

"Any progress while I was sleeping?"

"Rob and Maxwell jumped on the newspaper lead like flies on shit. Rob and Chief Braneni are hunting for a judge to sign the warrant for the paternity tests on the kids as part of the investigation, and Rob thinks he can wrangle just cause using his ragtag band of attorneys. I give it a fifty-fifty."

"Why is Rob involved so early? We don't even have a suspect."

"It's personal."

Shit, shit, shit. "The DA has a direct connection to this case?"

"Yeah. I found the link the other day, but I decided I'd keep my mouth shut about it."

"Open your mouth."

Sassy sighed. "One of the victims is a childhood friend, and they were rather... close."

"Any chance the kid was his?"

"Yeah. The one that wasn't matched with a newspaper scrap and didn't fit with the others is his as far as I can tell. Rob's going to sink if the paternity test goes through. Maybe he'll try for an exemption."

Fuck. I ran my hand through my hair and wondered what to do. "No birth certificate?"

"Last I checked, Rob was in process of having the birth certificate altered so his name was added. He might wait a while, but I saw the papers when I was snooping around in his office. He's already put in for a paternity test."

Poor, poor Rob. "Was he paying child support?"

"Are you asking me if I, little old me, would snoop in the DA's financials?"

"Obviously."

"He was making some large payments to the victim on a monthly basis unofficially, and everything I've found points at them having a cordial relationship. The sexual part of their relationship ended about a year ago. Rob's looking to settle down, and I don't think she wanted to commit. That's all I could find out under short notice."

"He's going to kill you if he finds out."

"It's his fault for leaving me alone in his office for ten whole minutes without asking me to relinquish my lock picks. It took me less than a minute to bust into his drawers and snoop around. He also needs to not leave his bank statements buried under his work papers. I got all that in less than five minutes, although I had to do some foot work on his kid. He'll turn the world upside down to find out who killed his kid and why, Aaron."

In his shoes, I would, too. "All right. It's personal for the DA. Anything else I should know?"

"That's the worst of it. So, we have an invested DA, and the police are itching to catch this bastard. The DA's going to be a problem; he's going to be blinded by his need for justice for his kid, and unless someone reveals he's directly involved, he's going to be in the way."

"No, he won't be in the way. Rob's a lot of

things, but if he didn't want the correct justice, he wouldn't have approached us, Sassy. He knows I'm going to find the real killer and not just get some false satisfaction. If he wanted just anyone caught, he wouldn't have worked with Maxwell to hire us. He wants the real killer. And I don't mean the bastard who pulled the trigger. He wants the one behind it. I mean, he wants the fucker who pulled the trigger, too. But that's not the one who really killed his kid."

"And we tossed our attorneys for justice. He knows that."

I hoped Sassy remembered to bring my medications with her before carting me off on her evening adventure. I'd need them by the time we finished the conversation. "Exactly. Does he know you know?"

"I could see him leaving things out so I could find it and put the pieces together, but I haven't approached him about it."

"Don't. We'll work this quietly. As long as he doesn't screw with the investigation, he can hunt justice for his kid as much as he wants. We'll need to look into the legalities."

"He can't try the case according to the rules, but he's going to get one of his hotshots to do it for him. He'll be subpoenaed to witness, I'm sure."

My chest ached for the man. "That explains his comment about me being an uncle."

"His relationship with her wasn't casual, Aaron. I think he wanted her to be his wife, but she just wasn't interested in him like that."

Everyday tragedies were the worst kind. Some men stooped to violence in their frustration. Others withstood the storm and wondered about what might have been.

"Are we sure the DA isn't involved, Sassy?"

"He's not," Sassy whispered.

"How do you know?"

"He's got a picture of his boy on his desk among those killed, and it's far more worn. Until this week, I didn't know he could even cry. No, Aaron. I don't think he did it. I think he wanted the child in his life more than either of us can know. I walked into his office the other day and met a broken, tired man."

"No stone unturned," I whispered.

"Either way, we won't like what we find," she warned.

"That's the price we pay for justice."

SASSY PARKED my truck in front of a planation home nestled in a valley skirted with trees. Killing the engine, she stretched and smiled at the building and its immaculate yard, bathed in the golden glow of lamplights lining the driveway. "One of the pack alphas owns this, and he's letting me borrow it for a few days. He says it's sturdy enough to withstand romping wolves, so he thinks it should survive a pair of felines. It's stocked, so if you have your first shift while we're here, I'll be able to feed you."

After gorging on more barbecue than I imagined possible at dinner, it astonished me she thought I'd be ready to eat again. Ever. "Nice of him."

"I stole handcuffs from Maxwell. I will use them if you attempt to escape."

Yep. Sassy was a chip off her mother's block when motivated. "So, this is a hostage situation?"

"Yep."

"How long am I being held hostage for?"

"However long is necessary. Mom locked Dad in her basement for a month before he surrendered. I've been told I have as long as needed. The alpha I borrowed this from is aware you may be stubborn."

Cheetahs. I swallowed my urge to laugh, unbuckled, and eased out of my new truck. As I hated the idea of lying to her, especially after everything that had happened, I saw one realistic choice I could make: I would tell her the truth and nothing but the truth.

"I punched your father because he'd jumped the gun and infected me before I asked him to arrange for some sort of accident so you wouldn't have to break your word about dating a lycanthrope. I suspect your brothers are mad they were robbed of a chance to involve me in some horrific and bloody accident of their making," I confessed. "We were on the way to the lumber yard to buy supplies so I could play with power tools to ensure such an accident occurred. I would've preferred to have skipped the crash, but the results were already on my schedule."

Sassy gaped at me. "You were *what?*"

"Stealthily making arrangements to become infected so you wouldn't have to break your word about dating non-lycanthropes."

"You're serious."

"I'll understand if you get upset and don't want to talk to me for a while. I'll also understand if you opt to lock me in a basement until you feel I've paid penance for my crimes. Does confessing get me off with a misdemeanor?"

"You were *planning* on contracting lycanthropy?"

"Sassy, I bought you really expensive shoes and a purse hoping you'd forgive me, and after I bought the shoes, I willingly went to your father's house. What happened the last time I went to your father's house?"

"He punched you in the mouth and broke your teeth."

"And masked the fact he'd bled on me to

optimize my chances of contracting lycanthropy. That old ass planned it from the start. And I'd been wondering why he hadn't wanted to kick my ass the instant I knocked on his door."

"Because he knew he'd likely infected you, and he'd toed the line doing it so your virus would be slow to mature."

"That's what Joe thinks. And the infection was so slow we didn't notice any changes in my personality, but when Joe checked, *he* could tell."

"Because Joe knows what it's like to be a lycanthrope and could identify the symptoms. Him looking that far through your memories would give him a good idea of probability of infection."

I nodded. "So, that's where we're at."

"You tricky bastard."

"Remember Jolie?" The mention of my last ex would likely infuriate Sassy, but I needed to make it clear what I had in mind for the foreseeable future.

"The cheating bitch who dyed her hair every time she cheated on you?"

"Yeah, her."

"I put dog shit in her shoes after you broke up with her."

Well, that explained a lot. No wonder Jolie had been extra mad at me. "I think she blamed me for that."

"Technically, it was your fault. You were a participant in that train wreck of a relationship."

"I gave up on women entirely at that point. Then your dad socked me in the mouth."

"And?"

"If you want me to be stubborn, you're going to have to tell me. Otherwise, I'll probably just do whatever you want without argument or complaint."

"But Mom had to lock Dad in her basement for a month."

"Your father was also a coalition cheetah. I'm not."

"What are you?"

"Your cheetah-to-be, obviously." I pointed at myself. "I'm also proof cheetahs *can* win, thank you very much. I've won this war. I'm just waiting for you to figure that out. Don't worry, though. I can be patient."

Her eyes narrowed. "You're rather relaxed about this. I brought you to a remote location to be held hostage."

"It's not a kidnapping or a hostage situation if your victim is a willing participant. It's a vacation. And after the past few weeks we've had, I think we've earned it. If you want me to put up a fight, I'm happy to do so. If you want me to chase you so you can put up a fight, well, I've heard a few too many lectures about how I shouldn't try to be a gentleman with you. That's the real question here. How do you want it?"

It could mean a lot of things, and her eyes narrowed to slits while she thought about it. The soft rumble of her purring promised my favorite sort of trouble in the near future. Relaxing, I leaned against my truck and watched her over the hood.

"What makes you mine faster?"

"I figured I was yours around the same time I started bailing you out from bad dates and arranging my schedule for rescue efforts on a daily basis. You have no idea how much those cheetahs pissed me off, Sassy. Some days, I wanted to go pick a fight with them for upsetting you like they did. How many pairs of shoes should I budget for? I'm not sure if our new salary will give me a lot of shoe shopping room."

"We get a nice bonus package and hazard pay because we will have to deal with a lot of pissy lycanthropes. I figure one moderate pair of shoes a week would fit within the budget."

"Whose budget?"

"Ours."

"Power tools?"

"I'm sure we can fit tools in the budget, and I'm sure you can con some poor suckers into paying you for hauling shit for them and helping them with their construction projects. Charge them in new tools." Sassy laughed, shut the door, and sashayed towards the house. "What do you think I'll like best, Mr. Clinton?"

"A little bit of this, a little bit of that." I peeked into the cab, spotted several bags waiting, and grabbed them before following after my feisty little cheetah. "I'm sure I can think of something."

"Think faster," Sassy growled.

I'd enjoy finding out how hard I could yank Sassy's tail before she snapped and took what she wanted. Some challenges couldn't be refused.

TWELVE

I needed to thank Joe for his
warnings.

SOMEONE NEEDED to hang a warning sign
around Sassy's neck so unwitting men, me
specifically, knew better than to taunt and
provoke her into ditching her restraints. Despite having been warned by her brothers,
her father, and even her mother in various
ways, I'd underestimated her. I'd underestimated her so much I emerged from her claim
battered, bruised, and exhausted. Most of the
battering and bruising I bore full responsibility for; I'd forgotten to account for how
fierce my little cheetah could be. Doubting
her determination accounted for at least half
of my bruises, too.

I needed to thank Joe for his warnings
cheetah females got rough during a claim as it
likely resulted in my survival of her plans.

Sassy handled her enthusiasm far better
than I did; she bounced out of bed like she

hadn't taken me for a twelve hour marathon I'd never forget. Skipping to the adjacent bedroom added insult to injury. I doubted I could crawl across the hardwood floor to make it to the tub. A soak sounded good. A soak might help me survive through the next few days.

"Mercy?" I begged. "Please? Sassy, come on. You're going to kill me."

"Daddy said I wasn't doing it right unless I made you beg. Mom agreed. I got the talk several times."

Her father's days were numbered, and I'd enjoy beating a matching set of bruises into him. "Your father's a jackass. I'm not saying anything about your mother as she'd win the fight if I started one, so we'll just say she's right."

She leaned out of the bathroom, a toothbrush shoved into her mouth. "What? You liked it."

While true, the bruises would remind me I needed to learn how to moderate even good things. "I match my truck."

"That's nothing new. I have a blood pressure kit in our bags, and one of the wolves works with Joe. Grover. You met him a while back. Short, quiet guy with a temper. If you need a transfusion because I got too rough for you, we're set. Honestly, that was a part of my plan. I just didn't plan on you being so enthusiastic."

She was calling *me* enthusiastic? Crazy cat. "How could I not be enthusiastic? You brought six pairs of shoes. Six pairs. And you kept showing them off. I'm just a man, Sassy. You can't do that to a man and expect anything other than what you got."

Her smile informed me she'd been planning on my reactions. Smirk firmly in place, she vanished into the bathroom to brush her teeth.

Damned. Cat.

"You're such a feline, Sastria."

"Oh, now that's hot. I got you to use my real name in that flustered tone. Do it again."

"I don't know if I have any places left for you to bruise."

"Do you need me to be gentle and kiss it all better?"

What sort of question was that? "Yes, obviously."

She laughed. "I've been told I have to feed you or you'll be useless to me. Go take a shower, hostage. Make yourself presentable while you're at it. I'll give Grover a call and have him check on you. Joe promised if I claimed you thoroughly enough, I get to give you a transfusion, which will secure my claim better."

"Why aren't you bruised? Anywhere. Not a bruise. Anywhere. I checked when you strutted to the bathroom."

"Post-shift lycanthrope, Aaron. It's a major advantage. Sure, I'm incurably diseased, but I heal bruises as fast as you give them to me. You'll have to try harder than that if you want to leave a mark."

Damn. "Well, I guess I don't have to worry about getting too rough with you."

"That is a fringe benefit of lycanthropy."

"Anything else I should know?"

"Daddy suggested I give you a break once I tired you out enough you started to whine. He also said I needed to be gentle." She emerged from the bathroom wearing a silky pair of pajamas. "There's pajamas in the bathroom for you. You clean up and get mobile while I get Grover over to make sure you won't drop dead on me. After, we'll get some work done."

Did the woman forget about the existence of sleep? How the hell did she expect me to work after so long spent in bed? If my sore muscles were any indication, I'd pass out the instant I sat somewhere comfortable.

"Shouldn't you have been worried about that earlier?" I eyed the floor, sighed, and eased out of bed. I ached, but I managed the short walk without falling on my face. "We need to have a talk about what it means to be gentle."

"You liked it. That's good enough for me."

"You're so damned sassy."

"Well, there *is* a reason you call me Sassy, and it's not because my first name is Sastria. You only have yourself to blame for how this worked out. If you hadn't been so irresistible, you'd probably be uninfected and bored and lamenting over how other women use you and leave you for other men. Idiots, those women."

"You're good for my ego," I acknowledged, flashing a tired smile at her. "Do that some more."

"You're so tired. Food first, then Grover, then you can take a nap. It's no good if you fall asleep on me."

Somehow, I'd unleashed a devil of a woman on a sexy mission. "I'm just going to agree with you on this one."

"Smart move. Move it, Aaron. We don't have all day."

I checked the clock on the nightstand. "Sassy."

"What?"

"It's six. In the evening. There's basically no day left."

"Huh. Fancy that." Sassy placed her hands on her hips. "Shower and dress, Aaron! What's left of today is wasting. I'm going to wrangle some wolves and make sure Grover's ready to do his doctor business so he goes away and leaves us alone."

"You have no idea how long it takes to do a transfusion, do you?"

Sassy frowned. "Well, no."

"Get our paperwork for investigations and be prepared to sit still for two to three hours while the wolf monitors us both. Also, the line hurts like hell inserting and it doesn't get much better throughout the transfusion."

"You're serious?"

"Very. And he'll have to check your virus levels. If you're spiking, it's fine, but if your virus levels have dropped, he won't let you donate. I'll just have to suffer until there's a compatible donor with the right virus."

"I have to sit still for up to three hours?"

"Yep. It's no fun. I've done this too many times for my liking now. It's not all bad. We can get work done while Grover monitors us. Then we'll be expected to eat as much as we can stomach and rest until your virus does its job."

"This is not how I envisioned my evening going." Sassy pouted. "All right. I can handle some work and be patient."

"We have to sleep, too. The restful kind."

Her shoulders slumped. "That's not fair."

I smiled. "It's not like I'm going anywhere."

"I'm holding you to that, Mr. Clinton."

I ENJOYED two hours of peace and quiet during the transfusion. Within five minutes of Grover setting up the line, Sassy passed out. Grover chuckled, shook his head, and assured me there was nothing to worry about.

Having slept through a few transfusions, I didn't blame her at all. While she slept, I read through newspapers in search of more pieces of the puzzle. Sassy's speculations were almost correct regarding Tom Heatherow's presence in the newspaper on my birthday. Instead of the shining recommendations I expected, I found a rape accusation of a classmate. Like with Renata Kirkville, the picture the newspaper featured included him together with the victim. The article claimed the case had been dropped due to insufficient evidence. The woman, one Felicity Jasper, showed up again in an article several years later, the victim of a hit and run. A quick search of the internet revealed no one had ever found the vehicle responsible, or its driver.

"If you're going to get pissy over your work, keep your heart rate somewhat tolerable. Don't screw up my transfusion being moody."

I snorted but put aside my tablet so I wouldn't be tempted to chuck the thing across the living room. "Riddle me this, Grover."

"I hate riddles. They give me a headache."

"Yeah, this one is going to give me a migraine, too."

"All right. Hit me with it."

"What kind of killer leaves a bunch of clues incriminating someone with old newspaper articles?"

"The kind that doesn't like the job he's paid to do and wants to see his hire sink."

The immediate answer startled me, and I frowned, glaring at the tablet. "That's not stopping this fucker from killing a bunch of kids."

"You're right. It's not. Depending on where the killer was hired, mercenaries have a code, and it's punishable by death if they violate it. If the guy was paid to kill fifty people, he's going to kill them or die trying. If he's hired to make sure someone is out of the way for a set period of time, he'll do it. We see it sometimes in military ops, and they're the worst sort. Do or die for them. And they may not know who they're killing before it's time to start the assassinations. If the hire's smart, he wouldn't list the kids until after payment was made. At that point, the code kicks in and they'll do it—or die. This guy might be ethical enough to try to sink his hire in a creative fashion. Or he was hired to make it flashy. Or he was hired to cover his tracks. How hard was it to find these clues?"

"Well, I had to count nine months ahead of the dates on the evidence. That's all, really. Then read the newspapers."

"So, it was a message within a message."

"Right."

"Have you fully evaluated the newspapers on the date reflected in the evidence?"

"I haven't found anything in them. That's why I tried my birthdate; I was born right on due date."

"So, you're the control."

"I wasn't the first targeted, Grover."

"No, but you're probably his lynchpin hit. He was probably ordered to get you out of the way for a while, so instead of killing you outright, he does as ordered: gets rid of you for a while in a flashy way. That accident was flashy, Aaron. He carpeted the highway with scraps. He wanted everyone to know you were in the way. They know, for certain, your birthdate. You're the right number of days, forty weeks on the nose. If you use forty weeks as the metric, I bet you're going to find a lot of interesting articles to read. Guys like this are methodical. They have a strong ethic, and when you piss one off during a contract, they'll find any loophole possible to get back at their hire."

"You've seen this before in the military?"

"Yeah. We had a guy sniping medics when I was overseas. That struck a nerve with the

guy, who ultimately started writing letters on
the corpses with bullets. By the end of his hit
list, we had the coords for their camp. We
wiped the bastards out; the mercenary got
away, but we got the hire and his band of terrorists hoping to wipe us off the map."

"That's a gruesome method of making a
loophole."

"Doesn't bring back our guys, but we got
our payback at the end of it. This reminds me
of that op. And if he's half as good as the guy
who nailed our medics, you aren't going to
prevent any of the killings, but you'll have a
yellow brick road leading you straight to the
hire. It doesn't stop him, but at least you'll get
the main player."

"So you don't think the clues could lead us
to other victims?"

"He's probably done. These guys move fast
once they move. In and out, killing off as
many of their targets as quickly as possible.
When was the last shooting?"

I reached for my phone, unlocked it, and
checked my mail for updates on the shootings. "Two days ago."

"And before? How many"

"Multiple shootings a day."

"Hitting every opportunity he can after
learning their habits."

"There was someone stalking single
women," I muttered.

Grover frowned. "Do you got a list of people being watched?"

"Yeah, we've got a list, but none of them were killed that I know of."

"Red herring or a coincidence, maybe."

"Maybe." I had my doubts, and I opened the list of women who'd reported someone following them, browsing through their names. I didn't recognize any of them. "But how would he find a newspaper for every single victim?"

"A lot of research, which is another mark it's a serious professional. I know you're going to hate hearing this, but your job is to find the hire. You're not going to find this guy unless he wants to be found. Frankly, he seems like the type who doesn't make mistakes."

"And he's using magic to cover his tracks," I muttered.

"Yeah. We heard about the truck. Smart move on your part having Joe go over it; he's the best I've seen for seeing through shit like that. There aren't a lot of memory hoppers around, but he practiced until he can get anything he wants out of someone, and he's got the balls to dig through years. Don't underestimate Joe. If he gets a hold of anyone responsible, he'll hop back as far as he needs to get the intel, and he won't care if he leaves a body when he's done."

Having experienced Joe's work, I grimaced. "That would not be a pleasant way to go."

"How far back did he go with you?"

"A few months."

Grover winced. "Beyond the crash?"

"Yeah."

"You're one tough son of a bitch."

"I think the lycanthropy virus helped."

Grover nodded. "I don't even need to do a test to tell you're spiking to hell. You flashed your teeth at me when you spotted me. That's pure feline disapproval. I'm surprised you didn't hiss. You kitties get almost as territorial as us wolves. Actually, the breeding males are worse than we are. With one lady per fifty or sixty males, it's no wonder."

"I think there are fewer than that. Sassy has a lot of brothers."

"Yeah. And they're all annoying bastards. Most breeding couples never manage to get a girl. That Sassy wanted you without the virus helping out is pretty remarkable."

"Long term exposure and I tried not to be an ass to her."

"That would definitely help your cause."

While I wanted to smack Sassy's father around a few more times, I shrugged. "Infection became ideal for me, so I have no complaints with how this turned out, I just wish the crash hadn't happened."

"Yeah. Your body has been put through the wringer. Joe's done a lot of work on you."

"You can tell?"

"It leaves a mark. We're trained to detect when someone's undergone a lot of intensive care. I've seen Joe's work enough to recognize it. Just how long was he working with you when you landed in his hands?"

"I guess five or six hours the night I was released from the hospital?"

Grover's brows rose. "Really."

"Yeah. He had a transfusion line hooked up for most of it, too. He'd gotten CDC clearance for Sassy's father to donate."

"For five or six hours?"

"Yes."

"Why the hell were you out of the hospital? That's critical level care, Aaron."

"So Joe said. He's looking into a malpractice suit."

"Have fun with that. I'm going to run the line for another twenty minutes, and then we'll wake your mate and see how she's feeling. Frankly, I'm impressed you're not passed out right along with her. She kept you busy all night and then some."

"He was a lot of frustration for one woman to enjoy," Sassy muttered.

"It seems we've been busted," Grover announced.

I reached over with my left hand and

flicked Sassy's hair out of her face. "How're you feeling, Sassy?"

"Are we at the eat-the-horses stage of our night yet?"

"We're not eating any horses. Horses are for riding." I rolled my eyes. "You're going to have to accept whatever is in the fridge."

"The grill's ready for you to fire up, and there're enough steaks and chicken in the fridge to satisfy you both. Just make sure you take out enough from the freezer to replace it so you don't starve tomorrow. How much of our conversation did you catch?"

"You woke me up talking about the medics being shot."

"Well, that's the important bit, so good. This guy's accuracy is top-notch, though. It really would not surprise me if it's the same outfit—or the same sniper—that was killing off our medics."

"How much would one of those mercenaries cost?"

"I'd ballpark it at around a hundred thousand a kill and fifty thousand for removals. You'd be classified as a removal."

"That seems backwards to me. The shootings were far easier to pull off, weren't they?"

"Yes and no. Guys like this charge less for the removals because they don't necessarily want to leave bodies. Yeah, there was a fatality in your crash, and it's entirely possible you could've died if Chetty hadn't bailed your ass out, but the more I think about it, the more I think it's a high-grade outfit."

"So, you think it's more than one killer?"

"And they're working together to make it look like one person's doing the work. The timing would have to be impeccable, but that's how those outfits work. They're mercenaries, and you may as well call them terrorists for hire. They'll work for anybody, but you offend them, and well, shit's going to hit the fan and it'll backfire."

"They targeted me for investigating. Do you think they'll do the same for others?"

"Inevitably."

Maxwell came to mind with Rob as a close second. "Shit. Will they target cops?"

"If they're paid to, yes. They'll target anyone, even kids. They won't care about the cops like they will the kids, but it is what it is. Ethics and morality are ignored if the price is right." Grover sighed and shook his head. "And if they decide to target a cop, it's going to be like the rest of the murders. In and out, confetti raining down, and another clue to point you in the direction of a cop-killer. We've already come to that conclusion, and frankly, I've already put in some calls."

"Including warning Maxwell?"

"He's the first I suggested Joe and Mark warn."

"How about Mark?"

"They'd be idiots to target Mark. If they hit him, they'll have the entirety of the United States military out for their blood. He's high enough rank they will not let it go. He's safe enough; those outfits would charge in the millions for a hit like his. Medics and support staff are cheaper."

I hated the casual, no-nonsense way Grover discussed the price of life. "How much cheaper?"

"We figure the hundred and fifty thousand mark a head, from the money trail we were able to identify."

"Isn't that classified information?"

"You're classified to hear it. Do you think I'm here by mistake, that Joe's here by mistake, and that Mark's still around for no reason? No, the military is hot on this case because it has the same markers of the outfit that's targeted us. You're just a very good excuse for us to be here."

"You and Joe were deployed, weren't you?"

"Right up until an hour after we got the call you'd been targeted."

Sassy growled. "Your brother lied to you."

"I wouldn't call it lying. I'd call it a clever redistribution of the truth, Sassy. If his job is to make it look like he's here for me and not this potential outfit, he made the right call." I chuckled. "Think about it this way. He handled the payments for the truck, right?"

"Well, yeah. He bought the whole thing. I have your insurance payout, and he wouldn't let me pay him back. Won't give me his banking details."

"That's how Mark apologizes for shit, Sassy. He buys stuff because he's a terrible human being." I laughed. "A really terrible one."

Grover's expression turned sheepish. "I feel like I should argue with you on his behalf, but you're not far off from the truth. When he's provoked, he's the kind of guy who makes heads roll, and to hell with the consequences. There's no better guy you want at your back, but he doesn't play fair, he never has, and he never will. But when it comes to kids and civvies? There's some lines he won't cross, and that's that. Mark'll fuck around with you because you're his family, but he's going to fuck up anyone who fucks with his family. He's half-cocked and ready to rumble, and the instant he has a target, well, may God have mercy on their soul because he won't. Your brother's one scary son of a bitch when he needs to be."

"Well, he's been terrorizing me for as long as I can remember."

Grover snorted. "That's what older brothers are supposed to do. But he's the only one allowed to terrorize you, and that's that. And how much you love your truck is legendary. We've all heard about you and your fetish for your trucks. Hell, I'm surprised you found a woman capable of holding your attention for more than a few minutes at a time."

Sassy cocked a brow. "What do you have to say about that, Mr. Clinton?"

"I like your shoes more than my truck, but I only like your shoes when you're wearing them, and if you happen to scratch my paint or leave a dent sitting on my truck while wearing your shoes, I doubt I'll even notice."

"And that would be my cue to check your virus levels, Aaron, as that was ridiculous even by your standards," Grover announced.

Sassy grinned. "What can I say? I'm convincing when I want to be, and I did a lot of convincing last night."

"Try not to seduce him again quite yet, Sassy. I need to check his virus levels, I need to check your virus levels, and I need to get as far out of the area as possible before you start up again. Please."

"Wussy wolf," Sassy muttered. "Run your scanner and make yourself happy. And I promise to feed him. I do not promise anything other than that."

"He needs to sleep, Sassy. However much he'd love to cater to your every desire, he'll be useless to you. I'd also rather he not fall over dead. Mark would not take it well if his little brother died during your claim. He's the only breeding male of your species in the city, Sassy. Don't break him."

"Fucking cheetahs!" Sassy howled.

I laughed and shrugged. "Not going to hear me complain. I get the girl. The other guys can keep each other company."

Grover glared at me. "You're not helping."

"No, no, I like my current situation. I got the girl. And I socked the girl's father in the mouth, too. That's going to be a highlight of my life."

"You really punched Chetty in the mouth? Joe mentioned it, but I didn't believe it. After he busted your face up a few years back, your unwillingness to keep him company became legendary. Frankly, we're still shocked he was in your truck with you."

"Honestly, I'm grateful he was. I'd be in a casket right now otherwise. I was supposed to thank him, but I punched him instead."

"I'm sure Daddy got the message." Sassy giggled. "I didn't think you had it in you, but sure enough, you whacked my daddy like you meant it."

"I really, really meant it. It was a manly way of saying thank you. Do try to convince him of that before he kills me?"

"I don't think he went through that much

work and effort to kill you, but I'll make sure he knows you were creatively thanking him. Your virus was obviously confused and needed to establish you have territory. I'm your territory."

I wasn't going to argue with her. "How long have I been your territory, anyway?"

"No comment."

"How many of those dates did you go on just trying to get my attention and drive me crazy?"

"More than one."

"How many more than one?"

"How many dates have I been on for the past, say, three years?"

"Too many."

Sassy grinned, and she refused to look me in the eyes. "That's how many dates."

"You are such a cat."

"I'll have you know, your reactions to it were equally catty, thank you very much. You got hissy every damned time. And on the bad days, you'd put up with my shit. Obviously, I had to mark my territory."

I remembered the night she'd tried to lick the skin off my face along with her snack of chocolate syrup. "With your tongue."

"Oh, that. No, you were just delicious."

"You mean the chocolate was delicious."

"No, I'm pretty sure I just said you were

delicious." Sassy smirked. "I look forward to enjoying my living delicacy more later."

"Much later, please. Much, much later, after I leave," Grover muttered. "Now, you two please stop flirting long enough for me to run these scans."

I held out my left hand for him, and he stabbed me with a needle. The scanner squealed an alarm, and I scowled at the shrill sound. "According to that sound, I'm about to fall over dead."

"That's the 'holy fucking shit, shift already' alarm. Judging from her behavior, Sassy's spiking, your virus is trying to assimilate her virus while attuning to it at the same time, your virus is doing a great job of it, and it's working overtime to fix this suspicious bruising you've developed."

Sassy turned her head, but I caught her smiling.

"I fell down the steps, obviously."

"And just how many times did you fall down the steps?" Grover snickered, put the scanner away, and began his work to remove the transfusion lines. "Feed him and let him get sleep, Sassy. I know he's tempting, but you need to give his virus a chance to settle. If you don't want to give his virus a chance to settle, start startling him until he shifts. With these virus levels, it could happen at any time. I'd rather it happen here. And after he shifts, keep him as a cat for at least twelve hours. That'll make sure his virus levels stabilize. Actually, if he shifts, take him to your father's house, let him loose, and let him work out his nerves with your brothers. They can handle a breeding male needing to learn how to socialize with other cheetahs. Once he shifts back, he's going to be sicker than hell. Call your brother in for directions. He's got a better handle on the early onset symptoms than I do."

"How sick?" Sassy demanded.

"Sick enough you're going to panic. I'd tell you to not panic, but it won't do any good. You're going to panic until he's healthy. If you want him healthy, keep your hands out of his pants for the rest of the night, let him get some rest, and don't make him run a marathon. You've claimed him. He's yours. He has no competition, either. So, you need to cool your heels. Seduce him after he's had a chance to recover."

Sassy scowled. "Fine."

"Go feed him. And I'm serious, Sassy. He's yours. Save your displays of tender loving care for after he's had his first shift. Once he's shifted for the first time and his virus has recovered, he'll be able to handle anything you toss at him. Until then, try to be gentle. You don't want to tax his virus before he's had a chance to shift."

"I'll behave," she promised. "I won't like it, but I'll behave."

"Of course you won't like it. You're staking your claim. Consider it staked. If you need any evidence of your stake, consider this: I'm an unmated male and he only gave me a hint of a glare before he figured out I wasn't a threat. If he can deal with me in the room without being a threat to you, you don't have to worry. Anyway, there's no female cheetahs to steal him from you. Remember that, and you'll be just fine."

Sassy blinked, and I got the feeling she'd forgotten how rare cheetah females were. "Oh."

"I swear. The instant a pair mates, their common sense wanders off for at least a week. Relax, Sassy. Aaron, just reassure her you're not going anywhere. That'll help."

There was only one way I could think of to convince her I'd be sticking around. "If you want a fancy wedding ceremony, you're going to have to do the planning, but I hear court houses work pretty well for securing legal claim on your partner."

Sassy's brows shot up. "Well, that was blunt."

"No one told me romantic was required! He said to reassure you I'm not going any-where. That's the only thing I could think of."

"Just give it to him, Sassy. You obviously

rattled his brain in his head. I'm going to leave now. Feed him first if you can't keep your hands off him," Grover ordered.

"I will ensure he's well fed," Sassy promised.

Grover shook his head, packed the scanner, and left.

I rubbed my right arm, which bled far less than I expected. "Was that reassuring? I tried."

"After roughing you up last night, I should be grateful you'd even consider a courthouse."

"I like the ridiculously expensive clear pair with the red soles. Those ones are special. We should go to the court house while you're wearing those."

"That's just sad, Aaron."

I grinned. "It's only sad if you don't go along with it. I like the idea. If any of those other men try to make you go on a date with them, I'll beat them with our finalized marriage license until they leave you alone. And as I'm such a considerate gentleman, I'll still play by your rules and go on a date with you every time you're forced to reject another man's advances."

"Deal. But be warned. Daddy's gonna whoop your ass when he finds out you took me to a court house for our wedding."

"We can do one of those formal events after. You wanted assurances of your claim. I'm offering them. I have no idea how long it takes to whip together a wedding," I confessed.

"With my family? Twenty-four hours."

I grabbed my phone and checked the state rules for the marriage license. "Bad news, Sassy."

"What?"

"They have a seventy-two hour waiting period."

Sassy retrieved her phone, and several moments later, she spat curses. "Fucking bureaucrats!"

I checked the rules in New Mexico and smiled my satisfaction. "We can either wait and let your family plan something, or we can skip to New Mexico and get a license there. No waiting period. We'd just have to hope a judge can see us."

"Daddy really will kill you if we skip town like that to get married."

"We just won't tell him."

"But we can't get married in two states."

"Why the hell not?"

"It's illegal."

"That's a pretty dumb rule," I muttered.

"I'm sure seventy-four hours won't kill us." Sassy frowned. "Maybe. But it'd be seventy-four hours from tomorrow."

I sighed and pointed at the door. "And we'd have to sneak past a pack of wolves to bail to town. It's better just to wait."

Sassy's expression brightened. "But busting out from a bunch of wolves sounds like fun."

"We can't bail to town, Sassy. We need to hunt for this killer's hire. However tempting, we need to prioritize. Dumping a wedding on your father's lap is a little like revenge, too. He gets to foot the bill if you dump it on his lap."

"Ah, the sweet, sweet taste of fiscal revenge," she purred, dialing a number on her phone. "Oh, Daddy!"

I bit my lip so I wouldn't laugh.

"What? No, Daddy. Everything's fine. Mostly. I need you to plan a wedding. Aaron won't ditch town and go to New Mexico because he's convinced you'll kill him if we do. Huh? What? Oh. Okay. Hold on." Sassy lowered the phone. "Daddy wants to know which town in New Mexico."

"Hobbs."

"Hobbs, Daddy. Are you nuts? You're nuts. Okay. Fine." Sassy hung up. "Daddy says, and I quote, 'There ain't no way in hell I'm paying to feed a first-shifter. You want to go to New Mexico? Fine. We'll meet you there in the morning.' I don't think he wants to bother with planning a wedding, Aaron."

What had happened to my quiet, almost normal life? Ah, right. Sassy's father had socked me in the mouth, busted out my teeth, and given me the gift of lycanthropy. As I liked the end result, I swore I wouldn't complain much. "Want to sneak past the wolves for fun?"

"Hell, yeah. Dinner, some sleep, and then a road trip?"

"I have no idea how we're going to sneak past a bunch of wolves in my truck, but let's call it a plan."

As I'd known from the day I'd met her, I loved Sassy's special brand of trouble and always would. Perfect worlds didn't exist, but I'd hope nothing would change between us with the exception of superior sleeping arrangements and the inclusion of extracurricular activities she desired as much as I did.

The only thing I could do was work each and every day to never give her a reason to regret having picked me.

THIRTEEN

Go away. We're busy.

I LONGED to give Sassy's father a whooping he'd never forget. Our plan to dive for my truck and run to the border ended with a knock at the door, and my brother, several of her brothers, Maxwell, Rob, and an assortment of wolves prowled outside waiting for us to let them in.

"Open the door, Aaron. I know you're in there. I can hear you growling at me," my brother said, and he pounded on the door.

"No. Go away. We're busy."

"Busy doing want? Eloping? Your elopement plans have been cancelled. We have a lead."

Shit. Leads meant work, work meant a definite cancelling of elopement plans, and since Rob had joined the fray, it was a lead that might take us somewhere productive. "What sort of lead?"

"We have a potential list of targets, and we

need you and Sassy to partner up with Maxwell and his partner to check into one of them. I'm going with another team to keep an eye on Sharon Gray. We've got three other teams, each partnered with some lycanthropes, to keep an eye on the others."

Shit, shit, shit. I unlocked and opened the door. "Where are they, and how long do we have to get into position?"

"With how this bastard is operating, we're not sure," Maxwell admitted, leading the charge and invading the house. "We're on the least likely of the targets since you're close to your first shift?"

"According to Grover's meter, yeah." I shrugged. "It is what it is."

"We'll make do. We keep a stock of neutralizer in the trunk for emergencies, so we can do any cleanup required, and if it's bad enough, I can call in the CDC. Sassy, you think you can keep him in line if he shifts?"

Sassy snorted. "I weigh eighty pounds on a good day, Maxwell. He'll probably be able to drag me around without thinking about it when he shifts. Most lycanthrope cheetahs weigh in closer to two hundred. I can occupy him with my feminine charms, but that's the best I can promise."

"Just wear nice shoes," Maxwell muttered.

"As a cheetah? You're nuts. I'd snap my neck trying. Also, I don't have four of the same shoe, and I refuse to wear mismatched shoes. Absolutely not."

"Now's not the time for jokes," Rob snapped.

"Now's the perfect time for jokes." Joe shoved the DA out of the way and cuffed the back of my head hard enough I yelped. "That's for sleeping with my sister."

Idiot. "You told me to!"

"You could have at least made her chase you for a day or two. What sort of cheetah male are you?"

"A happy one," Sassy announced, kicking her brother in the shin. "Stop bothering Aaron. And yes, he most certainly did sleep with your sister, and I have it on the best authority she liked it."

Lycanthropes. Was nothing sacred or private among them? Right. No. I was a fool to even hope for that.

My brother sighed. "Too much information, Sassy."

"No. There's a bunch of unmated males here. Absolutely not too much information. I have to make it clear he's mated. To me. Or the unmated males will bother me. And if an unmated female tries anything, it will not end well for her. He's *mine*."

"The unmated males here are either your brothers or the wrong species," I reminded her.

"You're still mine."

"I'm not disputing that. I'm just saying the unmated males here are either your brothers or the wrong species. We'll be working, so you won't have to worry about anyone getting any ideas. If time allows, we'll get a license while we're out."

"Possible but unlikely," Maxwell admitted. "We'll see what we can do, but we have reason to believe the killer will probably start another wave of killings soon."

"How many potential victims do we have, how did you find the leads, and what can we do about it? These guys are professionals."

"Guys is plural," Rob said, his eyes narrowing.

Grover sighed. "You're a bastard, Aaron."

"You give me information, you should expect me to use the information. That's how this works. If that information gives us the edge we need to stop the next killing and find the hire, I'm going to use the information."

Joe and Mark glared at the wolf, and my future brother-in-law and new doctor growled, "You told him about the mercenary company?"

"Joe, his virus is spiking to hell. Sassy could sneak up behind him, blow on his ear, and quite possibly induce his first shift. He's so wired to protect kids if I didn't tell him he'd run an even higher risk of snapping. If I didn't know better, I'd say a wolf had initially infected him despite him having most behaviors of a cheetah. He's not stupid. He's already figured out it's a professional outfit. He needs to go in knowing exactly what sort of outfit it is. These guys don't want to be caught, but they sure as hell want their hire to rot in hell. They made it just hard enough to link the clues together to make it clear they couldn't betray their contract. It's the same method in a different way. They're spelling out the coordinates for us, and I'd be a fool to ignore the similarities in those cases."

"What are you talking about?" Rob demanded.

"A few years back, a group of terrorists hired a mercenary group to take out military doctors. The mercenaries didn't like it, so they left clues. We never caught the mercenaries, but this is very similar to how they operated," Grover explained.

"Copycat?"

"The assassinations were never publicized, and it never hit public channels. It's very unlikely. We wiped out the entire terrorist cell after we got the coordinates from the mercenary group. This is one way these outfits operate, Rob. The ethical ones backstab their hires when they cross a line. Targeting doctors and kids? That's crossing a line for them. Women, children, and support staff are among those they don't want to target. They'll do the job to the letter, but they'll find some way to get revenge."

Rob's expression darkened. "Probability of catching the mercenaries?"

"Near to zero. We'll have to find the hire. If the hire—and the money—dries up, *if* it's this group, the killings will stop. Death of the hire typically nullifies the rest of the contract."

Rob spat curses. "Are you seriously telling me we won't be able to get them?"

Joe sighed and bowed his head. "They're using high-grade magic to pull these off, Rob. I already evaluated Aaron's memories. With these guys, nothing is as it seems. The white truck, for example."

"Red with produce. Yeah, we've been working that lead. We found the truck," the DA announced.

"You did? Where?"

"At the bottom of Lake Ray Hubbard. Only evidence we have is some paint transfer and scratches confirming the truck was the same one used to crash your truck, Aaron. It's a useless find. They left no other evidence. Police can't find jack shit, the FBI can't find jack shit, and the CDC brought in some specialists trying to find something, and they can't find jack shit, either. We even hired an angel. Whatever the fuck they're doing, it's strong enough not even an angel can pierce the illusions to get anything useful. There was one humanoid in the vehicle."

My mouth dropped open. "An angel couldn't get anything?"

"We might try asking for an archangel, but we doubt we'll get one. They don't like to meddle at all. We're at another dead end. The best we have is speculation from ancient newspaper articles."

"Featuring images of Tom Heatherow in the background?" I guessed.

"Bingo. What we can't figure out is if someone is framing Tom Heatherow, or if he's the one behind this."

And with his child a victim, I understood why Rob wouldn't act until he had no doubt of who was behind the murders. When he did, it'd become personal.

Justice would be served, and when it came time for justice to be served, I doubted Robert Allamant would be happy with the results. No, I knew he wouldn't be. Perhaps he hadn't been a large part of his son's life, but he'd always seemed like a family man to me. A father would never be satisfied with jail time or even death. Neither would bring back his son.

"Who do we have as possible victims?" I demanded.

Rob's expression turned neutral, but

something about his eyes warned me the man grieved. "Sharon Gray is our top concern, but we suspect Mark's efforts to play her old lover might bear fruit. We've had some incidents around her, but they've lessened in frequency following Mark's arrival. I came up with an idea that might work best at protecting her. Your brother and Miss Gray pretended like they were mourning the loss of their children, born in the appropriate age ranges. She's played the part, and while we can't confirm it's working, there's a good chance it might. They've been seen in public together, and they've been talking about trying again and doing better next time. Acting like parents who've lost their kids."

I gave my brother my full attention. "Mark?"

"She's one hell of a woman, and the local wolf packs are keeping someone with her at all times. She's got more suitors than any one woman needs, but she's having a great time. She understands she's a potential target, but she doesn't go out anywhere with her kids, who aren't even aware they're hers. She's going to avoid them until this is resolved. If there aren't any kids near her, we don't think she'll be targeted. They don't care as long as the evidence of wrongdoing is gone, and they seem to be limiting the evidence of wrongdoing to actual kids produced, not his sexual dalliances. He was single at the time, and there's nothing in the political rulebook stating single men can't sleep around at leisure. It's only when they sleep with married women it's an issue."

The more I learned, the more I wanted to take Tom Heatherow over to the Chetty house and let Sassy's father handle the matter permanently with a little help from me. "And none of the women were married?"

Rob grunted. "Tom Heatherow seems to have been very careful to avoid sleeping with married women."

"Political aspirations from the start?"

"It's highly probable. He was involved with politics in some form or another since college. On the surface, he looks like an activist. The deeper I dig, the less I like his activities," Rob admitted. "Still, this stinks of a setup. But who would set him up and why?"

"And why would he hire us to look into Sharon Gray unless he's somehow involved with her? Mark's idea he was hoping to find intel on Sharon and the possibility of children is sounding pretty plausible to me. I think we need to figure out why Sharon Gray is so damned important to Tom Heatherow that he'd pay us a fortune to get intel on her. Initially, I thought it was due to her relations with Senator Sterling, but that's a questionable lead at best. Senator Sterling can handle his bedtime activities in the public eye just fine. Everything we provided on Senator Sterling isn't going to do jack shit against the man in the court of public opinion. He treats his women well, men want to be him, and he doesn't cross the wrong lines."

Rob's expression darkened. "In short, he's a player but not a rapist."

I could always trust Rob to get blunt when discussing sensitive issues. "Exactly."

"That leads me to a very important question: do we have any actual evidence Tom Heatherow might be a player *and* a rapist? Because having a bunch of illegitimate but consenting children is a lot different from having a lot of children that are the product of rape." Rob flexed his hands. "And the only people who know for certain are dead."

"Except Sharon Gray."

Rob sucked in a breath. "And if he raped her, it won't matter if the kids are alive or dead. He'd want her gone to keep her from being able to testify against him."

I loathed the idea. "That's a strong possibility. Mark?"

"What?"

"We should go pay your new girlfriend a call, and if I go with you along with Sassy, she might talk to Sassy if she won't talk to us."

Sassy grimaced. "I'm not good at this sort of thing, Aaron. I'm really not."

"Who is? You're a lot of things, Sassy, but you're the best friend anyone could have. If we want to get to the bottom of this, we need to find out what actually happened between Tom Heatherow and the victims, and you're our best bet. Maxwell can come with us; however much as it disgusts me, he comes across as a fatherly figure. People just like him. Sharon can pick the best person to tell her story to, and we'll get to the bottom of this and protect her."

I just hoped we could get answers before more women and children lost their lives to a fatally flawed political system run by the worst sort of men seeking power over the majority.

WHILE I THOUGHT it was a good idea to take Sassy to visit Sharon Gray, somehow, I'd gotten saddled with Maxwell and only Maxwell, and I got to ride in his personal vehicle because Sassy owned my truck and was going to pay one of the other potential victims a visit. Sharon Gray had met me before, and once I introduced myself as Mark's brother, Mark thought she'd cooperate. With Maxwell playing the good cop in casual clothes, he thought we could get results.

Joe thought it'd be a good idea for Sassy

and I to spend a few hours apart to encourage our viruses to bond better.

"This is not how I was planning for my day to go," I informed Maxwell, buckling in and wishing I could hide in the bed of my truck and go with Sassy. "Am I the only person who thinks this is a recipe for disaster? According to Grover's scanner, I'm going to shift soon."

"It's good to get you used to working with a partner who isn't Sassy, and it'll happen at times, especially once you have your first kid. She'll need the time off, and you'll need to rotate in as a temporary for people who can't show up. And while I'm sure the local coalitions will love to kitten sit for you, she needs to be able to take time off to be a mother."

That even Maxwell was planning my kids amused me, as while I hadn't really put thought into having children, as long as they were with Sassy, I'd have as many as she wanted.

I foresaw needing a large house built ready to withstand a lot of kittens. I laughed. "I haven't even gotten that far yet, Maxwell."

"Of course not. Last week, you didn't think you had a hope in hell of having Sassy to yourself. I told you. You two were made for each other from the start."

"What do we have on Sharon Gray, Maxwell? Give it to me straight."

"We worked around the clock to read through the newspapers you identified as possible leads. Eight and a half months before her twins were born, Sharon Gray attended a fundraiser for Tom Heatherow's biological father. She was partially active in his failed campaign. Tom Heatherow wasn't supposed to be in attendance, but the picture shown in one of the newspapers has him in the background looking at Miss Gray. We managed to get a copy of the guest list for the fundraiser. She was on it. He was not. Miss Gray contributed a hundred dollars, and she was starting to get a real feel for the politics of campaigning. Over the next few months, several other newspapers either had mentions of Sharon Gray as a campaigner for the Presidential bid *or* a photograph of her in the background. Those pictures stopped after three or so months."

"Her pregnancy started showing?"

"That's what we think. The article forty weeks following the fundraiser is disturbing at best." Maxwell sighed. "And it's why I fear she'll be targeted no matter what we do."

"Explain," I ordered.

"It was the day Tom Heatherow's father announced he was pulling out of his campaign for the Presidency. Miss Gray wasn't mentioned, but that's a coincidence no one is willing to overlook at this point."

Shit. "That's one hell of a coincidence. Does the birthday of her twins and that announcement match?"

"No. Her twins were premature. But the killers aren't using the children's actual birthdays. They're using the suspected conception date. And we're finding more articles that match both the conception date and the forty-week mark. It's a really clever method. They're taking the guesswork out."

Grover's story of the mercenaries who'd riddled the coordinates of a terrorist camp into their victims matched far more than I liked thinking about. "They want us to know the story."

"Ethical murderers. Professionals stuck in a shit job but honor-bound to complete the job."

"They're being really flash about it. Why? Is it a setup?"

"It's either that, or there's a lot more to this story than we're guessing. There are a lot of references to Tom Heatherow's biological father in the articles we're finding along with mentions of him."

"His father seeking revenge for his failed Presidential bid?"

Maxwell shook his head, started his car, and headed down the long, twisting roads that would take us to Dallas. "I don't think so. I think Tom Heatherow's father is a puppet master pulling strings and Tom Heatherow is the puppet. And I think the puppet is backed into a corner and is killing off his children so the cycle ends. None of his potential children could be of use to him, either—and they could ruin his potential campaign. Tom Heatherow's father was—no, is—an ambitious man. That's clear from his run. His son ruined his Presidential bid. But I have no doubt it didn't slake his thirst for power. How better to get a taste than coerce or blackmail his son into making a bid so he can rule from the shadows?"

"That's a bit far-fetched, Maxwell."

"It happens in politics all the time, Aaron. Behind every politician is someone pulling the strings. The question is always, always who is pulling the strings and how much money is being paid out. I've been there. I've lived it. I'm as guilty as the next man on that front. I just chose to try to make up for everything I've done. Most don't. In the game of politics, you need to look behind the politician to see the mastermind. Tom Heatherow is likely guilty of some crimes. But which ones? That's something I can't tell you, and those who know are dead along with their children."

"Except for Sharon Gray."

"Exactly. We just have to hope we reach

her first and find out the truth before she's silenced forever."

"And that getting to her first makes sure she isn't silenced forever."

Maxwell sighed. "Don't get your hopes up, Aaron. These guys don't make mistakes."

"I'd say they most certainly have."

"How so?"

I clenched my teeth. "I'm still alive, and they're going to regret that by the time we're finished."

"Are they going to be alive to regret?"

"That's a very good question, Maxwell."

FOURTEEN

Should I flap my arms now and run
in circles?

SHARON GRAY LIVED in a tiny apartment in one of the worst neighborhoods in Dallas, and it amazed me the building hadn't toppled in a stiff wind. "All right. This is not what I was expecting, Maxwell."

"From my understanding of the situation, she prefers to limit how much she wastes on rent so she can indulge in luxuries."

The state of her windows worried me despite living on the second story. It'd only take one determined sniper on the neighboring building to get a shot at her. "That's not secure. At all. Sassy could break into that in five minutes flat, and those windows are optimal for a shooter."

"That thought had crossed my mind."

"And the apartment's probably small enough she won't be able to avoid the windows."

"Heavy curtains could block the view. That might be enough. If she wants them, we can get them on her behalf. Wouldn't be the first time I've done something like that."

I didn't ask. Some things were best left unspoken. "Take the lead?"

"You know what to do almost as well as I do. You've been questioning people for years. You've met her before. Don't stress yourself over it. It's no different from how you'd approach someone when you're working for the defense."

"This time, I have a cop breathing down my neck."

"Aaron, you're going to be a cop within a year. Now's a good time to get used to it. You're no spring chicken, so don't act like one now."

"Should I flap my arms now and run in circles? I can."

"Get your ass out of the car, Aaron."

I sighed but obeyed. Closing the car door, I stared at the rickety staircase leading to her front door. "Maybe they don't think they have to do anything. That looks like it could come down any moment."

"That had occurred to me."

As Maxwell wouldn't leave me alone until I did what he wanted, I climbed the staircase, flinching at the groan of strained metal beneath me. "This can't be legal, Maxwell."

"I'm thinking I should call in for an inspector. I think you're right. I'll do it after we're done here."

Worried the whole thing would come down under our combined weight, I knocked on Sharon Gray's door. She didn't leave me waiting long, and her brows rose while she looked me over. "You're looking good for someone who was in critical last week. What can I do for you?"

"Can we come in?"

"Sure. Mark warned me I'd likely see you. I wasn't expecting it to be this soon, though. Way he told me, you about died in that crash."

"Early onset lycanthropy helped a lot."

"Well, I'll be damned. What strain, sugar?"

"He's a cheetah, and he's newly mated."

"That didn't take long. Who's the lucky lady? Come on in and make yourself comfortable." Sharon got out of the way, and I slid inside with Maxwell on my heels. "You're a cop?"

"Yes, ma'am."

"This isn't a pleasure call, then. Have a seat."

Maxwell and I looked at the windows, which were obscured with light drapes that partially obscured the view of the neighboring building. I smiled and shook my head. "I'll stand if you don't mind. I've been sitting a lot lately, and it feels nice to be on my feet for a while."

"Why are you here?"

Maxwell glanced at me and nodded.

Damn it. "You've heard about the murders of women with their children, I presume?"

"Yes. Who hasn't?"

"We have reason to believe that you might be a target, and we wanted to speak with you about certain circumstances."

The color fled from the woman's face. "Mark already warned me about this. That's why we've been doing what we have been. But why are you here and not him? What's going on?"

"Mark's trying to help another woman avoid being the next target," I admitted.

While her face remained pale, she relaxed. "He seems like the type."

"To what?"

"Help people."

I laughed. "Ma'am, my brother's in the military. He kills people for a living, and he's good at his job. He wouldn't know how to be loyal to a woman without the help of the lycanthropy virus from an ultra-conservative wolf. But he tries to do the right thing when he can."

Maxwell cleared his throat. "It doesn't hurt that someone tried to kill his little brother. Mark doesn't take things like that lightly."

"I could help him out on the lycanthropy virus front."

I'd have to warn Mark he'd gotten into Sharon Gray's sights. "That's between you and him, ma'am, but I wish you the best of luck should you try. He's a player."

"He's honest about it. I'm a player, too, Mr. Clinton."

Yep. She'd gotten information out of my brother about me. "What can you tell us about Tom Heatherow and Abraham Sarmassen?"

Her eyes widened. "That old political campaign? What could you possibly want to know about that?"

"A picture of you with Tom Heatherow in the background at a campaign fundraiser was published in a newspaper. We wanted to find out what relationship you had with both gentlemen."

"Relationship is a stretch."

"Is it a stretch you can talk to us about?"

"Can I? Yes. Will I? That depends on why you want to know."

I'd either blow the questioning session or open the waterworks, but I couldn't afford to dance around the subject all day. "What if I told you that every woman murdered with her children had also been photographed with Tom Heatherow and had the pictures published in newspapers around the time your twins were born?"

Sharon's explosion of cursing startled me enough I hopped back a step, and Maxwell clapped his hand to my shoulder. "Miss Gray, if we could avoid startling Mr. Clinton into his first shift, that'd be ideal."

"That worthless sack of shit!" the woman snarled, and she grabbed a vase from off her coffee table and flung it across the room. It shattered on the wall. She searched for another fragile object to take her wrath out on. "He just refuses to give up and die like a decent man."

Well, I couldn't deny something had happened between the two. "I take it Mr. Heatherow is a dishonest player?"

"He's the type of dishonest player who spikes drinks and gets what he wants. Yeah. He's a player. He's a player you don't trust near your glass, but no one could ever prove a damned thing because he'd partner his cocktails of choice with pixie dust."

If I ever got Tom Heatherow alone in a dark alley, I worried I'd become the next murderer to infest Dallas. "Is that something you'd be willing to testify about in court, Miss Gray?"

"It's been tried. We're gaslit because of the pixie dust. We're called whores and worse because we slept with him. It doesn't matter that he spiked our drinks, not to the juries. We've been there and done that. Not with him, but others like him. It won't get anywhere fast. All an angel is going to do is confirm that my drinks were spiked, and he used enough pixie dust to make consent easy for him to get despite us not really wanting to give it."

"You know the other victims?"

The anger left Sharon's body on a pained sigh. "Some of them. It's a thing, you know? We've all walked in those same shoes, and we can't do anything about it. Nobody will believe us. He walks. And now he's getting rid of us because we're inconvenient. He's going to be making a bid."

"For the senate," I confirmed. "He was after Senator Sterling."

Sharon Gray snorted. "I wish him the best of luck with that. Sterling's a player, but he's an honest one. They're the best kind. I know exactly what I'm getting out of that relationship, and it doesn't require the help of a battery-operated toy."

Maxwell coughed and fought to keep from smiling. "There's nothing wrong with that, ma'am. And for what it's worth, I do believe you. That won't help you in front of a jury of your peers, but I don't doubt your word."

I'd been a private investigator too long to doubt men and women alike found ways to circumvent consent to get what they wanted.

"That's new. Mark said you're a private investigator. What's a private investigator doing with a cop?"

"Trying to make sure no one else is killed."

Sharon's sad smile hurt, and the pain centered in my chest. "He's not the type to stop, Mr. Clinton. I trust you understand that. It's not about our children. It's about us. We're the ones who, like his mother, ruined his life."

"Bullshit," I snapped. "You ruined no one's life."

While still sad, her smile brightened. "The world's black and white for you, isn't it? If we hadn't been there, if it hadn't been so easy, he wouldn't have been able to do it, right? That's all on us. We were available. That's how men like him think. That cat you sent to the mixer? That's the one who sank her teeth into you?"

"Sassy."

"Such a strange name, but it suits her. I got the feeling you were the one. A man doesn't buy shoes like that for a girl like her unless he's serious."

"You should see the ones with the red soles," I muttered.

Sharon laughed, a sound without life or warmth. "A man definitely doesn't buy shoes like that unless he means business. She's lucky."

"Tell me why, please." I wanted to understand.

In understanding, I might find the next piece of the puzzle.

"The first time I heard of Tom Heatherow, we'd found out he was Mr. Sarmassen's son. That was right before the start of the campaign. Mr. Sarmassen warned us then it would likely end his bid but he'd try anyway. He acknowledged the truth of it to those involved with his campaign from the very beginning. We were told to keep it quiet, which we did. Someone talked."

"Someone always does," Maxwell said, and his tone was the match of hers, lost.

I wondered how so much anguish could fit in so small of an apartment. "What can you tell me?"

"If I tell you everything, he'll want you dead, too. That's what he does. He kills people. Sometimes, he kills them but leaves them still breathing. Sometimes, he leaves their bodies cooling on the steps of a shopping center as a warning. No, as a promise. You're next, those bodies said. You're next. But I wasn't next. He went after Rachel and Emery. He went after Patrice and Carol. He went after Gemmy and Daniel. They're the ones who'd found new lives after he'd killed them but left them breathing, Mr. Clinton. He enjoys destroying lives, and he hates when his victims move on from what he's done to them."

"And you?"

"Do you think your brother was the first one to come up with the idea of claiming that my babies had died, Mr. Clinton?"

I sighed. "Did it do any good?"

"It won't, not if he's making a bid. He thinks he left me breathing but dead inside, unable or unwilling to speak out against him. I hadn't interested him. Until now." Sharon glanced towards the window. "They're probably watching even now. Waiting for me to tell you the important parts so I can be silenced. But not before I give you what you need."

"You sound confident." Her confidence terrified me.

She expected to die, and I had no idea what I could do to stop it.

"I can feel them watching me. You're a lot like your brother. You want to stop the inevitable."

"Magic?"

"It crawls over my skin when they watch. I can't see them, but I know they're there."

Illusions. Illusions Joe could see through if I allowed him to poke through my memories. I'd become living evidence if I could only find where they watched. "Can you show me where?"

"I expect I won't live beyond pointing if I did that, Mr. Clinton. It's one of those things, you know?"

"Can you tell me why you're so confident, Miss Gray?"

"I hear and see things I shouldn't sometimes. That's what I'm best at. I show up, and I listen. The fundraisers. The political mixers. The speeches. There's a lot of money to be had tipping off the newspapers, you know? That's what I do. I tip people off on what the politicians are up to. It's good money."

My eyes widened. "You were watching Senator Sterling?"

"Of course. I was watching Heatherow, too. Make no mistake. Should I live through this, it would be my honor and privilege to sink him. I would leave him dead but breathing, too. If I have to accomplish that through death, it would be worth it. Filth like him needs to pay. That's what I do. I make sure they pay. All of them."

Maxwell stared at the window, glancing at Sharon, his eyes narrowing as he examined the curtains and the angle to neighboring buildings. "Then help us, Sharon. We'll do everything we can to make sure you're safe."

"Don't make promises you can't keep, sir."

"Maxwell."

"I know who you are. You're the first politician I've ever met who actually meant it when he claimed he was sorry for what he's done. You? To become a cop? I never would've believed it if you hadn't done it. To go from the top of the hill to working the streets? No. You're idealistic. It won't help. Not against the sort of money they're throwing around to get rid of us. They'll succeed. It's just a matter of when."

"Or we cut the head off the snake and the money flow ends."

"How many people are you willing to kill to make the money vanish?" Sharon smiled. "This is bigger than you could ever guess."

"That's frighteningly cryptic."

"I'm good at cryptic. I'm almost at good at cryptic as you are at false sincerity."

I allowed myself a grim smile. "When did you think I wasn't sincere?"

"The shoe store."

I snorted. "I was very sincere in that store. You looked like you were going to eat that poor store clerk for breakfast. I went in to rescue her from you."

"You're serious."

"Had I gotten my way, I wouldn't have even stepped foot into that store, Miss Gray. But, that's how we got here. I need a motive, and I need names of who would want to make you and those other women disappear.

What did you see that could make a difference *now*?"

"It's not that simple."

Nothing ever was. "I'd like to understand."

"Would you swear an oath to me, Mr.
Clinton? If I tell you all I know, that you will
stand on my behalf when I'm gone, witnessed
by an angel, to tell them what I told you?
Would you? Even if you knew my blood
would stain your hands forever?"

How could I change the fate she viewed as
inevitable? That she believed herself dead already disturbed me. "I'd do more than allow
an angel to hear the truth of my words,
Sharon."

"What would you do?"

I stepped to the window, pushed aside the
curtains enough I could get a good view of
the neighboring building, and I took my time
examining every nook and cranny. I checked
the street below, the windows, and everywhere a sniper might be able to get a shot at
the woman. Once satisfied I'd gotten a good
look at the possible routes, I positioned myself where a shooter would have to go
through me to get her. Sassy would kill me
herself if she found out I'd deliberately put
myself in the line of fire Then, I turned my
back to the window. "Whatever's necessary to
get the job done."

"When Abraham Sarmassen found out his

bastard son would ruin his Presidential campaign, he started making plans. If he couldn't be President, then he'd groom the next best thing: his son. Tom went after us trying to destabilize his father's campaign and put an end to the bid. Revenge. That's what this is all about. But if Tom's after the senate, the Presidency is next. That's how these assholes work. If they can't get the seat themselves, they put someone they control in their place. So, Tom decided it'd be a good idea to try to ruin his father so he couldn't even have that. But that's all blowing up in his face. Abraham Sarmassen's a bastard even worse than his son, Mr. Clinton. Never believe anything otherwise. Killing us off to protect his son's bid for the Presidency would only be his first step, and if his son takes the fall for it? That'd make him happy. But really? They're probably working together because if Tom doesn't, he'll probably join us in the grave."

"I need proof."

"Tom's not the only unethical player, and not all of us slept with Tom. Some of us slept with his father."

Holy hell. "If you don't mind me asking, how about you?"

"Ask Max."

"Before or after you got hitched, Max?"

"Before, of course. I don't cheat."

"He's already a unicorn among politicians.

I sleep around, Mr. Clinton. Do you have a problem with that?"

"Not at all, ma'am. I slept around before I really got to know Sassy."

"How long have you been waiting around for her?"

"It's been a few years," I admitted.

"That's a lot of man to enjoy. Lucky woman. This is what didn't hit the papers, Mr. Clinton, and this is probably what's going to get me killed no matter what you do. Abraham Sarmassen entered his campaign knowing that all the funding he gathered wouldn't be going to his campaign. He black-mailed and coerced his way into free adver-tising, venue usage, and so on. He called in favors. Right from the beginning, he under-stood Tom Heatherow's existence would hamper his campaign. No, he knew it would end it. It's campaign fraud, pure and simple. He gathered millions for his run and didn't spend a cent of it on his run. He had the venues bill him and mark the invoices as paid for records, and he kept all the money for himself. Planning for his next attempt. He's been buying off politicians ever since. It's what sank you, Max. You wouldn't play the game he wanted, so he made everyone know about the true price of your bills. A price you hadn't even realized women and children would pay until it became law because he had his allies write in clauses to make you, the bill's sponsor, take the fall. He didn't anticipate you becoming a cop. No one did."

Maxwell's cheek twitched. "I knew something was up when those clauses showed up. They weren't written by hand, but yes. I'd sponsored that bill. It was my responsibility."

Everything I'd thought I'd known about Maxwell shook on its foundations. "You weren't behind those inclusions, Max?"

"No, I wasn't. But it was slipped under the wire. It was easier to just take the fall than it was to try to salvage my political career at that point. I became a cop instead. Even if I found out who'd slipped in those lethal clauses, none of us really understood what they'd do in application. I didn't figure it out until after it started taking lives."

"You were in the way, Max. It's as simple as that. Abraham Sarmassen has always had one goal, and that was to change the world. But not in a way most of us think of it. He wanted to change the world in a way that suited him best. He's only one of the players in this game. Tom Heatherow's another player. If his father gets his way, he'll be President. In name only, but President. He'll get the visible glory, but he'll be doing his father's bidding. Then there's everyone else beneath who gets a share of the glory, too."

I fought my urge to start cursing. "Can

you name them all Sharon?"

When she started naming names, cold shock enveloped my heart. From judges to senators, she left no branch of government untouched, and when she named the police commissioners of Dallas, Houston, and Austin, I wondered how anyone could stop the tide of corruption.

No wonder she lacked confidence in the courts. The local judges belonged to the men she'd never be able to touch.

How the hell was I supposed to investigate so many men and women, who all answered to Abraham Sarmassen, Tom Heatherow, and those seeking power to change the world to their liking?

I turned to the window and wondered if the killers knew just how deep the corruption ran and if they truly believed scraps of news-paper and subtle clues could make such an empire fall. Movement from the neighboring roof drew my eye, and Sharon's warnings sliced through my memories.

I pivoted, whipped my arm out, and caught Sharon in the ribs, putting every bit of my strength into the blow and followed through with a shove in the direction of the kitchen. Maxwell spat curses and dove for the window.

Shots rang out, glass shattered, and Sharon's apartment fell into darkness.

FIFTEEN

You tried.

BEING SHOT HURT LIKE HELL, and my arm wouldn't be the same for a while, but the pain came second to the reality that Sharon had been right all along.

I hadn't moved fast enough.

It took one look at her to realize seconds mattered and slipped away. Pre-shift lycanthropes weren't much sturdier than regular humans, and I had no idea how I'd staunch the bleeding from two chest wounds. Her breath bubbled, and blood seeped from the corners of her mouth.

Her dulling eyes focused on me. "Told you," she choked out in a whisper.

Why couldn't I be Joe? Why couldn't I be Grover? Either would've known what to do.

I couldn't let her last words be a pained 'Told you.' I couldn't let it end with blood in a tiny, cramped apartment in the seediest part of Dallas.

Something changed in Sharon's face, a determination to not fade away until she finished what she set out to do. What that was, I couldn't guess. Ignoring the burn in my arm, I ripped my shirt pulling it over my head and applied pressure to the entry wounds. "You're not dead yet, Sharon." I growled the words, and my entire body shook from the growing fury deep within.

She'd been right, and I hadn't been fast enough.

Some stains wouldn't wash away, and her blood covered my hands.

"You tried," she said.

She stopped breathing, so I breathed for her. I had no idea what CPR would do with gunshot wounds in the chest, but it was the only trick I had up my sleeve, and until someone who knew what the fuck he was doing told me to stop, I'd keep trying.

I didn't want those being her last words, either.

Sirens screamed, and it wasn't until someone pulled me off Sharon that I comprehended we were no longer alone. Blood covered everything, and the reality of what I'd become hit almost as hard as the presence of the paramedics taking over. "We're infected."

Then I remembered Maxwell, and I twisted towards the window.

Death came to us all, and one day, I might

find comfort in Maxwell's end. The shooter hadn't taken any chances with him, and his life had fled from his body long before his body had hit the floor. His open, unseeing eyes would haunt me, already clouded.

My chest hurt as though I'd been the one shot, and I struggled to breathe.

Someone cursed, but the crash of thunder in my ears drowned all other sound. The fire in my arm spread and consumed me from within.

Time stretched and snapped, folding in on itself and dumping me from the reality of Maxwell's death to a sterile, white room splattered with blood and the metallic stench of blood mixing with the harsher fumes of disinfectants. In spots, the walls shimmered where someone had thought to use neutralizer and likely gave up on the idea, leaving the room to its fate.

I growled with every breath.

"I have no idea how you expect me to treat a lycanthrope who won't let anyone near him," a man's voice announced. "How many people do you want to sacrifice to him? I don't have any infected on staff. This is a hospital, not a veterinarian's office."

From the day I'd met Sassy, I'd learned the hard way about the prejudices she faced, then his words sank in, and I froze, lowering my gaze to my hands, shivering as I confirmed without a shadow of a doubt I'd sprouted a fur coat and exchanged hands for paws.

"Doctor, sir, we swore an oath. He's been shot several times. We may not be a veterinarian's office, but he's here. We can't just let him bleed out in our ER."

"That argument got the other lycanthrope into my ICU ward. I don't know what you expect us to do if he won't let any of us near him. At least she was in a human form so she could be treated. We don't even have an ID on him."

"Let me try," the woman replied, her tone firm.

I recognized that tone. The woman would get her way, and she'd kick the ass of anyone who tried to stop her.

"I am not responsible if you contract lycanthropy," the doctor warned.

"If you won't treat him because you're afraid of contracting lycanthropy, I will," she countered. "It's no different from treating any other patient with a contagious disease, sir. Don't lick his blood, don't get cut, and it's not a problem. It's not an air-borne illness."

"If he cooperates long enough for us to sedate him so we can work, I'll treat him, but I don't know what you expect me to do. I'm trained in the surgical care of *humans*. That is not a human. That is a very large and angry cat."

"How else do we treat gunshot wounds? We remove the bullets and do what we can to stop the bleeding and repair the damage. You have magic, sir. Use it. That's what you're paid to do. The rules are clear. If we don't have insurance information on critical injuries, we treat and worry about it later. This is a treat and worry about it later situation."

Without any sign of fear of the blood decorating the room, a woman in green scrubs strode in and approached me, and she went to a tray containing syringes and clear, glass bottles. "If you'd please keep your teeth and claws to yourself, sir, this will only take a moment."

Once again, the nurse's tone implied if she didn't get her way, someone would pay, and as she was talking to me, I would be the one to pay the price for her wrath. My ears twitched back, and I stared at her. I'd heard cats couldn't see colors the same way as humans, but the woman seemed as I expected, green scrubs and all.

Perhaps lycanthropes borrowed from humans while in their animal forms.

She approached me, tapping the air out of her syringe and depressing the plunger until fluid beaded on the needle's tip. "Where do you suggest the best injection site to be, doctor?"

"My vet stabs my cats on the back somewhere."

"Your cats are also clones of Satan and rule Hell. Where do you think is the most effective place?"

"Try his shoulders near the neck. That should spread the sedative around faster. That's just a guess. The last time I worked on a cat, it was dead and a part of an anatomy lab."

If the doctor was trying to instill confidence in his skills, he needed to rethink his strategy.

The nurse approached, and when I kept still, she dropped to a knee, not caring that my blood got onto her scrubs. "Please lower your head, sir."

Given a choice between bleeding out in the ER and being treated by a doctor who likely didn't give a flying shit if I died in his ER, I took my chances with the nurse and hoped she did a better job than the prejudiced asshole in charge. Moving hurt, and I hissed at the pain, which engulfed my chest and arm. Did the forelegs of a cheetah count as arms?

The instant I placed my head on the cold tiles, the nurse jabbed me in the shoulder, rose to her feet, and backed away to give me space. "See, sir? That was not nearly as bad as you thought it would be."

"He's been hissing and spitting at us since

he was hauled in here. He took a swipe at me. At *me*. In my ER."

"You also act like you own the place when you have a riled up predator fresh from a traumatic event. You heard the paramedics, sir. The only reason our Jane Doe reached the hospital alive was because he administered CPR until paramedics arrived, despite having been shot several times. The trauma induced his shift. Jane Doe's virus levels are too low for a shift."

Several times? I'd only noticed my arm. Where else had I been shot?

I couldn't save Maxwell, but that Sharon had made it to the hospital alive eased some of the tension in my chest.

Within minutes, the nurse's injection kicked in, and it packed a harder punch that Sassy's father did.

When coherency returned, I'd been hooked up to machines again, someone had rigged a mask to fit over my muzzle, and I had several lines going into my foreleg. To add insult to injury, I wore a collar, and it was lashed down to an operating table to hold me in place, and my paws had been subjected to similar treatment to keep me still. I lashed my tail at the restraints and growled, which caught the attention of the green and white clad figures in the room.

"I'm not moving the lycanthrope from this

room," the doctor announced. "It's already heavily contaminated with the lycanthropy virus, he's stable, and secure. Until we can neutralize the room and get someone here specialized with lycanthropes, there is zero chance I will put the other patients in this hospital at risk of infection."

While a prejudiced asshole, I'd deal with the annoying doctor and accept my humiliating state as a necessary payment for still breathing. I blinked and tried to force my eyes to focus, but my vision wavered despite my best efforts.

"Sir? The police are here about the lycanthropes. They're demanding to put an armed guard with our Jane Doe, and they claim they have IDs for both patients," a man announced, and I focused on the green-clad figure, identifying him as a nurse or a doctor who'd ditched the white coat for more sensible wear. Like much of the room, his scrubs were stained with red.

"Get out of those scrubs and spritz down with neutralizer, and no one who isn't cleared goes beyond the door. We must keep the contagion contained."

Within five minutes, the police invaded the ER and disregarded the doctor's orders to stay out of the room, and Joe accompanied them armed with his bag of medical supplies. "I sent Grover to the ICU ward to help with

Miss Gray," he announced. "Sassy is on the way. You heard about Maxwell?"

Collared, obstructed with a mask I assumed was helping me breathe, and trussed to the table, all I could do was flatten my ears and stare at him.

"There's nothing you could have done for him, Aaron. The first bullet killed him instantly. The others only made sure of their mark. You're going to blame yourself later, but you did everything just right. I've already heard the story from the paramedics and the cops who arrived at the scene first. Grover's even better at trauma care than I am, and if he can't stabilize her, no one can." Joe looked me over, frowned, and turned to the hospital staff. "Why is he tied to the table?"

"Who are you? What are you doing in my hospital? This is not an open clinic."

"I'm his primary care physician and a military field surgeon, and if you raise your voice to me one more time, I'll have the police throw you out of your own hospital and put you under investigation for risking a patient's life." Joe's cold delivery ushered in silence. "Why is he tied to the table?"

"We didn't know when he'd come out of sedation," the doctor answered. "We are not equipped to handle an animal in here."

"What care did you give him?"

"We removed four bullets and stopped

bleeding at the injury locations. We aren't sure what else we're supposed to do with a cat."

"Chief? You want to get these folks questioned while I take care of Aaron? As soon as Sassy is here with his truck, we'll relocate him to her father's house and handle his treatments there. I'll sign off for the waivers and liabilities. Get ahold of the CDC and get a proper medical team to back Grover up. You'll also want to contact the local wolf packs and identify six to ten unmated male wolves willing to gamble that have her blood type. You need to boost her virus to get her through the operations, and it's probable that one of the viruses will stick."

"Why not mated female wolves?"

"If you can find them, bring them, but I wish you luck convincing their males to let them do the transfusions. Who knows? Maybe you can find six to ten who are willing and have the right blood type. But however it works out, Grover is going to need six to ten donors to rotate. Human blood isn't going to cut it."

"How about Aaron? Will he need donors?"

"The Chetty family already has donors lined up; his brother's already handling the basic footwork to make sure everyone's ready for him when we arrive. Sassy will do the first transfusion, and we'll see where his blood pressure is at after that. I'm going to need a gurney and several nurses who aren't chickenshits to prep him for the trip."

"I'll help," the nurse who'd handled my initial infection announced.

"Good. You know how to neutralize this place?"

"Yes, sir."

"Excellent. Once we have him loaded up in the truck, I've already requested the neutralizer you'll need to detox your operating room. It'll be out of commission for a few hours, but then you'll be ready to go. Cleanup crew will handle the work, and your machines will be fine." Joe grunted, put his hand under my chin, and lifted my head. "Who rigged this mask?"

"I did, sir," the woman replied.

"I'm taking an oxygen tank and this mask, and I'll have them returned when I'm finished with them and they've been decontaminated. If you need authorization forms to take the equipment, call the CDC. They'll provide the documentation. I have a list of other supplies I've been authorized by the CDC to take to treat him outside of the hospital."

"You're taking full responsibility for him?" the doctor asked.

"You're insufficiently trained to handle this patient, so I recommend you get out of my way. And if this cheetah scares you, when

I shift, I outweigh him by at least fifty pounds. He has some growing to do."

"What supplies do you need?" the nurse asked.

Joe pulled out a sheet of paper from his back pocket and handed it over. "Thank you, ma'am."

She hurried off, shucking off her bloodied scrubs as she went and tossing them into a corner.

"All right, Aaron. Let's get a look at you." Joe muttered curses under his breath and unbuckled the cuffs around my legs, tossing them aside. "Entry wounds?"

"Two chest, one shoulder, two in his arm," the doctor reported. "The chest shots may have been ricochets; they didn't penetrate beyond the breastbone and were easy to pluck out. The shoulder was a heavy bleed, and is the primary source of the damage. One bullet in his arm lodged against the bone, the other went fully through."

"Damage to the shoulder?"

"We're uncertain. He hasn't been scanned yet, and I don't have the right sensory abilities to judge. I'm specialized in soft tissue repair."

Joe's brow rose. "How specialized?"

"I'm specialized in hemorrhage control. I can't manipulate or repair muscle and organs, but I can control the bleeding, which is what I did."

"I'm going to need a full surgical kit and casting materials on top of everything else on my list, depending on what that bullet did going through his shoulder."

"It couldn't have damaged too much," the nurse said, sticking her head back into the room. "He performed CPR, and the paramedics claimed he was fully mobile until he shifted."

"Where'd you pull the bullet out from?" Joe demanded.

"Against the bone; I could verify some light cracking without the use of imaging machines."

"Likely another ricochet." Joe nudged my head to the side and prodded at my chest, which hurt enough I growled. "Sassy's going to be thrilled when she sees this. You're a walking sieve, Aaron. At least you're not leaking for the moment. What sedative did you use on him?"

The doctor named a drug, and Joe nodded his satisfaction. "Good choice for lycanthropes. Lasts long enough for the base treatments and tends to calm the virus without tapping it out. Make sure you keep a stock of that flagged specifically for lycanthropes, and make sure it's fresh. You don't want any risks with that. If you're having trouble administering it, use a dart gun. That's how we handle it in the field. When treating a lycanthrope, you'll want to monitor their virus levels in half hour intervals. You want their virus to help, so you can't drug it into submission."

Joe resumed poking and prodding at my fur, and I lashed my tail each time he touched too hard or located a gunshot wound. "All right, Aaron. Until I get to see how badly those bullets damaged the bones, you're to stay off your paws. If we need you to move, we'll move you. Once Sassy—"

"Once I what?" Sassy demanded, and a moment later, she leaned over me, her eyes narrowing as she examined the mask around my muzzle. "His eyes are dilated to hell, Joe."

"He's high on sedatives, which is a good thing. It'll make it easier to get him home. They sedated him so they could remove the bullets and stop the bleeding. They patched the leaks, and at cursory look, his virus is hard at work repairing the damage. You stay with him, keep him calm, and don't let him off that table. He took a round to the shoulder, two to the chest, and a pair to his arm, and I have no idea how much actual damage the rounds did. I'm hoping ricochets, but I don't know yet."

Sassy dug her fingers into the scruff of my neck and held on tight. "Can do."

"This lady here is Aaron's mate, so I recommend you keep your tones pleasant, your manner courteous, and treat her like the lady she is, as I'm not going to be responsible if either one of them go after you for crossing their lines right now. She'll keep him calm, but they're newly mated, so that means if you don't treat her properly, he's going to disregard all my advice about staying off his paws and educate you on why you treat a lycanthrope's lady properly."

I liked Joe's opinion of the situation, and I lashed my tail to make it clear I'd live up to his expectations.

"You're giving him ideas, Joe." With her free hand, Sassy scratched behind my ear. "Settle down, Aaron. You can't maul any doctors or nurses today. As soon as Joe clears you, I'm taking you home, and we'll make sure you're all right. There's a bunch of cops guarding your truck along with a few of my brothers. Daddy's at home making sure they're ready when we get in. I took care of calling your parents, and they'll probably be at the house when we arrive." She bit her lip and bowed her head. "They told me Maxwell didn't make it."

"Killed instantly, Sassy, and I'll keep telling you and Aaron that until you believe it. And don't you start about what would have happened if you'd been with them. You would've been shot, too." Joe cuffed his sister's ear before pulling her into a hug and kissing the top of her head. "You take care of Aaron while I get everything prepped. He'll be fine. He's conscious, he's beating the table with his tail, and he's alert. Maybe they don't know how to treat lycanthropes here, but they covered the important parts, and I can take care of the rest at Dad's place."

ACCORDING TO JOE, early onset lycanthropy and my first shift saved my ass in more ways than he could count. One day, I might understand how he could touch someone and identify everything wrong with them. While cracked, my shoulder emerged relatively undamaged, and he called in a favor from a few of his military buddies to repair the damage so I wouldn't need a cast.

The wounds would take a few days to heal, and I'd spend the time as a cheetah, but I'd recover.

It wasn't until Joe's military buddies left that it really hit me that Maxwell had laid down his life trying to keep my promise to Sharon. I'd come within a hair of doing the same, too.

Bones could be knit. Gunshot wounds could be closed.

No one could raise the dead. I supposed God could, but he wouldn't. I supposed God's angels could, too, but they wouldn't, either. Everything had a season and a purpose under Heaven, and just as there was a time to live, there was a time to die. No one could stop the inevitable march of time until the end of days and the cycle began anew.

And just as there was a time to live and die under Heaven's watchful eye, there was a time to kill, a time to heal, a time to break down, a time to build, a time to weep, a time to laugh, and a time to mourn.

Sassy cracked and broke first, and she wept into my fur, shuddering from the force of her sobs. With the same undeniable force of winter's first breath through the trees, we all fell to our grief in different ways. Cheetahs couldn't cry, and the pressure built in my chest adding to the physical pain Joe's drugs couldn't quite touch.

Silence reigned, something I understood far easier than the senseless loss of life.

What could any of us say? I'd hated Maxwell for so long for what he'd been part of, but he'd done something so few did. He'd taken up his cross and tried to make up for what he'd done. To learn he'd been just one puppet among many worsened the blow of his loss.

He'd carried his cross for something he hadn't been fully responsible for.

Nothing I could say or do would bring Maxwell back. All any of us could do was try to fill his shoes and hope we didn't fall short. When had he gone from someone I'd distrusted and believed a lesser man, to someone I aspired to be like? Somewhere along the way, I'd changed course, so subtle it took the man's death to realize I'd begun trying to wear his shoes despite my apprehensions.

I couldn't bring him back, but I could do one thing. I could find justice for him and the others lost. They wouldn't notice from their graves, but everyone left behind would. While I wanted to rend them with my teeth and claws, I'd set aside my desire for revenge and topple the empire responsible for so much grief.

Maxwell's death would not go to waste. That much I could do.

The hours stretched on, and when Sassy's grief made way for exhaustion, I listened to her breathe and felt the rise and fall of her chest against my back. Her weight offered small comfort, but I took what I could.

Sassy's father crouched beside us and covered his daughter with her blanket, one that still carried hints of my scent on it. "She'll be all right."

In time, we all would be. Time did that

no matter how hard we fought against it. Tomorrow, the cut of Maxwell's death would heal enough to make the weight of grief a little less smothering. The day after, the fury would take root, and we'd wage a different battle, one I believed would test our limits.

A thin line separated justice and vengeance. Revenge fit in somewhere, too, although I wondered if we could ever find peace if we dipped our toes into those bloody waters. No, we wouldn't.

It might take days, months, or even years, but we would have to satisfy ourselves with finding justice any way we could.

Vengeance would have to sit on the sidelines.

The deepest cut of all was the realization Maxwell had been the one to teach me that bitter lesson.

He could have sought vengeance for the loss of his old life, but instead he chose to seek justice and liberty for all.

Sassy's father rocked back on his heels, rested his hands on his knees, and regarded me with narrowed eyes. "How's he doing, Joe?"

"All things considered, good. He'll be back on his feet in no time. Aaron, I know you're not going to like this, but I'd like to check your memories one more time. You're going to relive the shooting. I can't help that. If I could take that away from you, I would."

I shook my head.

Joe considered me with a frown. "You don't want it taken from you?"

I nodded.

Something in his eyes shifted, some sort of lingering pain time hadn't healed for him and might never fully erase. "You were never the kind to run from difficult things. Are you willing?"

Joe needed to know the names, Sharon's fears, and Maxwell's last moments, too. He could do the one thing I couldn't: he could speak. I nodded.

"All right. Dad? Hold his head steady. I don't know how he's going to react to this, but I'd rather he not thrash. I'll try to be quick, Aaron."

I nodded and rested my head on my paws.

With the memories so fresh, what could Joe do? I already relived Maxwell's final moments, replaying his last breaths even as I'd tried to get Sharon out of the line of fire, too.

We'd both been willing to lay down our lives for Sharon's sake.

I refused to regret my choice despite the price I'd pay for years to come. Men like Maxwell weren't easily forgotten, and I found his sacrifice easier to accept when I acknowledged neither of us would have changed anything, even if we'd known the outcome.

Sassy's father rested his hand on the top of my head, and Joe touched my shoulder.

I'd been right. Joe delving into my memories hurt no more than what I already carried, and in the wake of his magic, I found relief and an almost gentle sense of peace. Later, I'd cycle through the stages of my grief, but I could carry the burden without breaking beneath its weight.

Maxwell's death wouldn't be wasted.

"Jesus Christ," Joe whispered.

"What?"

"Get on the horn with the cops and tell them to check Sharon's apartment. There has to be bugs planted in there, and if we're lucky, the memory chips are in the cameras. If we get that, we have some good leads. It was a planned killing, and they waited until Sharon told Maxwell and Aaron what the articles and the killings were really about. It's bad, Dad."

"How bad?"

"Bad enough. I don't know if they meant to leave Aaron or Sharon alive, but I have no doubt Maxwell was their main target after what Sharon told them. Maxwell knew too much, too. I think they meant to kill Sharon Gray but Aaron got in the way. From what I can tell of Aaron's memories, they targeted Maxwell before spraying the apartment. I can't tell how Aaron was shot; the entry and exit wounds on his arm match from being hit from behind, but his chest shots were either ricochets..."

"Or someone was in the apartment?" Sassy's father asked.

"If there was someone in the apartment, Aaron didn't see them, but he *did* see the shooters without realizing it. I can get composite sketches done. They were on the roof and in a second-story apartment across from Sharon's. And I can tell you one name without needing the sketches, and it's bad news."

I'd seen someone? I tried to lift my head, but Sassy's father applied pressure and held me down.

"Who?"

"Maxwell's partner." Joe's expression darkened. "And I'm willing to bet he's the bastard who tagged Aaron's truck. He was at the station the same time Aaron was before the crash. He'd been around his truck."

Sassy's father growled. "Just how far back in Aaron's memories did you go, Joe?"

"As far as he let me with his permission, Dad. I got his permission. I swear. Aaron?"

I bobbed my head, forcing Sassy's father to release me. I reached out with a paw and touched his shoe.

"All right. Did you see the Park Lane

shooting?"

"I did."

"Anything out of place?"

"I'll have to talk with Aaron about it and refer to his photographs. I don't know what he didn't see versus what he did see. We'll have to figure it out after he shifts back. Sorry, Dad. It's not infallible. Some things are easier than others. When he doesn't think he sees anything, but I clearly see figures through the window and on the roof, I know magic was at use. But I don't know who he thought he saw at Park Lane and who he didn't think he saw. It'll have to wait."

"Anything else?"

"As I absolutely refuse to look through his memories beyond the shooting, no."

"Why not?"

"Dad, they made the wolves uncomfortable. I don't want a front row seat to what Aaron did with my sister."

"I think it's obvious what he was doing with your sister. That's what mated pairs do. Really, Joe. You're an adult. A little sex isn't going to kill you."

"When it involves my sister, yes, it will!"

"I want names, Joe. And when I get them, we put an end to this once and for all."

"No, Dad."

"Why the hell not?"

"We aren't getting justice for Maxwell by

indulging in murder, however much they deserve it. No, we're going to give them something far worse."

Sassy's father growled. "Explain yourself, son."

"Sorry, Aaron." Joe sighed. "I get more than just memories when I use my magic, Dad. Every thought, every feeling. It's a part of the package. Sure, I can dodge the worst of it when I want. I can shield myself somewhat, but when it's so raw, it's hard. Maxwell wouldn't have wanted us seeking revenge. He'd want justice. There's a difference, and this time, we'll have to play it Maxwell's way. It's not our way, but it's the right one. We'll just have to make sure our case is so strong, those guilty have no hope of escaping justice. And well, if justice also involves a little vengeance, that's fine, but we stick to the spirit of the law as much as the letter. We beat them at their game, and we beat them fairly. And when we tear their empire down around them, we'll walk away with clean hands. It's harder that way, but that's what we're going to do."

Sassy's father drew in a breath, closed his eyes, and nodded. "I can live with that."

"It's not our choice. It was Maxwell's."

No one could raise the dead, but for a time, he'd live on through us, and that would have to be good enough.

SIXTEEN

You're going to mat his damned fur.

GRIEF WORKED IN MYSTERIOUS WAYS, and while mine washed away and crystallized into new purpose, Sassy fell beneath its weight. She clung to me except for rare moments dictating we be separated, but she always came back with her steps dragging, her head bowed, and the life beaten out of her. It took me a while, but realization sank in.

For all we'd investigated crimes and dug into the secret lives of people in the search for justice, I'd always sheltered her from the worst parts of our job, carrying the burden of it so she wouldn't have to. I'd walked in her shoes the first few murder cases we'd pursued on behalf of the defense, and I'd accepted more than my share of the work to keep her from experiencing the bitterness of life at its absolute worst.

My caring came at a price, and she paid it in a blow so heavy we'd all falter for a while.

I couldn't protect her from everything, and I hadn't done her justice in sheltering her. Her father carried some of the responsibility as well, although I'd never blame him for trying to safeguard his little kitten for as long as possible.

Sassy wilted, but when she worked her way through her grief, I'd watch her grow and blossom into someone new and ready to face the world. How she would emerge would dictate a lot about our future, and I held my breath in anticipation of the moment she progressed beyond mourning.

Sassy's father tired of his little kitten's grief by breakfast the next morning, and he decided to take matters into his hands, scruffing me and dragging me off while Joe contained his struggling sister. "I'll return him. You're going to mat his damned fur sobbing on him all the damned time. The damned holes are closed, he ain't got no broken bones, so stop treating him like a box of tissues already!"

Someone needed to tell Sassy's father a swift kick in the ass and a short-term kidnapping wouldn't stop his daughter's grief.

Within twenty minutes and one future father-in-law induced transformation, which also featured a scalding hot shower to get the blood off, I contemplated killing the bastard for running me through a wringer and dumping me on his bathroom floor. He dropped a towel on my head. "As no one except my daughter would ever want to see you naked, dry off, wear the bathrobe on the vanity, pull yourself together, and stop that train wreck. I don't care how you do it, just make the crying stop!"

"I thought Joe said three days." I groaned and debated if I had the energy to wear the damned bathrobe. My chest ached the worst, but after a brief inspection, I'd emerged from the shooting with dark bruises. My shoulder screamed protest when I tried to put the towel to good use, managed to tolerable levels, and struggled to shrug into the bathrobe. I ultimately needed help to get into it. "That was not three days. That was a single night."

"And my little kitten spent the entire damned time sobbing her heart out because she doesn't know how to handle this."

Who did? "I'll do what I can."

"You always have. Now get your ass out there and make the crying stop."

I secured the bathrobe, sighed, and worked the kinks out, wondering how lycanthropes dealt with shifting when it hurt so damned much. I wanted to find the nearest soft surface and flop onto it without moving for a week. With a little luck, I could make Sassy the soft surface and keep her from driving her father insane.

I recognized a lost cause, so I gave up hope of making the crying stop anytime soon and braved the storm.

Joe still fought to keep his sister contained, and I closed the distance between us, wiping her cheeks with my thumbs. "Your daddy's mean," I complained. "I'm going to need you to dry those eyes and start getting ready for work, Sassy. We've got names, so instead of tears, we're going to give them the balance of heartache and make them regret the day they thought they could get away with this. And however tempting, we won't be getting revenge. That's not what Maxwell would want. If you want to cry, wait until the funeral. There'll be time enough for that then."

"I'm so mad."

Ah. I reevaluated my opinion about her state of mind, and had I been thinking clearly, I would've remembered Sassy's response to frustration in safe places was to cry it out since murder was illegal. "We still can't kill them."

"That's why I'm mad."

I shot a glare at Sassy's father. "I think she's moved on to the anger stage of grief."

"We're all there," he replied. "And don't you look at me like that, boy. You couldn't tell that was angry crying, either."

While he had a point, it didn't stop me from giving him another dose of my glare.

"Daddy, he's a first shifter," Sassy whispered. "He's a territorial first shifter. And you're turning gray-green, Aaron. Go sit down."

"Remember that part I warned you about when he first shifted, Sassy? It's starting, and he's going to be miserable. Nausea, fever, chills, you name it, he'll experience it. You have two jobs to do."

"Two? What two?" she demanded, and after consideration, she placed her hands on my hips to direct me to the living room couch. "Your sides aren't hurt, right?"

"My back's fine," I told her. "And I'm feeling more bruised than anything else."

All in all, I'd gotten lucky. I supposed I would never learn if I'd gotten lucky, or my lively state had been by design.

The instant I sat, Sassy stretched out, used my lap as a pillow, and passed out. I lifted my hand and pinched the bridge of my nose. "Joe? Can you grab me a pillow and her blanket? What were her two jobs supposed to be, anyway?"

"Keep you calm and feed you whenever you can keep something down. I'm exaggerating on how bad it'll be. I have several pill bottles with your name on them. You'll have the fever and chills, but the nausea should be manageable and the pixie dust will make sure you don't give a shit you're miserable." With a little help from Sassy's father and brother, I made myself comfortable and tucked Sassy in so she could rest. Even in sleep, her expression seemed pained, and I stroked my hand over her head, not sure what anyone could do to give her respite from everything.

"I don't use pixie dust often," I admitted. "It's not my thing."

"You're a restrained, sober man. We can barely get you to have a beer. We know. But you're going to have this pixie dust. It'll help you keep your temper controlled, and the last thing we need is you getting snappy. I'll start you off on a light dose. We want you in a decent mood, not higher than a kite."

"As long as I'm not impaired for this."

"It'll hurt," he warned.

"I'd rather hurt and be functional. I need to be able to think."

"If you change your mind, let me know."

I nodded. "I'll take some painkillers, but we'll leave the dust for if I start going for someone's throat. Deal?"

Joe chuckled and shrugged. "Whatever you want, Aaron. I'm not going to argue with you over it, not when you're itching to catch these bastards."

"What do we have on them, Joe?"

"A lot of names, recording devices like I

hoped, and some interesting evidence left in Sharon's apartment. I don't know where Sharon got it, but we have some non-circumstantial evidence to work with."

Non-circumstantial evidence, glorious, wonderful, hard, useful evidence sounded better than even painkillers. "What type of non-circumstantial evidence?"

"Financials. Bank accounts, amounts, more names, and more than a few of them match what Sharon told you," he announced.

In so many investigations I'd participated in, the financials often told the most accurate story, leading to convictions, exonerations, and in one case, even a complete overturn of an old conviction. "How does that fit with what we know of Sharon, the outfit, and our culprits?"

"If accurate, planted evidence is still evidence, and the police have the evidence. Maxwell's partner has already been arrested on a charge of conspiring to murder a law enforcement officer. Rob's been feeding me intel."

That led me to a concern I didn't want to think about too much. "Is Rob part of the conspiracy?"

"Not as far as I can tell, but anything's possible at this point," Joe admitted. "Your brother's looking into it. Several police commissioners are being arrested by a mixed hat of the CDC, the FBI, and the military police for their part in Maxwell's murder. A lot of the evidence seems to be a paper trail leading to Maxwell's murder."

"He was the target?"

"It looks like it, and you and Sharon were just the extras. Perhaps they didn't account for the lycanthropy virus? The virus is a major contributor to why Sharon made it to the hospital, taking a close second place to you administering CPR. And yes, I saw everything. You did the only thing you knew how to do, and while you got fucking lucky, you made a difference. Try to focus on that in the days moving forward. Also, if you could stop petting my sister, that would be great. It's making me uncomfortable."

"Joe, I'm going to be marrying your sister. I recommend you get used to it." To prove I refused to be cowed by him, I kept stroking my hand over her hair. "She's had a hard few days."

"You marrying my sister is also uncomfortable."

"Maybe you need to see a doctor. You're the one who wanted this to happen."

"The consequences of such actions weren't yet apparent when I opened my mouth and encouraged you."

I rolled my eyes. "You'll probably survive."

"Wait. You're going to be marrying my sister?" Joe scowled. "Cheetahs don't marry."

"Like hell we don't," Sassy's father muttered. "See this ring?" He held up his left hand. "This ring is evidence that cheetahs definitely do marry, and if you had a single functioning brain cell in that skull of yours, you'd drop it. If your sister hears you, you'll never hear the end of it. Also, as you're giving Aaron a hard time, you can help plan the wedding, since their elopement plans are officially canceled. It'll give Sassy something to look forward to after the rest of this mess has been sorted out."

"I have to return to work."

"If you even think of skipping your sister's wedding, you will be returning to work in pieces."

While I really doubted Sassy's father would kill Joe, I worried enough I rested my hand on Sassy's shoulder and stared at him. "I'd give up now."

"I should've just told you it was better to be a coalition male. Damned breeders."

"I'd watch your mouth, Joe. He wasn't born a cheetah. They might have nothing but girls. Then you might be surrounded by nothing but breeders. And if their children's children have daughters, you coalition males are going to rue and lament the day you made fun of him for loving your sister."

Joe scowled. "They'll be lucky to have a single girl."

"Don't count your eggs until they hatch. Your sister's more stubborn than a rock, and her male's not much better. They'll have a bunch of baby girls just to spite you."

"That's not even biologically possible, Dad," Joe complained.

I knew one way I could make it biologically possible. "Don't worry, Joe. I'll just ask a succubus and incubus for help. I'm sure they'd be delighted to help with the conception of many little girls to help boost the breeding cheetah population in the city."

Joe's eyes wouldn't. "You wouldn't."

I cocked a brow. "Try me. Keep complaining, Joe, and we'll see what happens. Now, being serious. Where are we at with the investigation? How can I help?"

"The first problem is the infiltration into law enforcement. Losing several commissioners and a handful of cops involved with the original investigation hurts. Add in the fact that several of the judges who issued warrants will face accusations for their involvement, and this is turning into a mess. In good news, the judge who approved Rob's warrants seems to be outside of the conspiracy. The FBI, CDC, and military are cleaning house, and they're armed with angels. Because they're law enforcement officers accused of the murder of another law enforcement officer, a lot of those pesky human rights laws simply don't apply. If they can't claim they weren't involved, they'll be questioned until we get the information we need. The angels will see it's done fairly, but while they retain their right to remain silent, doing so is an automatic imprisonment without bail until the completion of the trial."

I grimaced. "And it's essentially an admission of guilt if they can't verify to an angel they are not guilty of the crime."

"Right. Not very satisfying for us, but we catch the bastards. Maxwell's death ensures they'll live the rest of their lives in prison. And if any of them have the talents required to pull off the murders and mask the truth, well, it wouldn't surprise me if Texas temporarily revived the death sentence specifically for this case. It'd drag out in the courts, but with so many women and children dead, it might happen. And if they don't, they'll be locked in maximum security, and kept in a cell that nullifies most forms of magic. Either way, they'll have hell to pay."

"Will eliminating the law enforcement participants and judiciary participants be enough to bring the mountain down?"

"It's only the first pebbles of the landslide. We've cut off their easy way of obstructing the investigation, though." Joe paced the living room.

Someone knocked on the door, and Sassy's father went to answer it. Moments later, my parents stepped into the room with my brother in tow. I lifted my hand off Sassy's shoulder and waved. "If anyone else cries today, I might snap. Please no crying. I'm done with crying for now. Thank you, Mom."

My mother sighed and shook her head. "All right. I got it out of my system last night, anyway. How are you feeling?"

"Bruised but otherwise fine."

"I'm sorry about your friend, baby. How's Sassy holding up?"

"She had a rough night."

"So much crying," Joe muttered.

"Couldn't kill anyone over it, got frustrated?" my mother guessed.

"How'd you know?" Joe blurted.

"We're southern women, Mr. Chetty. When we want to start with the killing and can't, that's frustrating. Someone tried to kill my baby twice. You better bet I was frustrated. You've got a lot to learn about women, bless your heart."

"He's a coalition cheetah, Mom. He can't help it."

"Ah, yes. I've been learning about you coalition males. From my understanding, you

are relentlessly into other males unless a female forcibly evicts you from the coalition?"

Heaven help us all, my mother had taken
an interest in cheetah breeding habits. "Good
luck, Joe."

Sassy's father grinned at my mother. "Yes,
Mrs. Clinton, that's exactly how it works. My
little kitten wisely captured her breeding
male before his induction into a coalition. I
raised her to be smart. Her momma's mad she
didn't get to wrangle him properly, but I
figure she's been wrangling him for years."

I wouldn't tell my mother the bastard had
popped me in the mouth to help his daughter
get what she wanted.

"I will hope they have many daughters despite the odds being against them. I know a
succubus. She owes me a favor. We could
arrange for a girl or three. Cheetahs need
more girls. I'd be helping your species out a
little."

Sassy's father turned his attention to me.
"I see your threats about sex demons was not
an idle one."

I shrugged and held my hands up in surrender. "I had no idea Mom had any dealings
with demons."

"Just because they indulge in sin doesn't
make them monsters," my mother replied.
"No, there are other monsters worth wor-
rying about, and they've tried to kill you

twice. Is there anything we can do to help? Also, if you need a succubus and incubus for the strategic planning of my granddaughters, I know a pair who'd love to meet you."

I smirked in Joe's direction. "Try me," I mouthed at him.

He flipped his middle fingers at me.

Sassy's father excused himself, went into the other room, and returned carrying a box, which he set on the floor with a loud thump. Five more trips later, and he patted the stack. "This is a complete newspaper archive of all dates we think are relevant from the murders. We need a complete collection of any articles that may involve those on the list Aaron got from Sharon Gray. In addition to this, we're trying to form profiles on all political activities of those involved. We're hoping to get a complete picture of what led up to the mass murders. Hopefully, we will also catch the killers hired to pull off the killing, but I doubt we'll have the resources. We also speculate they're providing some of the information to make sure their hires are brought to justice."

"With one hand they giveth, with the other they taketh away," my mother grumbled.

"On our breaks, we can plan a wedding," Sassy's father announced.

"I brought a binder."

I rolled my eyes so hard I hoped to give

myself a concussion, but I remained conscious. "No marriage license, no wedding. That's how it works."

"I'm friends with one of the county clerks," my mother chirped. "I'll give her a call. I'm sure she'll have no problem sneaking out of work with the seal and all the information you need."

"Mom," I complained. "We can handle going to the courthouse on our own to get the paperwork when needed. There isn't going to be a wedding until *after* we've caught these bastards and made sure they're so ruined they'll wish we'd killed them."

"That's my boy. What can we do to help so we can get to the wedding planning?"

I considered my parents. "You'd take on a bunch of ultra-wealthy politicians and conspirators if they're in the way of a wedding, won't you?"

"Well, that other son of mine isn't getting married, so if I want a wedding, I have to get rid of a bunch of corrupt politicians. And those corrupt politicians hurt my baby boy. What do you think?"

I coughed. "I think I should have just dumped the case on your lap from the start."

My mother shot me the look, the one that meant I'd skated out onto thin ice and was a single step from regretting it for the rest of my life, however short that might be. Very short, according to her expression. "I love you, Mom."

"I knew you were always smarter than your brother." My mother snagged one of the boxes, set it beside my feet, and joined it on the floor. "For the record, I have a strong dislike of politicians, I will enjoy this far more than I should, and I know how to use a gun."

"You're a Texan, Mom. Most Texans know how to use a gun. It's in the guidebook on how to be a Texan. You told me this when I was four, which was when you told me I'd get a switching I'd never forget if you caught me treating any gun like a toy."

"You were one when I first told you that, boy, and I told it to you every month once a month, while slapping my leg with a switch I'd picked just for the purpose of scaring obedience into you. It worked. I'm still a better shot than you are." With a delicate sniff, my mother removed the cover from the box and pulled out a newspaper. "List, please."

"I'll go print a copy, ma'am," Sassy's father said, leaving the room.

Mark plopped onto the couch next to me. "How's Sassy holding up, really?"

"I forgot she'll cry if frustrated enough, and she's probably frustrated she can't indulge in multiple cases of homicide. Add in Maxwell, and well, what were you expecting? Her father got tired of it not long before you arrived, dragged me into the bathroom, made me shift, and demanded I make the sobbing stop. I guess it counts if she passes out from exhaustion?" I smiled at Sassy and brushed her hair away from her face. "She had her spats with Maxwell, but..."

I shrugged.

Sassy's father returned with several printouts, which he handed around. "She's Sassy. She liked she could sass him without fear of rebuttal. She could be herself around him, and that's rare for her. All of the cheetahs she knows wouldn't give her the time of day most of the time. Coalition males do not pay much mind to breeding females, and they don't handle her sassing very well. He did, and that hit her hard. To almost lose you, too? She needed to get it out of her system. When she wakes up, all hell is going to break loose."

Keeping Sassy from taking over the world in her quest for vengeance would occupy me for a while. "We just have to convince her that sinking them is the best we're going to get."

"She'll be fine," her father assured me. "She'll be pissy about it, but we're all pissy about it. These fuckers killed a good man for no other reason than disliking his politics."

The truth would hurt for a long time. "No, they killed him because of his ethics. He's the type of man who would've worked relentlessly to stop them. He dedicated his life to making up for a bill he wasn't even fully at fault for." I regretted not learning that truth sooner. Things might've been different.

Sassy's father sighed. "And had they been smart, they would've made sure you hadn't survived the shooting, because you're cut from that same cloth. You tossed your career down the drain just like he did for the same reasons. Justice will be served one way or another. There's a lot we can't do without a badge, but there's a lot we can do. Working with the DA is untraditional, and we'll step on FBI toes, but we can present enough evidence to point the FBI in the right direction, and that's what this is all about. We won't get our share of the glory, but we *will* make certain every last one of those asses pays."

"In blood would be nice," I muttered.

My brother yanked on my ear. "No. You may not indulge your lycanthropy virus with brutal violence, no matter how satisfying it might be. I had to turn in my gun until it was determined I would not participate in vigilante justice."

"Be nice to your brother, Mark," my father ordered.

"For the record, I find your favoritism disturbing," my brother complained. "Why are you siding with them, anyway? They took my gun!"

My mother smiled. "You do not need to

carry around that nasty rifle everywhere. And as for your brother, he was always the nicer child, that's why."

"You suck, Aaron."

"How is the loss of your rifle my fault?"

"You got shot, and for some reason, my commanding officers determined I would leave a pile of bodies in my wake if I got a list of the assholes responsible. They found out I had a list of the assholes responsible. Joe? Tell them I can have my gun back. They seem to think you can handle a psychiatric evaluation."

"No. And you're not going into the field until *you* have a high-sensitivity lycanthropy scan done. You're as vicious as your brother, and he's fresh off his first shift. With the way you sleep around, you probably got infected years ago. That'll serve you right, too. And if you did get infected, I bet there's a cranky lady waiting for her chance to land you permanently. So, Mark. Have you had any cranky ladies hanging out in the wings lately? Maybe a reoccurring dalliance somewhere? A favorite brothel?"

I relaxed and waited for the real show to begin, one where two military-trained assholes went in for gold and emerged battered and bruised. I put my bets on my brother; he needed the vent before he burst. "I'm not sure I classify as vicious, Joe. I'm with you on my brother being short a few cans of a six pack, though. If you're going to go bust him up and make him a cat, too, do it outside. Keep the infections to the younger generation."

"For that, you're not getting pixie dust *or* painkillers until you're begging. Anyway, you're really non-violent for a first shifter. You were remarkably well behaved at the hospital. Good job, by the way. The one nurse said you'd limited your aggression to flat ears and hissing. No swipes, and you kept your blood to yourself. You score full points and a best first shifter award."

"There's an award? What do I get?"

"One get out of ass-kicking free card. You need it. I don't know what the hell you did to my sister, but she wouldn't stop purring until we got the call you'd been shot. You get a second card for your work with Sharon. You might need two. My sister wouldn't stop purring. It was disturbing."

"Maybe if you were better to your coalition buddies, they'd purr, too," I countered.

Sassy's father howled his laughter. "You just lost that one, son. Give it up. Your sister was purring because she was happy. She's been waiting a long time for him. Let her be happy. She'll start purring again once she feels like she's able to do something. And she probably won't stop for a while."

"After the first few kids, maybe," Sassy's

mother said, striding into the living room carrying a tray loaded with mugs, which she set on the coffee table. "I've soup warming for you in the kitchen, Aaron. There'll be barbecue in a few hours, but the soup should tide you over while you do your reading and planning. Joe, I don't want to hear you getting mouthy with the guests again."

"Aaron doesn't count. He's stealing my sister."

"Boy, you're so jealous you can't see straight," Sassy's father scolded, grabbing Joe by the ear and dragging him towards the kitchen. "We've mouths to feed, and when your mother says we're having barbecue, that means we get to make it. Leave Aaron alone. You've checked him over plenty, and your sister's fine, too. You're just mad she went to him and not you, and your delicate big brother sensibilities are offended. Don't you be minding him any, Aaron. I swear, some days, this one wants to be a breeding male and is too much of a chicken shit to tell his coalition he wants a lady to catch him so he can raise a litter, too."

"Dad!"

"Don't you 'Dad' me, you brat. March. Your momma wants her turn helping with the hunt, so we get to provide the meat so she doesn't come after us when she's hungry in a few hours, and you know how your momma gets when she's hungry."

I waited for them to leave before grinning at Sassy's mother. "Thank you kindly, ma'am."

"You're welcome. Now, you just tell us what we need to do so we can get the real work done while the boys play in the yard."

"We need to get as much dirt as we can on these assholes so we can bury them with it," I said, pointing at the boxes of newspaper articles. "And we start looking there, because there's nothing newspapers love more than getting dirt on filthy politicians."

SEVENTEEN

Dump chocolate on their heads and
leave the ants on their yard.

"FIRE ANTS," Sassy mumbled, stretching on
the couch and rubbing her nose against my
stomach. "Kill the bastards with fire ants."

Hours of reading with a short break to
scarf down ribs and brisket had earned us a
pile of newspaper articles and a list of re-
porters, some whom still lived in the area,
who might have more intel on the men and
women on our list. I considered the stacks,
which took up most of the living room floor,
fighting my urge to smile. "That's a pretty
good idea. How do you propose to kill the
bastards with fire ants?"

"Dump chocolate on their heads and leave
the ants on their yard. Ants can figure it out.
Ants love chocolate." She yawned, wrapped
her arms around me, and held on tight.
"Warm."

The prophesied fever had something to do

with the warmth, and Sassy's father kept changing the temperature when I rotated through the various stages of sick, trying to keep me comfortable without a care in hell about what anyone else thought about it. "There's lunch in the fridge for you if you're hungry."

Sassy growled and bit on my bathrobe, which I translated as hard evidence of her hunger. "Bathrobes aren't food."

She didn't agree with me, as she tried to take several more bites before hissing her frustration.

"And that would be my idiot sister still mostly asleep," Joe announced. "But find out more about those fire ants."

Grinning, I poked Sassy's shoulder. "Do fire ants even like chocolate?"

"They better. Chocolate's delicious. You're warm enough to melt chocolate on."

Joe snorted. "That's because he's running a fever, Sassy. Also, let us never discuss you melting chocolate on Aaron ever again, thank you."

"Since when did you become such a wuss?" Sassy hissed at her brother, eased off my lap, and lurched upright. She eyed my bathrobe. "Why aren't you wearing clothes, Aaron?"

"Your father gave it to me, then you fell asleep, and I wasn't going to wake you. This is what I'm wearing now." I smiled at her and pushed her hair out of her face and tucked the wayward strands behind her ears. "Are you feeling better?"

"Are fire ants an option? We could get thousands of them and let them loose on their lawn. Get entire nests of them."

"I don't think we can assault them with fire ants, Sassy."

She scowled. "We wouldn't be assaulting them. We'd just be letting nature run its course. We'd just provide some chocolate to help encourage them."

"Why waste good chocolate?"

"We have to guarantee the fire ants attack them. It's the only way to be sure."

"I have no idea what you were dreaming about, but should I be concerned?"

"I will not use chocolate on you in that fashion. And I'd use the best quality chocolate on—"

"No," Joe snapped. "No. No. No. We are not discussing what you would do to Aaron if you slathered him in chocolate."

Sassy's brows rose, and she blinked at her brother. "Maybe you shouldn't be thinking about my mate like that, you insufferably male cheetah pervert. He's mine. If you want to be slathered in chocolate, go find yourself some other female. It's not my fault you coalition males are so damned tame."

In what universe were coalition males, who had a reputation of sleeping with anything male that moved, tamed? "Yeah, go find some other female, Joe. I'm sure my mother would be delighted to introduce you to some classy ladies. That's the only type of lady my mother bothers with. Classy."

"I know a few wolves," my mother agreed. "Single wolves. Of the female variety. They come to church sometimes. I know a cat, too. Not sure what breed, she's too shy to tell a soul, mind you. She brought an angel to church with her, surprising us all something fierce. Turns out the poor dear hasn't been taking to lycanthropy well, and her momma put it in her will to pay an angel to help her get all settled. The angel refused payment, and well, she's just not comfortable and all adrift. She'd love to tame herself another cat, I'm sure. She won't come within five feet of us normal folks, terrified of passing on her infection."

I leaned forward for a better look at my brother, who sat on the floor still flipping through newspapers. "When did our mother start hanging out with lycanthropes, Mark?"

"Around the same time it was obvious the only way she'd get grandchildren was if she got over herself and accepted grandchildren were only coming through a severe case of infectious, incurable disease. After that, she dove right on in. Then she changed churches because they wouldn't let any lycanthropes in the door, and that didn't sit right with her. I'd call it three years ago. You really should visit them more often."

"I'm sorry, Mom."

My father chuckled, dumping a newspaper into the read pile and grabbing another. "She was hiding it from you expecting to have to swallow some bitter pills. Your brother only found out because she made him go to church with her the last time he came to town."

"Joe should totally go get laid by someone of the female persuasion," Sassy said, rolling her shoulders. "I need a shower. I think I'm still wearing some of your blood, Aaron. You're probably wearing some of your blood, too, so you should come shower with me."

"Stop it!" Joe howled.

"Bless your heart," my mother murmured, shaking her head. "Go take a shower, and take your time about it. Your brother's been so offended he wasn't the one to coddle you, he's been rather hissy. I've noticed the felines hiss often. It's rather endearing, really." My mother's smile brightened to a huge grin. "Please. Take your time."

My mother was on a mission for grandchildren, and I didn't have the heart to tell her I'd probably end up snoozing on the nearest appropriate surface rather than doing what she wanted.

"Come on, Aaron. Your hair's a mess." Sassy grabbed my hand and tugged until I rose to my feet. "You'll feel better after you're cleaned up."

While I likely did have blood in my hair, I doubted I needed another shower, but I co-operated with her anyway, following her up-stairs. The instant we reached the top of the staircase, she checked behind us. Huffing, she dragged me to the master bathroom typically reserved for her parents.

"You're testing your luck."

"Daddy won't care and Mom will accept it as inevitable. You need to relax and soak, and they have the good tub. It fits both of us. The others don't. But I'll shower first while you lounge." To make it clear she wasn't accepting no for an answer, she stoppered the tub, got the water running, and adjusted the tempera-ture to her liking. "Soak, Aaron! I was lying about the blood in your hair. Daddy got it all out from the looks of it, it's just messy."

That was something. It took me a few mo-ments to realize Sassy shimmered in the bathroom lights. "You seem to have been hosed down with neutralizer recently."

"You don't remember? We all got hosed down before getting into your truck. We'll have to clean the seats and bed; it's pink and sparkly right now. Sorry. They get pissy about potentially spreading the virus."

"I'm sure my big, manly truck will survive."

"We can spend some quality time together in it to make up for the pink glitter."

Did she really think I'd say no? "That sounds like a great idea. We'll have to schedule it after we take care of a certain list of names. I'm interested in hearing more about your chocolate and fire ant plan."

"I don't think we can get bullet ants. I'd rather use bullet ants. They hurt more."

"Where would one get bullet ants?"

"No clue in hell. It's easy to get fire ants here. Hell, Daddy can't get rid of the damned things from the far back of the yard. He'd be thrilled if we could evict those bastards. We can get them in the thousands. Maybe even the hundreds of thousands. I'd sell shoes to get my hands on as many of those little shits as possible."

"I'm not sure Maxwell would approve of us terrorizing his killers with fire ants."

"Maxwell would fucking love it, but only if we didn't get caught."

"All right, I'm going to listen to your pitch. You make this good, Sassy, and I'll even think about how we can legally inflict fire ants on those bastards."

"With my chocolate syrup?"

"I can think of better things we could be doing with chocolate syrup and whipped cream. Why waste good chocolate when sugar water will do? What if they like chocolate?"

"You're right. They might like chocolate. Sugar water is obviously the right way to go about this."

"And sugar water is rather hard to detect if we spray it down and try to lure this hive of angry fire ants to the appropriate locations. Are there laws against escorting fire ants to a new home?"

"I really don't know, but if there's not, there should be." Sassy wrinkled her nose, ditched her clothes in record time, and hopped into the shower. I disapproved of the frosted glass. "That's why we should do it before it's against the law. We should check. If it's not illegal to spill sugar water in a path to a location and strongly suggest the fire ants relocate, we can't be busted for jack shit."

"Think your mother would mind if we snitched some of her bubble bath?" I asked, eyeing the bottle perched on the tub's ledge.

"She won't mind at all. Make yourself cozy, Aaron. Wait until I join you to fall asleep. Oh, and don't mind my idiot brother. He's just mad you actually did what he wanted. He was so damned sure you'd run away like a little coward rather than take the dive. I think he was hoping you'd run so I'd have to work to earn you. He's been striking out with his boyfriends lately."

"Oh? How so?"

"The coalition males are dicks, that why. They like their boyfriends young and rowdy. Joe is old and cranky. Your mother's going to have fun matchmaking for him, and bless his little heart, he's going to be a mixed species breeding male within a year. And I will enjoy laughing at him. If he's smart, he'll settle down with someone who doesn't have the infection and bring in a new lady to the lines. We need fresh blood. Your contribution only goes so far, and Joe is so not the nurturing type. I'm going to try to rescue your mother's feline. I know some cats."

"I'm aware. You know *all* the cats."

"It'll be useful when we become cops. Lycanthropes stick together, and if they see something, they'll let me know. They'll eventually get to know you and come to you, too. The parents will come to you, particularly."

"Why me?"

"You'll be more likely to want to murder anyone who hurts a kid. I'm the one they'll come to if they have a kid needing protection. Males will do anything to eliminate threats to the children. And you were like that before lycanthropy, too. We'll both get swamped whenever there's a crime involving kids.

That's going to be rough, but someone has to do it. It's best if it's us, right? We'll do the job right."

Even over the shower, I could hear the worry in Sassy's voice, and all my misgivings over the years and the occasional comments I'd made about not envying the police for the work they did, all came back to haunt me in one way or another. I tossed the bathrobe to join Sassy's clothing and slipped into the tub, adding a liberal splash of bubbles. "We'll do the job right," I promised. "But it might mean we don't get to lure fire ants to new homes if we can't find a way to do it without breaking the law."

"We can get creative, right? There's nothing illegal about spilling sugar on the road. We just have to leave a really good sugar trail and evict a bunch of ants. We could get every lycanthrope in the damned city to help out, too."

As I could see Sassy coordinating a mass relocation of insects to secure revenge on those who'd murdered Maxwell, I worried. "It's probably not wise."

"Fire ants aren't lethal. They're just annoying as fuck. We'll only send a few. Just enough to make the fuckers suffer while we sink them in the court of public opinion and ensure their political careers are over forever. Max was a good guy. Sure, he fucked up, but he was a good guy. A lot of people liked him. They'll be labeled cop killers and be fucked. Fuckers."

"I'll look into the legalities of fire ants, but I'm not promising any more than that. *If* I can find a way to do so that's…" I blinked, then I narrowed my eyes. "Hey, Sassy?"

"What?"

"Do you believe in ghosts?"

"Well, no. Not really."

"I read a book once that had a vigilante cop who couldn't get the evidence he needed to sink a bastard for his crimes. A murder. So he figured out a way to get the guy to confess."

"I've read it. I was bored and you had it out at your apartment. He recorded voices that sounded like the victim and played them while he was sleeping to freak him out. The guy went mad and turned himself in, claiming he was being haunted by his victims. There's a lot of problems with that plan, Aaron."

"Like what?"

"Breaking and entering to set up the players is definitely illegal."

"It's only illegal if you're not invited. There's some cool toys out there that can play sounds and make it difficult to hide. You know, those annoying damned beepers you set up in my apartment that one time?

They're small, hard to spot, and can make a lot of noise. If we can program something like one of those to play back voices, give them to someone who has been invited to their place, and plant them, maybe we can copycat that book."

Sassy turned off the shower, marched across the bathroom, and joined me in the tub. "Tell me more," she purred. "That sounds even more evil than the fire ants. No, not just evil, useful. You could get them to confess just to make the voices stop."

I considered it, and then I smiled. "And I think my mother might know the absolute perfect accomplices who'd love to get involved. While it was my idea at first, she's obviously been wanting granddaughters and has realized girls are few and far between. It's to help cheetah lycanthropes around the world, or so she'll say."

"What? Who?"

"A succubus."

Sassy's eyes widened. "A succubus? Your mother knows a succubus?"

"From what I've gathered, she knows an incubus, too. I think she really wants litters of granddaughters and has been doing her research. If you're aiming for specifics, they're who you go to. And honestly, since the boys versus girls issue is my contribution, I'll just pay an incubus a filthy amount of money to help increase the odds of a girl. I'm not too keen having my time with you be a group activity, either."

"You can do that?" Sassy gasped. "I had no idea."

"They're walking, talking fertility clinics, Sassy. They live and breathe sex and reproduction. They can make barren women fertile when motivated enough. Same with infertile men. I'm pretty sure they can reverse full hysterectomies if they really want. That's what they do. If you want ten daughters, I'll do whatever it takes to give you ten daughters."

Sassy's eyes narrowed, and she smiled. "For starters, we can let nature do whatever it is nature wants to do. I see you're not put off by the idea of children."

"Sassy, you're naked in the same bathtub with me. What were you expecting?"

"Good point. I was thoroughly corrected about my misconceptions regarding your lack of interest. There is definitely no lack of interest. You're very interested. This made me very happy."

I grinned. "You purred so much you pissed your brother off."

"I couldn't help it. I was looking forward to seeing you, and I got excited, so I purred. But then we got the call."

"It won't bring him back, but we'll have to have one boy so we can name him Maxwell, then we'll have to do the whole parenting thing right so he grows up wanting to be a cop."

"Not a politician?"

I shook my head. "No. Maxwell was a lot of things, but I think he'd missed his calling all along. Sure, I liked bitching about him, but he did the cop thing well. He shined. He just got lost along the way."

"You got a little lost along the way, too. You'd make a better cop than a private investigator."

Enlightenment struck me, and I relaxed in the tub, unable to stop my smile. "No, I'd only make a better cop right now because I was a private investigator first. And maybe the reason Maxwell made such a great cop was because he was a politician first. Those who killed him won't get away with it, that much I swear. We know who it is. We just need to ensure everyone knows what they've done and close off all routes of escape, even if it means we can't dunk them in chocolate syrup and feed them to fire ants."

"I thought we weren't wasting chocolate syrup on them."

"Chocolate syrup sounds more interesting than sugar water," I admitted. "If we're going to make headlines, it should be flashy."

"Go big or go home?"

"Exactly." I smiled at her. "Your father has

banned eloping, and is in full plan a wedding mode. How do you feel about that as the future Mrs. Clinton?"

"It'll keep him busy while we look into legal methods of acquiring confessions. Tell me, Aaron. Do *you* believe in ghosts?"

"As a matter of fact, future Mrs. Clinton, I most certainly do right now. But, before I worry about any ghosts, I think you need to thoroughly reassure yourself I'm intact from head to toe. Take your time. I'm a patient man."

"Yes, you are, and I think I've had my fill of being patient, Mr. Clinton," she purred. "But I will accept your offer to thoroughly reassure myself you're intact. From head to toe."

I pointed at my shoulder, which still ached despite Joe's work. "This spot hurts. I bet you could kiss it and make it all better."

"Don't worry, Mr. Clinton. I'll get there. Eventually."

WHILE I ENJOYED DOZING in a bubble bath with Sassy, I was less than thrilled with the invasion of her mother, who went about her business, which involved gathering up the clothes we'd left on the floor and straightening everything we'd disturbed. "Are you finished taking your time? There's several coalitions of hungry males downstairs whining because I'm not going to serve them supper until you two are finished getting cleaned up. Sassy, what have I told you about napping in the tub?"

"It doesn't count when I'm sleeping on Aaron. He was awake."

"He was about as awake as the hordes ten minutes after Christmas dinner. If you two would like to sleep, take yourselves up to bed, and I'll keep a plate for you."

"We'll be down in a few minutes," I promised. "Who all is downstairs?"

"Numerous coalitions of cheetahs, representatives from every wolf pack in the city, I lost count of the felines, more police officers than I can shake a stick at, Chief Braneni, and several district attorneys from all over the damned place. Your friend Rob's around, and I ain't seen an unhappier man in a long time."

"He's had a hard time lately," Sassy mumbled, stretching and yawning before resting her cheek against my shoulder. "Anything important?"

"They were itching to question Aaron, but your brother spoke up and said he'd already poked around and could answer the questions on Aaron's behalf, so they'll do a cross-examination as soon as you're downstairs to compare what Joe saw versus what you thought you saw, Aaron. They're hoping to get more information beyond what Joe's already reported. Those cops are really unhappy. There's been a lot of arrests, and the local law enforcement crew is down by almost twenty percent."

I sucked in a breath. "That many?"

"There's going to be a lot of happy lycanthropes. Because of the high number of arrests that will ultimately lead to imprisonment, the CDC is pushing to have the test of the lycanthropes in the force here accelerated. You two will still be the flagship pair, but they're going to open a special academy session a month or two after your session starts, or so Chief Braneni claims. That's part of why we've got so many here today. They're handing in the names of those interested in signing up."

"The chief is handling it directly? That's odd."

"CDC's orders, as they need to verify potential candidates, run virus checks, and otherwise do evaluations on suitability. The CDC really wants this to work. Too many lycanthropes, not enough lycanthropes policing them." Sassy's mother shrugged. "I'll go fetch you some clothing, so start thinking about getting out of there. There's a lot of folks wanting a chance to talk to you."

I waited for Sassy's mother to leave before

stretching and beginning the tedious process of working the kinks out. "We're going to have to buy a house, and it needs a tub better than this one," I announced.

"I like your priorities. I also warned you we're not body shy, right? We're going to need really good locks on our bathroom door if we ever want privacy. I would've locked the door, but my mother would've just asked Dad to take off the damned hinges to bust in; he installed the hinges on the other side specifically so we couldn't lock ourselves in the bathroom."

"Good precaution. I'll be borrowing that."

"Aaron."

"What? It's true. Children and unsupervised tub usage is a no-no." I considered it. "And the bathroom door will have a proper key adults can easily access."

"I see you've been corrupted by my father already."

I smiled at her. "You can blame my old man for this. He may not be a lycanthrope, but he's got hover-parent tendencies. It's genetic, I'm sure."

"I just thought you should know that lycanthrope women can have children into their early hundreds from the looks of it. There are emergence women who were infected later in life still having children. I thought you'd appreciate some warning."

"What I'd like to know is how the CDC knows this crap when emergence wasn't even a hundred years ago."

"Well, not quite. Magic has been here all along, but it floods the world in waves. We're in the middle of the flood right now. They know because there are people who survived between the waves in the limited pockets of magic left. Add in the divines, the angels, and the demons in disguise, who'll talk about how the world used to be if the price is right, and the CDC can learn a lot without having to have people experience it. Lycanthropes are easy. They're always in high numbers during the waves. But it's higher than any other wave. That's what the rumors claim, at any rate."

"You believe the rumors?"

"Yeah, I do. Mom and Dad were from the emergence, and it took their viruses a long time to mature. Mom's thinking about having more kids down the road. She'd like another girl."

With a single look at Sassy, I could understand why. "If I were your father, I'd want another kid just like you, too. But your brothers are good men."

"She wouldn't mind a few more boys. The house is too quiet."

"Is this a cheetah thing I should be worried about in a few years?"

"Only if you don't like children." Sassy grinned and poked my chest. "And you can't even try to trick me, Mr. Clinton. You adore children."

Only someone blind wouldn't notice. "I've been thoroughly busted, I see."

"Not rocket science, Aaron."

Sassy's mother invaded the bathroom long enough to leave clothes before excusing herself, and I sighed at the inevitable eviction from the warm water and Sassy's intimate company. "They're going to invade in packs if we don't go downstairs."

"They really will. Still, I'm sorry, Aaron."

"For what?"

"My father infected you."

I smiled and stroked her back. "Sassy, I came over here with those damned shoes and a purse and asked him for help. I was tired of watching you be miserable, and I didn't want you to have to go back on your word, so I was going to take all the risks and go back on mine. The shoes were hoping you'd forgive me. Don't be sorry."

"He punched you in the mouth."

I pointed at my teeth, which had emerged better than before he'd cleaned my clock and knocked a few out. "And they're just fine now. Dental surgery can work miracles with a little help from magic. And I didn't even have a big bill. It worked out. If I'd known all it would take is your father socking me in the mouth to win you, I would've been presenting myself every morning for my daily beating. By the time I visited your father, I was scheduling my life around when I needed to rescue you from bad dates. I was getting desperate, and I wouldn't ask you to budge on your conditions for who you'd date. And you were right to do so. Lycanthropy isn't a virus to screw around with. I had to want you bad enough to fully accept it. And I did then, and I still do."

"We would've been spared a lot of anguish if I'd just bent," she whispered.

I smiled and held her close. "No, Sassy. There's a lot to be said about the journey being just as important as the destination. Let's make the most of it, and when we get around to having litters of brats of our own, we'll leave them with our parents as often as possible so they hopefully neglect to have additional children of their own because I'm not sure I'm quite ready to handle that yet."

Sassy snickered, splashed me with water, and pulled the stopper from the tub. "You're something else, Aaron."

"I try."

EIGHTEEN

Texans. I could always trust them to
try anything once.

CHAOS WAITED FOR US DOWNSTAIRS, but for
whatever reason, the hordes descended on
Sassy first, leaving me time to reclaim my
spot on the couch and start doing some investigation work for tempting but probably
illegal behavior. To my amusement, while it
was illegal to transport fire ants and other
pest species by vehicle, nothing on the books
stated they couldn't be evicted from their established nests with reasonable force, which
included magic. There were also no laws on
the books banning the clever usage of sugar
water or other non-regulated substances to
encourage pest species to move. There were
some curious bylaws banning the spraying of
chemicals into yards, but none of them
barred non-toxic substances from being
sprayed from the sidewalk.

At some point in time, someone must

have decided to turn a house into a chocolate sundae as there were laws banning the use of whipped cream and chocolate syrup on someone's yard without express permission of the homeowner.

Texans. I could always trust them to try anything once.

To my delight, nothing on the books barred me from mixing sugar water and using them to attract an assortment of critters. There was even a law allowing people to install hummingbird feeders on city property if they met certain requirements. I'd have to check if Tom Heatherow's property had a sidewalk skirting it or a city-owned tree. If there was a city-owned tree skirting his yard, Sassy's hope of using fire ants could be realized with a little work on my part.

However childish, I thought Maxwell would appreciate the effort we'd put in on his behalf. He'd had an odd sense of humor about things like that.

In theory, with a lot of work and finding nests needing to be moved, I could lead innumerable fire ants to Tom Heatherow's home and encourage them to take up residence in his yard without worry of criminal charges.

Luck would dictate if they took offense to his presence, but I'd take what I could get.

"Aaron?" Sassy asked.

I lifted my head. "Yes?"

"I don't think we're going to be able to use chocolate syrup or fire ants."

"We can't use chocolate syrup or whipped cream on private property without home-owner approval, but there's no bylaws barring it from public spaces as long as it's accidental. There are no laws in place against sugar water. There are laws against trans-porting invasive or nuisance species by ve-hicle without permit, but there are no laws barring their relocation through natural means. It's completely legal to create a trail of sugar water along a road and encourage them to move into someone's yard. In other news, there are no laws barring the use of magic to encourage pests to relocate away from some-one's property, but the homeowner must ap-prove the removal of the pests. Fire ants are classified as a pest. And no, we can't ship in bullet ants for the purpose of leading them to an asshole's house."

Every cop in the room, including Chief Braneni, stared at me. I held up my hands in surrender and couldn't smother my grin. "I'm an asshole, ladies and gentlemen. I'm an ass-hole who has been a private investigator for years, and I use the laws for my convenience during investigations. It's not *my* fault there are no laws on the books barring these things. I just figure if we need a confession to catch these bastards, a heavy dose of karma, and the appearance of a curse might help get the confessions we need. Tell me, do you believe in ghosts?"

I truly did love the sound of silence.

Chief Braneni's eyes narrowed, and he crossed his arms over his chest. "I'd love to hear why you want to know if we believe in ghosts."

"I'm a fan of clever ways of getting confessions out of people. Legal ways," I clarified. "I'm also stealing from a novel. Essentially, the investigators needed a confession, so he put together a profile on all the victims and created sound files played during the perp's sleep to make him believe the ghosts of his victims were haunting him. I thought we might do something similar."

"If it's legal, I don't care what you do if we catch these bastards. We're getting confessions aplenty from some elements of this group. It helps that the law allows us to call in angels for the questioning sessions. The angels… are rather cooperative."

My eyes widened. "Cooperative how?"

"They're suggesting questions for us. You know how angels get, Aaron. They're almost as obnoxious when it comes to the cases involving kids as you are. Children are sacred to them, and these fuckers are responsible for the deaths of many innocents. They're invested."

My eyes widened. Angels had their own laws to follow when it came to interactions with humans, not that it did human law enforcement any good; angels came and went as they felt like, and the only reason most of the laws worked was because the angels followed them of their own volition. When they opted to break human laws, they paid the fines as needed and reminded humanity they obeyed a higher power.

"How many angels?"

"We've had five helping us with the questioning sessions."

Five? I whistled. "That's something else."

"We've had some demons show up asking if they could be of use, too. You know something's bad news when those sides join forces. This case is going to move fast. Angelic verification will help make sure we can get a case rolling, but we need more than what we have. How legal can you make this haunting, Mr. Clinton? You've been a pest from the moment you started your investigation business, and we've lost too many bodies to dick around on this. How many lines can you toe?"

"I won't be toeing any lines, sir. It'd all be fully legal."

"Testify before an angel legal?"

I smiled. "That's what I do, sir. I always have. The way Rob tried to sink me? I had to do everything by the book."

"It's exceptionally frustrating, and I never thought I'd see the day where I'd be encouraging him," the DA said.

"I just don't have enough to sink these bastards yet. None of the leads we have give us a direct link to the top of the chain. We've only knocked down a small facet of this group, and we don't have the person tying law enforcement to the power players in this case. We know who they are, we just don't have the damned link."

"We're missing someone?"

"Or we're just not asking the right questions, and while the angels are helping us, they can only nudge us when the person we're questioning makes a mistake from the questions we do ask. That's where we're running into problems. We've gotten enough on them to make sure they stay in prison until trial without bail, and we have enough to convict them all, but we don't have enough to get them all right now."

Shit. "How high do we go?"

"The judges. That's where the trail runs cold. The people working with the judges have done so in anonymous fashions; directions on how to manipulate the courts and laws have been issued through anonymous mailings, letters, and so on. All we have are some post marks showing where the communications came from."

"We have a list of names. Let's see who lives or works near there, and we'll start investigating in that general area. We'll talk to the postal workers there. How many communications?"

"Enough of them that we were about to take the investigation to the post office already," Chief Braneni replied.

"It's like you know how to do investigations work." I rolled my shoulders, closed my laptop lid, and set it aside. "Are any of those angels accepting private contracts for work, Chief Braneni?"

"One will do private work if the price is right, but he doesn't come cheap."

"He?" Most angels didn't really have a gender, sounding neutral when they spoke. How they spoke without a head still baffled me, but I figured they had a reason for leaving their heads at home.

"He's an archangel."

I choked on my own spit. "You have an archangel?"

"We do, and he's the one who has been nudging us with certain questions."

My mouth dropped open. While I certainly thought the case important enough to pay high prices to see those behind the murders fall, I'd never dreamed it would attract the interest of an *archangel*. "Is there a chance I can speak with him?"

Chief Braneni pointed at the backyard. "I see no reason why not. He's helping with the grills right now."

"Please excuse me, ladies and gentlemen. I have a few questions for the archangel." I refused to question why a being without a head would have interest in grilling, but I'd take it. I hopped to my feet and strode for the backyard.

Every time I met an angel, something about them put me on edge, and the sensation rippled over me. Deep inside, the awareness the winged being could wipe us all from the Earth with a snap of his perfect hand shivered through me. From behind, he resembled an ancient statue carved of alabaster with wings of silver, white, and gold.

"Hello, Aaron," the archangel said without turning. "I was wondering when you'd seek me out."

Exposure to angels had taught me they enjoyed a certain amount of human humor spicing their lives, and I decided I'd treat the archangel no differently from his brethren. "Didn't check into the future to find out when?"

"Some things in life are best left as a surprise even to those such as I. You have questions."

"What human doesn't?"

The archangel's laughter chimed. "Perceptive. Tell me what you wish to know, and I will tell you if it can be done."

Since when did angels make it easy? I frowned. "I feel like I'm missing something here."

"I'm easily offended, and I've found my delicate sensibilities quite offended of late. Some say angels do not meddle in the affairs of humans, but we do when *He* says we may."

The last thing I needed was being involved with a divine of any stripe. "That sounds terrifying to me, truth be told, although my mother is rather devout and would just love to hear more about that."

"And you are not so devout, despite the evidence of your eyes."

"I'm a freshly minted lycanthrope. Do you know what they do to freshly minted lycanthropes in churches dedicated to the devout? I've no interest in experiencing crucifixion personally. I think I'll stick to non-devout. I get the bonus of watching my mother question how she'd managed to produce two non-devout sons after trying too hard to make sure we walked the path she wanted."

"Free will. It's humanity's most obnoxious trait."

"I never thought I'd be asking an archangel this, but do you believe in ghosts?"

The archangel's chuckles touched something deep within, and a tension I hadn't known plagued me washed away. "When it suits me. Ghosts are interesting things, Mr. Clinton."

"Are they? How so?"

"They exist when needed the most, fade at the most unexpected moments, and return when necessary. Hauntings, as humans often think of them, don't happen in the way humans believe. No, souls don't usually get lost on the way. They can be bound, chained, and forced to remain, but that is a deliberate act. The human mind so often works in mysterious ways. Tell me. Why do you need a ghost?"

"Ghosts," I corrected. "I figured if we couldn't find enough hard evidence to implicate those responsible for the recent murders, we'd find another way to make the mountain fall. And it only takes one to make the mountain fall."

"Ah, yes. I know of who you mean. Please understand I will not reach into your mind and take what you want me to know. I've seen the marks where you've endured this already. While I will never understand what it means to be human, I find no joy in inflicting pain upon those... undeserving."

"And those who are deserving?"

"*He* rather enjoys when those who have wronged many get their just desserts, and he finds the idea of chocolate syrup, whipped cream, and fire ants rather amusing. Perhaps, as the woman close to your heart desires, bullet ants. Miracles do happen, you know."

"Can the chocolate syrup, whipped cream, and ants come with a side dish of angry ghosts?"

"Those who have lost their lives have moved on and rest easy until their seeds of life are reborn into this world." The archangel turned to face me, clicking his grilling tongs together. "The dead won't rise. I can't offer you that."

"Wasn't asking for that. I'm working for the one thing I can give them."

"There's a fine line between justice and revenge, and at times, they can blur together where it's possible to have justice, along with revenge without crossing over. That's what your heart desires, is it not?"

Why did the truth hurt so often? "Only because it's so fresh. Justice will have to be enough, as long as it can be secured. I'll toe as many lines as needed to give them that. I won't let Maxwell's death be for nothing."

"It's rare for humans to be so truthful about the state of their heart. You learned that quickly. How curious."

"If I could curse them to hear the voices of those they'd killed, if I could entice every damned fire ant in the state to converge on the guilty, I would. If I could make it rain chocolate syrup and whipped cream on them whenever they stepped outside, I would. If I could have the fires of hell scald their feet with every step they took that led them towards killing innocent women and children, I would. If I could have them hear the voices of those they've killed whenever they closed their eyes, I would. If I could have them see the blood, feel the pain, experience what it was like to die, I would. If I could have them stand in the shoes of those they'd killed in their final moments, I would." I drew in a deep breath, shrugged, and shook my head. "But I can't. Tomorrow, I probably wouldn't even if I could. Maybe the day after, or the day after the funeral. However long it takes. But even if I could right this moment, I probably wouldn't. It won't bring any of them back."

"Nothing will. I can't take that pain away from you. But you don't have to carry the burden of the faces and names of those you didn't even know. Their deaths are not your fault."

"Someone has to care what happened to them. That person is me."

"Because you decided it is you."

"I guess. I'm not a nice man sometimes. Wanting to drown the bastards in chocolate syrup and whipped cream and set hordes of fire ants on them? That's the anger talking. I get that. I'm human. But it won't do any good unless they fall and can't repeat history. I can't even say I wouldn't drown the bastards right now. If I met them in a dark alley with a sufficiently deep puddle, I'd probably try. But it's a good thing I'm not devout *or* an angel. I don't have to forgive them for what they've done. I just have to seek the truth and make sure that they never have another opportunity to do what they've done again. That's what I want."

"Trails of sugar water and eviction of fire ants, while amusing, would not be effective."

I sighed. "I figured as much."

"What if chocolate syrup, whipped cream, and fire ants could rain down from the sky?"

"I'd probably ask if we could use bullet ants instead," I replied. "Then I'd ask how much it would cost to add ghosts."

"Do they have to be real ghosts?"

"No, I suppose not."

"Magic works in mysterious ways, and you never know when *He* is listening. But I would advise you of one thing: be careful what you wish for. You might get it."

"A cherry on top seems appropriate, if I'm going all in with a rain of chocolate syrup, the whipped cream, and bullet ants with a few fire ants tossed in for good measure. If I had to be careful about what I wish for, it's very simple. I'd wish for justice. That's it. The chocolate syrup, whipped cream, and fire ants aren't necessary. Texas doesn't really consider the death penalty anymore, so I'll have to get whatever justice the courts allow and hope for the best. Frankly, I'm angry enough over this I'd probably crack open a beer should the rain of chocolate syrup, whipped cream, and fire ants turn lethal for those who'd desired the death of fucking *kids* to cover their political ambitions. No matter what I do, those who are behind this might walk anyway. That's an unfortunate reality. The best I can do is my best, and that pisses me off."

"Tell me this, Mr. Clinton. If you could offer those mothers and their children and your friend a second life, would you?"

I held my hands up in surrender. "Hell no. No offense there, but I've been told it's a life for a life. They preach that seriously. The whole crucifixion thing. One life in sacrifice for many, except life's not that tidy. There's a reason the dead can't be brought back to life."

"Ah, I didn't mean it quite like that. You humans jump to interesting conclusions. No, this would not require you to crucify yourself, or anyone else for that matter, but it would result in a lot of daughters who'd one day have children of their own. They won't be the same people, but it's possible to shepherd their seeds of life for a second chance on this Earth. That *is* something I can offer you. You said it yourself. Every season has a purpose under Heaven."

"I didn't *say* that."

"No, but you forget an important truth, Mr. Clinton."

I frowned. "What truth?"

"Life is a prayer, and *He* is always listening even when you don't choose to believe in him. The other divines are listening as well, however much it annoys me that I must acknowledge their existence. That's an inconvenient truth. That's both the beauty and darkness of free will. It doesn't matter if you believe or not. Your life is a prayer, and that is the prayer *He* listens to above all."

"That sounds like the behavior of a stalker."

The archangel laughed. "You're a bold human. Calling *Him* a stalker?"

"I can't help if it's true."

"What an impetuous human. Do you have any more questions for me?"

"If I asked for that rain of chocolate syrup, whipped cream, and the Earth's most painful ants with a cherry on top along with pseudo-ghosts, what would happen?"

"Ask and find out, Mr. Clinton."

I glanced towards the house and wondered what Maxwell would do. Technically, asking an angel for a miracle wasn't illegal, and ultimately, the angel held responsibility for listening to any prayer. Divine intervention could happen. I wasn't breaking any law asking.

It didn't make me a nice man, though.

"Those who killed those mothers, those children, and Maxwell. Those behind the killings, the ones truly responsible for those deaths. Could they please be subjected to a rain of chocolate syrup, whipped cream, and the world's most painful ants, pretty please with a cherry on top? And should they want mercy for what they've done, well, they'll just have to show up in court, confess their sins, and leave nothing of their crimes out and get the justice they deserve. That seems fair to me."

"And should they perish in such a rain, Mr. Clinton?"

"That might be a mercy," I admitted. "I can't imagine life for them would be very good in prison once the other inmates found out what they've done for the sake of their politics."

"Tell me, Mr. Clinton. Which would you choose? Mercy or justice?"

I hated that question, and I sighed. "Why can't it ever be both?"

"Life rarely works out that way."

I could think of one answer that might annoy the archangel, but fit better than the alternatives. "Mercy as long as justice is still served."

Something about the archangel's posture changed, and I got the odd feeling he smiled. "Humans. You're so interesting."

He handed me the barbecue tongs, and with a flash of golden light, he disappeared.

AS GRILLING BEAT AN INTERROGATION, I took the archangel's place and worked to help feed the insane number of people taking over the Chetty house. I supposed Sassy must've warned the cops away as no one bothered me while I flipped meat, prodded the offensive vegetables hogging space on two entire grills, and otherwise ignored everyone I could. The normality helped me relax, but I worried I'd managed to haunt myself even thinking about indulging Sassy's desire for some Grade A just desserts.

Only an idiot would waste that much chocolate syrup and whipped cream.

"Talk with the archangel go poorly?" Sassy's father asked, taking a sip from his beer. "I'd offer you one, but I figured you'd just have to find some polite way to tell me no, so I figured we'd skip the dancing."

"I vented some of my temper out."

"On an archangel? You're nuts, boy."

"Yeah. Not one of my better moments."

"You're still standing, so you must not have offended him any. I see he left you to do his grill work, though."

"He probably had better things to do."

"Like what?"

"Summoning rains of chocolate syrup, whipped cream, and ants on a bunch of assholes?"

"I trust you didn't actually suggest such a thing to an archangel."

I shrugged. "It just popped out. It's been a hard few days."

"Well, shit. I would've been asking for death by something far more embarrassing."

"I didn't say anything about them dying."

"A man can hope." Sassy's father shook his head. "What did you actually talk about?"

"Ghosts, chocolate syrup, whipped cream, a cherry on top, and something about mercy versus justice. Honestly, the whole conversation disturbs me. He also had some commentary about the devout and non-devout when I informed him I didn't even follow his specific religion."

"Hey, Joe! Get out here," Sassy's father yowled.

Joe emerged from the kitchen armed with an apron and a pair of tongs. "What is it? I was about to get the corn off the grill."

"Aaron mouthed off to an archangel. He might still be suffering from blood loss."

"He doesn't look dead. If he'd actually mouthed off to an archangel, he'd be dead, Dad. Only an idiot mouths off to an angel. Aaron, you should probably get your ass inside. Sassy's getting anxious because you're not around."

I arched a brow. "Seriously?"

"Well, less that you're not around, more that she's trying to spare you from the interrogation going on in there. She's getting frustrated."

"The cops are telling her what protocols they have to follow in the investigation, aren't they?"

Joe's brows shot up. "Do you read minds?"

"No, I just know Sassy. She's probably trying to find ways around the rules so she can do more direct investigations without breaking any laws. She would've been better off plotting the malicious relocation of fire ants."

"You're probably right. Can you please derail that nightmare before she says something she regrets?"

I passed the tongs to Sassy's father. "All right."

In the time I'd been gone, the living room had turned into a war zone, complete with a digital murder board displaying a grid of all the victims killed. Maxwell's picture cut deep, but I found some comfort that Sharon Gray's image hadn't made it to the display—yet. "How's Sharon?"

The conversation ended, and Sassy popped off the couch and bounced to my side. "Grover says she's stable, but it'll be a while until she's out of the woods, and they needed a lot of wolves to donate because she had severe internal bleeding. They've stopped the worst of it. Grover's cautiously optimistic she'll make a good recovery, but until her virus matures and she shifts, she'll have impairments."

I frowned. "What sort of impairments?"

"A round went through her shoulder. You probably hadn't noticed because you were more worried about the chest shots. A lot of broken bones, but the virus will eventually repair it. She just won't have full mobility in her one arm for a while." Sassy poked my chest. "How is your chest doing?"

Ouch. "I sense a cranky Sassy. And yes, it's still bruised and hurts."

Narrowing her eyes, she pulled her hand back to jab me again, but instead of nailing me in the chest, she flicked my nose. "You ran away and left me with these... these... these *cops*."

"Are you upset they're cops, upset you're not a cop, or frustrated because you're hungry, aren't getting anywhere with the investigation, and otherwise want to go knock heads together and arrest people because you have names, but you don't have enough evidence to push through an actual arrest yet?"

"All of that with emphasis on the hungry part," she admitted.

"Your brother's about to take the corn off the grill, so you're about to be fed. Now, that said, where can I get one of those things and how much do they cost?" I pointed at the digital board. "I use a whiteboard and markers, and I need one of those in my life. I will buy it myself, but I *need* one."

Chief Braneni arched a brow. "Then you need to work your ass off and become an upper tier homicide detective. The lower tier detectives get whiteboards and shitty markers."

I laughed. "I like how you're honest about the marker quality. Noted. Bring my own markers... or buy my own digital board and share with people who give me coffee."

The cops snickered, and the tension in the room relaxed. While I'd seen most of the cops a few times, I hadn't had relationships with them like I had with Maxwell. At most, I knew their last names, and I sought out one of the older cops I'd run into enough times to remember his last name. "Officer Tulfield, you're in investigations. How's the board situation?"

"The digital boards make us all more efficient, so he's working on getting them for everyone. I'm sure there'll be one around when you get through preschool."

I expected a lot of ribbing from the older cops in the near future, so I forced myself to grin. "I can handle a whiteboard, but I'm not going to tolerate bad markers. That's condition for a revolt."

Sassy jabbed me in the ribs. "Aaron!"

"What? I'm spoiled. I can't investigate properly if I have crap markers, and if they're the ones that squeak, the entire station will hear whenever I'm working. That's just unacceptable. I bet the digital boards don't squeak."

"Aaron, take this seriously."

"What's the best way to sass you about this, Sassy? This seems to be a prime opportunity to sass, and I'm afraid you're usually the sassing party, so I'm going to need instruction to properly do this."

She stared at me, her expression less than impressed. "I don't know what you were doing outside, but you seem to have returned to me in an odd humor."

"I avoided death by archangel, and I may have embarrassed myself more than a little."

Her brows rose. "How?"

I told her how I'd informed an archangel I was less than devout as my opening volley, then I confessed my sins of wishing an assortment of cruel punishments on those responsible for the murders. "I didn't break any laws, but that wasn't one of my better moments. At least, I don't think I broke any laws."

"It's only breaking laws if you attempt to turn those wishes into reality," Chief Braneni said. "And frankly, that's tame compared to what most of us are praying for right now. There's a general trend, and it involves a dark alley and the perfect murder, but that's what separates us from the bad guys; we aren't going to act on it however tempting it may be. They'll get their day in court."

"Unless a rain of chocolate syrup, whipped cream, and ants kills them," I muttered.

"Aaron, you didn't."

"I'm going to blame this on Joe and the lycanthropy virus. Joe's medications removed the filters over my mouth, the lycanthropy virus obviously contributed, and you were so funny when you were mumbling about fire ants in your sleep. I asked for a cherry on top, though. I figured if I was going to go all in and vent to an archangel, I might as well do it right."

She sighed and shook her head. "However

satisfying that might be, that'd be a waste of chocolate syrup. I've acknowledged the errors of my thinking. I have a lot better things I can do with that much chocolate syrup."

Chief Braneni chuckled. "I don't want to know, but I'm glad you two are doing well despite everything. You're looking a lot better than I expected, Aaron."

"Having my first shift helped a lot. Joe took care of the rest."

"Still. You did good work in a pinch. There was nothing you could have done for Maxwell. There's no happy ending to this story, but there can be closure. This applies to you, too, Sassy. Once you start working the streets, you'll find there's as much heartache as there are triumphs." Chief Braneni sighed. "His funeral will be in three days, and I'm sure he'd like for you to be there. His wife asked if I'd talk to you. Everyone who isn't on duty will be in attendance, but we'll have our own farewell after this case is a wrap. It might be a while."

"What do you need from us to make that happen, Chief?"

"Keep your noses clean and do what you do best. You know the rules. Don't mess this up," he ordered.

Some things were easier said than done, but I'd make do somehow, as always.

NINETEEN

A rainfall of unusual composition.

IT TOOK until midnight before everyone left, and another hour after to help clean up the mess, dismantle the excess picnic tables, and otherwise restore the Chetty house and yard back to order. If I got my way, I'd make it to Sassy's bed, flop onto it, and sleep for several days. My phone, a replacement Sassy had picked out after the crash, rang. As nothing good came from a call after midnight, I answered the call without looking at the screen. "Aaron Clinton speaking."

"Chief Braneni here. I have a question for you."

"I could have sworn I just saw you an hour ago. What can I do for you?"

"When did you express your interest in a rainfall of unusual composition?"

That was one way to put it. "Maybe five minutes after I found out there was an archangel in the backyard."

"There are interesting reports of rainfalls of unusual compositions lighting dispatch up."

Shit. "You're serious."

"Rather. We've also had a few individuals of interest come into the police station eager to talk to us. Might you know anything about that?"

"Do I need to go to the station, sir?"

"No, no. That's quite all right. Obviously, it's absolutely impossible for a solitary lycanthrope fresh from his first shift to have anything to do with these curious and somewhat disturbing incidents."

"Is Tom Heatherow involved with any of these calls?"

"Not that I've heard yet, no. Anyway, I thought you'd want to know that your rather unusual method of requesting assistance seems to have borne some fruit for us. I recommend you watch the morning news. You'll find it very interesting, I'm sure. Do give Sassy my regards." Chief Braneni hung up.

I stared at the darkening display of my phone. "Hey, Sassy?"

"What is it?"

"I think I made a mistake, possibly. But I'm not sure it's a mistake. Are you okay to drive? There's something I want to look into."

"What could you possibly want to look into?"

"Tom Heatherow's house."

"Why would you want to go there this time of night?"

"I want to ring his doorbell and ask him a question."

"At one in the morning?"

I nodded. "Yes, at one in the morning." Tom Heatherow tended to stay at his home unless he had reason to go out, and he'd been staying at home a lot more frequently with the investigation going on, something I'd found annoying as he'd often requested we visit him. "Also, did he make you go to his place to give him the photos and discuss the contract?"

"Of course. He's too good to come to us. I should have told you, sorry. My brothers tagged along for the ride, but it didn't take long and I didn't go inside the house. Told him I had to get back to the hospital."

"We have new information for him."

"We do?"

"We sure do. We're going to politely inform him that we have reason to believe Sharon Gray is heavily involved with the local lycanthrope packs, and because we're generous private investigators, we're going to give him some pointers on how to deal with the packs if he wants to gather more information about her. That counts as useful information following the conclusion of our contract, which we may feel is worth mentioning."

Sassy's eyes widened. "Daddy? Aaron's really aggressive, and it's starting to worry me."

"Pack the boy into his truck, let him do what he wants, and if you're going to be keeping him awake all night long, don't do it in my house, young lady."

"Daddy!"

"What? I'm an old man. I need my beauty sleep. Late nights are for the young. Take Joe with you just in case. Joe? Go with your sister and keep her out of trouble."

"I definitely won't be keeping Aaron up all night long if Joe's with us," Sassy growled.

"What the hell? Now I'm a birth control method? That's not cool," Joe complained, strolling over. "Beats putting the picnic tables back in the shed, though. Where are we headed?"

"Tom Heatherow's house."

Joe scowled. "Mark! Need you for a road trip."

My brother joined us, and some dumbass had given him a hunting rifle. I pointed at it. "Where did you get that?"

"Dad. He said if anyone looked at you or the future mother of his grandchildren the wrong way, I was to shove it up their ass and fire. I'll spare you the rest of the lecture." Mark patted the rifle. "I don't need a carry permit for this puppy, and it wasn't on my list of weapons I wasn't allowed to handle without adult supervision."

"I'm with you, Mark. I count as adult supervision. No firing unless I give you the order." Joe stared at my brother until he scowled and looked away. "Get your ass to Aaron's truck and sweep it for unwanted friends. You're good at that."

Mark jogged towards the front yard cradling the rifle like most people cradled infants. I worried my brother had finally snapped. "Unwanted friends?"

"Trackers. Happened once, it could happen again. Maxwell's partner hadn't been near your new truck, but there were plenty of people who were, so it's worth a look. It'll only take him a few minutes, and he likes the work."

"I'm going to have to suggest to Dad he shouldn't give Mark any more weapons until he has an evaluation."

"He's probably infected with lycanthropy, and he's riled up because he can't go on a hunt. He works with the lycanthropes in the field, so it's entirely possible. He'd shake out as a wolf, though."

"What's one more wolf around Dallas?" Sassy muttered. "When's he due for testing?"

"I'm going to take him in after things settle down. It's not like there's a cure, but he's definitely been snappier than normal and ready to indulge in violence. I can't say I blame him. I've been ready to take names and shove various weapons up asses this week. Why are we going to Tom Heatherow's house?"

"I'm hoping for a miracle."

NORMAL PEOPLE CALLED the excessive house at the end of the street a mansion, but Tom Heatherow preferred to think of it as his cottage. I supposed if I dumped the whole thing in the Alps, it might blend in as an over-sized cottage. It stuck out compared to the nicer homes on the street, most of which were ranch-style homes better suited for the Texas heat.

The lights were on, his Mercedes sat in the driveway, and I hoped a little harder we might see a real miracle happen before our very eyes.

I'd even deal with a few ant bites if it meant we could get a confession out of the bastard.

Sassy parked behind the Mercedes and killed the engine. "Are you *really* sure about this, Aaron?"

"I'd like you to hang back, please. This could get messy."

"Messy how?" she growled.

"Not bloody, if that's what you're worried about. Well, I hope. That's why Joe's here with Mark. If things look like they will get bloody, Mark can take care of it. But Mark? Unless shots are fired, I swear, if you put your finger anywhere near the trigger, I will kick your ass so hard Joe and Grover will have to work together to surgically remove my foot from your kidney."

"Ouch, Aaron. That's just wrong." My brother sighed. "I won't touch the trigger unless shots are fired or look to be fired. But if he's armed and points a gun anywhere near you, I'm shooting first. I'll accept the surgical removal of your foot from my ass if necessary."

"Sassy?"

"What?"

"There might be a splatter radius, and I'd rather your pretty shoes didn't get messy. You may want to leave them in the truck."

Sassy blinked. "You want me to do *what?*"

"Leave your pretty shoes in the truck. They're the blue ones. I really like the blue ones, and I'd be sad if they were damaged." I smiled at Sassy, leaned towards her, and kissed her cheek. "There might be ants, so you may just want to stay in the truck. Record with your phone. It might be worthwhile."

"What have you done, Aaron?"

"I haven't done anything. Scout's honor. I'm just seeing if there's any substance to what Chief Braneni called me about."

"What are you talking about?"

"Just humor me, okay? Take your shoes off if you're coming with me, and stay back, all right?"

"Why am I staying back?"

"You might lose your temper and try to strangle the bastard. If you're behind me, I can catch you before you indulge." I grinned at her and winked.

"That's... actually accurate. Okay." Sassy contorted behind the wheel, showing off her legs while removing her shoes. "I'll refrain from strangling him no matter how much he deserves it."

"Good." I slipped out of the truck and headed for the front door, considering how best to get the bastard to step outside. I strolled up the walkway, rang the doorbell, and took several steps back.

Tom Heatherow cracked open the door, and his eyes widened when he spotted me. "Mr. Clinton?" he blurted.

"Mr. Heatherow," I replied, lifting my hand to flick him a salute; I missed having a hat, as I would've dipped the brim instead. "I wanted to stop by to apologize for not notifying you myself of the circumstances and deliver your pictures in person. I know Sassy handled the deliveries, but I wanted a chance to talk to you myself." I made of show of admiring his house, something I'd done every other time I'd visited him. "Nice lighting here, by the way. It's my first time here so late in the evening. I would've come earlier, but I got sidetracked."

"I understand," he replied, and his expression turned puzzled. "Thank you for coming. I wasn't expecting to see you at all."

"I learned some new information, and it seemed fair I come over and talk to you about it." I took a few steps back to admire the lamp-lit flowers lining his walkway. "It won't take long."

Tom Heatherow stepped out of his house and closed the door behind him. "You have new information?" The eagerness in his voice matched his stride, which lured him out of his house.

"Some, yes. It's about Miss Gray," I said, lowering my voice. "And the company she currently keeps."

"Currently keeps? How is that important to me?"

I clasped my hands behind my back and wandered a few steps away to look over one of his flowering bushes, a rose as far as I could tell. "They're a possessive lot, so if they find out you were looking into her, they might cause you trouble. Suitors."

"Suitors?" The astonishment in his voice boded well for my ploy to lure him outdoors. "What suitors?"

"She's an attractive woman, and she's getting older. It's not surprising she's looking to settle down and possibly marry, and there are plenty of men willing to accept her for who she is and who she was. You were aware she's infected with lycanthropy, yes?"

"What? She's infected?"

"Yes, she is."

My confirmation lured him out of the house, and he stepped onto the path to join me. "How—"

When I thought of rain, I thought of drops falling from the sky. During a bad blow or a hurricane, it'd come down in sheets. Chocolate didn't drip, drop, or even sheet. It plopped, splooshed, and splattered, thick, oozing, and warm enough my skin crawled. I caught the edge of it, and I hopped a few steps back to escape the worst of it.

Whipped cream, the canned stuff that drove Sassy crazy because she couldn't help herself when it crossed her path, popped into existence over Tom Heatherow's head. In a flash of golden light, a single cherry landed on his head.

The ants didn't rain down from the sky,

but swarmed from the roof of his house and teemed over the sweet-ladened man. They glowed with a faint, golden light, and the instant the first one reached his feet, Tom Heatherow screamed, dropped to the walkway, and flailed as though the fires of hell boiled beneath his flesh. My brows shot up, and I debated offering to help him.

Then I remembered the truth of what I'd asked of the archangel, clenched my teeth, and listened to him scream.

"Jesus Christ!" Sassy yelped, and she stuck close to the car. "What the hell?"

"Tell me, Tom Heatherow. Do you hear their voices?" Ghosts, pseudo-ghosts, it didn't matter. Whatever landed the fucker in prison and kept him there until the end of his days. I'd have to thank the next angel I met for making certain justice was served. I reached over, plucked the cherry off his head, and popped it into my mouth. "Here's the funny thing about what you've done, Mr. Heatherow. Yeah, you got Maxwell out of the way, but there's always someone who is going to take his place. This time, that someone is me. And when I do, it's going to be treacherous men like you I turn over to the courts. Did you really think you'd get away with murder?"

In retrospect, I doubted the bastard could hear me over his screams, but I didn't care. I

pulled out my phone and took pictures of
him. One by one, the ants winked out of existence, although a few I recognized as good
old Texan fire ants stuck around and continued to take offense to Tom Heatherow's
presence.

None of them bit me.

"Aaron?" In her bare feet, Sassy ran up the
walkway. "What happened?"

"Just desserts," I announced. "Would you
like to give Chief Braneni a call? I'm sure he'd
just love to hear about this." While I'd rather
the bastard fell over dead, I kept an eye on
him to make sure he still breathed. Maybe
mercy needed to temper justice in some
cases, but if I could pick one man to stand
trial of them all, I'd always pick him. "You
might want to call for an ambulance, too.
Who knows what that many ant bites will do
to the fucker. We can start a betting pool to
see how long it takes him to start singing like
a canary. And once he does, he'll get his day
in court, and I hope he enjoys watching
everything he worked for fall apart around
him."

Sassy's eyes widened, but she retrieved
her phone, dialed a number, and said, "Chief
Braneni? I'm sorry to bother you, but Aaron
wanted to give Tom Heatherow some information, but when he—" Sassy's mouth
dropped open. "He really did? You're seri-

ous. He really did that? Aaron! How could you?"

I looked her in the eyes and said, "It was your idea. Except for the cherry on top. That was all me. Do I look like a miracle worker to you?"

Sassy blinked, lowered he gaze to Tom Heatherow, who continued to writhe and scream at my feet, and said, "Yes, you do."

"Just request an ambulance, Sassy. He does us no good dead."

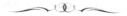

TOM HEATHEROW SURVIVED the hundreds of ant bites covering his body. He held out an entire week, all spent at the hospital for observation, before the haunting voices of the dead and a single visit from a pale but very alive Sharon Gray broke his resolve and he begged for the torture to stop. A single call from the hospital summoned the police and the archangel, and luck alone had me down the hall to be the CDC's guinea pig for various testing, to check on my virus levels, and otherwise determine I'd fully recovered from the shooting.

A quiet laugh from the archangel, a sound I suspected I alone heard, clued me in that luck had nothing to do with my presence at the hospital for the confession.

Tom Heatherow began with begging Sharon for forgiveness, claiming of all the women he'd been with, he hadn't wanted her to be hurt, but she'd known too much. Sharon's expression darkened, and she glanced at the archangel.

"You're under no obligation to forgive him for his sins, Miss Gray, but you might find the burden of your experiences easier to bear should you decide against carrying the burden of his existence on your shoulders. Is he worth scarring your soul? Only you can decide."

She nodded, watched Tom Heatherow, and said nothing.

Name by name, Tom Heatherow confessed his sins, and the waters had run deeper than we'd guessed. From victims to targets to accomplices, once he began to speak, he refused to stop until he'd aired every last one of them. Through it all, we listened, recorded his words, and waited for the archangel to confirm the truth of his words.

It took several hours for him to finish, and through it all, I worked through my grief and anguish, accepting the tangled mess that would one day become justice. It would take time, even with the word of an archangel driving the case forward. But one day, Maxwell would rest easy, as would the other victims

killed through Tom Heatherow's machi-
nations.

Tom Heatherow turned to the archangel
with wide, blood-shot eyes. "Tell them. Tell
them! I told the truth. Every word true. I told
them. Just make it stop."

I wondered what Tom Heatherow had
heard, and I wondered how much of it was
old ghosts, ghosts of an archangel's creation,
or memories haunting the man.

~*Memories are more potent that even ghosts,
and nothing a ghost could do would surpass what
he does to himself. Justice has been served.*~ The
archangel reached out and rested his hand on
Tom Heatherow's head. "You have spoken
every word true."

"Mercy," he begged. "Mercy, please."

I held my breath and waited for the
archangel's verdict, something no court could
overturn. Would the man live? Would he die?
Or would the archangel once again surprise
me with the unexpected?

"Then I take it all from you. Everything
you were and everything you are, I cast them
away. Justice has been served, but mercy has
been granted. Your life could never repay the
lives of those lost at your hand. You are now
a blank slate, and may you become something worth the air you breathe. When you
require his testimony, call for me, and I shall
stand in his place for he will never again be

the man who believed he could seize power through the blood of children." The archangel's declaration shook the hospital, and startled cries rang out from down the hall. Before I could even release the breath I held, the archangel vanished in a flash of silvery light.

Tom Heatherow's expression went slack, and in that moment, I understood the archangel's decree was an absolute, and nothing short of divine intervention would bring the man back. I wondered who he'd become, but I decided it didn't matter.

Justice had been served, and death wasn't the only mercy. A man who'd never understand the crimes he'd committed wouldn't face time in prison. His cause wouldn't haunt the judiciary system for long, either.

The CDC would take over the case, the man would likely disappear from Dallas, and he'd be molded into a different and better man, one who wouldn't ruin so many lives.

Sharon's eyes widened. "What just happened?"

Tom Heatherow's gaze slid to Sharon, and he smiled. "You're beautiful. Are you an angel?"

"No, I'm not an angel," Sharon replied, and her brows furrowed.

"Oh. You look like an angel to me. Will you be staying long?"

"No, I won't be staying long," she replied, her tone puzzled.

"That's a shame. You look like an angel."

The moment the woman realized what had happened to the man who'd terrorized her and almost cost her her life, her eyes watered, although no tears fell. "I'm no angel, but thank you."

I slipped out of the room and left the consequences of the archangel's decree for the hospital staff, and I wondered if anything remained of Tom Heatherow beyond our memories of everything he'd done.

I hoped not.

Sassy came down the hall, scowling when she spotted me at the door. "What happened? I've been looking for you everywhere. I swear, they sent me all over the hospital trying to figure out where'd you gone after testing."

"He confessed."

Her eyes widened. "He did?"

"About everything. There's cleanup to do, but as far as we're concerned, it's over."

"You got all the names from him?"

Mercy hadn't come in a form I'd expected, justice wasn't a conviction, but a promise the mountain would fall, and I found the combination both bitter and sweet. I wrapped my arm around Sassy's shoulder and turned her around so we could escape the hospital and the inevitable scrutiny I'd face from the police for getting their prized confession, the word of an archangel, and the complete loss of the man who'd wrought so much tragedy. "He'll never stand trial, but we've the word of an archangel he'll give testimony to make sure the case is closed in the courts. That'll have to be enough."

"Well, I guess what they say is true. Huh." Sassy leaned against me.

"What is true?"

"Angels are assholes."

They sure were.

Epilogue: I really needed to curtail her enjoyment of watching horror movies before bed.

NINE MONTHS LATER

HAD I known Sassy would need to deal with pregnancy and the rigors of the police academy at the same time, I might've attempted to veto our training cycle and earned myself an ass-kicking from my wife. Had I know she would go into labor during the graduation ceremony, which included our entire class of six lycanthropes, I wouldn't have bothered to leave bed. I would've stayed home, kept Sassy home, and left her in the capable hands of our mothers before our trip to the hospital.

According to my mother, my job was to accept I'd have a broken hand by the end of the delivery and do my best to convince Sassy our firstborn children weren't actually going to claw their way out of her belly and take over the world from birth.

I really needed to curtail her enjoyment of watching horror movies before bed. Every time she watched one, she concocted a new way our children would kill us all.

Twelve hours later, the twins we expected made their appearance along with one extra, a tiny boy who wanted nothing to do with being born. He voiced his complaints over his eviction from her belly in screams confirming he had healthy lungs. Our twins, the daughters neither of us had truly anticipated, cried as well, although they were easier to please.

They wanted their mother to nurse them immediately, and they were not having anything to do with the nurses who wanted to check their health. To my amusement, the babies won, although Sassy ultimately needed her mother's help getting both babies situated and cradled while they drank for the first time.

As though accepting his fate as the custodian of two sisters, Maxwell waited his turn for a chance to nurse with admirable patience, and gave Joe and the nurses time to measure him, check him over, and otherwise confirm he had all of his pieces in the right place.

All things considered, I could only think

of one thing to say. "I'm so sorry."

The look Sassy shot me promised retribution later. "You're exactly fifty percent to blame for this, Mr. Clinton."

"No, I'm pretty sure I'm at least seventy-five percent to blame for this. The blue shoes are taking the other twenty-five percent, as you're faultless." I regarded my hand, wondering if she'd ever release it but decided I didn't mind. When she let go, I'd need Joe to put my hand back together. Until she wanted me attending to my new fatherly duties, I'd stay where I was and do my duty as primary hand holder.

I had no idea how we'd manage caring for three infants completely dependent on us, but I was relieved neither of us was expected to begin working for three months. When we tested our new lives as cops, our parents would take up the roles as spoilers of grandchildren.

It still amazed me we'd managed to cram eighteen months' worth of education into eight months.

"You're so full of shit, Aaron," she whispered, and as I'd been warned, her exhaustion left her shaking and ready to check out of life for a while. My next job would be to keep her awake long enough to bond with our babies.

Smiling, I leaned over her and kissed her cheek. "You're perfect, and so are they, but you have mommy duties to attend to. After our voracious daughters are satisfied, little Maxwell needs a turn."

"How'd we end up with three?" Sassy shrugged. "Oh, well. What's one extra?"

I wouldn't remind her we'd never sleep again from my understanding of the situation. We weren't going to be sleeping with twins. Triplets would drive us to the limits of our sanity. "Exactly. What's one extra? I think we'll manage just fine," I lied. "There are four eager grandparents with like a million kids between them who'd just love to babysit for us."

My parents sighed while Sassy's parents laughed.

"You're right. Totally right. Now, I do believe we have an argument to resume, Mr. Aaron Clinton, as our entire list of boy names is now *completely fucking useless!*"

"If you're expecting me to be apologetic that we have two daughters as beautiful as you, you're going to be very disappointed."

"Aaron," she growled.

I smiled, lifted her hand, and kissed her knuckles. "Next time, please don't break every bone in my hand, okay?"

"Next time? Next time? Why are you already thinking about next time? And what the hell are you talking about? I didn't break your hand."

Joe, deliverer of his newborn nieces and nephew, laughed from the doorway. "You broke his hand, but he's been a great sport about it. I will say this much, though. Damn, woman. Next time Dad needs a vice, I'll just tell him to talk to you."

"The instant I can get up, you're a dead man, Joe," she snarled.

"He's teasing you, Sassy. You're fine, I'm fine, and the babies are fine. That's all that matters." The start of the rest of my life filled the room, and Sassy graced me with a tired smile. "Please don't kill Joe. I need him to put my hand back together," I teased.

"You will regret that, Aaron."

"But will you make me regret it while you're wearing the blue shoes? It's important."

"You are so lucky the babies are nursing, Aaron. So. Lucky."

Yes, I was.

Burn, Baby, Burn is the next book in the Magical Romantic Comedy (with a body count) series. These stories, with the exception of Burn, Baby, Burn (sequel to Playing with Fire,) can be read in any order.

About R.J. Blain

Want to hear from the author when a new book releases? You can sign up at her website (thesneakykittycritic.com). Please note this newsletter is operated by the Furred & Frond Management. Expect to be sassed by a cat. (With guest features of other animals, including dogs.)

A complete list of books written by RJ and her various pen names is available at https://books2read.com/rl/The-Fantasy-Worlds-of-RJ-Blain.

RJ BLAIN suffers from a Moleskine journal obsession, a pen fixation, and a terrible tendency to pun without warning.

When she isn't playing pretend, she likes to think she's a cartographer and a sumi-e painter.

In her spare time, she daydreams about being

a spy. Should that fail, her contingency plan involves tying her best of enemies to spinning wheels and quoting James Bond villains until she is satisfied.

RJ also writes as Susan Copperfield and Bernadette Franklin. Visit RJ and her pets (the Management) at thesneakykittycritic.com.

FOLLOW RJ & HER ALTER EGOS ON BOOKBUB:
RJ BLAIN
SUSAN COPPERFIELD
BERNADETTE FRANKLIN

CPSIA information can be obtained
at www.ICGtesting.com
Printed in the USA
LVHW030223100921
697457LV00007B/1219